Riding
For
Redemption

Bev Pettersen

Editor: Patricia A. Thomas
Cover Art Design: Vivi Designs

DEDICATION

In loving memory of Jan

CHAPTER ONE

Scott Taylor had a profitable investigative business, a medal of valor and a splitting headache. He squeezed his eyes shut, trying to contain the throb.

Belinda, his hovering assistant, pried a file from his hand and slapped it back on the mahogany credenza. "Your buddy from the jockey school left another message," she said, her voice sharp with displeasure. "I told him you couldn't talk, that you're *supposed* to be on sick leave."

"Garrett's an old friend," Scott said. "It's nothing to do with work." He rubbed the raised skin on the side of his forehead and forced a smile. Belinda had raised five boys and been a superb assistant for six years but ever since the shooting, her motherly instincts had kicked into overdrive.

"Hey, what are doing here, boss?" Snake filled the doorway, his shaved head gleaming under the fluorescent lights. "Thought you were taking time off. Did you hear what was hidden in that shipping container? Goddamn grenade launchers, some AK-47s, a Browning 50 caliber and one of the suckers even had a gold-plated skull."

Snake's gaze settled on Belinda's frowning face. He flushed and backed up. Even the formidable cobra tattoo on his neck seemed to shrink. "Sorry, ma'am," he added quickly. "I wasn't talking work. Just thought Scott would want to hear about the Tijuana shipment, you know...since he was right here in the office." He turned and shuffled down the hall, nearly three hundred pounds of muscle yet still muttering an apology.

"A gold skull." Scott blew out a wistful sigh. "I'd like to see that."

Belinda jammed her hands on her hips, her gray hair bristling. "You're supposed to be recuperating, not dropping by the office. No wonder the boys keep running to you."

The boys? Some of the toughest men in California, and Belinda ran them like a staff sergeant. "I am recuperating," he said. "It's just a little headache."

She jabbed a finger into his chest.

He instinctively grabbed her wrist, then froze in dismay, afraid he'd hurt her.

She poked him again. "It's not just a little headache," she said, her voice quivering. "You were unconscious for two whole days."

The last time he'd seen her so vulnerable was when her husband had been blindsided at a traffic light. He rose to his feet and wrapped her in a reassuring hug. "It'll take more than a trigger-happy punk to kill me," he said. "And the headaches are fading."

"But I've seen you, your problems..."

"What do you mean?"

"Sometimes you lose your balance," she said. "It's so unlike you."

"That's nothing." He gave a dismissive shrug. "Just a little dizziness."

She shot him such a skeptical look he sat back down and began scribbling notations on his yellow pad. "There's some blood restriction where they extracted the bullet," he said, staring at the paper. "But nothing to worry about."

She snorted, such an atypical noise from a proper lady that he smiled, almost forgetting his frustrating headaches.

"You're supposed to be off work for at least a month," she said. "That means no work. Not even to read cases." She resumed her zealous sweep of his desk, removing two more files. "Those are the doctor's orders," she added. "So that's what you're going to do. The office won't collapse. Snake and I can run things while you're gone."

"Dammit, Belinda." Scott groaned as his notes disappeared.

But she continued to stack files, and it was obvious she sided with the surgeons. Damn inconvenient really, because Belinda in a snit could make things difficult. Thankfully, there was no way she could monitor him at his house, and much of the information was already stored on his phone.

It would be simple enough to call Snake and direct the business from home, yet still appease Belinda and the doctors. Perfect, because there was no way the Taylor

Investigative Agency could function without Scott Taylor. The guys depended on him. Snake was good but T-Bone was still a few hours short of his license and they had that big surveillance job coming up. If the money laundering case imploded—

"So?" Belinda asked. "Do I have your promise?" She tilted her head, her narrowed gaze locked on his face. "Promise to stay away from the office for a month?"

"An entire month?" he said. "You're pushing this too far." She'd left him a perfect loophole but he made a show of protesting. Belinda was smart. She'd be suspicious if he agreed too readily.

He waited a moment then blew out an exaggerated sigh. "All right. One month max. I promise not to step foot in the office the entire time."

She gave a triumphant nod. Then in a move he hadn't anticipated she scooped up his cell phone and bolted toward the door.

"Hey," he called. "Give that back!" And now his dismay was very real. He needed his phone—it contained his contacts, his files, everything.

"I'll assign you an office phone," she said over her shoulder, not slowing a step. "And your doctor's number is all you need."

He half rose, then dropped back into the chair. Yelling only increased his headaches, but dammit, he should fire her. If she weren't irreplaceable—and very much loved—he most definitely would. He grabbed his pad and scrawled a note in block letters, 'FIRE BELINDA,' then stared morosely at his bare desk, unable to imagine a month cut off from the office.

He'd go nuts stuck at home, twiddling his thumbs. The desk looked pitiful, stripped of files. The liquid stains on the wood were clearly visible. Coffee no doubt. He'd been gulping way too much caffeine over the past several months...actually over the past several years.

He dragged a hand over the top of his head, still surprised by the unfamiliar bristle. His hair was growing back, slowly, but it hadn't been this short since the diabetes fundraiser for Belinda's son.

Maybe he did need time off, if only a week or two. He could fly to New York and go to Aqueduct with his dad. The track wasn't as beautiful as Santa Anita but they definitely had nice horses. He could stay in contact with the office from there. Snake was smart and trustworthy, although the man tended to scare clients.

He reached for his phone then remembered the confiscation, and hell, he couldn't remember his father's cell number. "Belinda!"

She materialized in the doorway, waving an unfamiliar phone and not looking one bit contrite.

"I need Dad's number," he said. "And a flight reservation."

"Your father is in England. Remember? You gave him tickets to the Cheltenham Gold Cup."

Scott dragged a hand over his jaw, vaguely remembering the gift and his father's quiet delight. Originally he'd been hoping to go too, but the agency had been overwhelmed with work, and as usual, it had been impossible to carve out the time.

But now there was time. It might even be fun. He could call Snake just as easily from Europe as New York.

"Check Dad's itinerary for me," he said, feeling more energized than he had all day. "And give me the number to that finance guy, Derek something. I'll follow-up on the background checks he wanted."

Belinda's mouth compressed and she remained unmoving in front of his desk.

"Maybe the man's last name is Burke," he added, perturbed by her stillness. Though Belinda was pushing sixty, she was usually a dynamo of energy and her silent stare made him uneasy.

"Are you an imbecile?" she finally snapped.

"Actually, I've rarely been called that." He gave an amused smile. His headache had vanished now, probably because he was looking forward to the trip. Besides, he never could summon up much annoyance with Belinda. She was like a den mother with a very needy cub. Still this name calling was unusual. An imbecile?

She stepped closer, her mouth dangerously tight. "Don't you remember what the doctor said?"

"Sure. No stress, no diving, no...flying." He groaned and cut off a curse.

She opened her hand and dropped a shiny cell phone on his desk. "Your dad's number is programmed in, but you can't fly anywhere. Please, Scott." Worry lines fanned her eyes. "For once in your life, just forget work. Go somewhere and relax."

He wasn't sure if he remembered how to relax, but he genuinely regretted causing her any concern. She had enough to worry about with her own family. He picked up his new phone, pressed some buttons and concentrated on the screen. "Who's Lucy?" he asked, scanning the pitifully few numbers Belinda had programmed into its memory.

"She's the last lady you took to dinner," Belinda said. "I thought you liked her."

He shrugged and deleted the number. Lucy had been okay but her friend was clearly using, and that strung-out look always made him edgy. Any involvement with women who associated with druggies was strictly avoided. He'd learned his lesson the hard way.

Thinking about it still hurt. He gripped the arms of his leather chair, pushing away the memories and fighting a wave of dizziness. Maybe he did need time off.

"All right," he said slowly. "I'll stay away for a month but I want regular updates. And T-Bone is a pain in the ass, but he's a genius with the computer. Make sure he doesn't quit." His voice softened. Belinda worked harder than any of them. "Maybe this is a good time for you to visit your son."

"I can't afford—"

"Book the trip out of petty cash," he said. "Take your husband too. And when I see you next month," he paused, forcing a scowl so she wouldn't argue, "you better be over this nagging. Or else." He grabbed his pen and tapped the 'FIRE BELINDA' notation.

She paid no attention, just blinked away tears of gratitude, the corners of her mouth wobbling.

"And please give me the number for Garrett," he added. "I want to call him before I go."

She dropped Garrett's number on his desk, already written up on a yellow call sheet, utterly efficient, as usual. Then she turned and walked from the office. Belinda was smart, opinionated and stubborn, but fiercely loyal, and without her the agency never would have grown to such a powerhouse.

Scott pressed Garrett's number, trying to remember when they'd last talked. A couple months, maybe more?

Garrett answered on the first ring. "Hey buddy," he said. "I tried calling the hospital. Heard you were clipped saving that kid. Forget the boy's name but glad he's okay."

"Robbie," Scott said. "His name is Robbie. And a lot of

people took part in the rescue."

A rescue that had almost turned tragic. The boy's terrified eyes still haunted him. Not the FBI's finest hour—or his. Robbie shouldn't have been placed at such risk. They'd been lucky.

"But you're the golden boy who took a bullet and received a commendation. Always the hero." Garrett's voice had a slight edge.

"The entrepreneur role was already taken by you," Scott said.

Garrett chuckled, sounding once again like his easygoing self. "Remember the money we made, sneaking your pony into the track? Selling rides to all the little kids?"

"Yes, Beauty was a trooper. And your idea was brilliant." Scott leaned back in his chair, smiling at the memory. No doubt, frazzled parents had merely wanted a babysitter while they lined up at the betting wickets, but Beauty had definitely made them pocketfuls of cash, that is until an irate security guard had banished them from the grounds.

Garrett's ideas had been daring and fun, but often illegal... And the fact that Garrett was pulling stories from so far back meant he wanted a favor.

"What do you need?" Scott propped his feet on the empty desk and made himself comfortable, deciding there were some advantages to Belinda clearing away his files.

"Just your esteemed name," Garrett said. "Our application is up for renewal but they're threatening to ban our Mexican students. I'd like to list you as one of our directors and educators. Boost the school's legitimacy."

"I don't think having an ex-cop on board will do much for your legitimacy. And I've hit a few trifectas but—"

"But that's exactly what will impress them." Garrett's voice rose. "We had an incident here. A drug dealer enrolled in the program. Trying to entice our students."

Scott's feet thudded to the floor. Like Garrett, he loved the race industry. However, there were inherent challenges, and riders—who faced danger daily—were too susceptible to drugs and alcohol. It was despicable for a low life to infiltrate a jockey school and prey on students. "I hope you busted his balls," he growled.

"Couldn't. The guy sneaked off when we shipped some horses to Mexico."

"You sending horses to Mexico now? Dammit, Garrett."

"Not for meat," Garrett said. "But there's a training center that's trying to restart Thoroughbred racing in the Baja. Some of their students come up for schooling—grooms, exercise riders, jockeys. They're scraping for racehorses. When I have a surplus, I ship the horses down and everyone's happy."

"This dealer was never caught?" Scott asked. "He just disappeared?"

"Yeah. Guess he stayed in Mexico. His family has been a pain in the ass. Wanted him treated as a missing person. They insisted on an investigation which caused all kinds of problems. Piece of shit really screwed the school. But with a PI and ex-cop as director—maybe I could even list you as teaching an addictions course—I'm sure our renewal would be approved."

Scott rolled a pen between his fingers. He wanted to help. Garrett was his oldest friend—the guy had been there for Scott's first bike ride, his first beer—but Garrett never worried much about rules, and some of his free-wheeling deals made Scott shudder.

"I can't advertise a class I have no intention of teaching," he said. "And I don't want to come on as a director. Too many liability issues."

"I was afraid you'd say that. You and your damn ethics." Garrett chuckled but his laugh carried a hint of desperation. "There's nothing to worry about. I've already had my lawyer look into the liability aspect. They'll make sure you're protected. We can work out a different title too. I only need some pictures of you on the brochure. Maybe that shot of you with the governor.

"And even if you'll just agree to set up the addictions course," Garrett went on. "Spend five minutes in the classroom then turn it over to my instructor. That would work. When the government sees we have an expert on board, someone like you who's made such a stand against drugs, and with that recent commendation... My God, man, you took a bullet for that kid."

Scott closed his eyes and leaned back in his chair, letting Garrett's persuasive words drone against the pounding in his head. The man was on a roll now. Even as a little kid Garrett had been a natural promoter. And this southern California school did sound worthwhile compared to many of his friend's past ventures.

One of Garrett's jockey grads had even made Scott some money, bringing in a longshot the first day of the Santa Anita meet. It was doubtful that Thoroughbred racing could ever be re-established in the Mexican Baja. Those glory days were gone. Still, he gave them full marks for trying.

"Garrett." Scott was finally able to slide in a word. "I'd like to help, but I don't want any misrepresentation. I need to be comfortable with this. But if you give the details to my assistant, maybe she can figure something out." There was no way he'd trust Garrett's lawyers, not when he had Belinda and his own legal team. "Hang on a sec," he added, rising from his chair.

Belinda's lips thinned as he summarized Garrett's request. "Sure, I'll talk to him," she said, reaching for the phone. "But I've always thought he was a bit of a schemer."

"Yes, but it's for a good cause so take it easy on him," Scott said. "It'd be nice to keep his jock school operating. Industry reports are excellent and he's putting out decent riders."

Belinda only sniffed, and Scott walked back into his office, feeling a twinge of pity for Garrett.

Twenty minutes later, she re-appeared with a handful of papers and a satisfied expression.

"All right," she said. "I've agreed he can list you as school consultant and special lecturer but definitely not a director. He thinks that will be enough...since you're going to live onsite for a month, teaching his new Addictions 101 class."

Scott jerked in horror.

"Don't worry." She positioned a colored printout on the middle of the desk. "He has a vacant villa with a pool, Jacuzzi and fully stocked bar. You'll teach no more than two hours a day, four days a week."

"Absolutely not!"

"Plus there are great trails and you can ride any horse you choose."

Scott tilted forward, unable to hide a spike of interest. Garrett always had a good eye for a horse. "Thoroughbreds or Quarter Horses?" he asked.

"Both. There might even be some cattle on the grounds. They run an occasional stock management clinic."

"And Garrett's satisfied with that? It's enough for government approval?"

"It's fine, although it wasn't exactly what he wanted. I did agree he could use your picture on his brochure as well as the Taylor Agency's name. The publicity will be great for business." She gave a rueful smile. "The racetrack industry always seems to need PI services."

"Doubt there'll be much need for investigative services at a jockey school," Scott said. "It'll probably be boring as hell."

Belinda's expression turned smug. "I imagine it will," she said.

CHAPTER TWO

Megan took a final bite of the chocolate bar, savoring the blend of caramel and pecans. After eight days of tofu and carrot sticks, the forbidden chocolate made her sigh with pleasure. She hadn't intended to dip into their supplies, not until she returned to her dorm, but the bars were hard to resist.

She folded the empty wrapper then checked the truck's cracked dashboard clock. Thirty-three minutes before her next class. Plenty of time to return to campus. She didn't want to be on the receiving end of her instructor's wrath. Only a week into the program and she'd already witnessed Lydia's tongue-lashing when a student was caught sneaking a cookie. The model-slim Lydia wouldn't consider a run to the store for junk food any excuse for tardiness.

Fortunately, Megan was enrolled in the exercise rider program and she didn't have to watch her weight as obsessively as the jockeys. Unfortunately, the cafeteria's menu was severely limited, and the closest store was ten miles down a winding country road.

She wondered if her brother had ever craved chocolate while he was here. Probably not. He'd been so keen to be a jockey, a real jockey with papers to prove it. Don't think in past tense, she chided herself. It was ludicrous to believe Joey had left the school and run off to Mexico. He'd always kept in touch with his family, even during rehab. And his text messages had been upbeat. Her mother had lived for those messages.

On impulse, she grabbed her phone and pressed her mother's number.

"Hi, Mom," she said, forcing a cheery tone. "What's new?"

"Not much. Nothing from the police. Myra dropped by with some of her cinnamon buns."

Megan could barely hear her mother's despondent voice. She switched off the radio, but the roar from her cracked muffler couldn't be silenced as easily. "How's Stephen?" she asked. "Did he get anywhere with Missing Persons?"

"No, the police can't help. Guess we just have to wait. And pray Joey comes home. All they can tell us is that he went to Mexico five weeks ago." Her voice quavered. "How's your design course?"

"It's fine. Everything's fine." Megan cringed at the lie but her mom and step-dad would panic if they knew what school she was really attending. "I haven't been doing much over the last week. Studying, a little exercise. I even lost a few pounds."

She forced a chuckle even though her aching muscles screamed. Jogging an extra mile every morning certainly hadn't prepared her for the rigors of riding school. "Did Joey make any bank withdrawals yet?" she asked. "Use his phone?"

"N-nothing." Her mother's quaver ripped at Megan's heart. "And his credit card hasn't been touched. Maybe the police are right. Maybe he *is* back on drugs."

"No! No," Megan said, calming her voice. "He would have needed money. I'm sure he was clean. And I don't care what the school said. Joey made some mistakes before, but not recently. I'm positive."

"It doesn't matter what kind of trouble he's in. I just want him to call."

"I know, Mom. Listen, I'll check back on the weekend. Say hi to Stephen. I love you."

She stiffened as a sleek gray car loomed aggressively in her rearview mirror. Please, not a cop. She didn't want trouble. Didn't want anyone at the school to know she was Joey's sister. She dropped her phone between the two seats—one of these days she'd get a hands-free device—and wrapped her fingers around the wheel.

She peeked again in the mirror and blew out a relieved sigh. Definitely not a cop. A Mercedes emblem was conspicuous on the hood. Cops didn't drive luxury cars.

She eased off the accelerator, pulling slightly to the

side of the twisty road so the car could pass. Maybe if her truck were ten years younger, she'd have gunned it. But she'd never had the time or inclination to go vehicle shopping. Her rueful gaze met the driver's, and he raised his hand in polite acknowledgement before cruising past.

Soon he was just a gray streak on the narrow road and once he rounded the corner—

Her eyes widened in horror. A huge pickup careened around the bend, straddling the centerline, headed for the car that had just passed. She jammed on her brakes, certain she was about to witness a head-on collision. But the Mercedes alertly swerved into the ditch, kicking up a flurry of gravel as it bounced over the rough ground for what seemed like an eternity.

The pickup slowed. Two heads swiveled. Then it sped up without bothering to stop.

She jammed her truck to a stop on the rutted shoulder, pried her phone out from between the seats and hurried toward the ditch, her heart pounding. She reached for the driver's door, clumsy with panic, afraid of what she'd see. Her CPR was rusty. She should have taken that first aid class offered in the fall, and not been such a recluse.

"Did they clip you? Are you okay?" a man asked, his voice a deep baritone as he opened the door and stepped out.

"I'm fine," she said, searching his face for signs of shock. "You can wait in my truck. Sit and stay warm. I have chocolate." Her fingers shook as she tried to press 911.

He pried the phone from her hands. "Don't bother the police with this. They have enough to do."

"But...that truck didn't even stop." She crossed her arms and realized she was shaking. "They didn't care."

"Typical punks." His voice hardened as he reached into his car, emerging with a pencil and paper. "What do you think? Late model Dodge pickup. Two-door?"

"I don't know. But the color was cobalt blue."

He looked up from the paper, amusement flashing in his cool gray eyes. "Cobalt. Okay, thanks. With the color and plate, the police can track them down."

"But I didn't get the plate. It happened too fast. I'm almost sure it was two guys though."

"That's okay. I got it." He scribbled something, head bent.

"You remembered their license plate? Even when you were ditching it?" She jammed her hands in her pockets and stepped back, feeling rather useless. "You must have a good memory."

"For some things. Not phone numbers." His smile was slow and deep, crinkling corners of his eyes and heck, she couldn't look away. Chiseled jaw, a hint of stubble, distractingly attractive.

"So," he asked, "what's your name and number?"

"Megan. Megan Spence," she croaked, flustered. She never gave out her phone number but had to admit it was no problem giving it to this guy. It wasn't just his numbing good looks but something else, an easy confidence that made her feel safe. "I live in L.A. though," she added. "I'm only here for a short time."

"Me too."

"Oh, well, maybe I'll see you in court or something?"

"Don't worry about court." His smile deepened. "I doubt the police will even call you. Is that your truck?"

She nodded, watching as he jotted down her license plate. Very efficient, she thought, studying him covertly. He was lean and handsome with short-cropped golden brown hair. Looked like an athlete or maybe a Special Forces type, except his skin was rather pale and there was a faint line on the side of his head.

"I think maybe you banged your head." She edged forward, straining to see. "Looks like a mark—"

"Old injury," he said, not looking up. His voice turned crisp and clearly the subject was out of bounds. "I'll report this, arrange for a tow and hopefully no one will bother you. I appreciate you stopping."

"No problem." She peeked at her watch. Lydia's class would be starting in exactly seventeen minutes. But it seemed cruel to leave him stranded on a lonely road waiting for a tow that might take hours. And she was quite certain he'd banged his head, despite his denial. He'd stiffened when he bent for the paper. Not exactly a wince, but something that revealed discomfort. Plus, he was damn good looking, and it had been a long time since anyone had stirred her interest.

She shoved back a tendril of hair, ignoring her ticking

watch. "It might be a while before the tow truck comes," she said. "I have a rope in my truck. Want to give it a try?"

"Sure. I'd appreciate that, Megan."

He wrapped her name in such a deep smile, her pulse tripped. She nodded and tried to walk gracefully toward her truck, aware of his very male scrutiny. Damn. She hadn't changed since morning gallops. She probably had helmet hair, but at least her shirt and jeans were passably clean.

She did a quick frontal check, wiping off some stubborn horsehair, then stepped up on her back tire, reached into the truck bed and pulled out a rope and shovel. She turned, almost bumping into him, surprised by his silent approach.

"I'll carry it." His voice had a calming effect. "A shovel too. Good. You must be a ranch girl."

"Not anymore." She passed him the heavy rope before jumping to the ground. "My mom and step-dad still live on the ranch, but I make jewelry now." At least she did when she wasn't trying to find her brother.

She paused, still holding the shovel, watching in concern as he abruptly splayed a hand against the side of her cab. His mouth tightened, as if in pain. "Are you okay?" she asked. "You went into the ditch pretty hard."

"I'm fine." He straightened with a curt nod. "I left the hospital recently."

"Then I'll fasten the rope." She pulled it from his hands, ignoring his protest, and hurried to the ditch before he could stop her.

"I'm smaller anyway," she added. Besides, he had the shoulders of a Greek god and she doubted they'd fit under any car. She dropped to the ground and wiggled beneath the bumper. "I helped my brother tinker around with a lot of machinery. And German cars are always great. It's never a problem finding a place to attach ropes."

She slid back out. "There," she said, rising and swiping the gravel from her jeans. "I'll just back up, hook on and see what happens."

He looked rather bemused but he did have the presence of mind to check her knot, and she guessed it was a measure of his pain that she'd even been able to grab the rope. He didn't look like a man who asked for help—more like someone who gave it.

She maneuvered her old Ford into position, attached the rope to her hook and stepped back into the cab. He gave a thumbs up from the tilted seat of his car. She slowly pressed the accelerator. One jerk of protest. Then the disheveled Mercedes emerged from the ditch.

Dented fender, broken headlight, cracked grill. Other than that, the car looked okay. By the time she'd stepped down from the cab and unhooked her end of the rope, he'd already replaced the unneeded shovel and was coiling the heavy rope.

At least he wouldn't be stuck waiting on the side of the road. And it was a lovely car, banged up but unmistakably elite, even beneath the layer of clinging dirt. "First time my truck has ever rescued such a beautiful car," she said wryly.

"First time I've ever been rescued by such a beautiful lady."

She shot him a look, searching for sarcasm, but his expression looked genuine. He didn't seem to mind her faded jeans. Or the messy braid in her hair.

"I'll be back in L.A. next month," he said, his level gaze holding hers. "I'd like to take you for dinner. As a thank you."

She hesitated, uncertain how long she'd be at Joey's school. This guy probably wouldn't call anyway. And the prospect of dressing up and driving across the city to a boring restaurant wasn't very appealing. There was no possibility of escape if conversation turned stilted.

"Or just coffee, if you prefer," he added, obviously a perceptive man.

"It's not that," she said. "Really, I'd like to meet you. But I live near the San Gabriel Mountains and there's a racetrack close by with great food. The horses are always fun to watch. April 30th is the last day of spring racing. Maybe we could meet there?"

"Santa Anita. Perfect. One of my favorite spots." His mouth curved revealing a dimple on the left side of his cheek. Or maybe it was a scar that was more noticeable when he grinned, but whatever he was doing was definitely making her insides melt. Heck. She was staring again, acting like a dork.

She turned and slid into the cab, her skin hot and tingly. He closed the door and leaned against the open window of her truck. It was impossible not to notice the muscles rippling in his forearms.

"My name's Scott. And I'll see you at Santa Anita in April." He spoke with such assurance she could only nod, sensing he was the type who really would call.

She fumbled with the shift and jerked the truck down the road, barely hearing its noisy muffler over the pounding of her heart. Wow. Her breathing was still racing and despite the cool blast of air conditioning, her palms stuck to the steering wheel.

He was gorgeous, sexy and nice and he was going to call. And although the last five weeks had left her in a wrenching hell, for now she was almost happy. She spent the rest of the drive humming along with the radio. And even smiling.

CHAPTER THREE

"Megan. What is the percentage of silica commonly found in the synthetic track surfaces of California?"

Megan tried not to groan but the looks shot her way by sympathetic classmates only raised her frustration. Lydia had been targeting her for the last half hour, ever since she'd rushed in late after towing Scott's car from the ditch. Usually she was good at making up answers, but this question was way outside her ranching background.

She shot a look at her roommate, Tami, who only shrugged and gave a trademark eye roll.

"I have no idea," Megan finally admitted. "I do know Santa Anita switched back to traditional dirt so maybe there wasn't enough silica?"

Lydia's eyes narrowed. "The correct answer is in yesterday's study handouts," she snapped. "In the real world, you'll need to know these details. The reputation of our school depends on each and every one of you. Unfortunately the caliber of our students this year seems vastly inferior."

Megan bit back her reply, aware it was folly to argue. Lydia didn't like questions or debate. Yesterday Eve, the pretty dark-haired girl with the flashing eyes, had challenged her on a point, and Lydia had summarily punished Eve by assigning extra barn chores.

Megan couldn't let that happen. She wanted as little schoolwork as possible. Needed all her time to trace her brother's tracks. If Joey had slid back into drug use, someone here should know and, if not... She shivered, not wanting to entertain the horrible alternative.

No, he was alive. He had to be. She nervously fingered her pencil, freezing when she realized the brittle teacher had just mentioned Joey by name.

"Our school has already taken a big hit because of traffickers like Joey Collins," Lydia said, her lip curling in distaste. "Drugs and alcohol are insidious. Be careful of unscrupulous people who will encourage you to experiment. It was criminal that he posed as an aspiring jockey when he really just wanted to set up dealers."

The pencil in Megan's hands snapped. She glared at Lydia. No one knew she and Joey were related—they had different surnames—but she hated to let anyone smear him like that. Nothing had been proven. He was missing, for God's sake.

"Joey didn't do drugs," Eve said, her voice loud and confident.

Megan twisted in her seat. She'd only been here a week and didn't know all the students yet, but this girl was definitely one she wanted to meet. Eve was supposedly a top rider and clearly courageous enough to challenge Lydia. Unfortunately Eve was also very reserved, almost haughty. So far, Megan hadn't been able to engage her in any type of conversation.

"Joey started school the same week I did," Eve said. "He didn't do drugs."

"For your information, the police confirmed he'd been in rehab," Lydia said smugly. "Several times, in fact. He's a crackhead."

Eve's eyes flashed and she squared her shoulders as though preparing to say more. Lydia's eyes narrowed to ominous slits.

"Who's Joey?" Megan asked, trying to keep her voice nonchalant.

"The student who almost shut down our school," Lydia snapped. "Dumped the horses in Mexico and deserted our driver." She shot another dark look at Eve and continued. "But Mr. Baldwin is committed to success and is fighting the stigma. He's added an addictions class, worth a full credit for university transfer. A famous instructor has been hired. Just don't expect this man to be as flexible as me."

Someone in the back snickered, but Megan wasn't sure if it was because of the flexible comment or because Lydia always flushed whenever she mentioned Garrett Baldwin. She seemed to idolize the school owner, primping and posing whenever he appeared.

Lydia sniffed. "No one will laugh next week. Mr. Taylor only has a forty percent pass rate. He'll weed out inferior students. Of course, that's assuming Mr. Baldwin doesn't send you home first. He's requested my candid assessments, and I've been very honest. Some new students—you know who you are—simply aren't cut out to be riders. It's a waste of time and money to let you stay."

Tami made a slashing gesture over her throat, but Megan shifted in her seat, fearing her cheeks had turned bright red. Only two students in the exercise rider program were still trotting in the field—doing baby circles with Lydia and the grooms.

And Megan was one of them.

She glanced over her shoulder at Peter, the other hapless rider. He seemed totally unconcerned, busy flirting with the slim redhead in the back. Of course, he'd already had his meeting with Garrett Baldwin. He'd been approved to stay.

Megan sighed but the minute hand of the wall clock seemed to move slower than usual, dragging along with the afternoon lecture. There was so much to do. Finish class, pick out stalls, feed, shower, eat and then meet with Garrett. Hopefully, it wouldn't be an exit interview.

She'd have to work harder. However, she was always exhausted. The days were strenuous and it didn't help that her roommate snored. Seven nights into the program and she still wasn't used to sleeping with Tami. Wasn't used to sleeping with anyone.

Lydia finally dismissed the class with a jerk of her head, and they filed from the room.

"Is your interview with Garrett tonight?" Tami asked.

Megan nodded. "I'm the last one. Peter went this morning. According to Lydia, Garrett sees the best students first, the worst ones last." She forced a wry smile, hiding her fear. It would be devastating to be kicked out after only eight days—she hadn't learned a single thing about Joey yet, and certainly was no closer to finding him.

"Don't worry." Tami nudged Megan's ribs with an elbow. "Rumor is, Lydia makes up most of this stuff, trying to scare us. You really have to suck to be kicked out of jock school. And Garrett likes pretty girls so you'll do fine. You're the only student with an evening appointment. My interview was at seven in the morning and my eyes were still baggy. I didn't impress him at all. Lost any chance of snagging a rich sugar daddy."

She gave such a mournful sigh, Megan smiled despite her very real fear she might be sent home. At this point, she was ranked as one of the worst riders here. But she had to stay in order to track down Joey. This was the second time her mother had lost someone she loved, and they both needed answers.

"If Garrett doesn't think I can ride well enough to stay as an exercise rider," Megan said thoughtfully, "I'll request a transfer to the grooms' program."

Tami's nose wrinkled. "Loser! You'd be stuck riding in the field forever and all the cute guys are on the track. Most of their lectures are at different times too. You'll never get to hang out with the cool people."

"True," Megan said. Tami made no secret of her interest in the jockey students—an interest that rivaled Megan's own but for totally different reasons. Joey had been in the jock program for almost seven months. The people that knew him best were the jockeys.

"If Garrett offers you a drink, you'll get to stay," Tami said. "And it wouldn't hurt to change into a low-cut shirt. Maybe wear that silver and amethyst necklace too. I'd kill for jewelry like that. It must have cost more than your truck."

"You can borrow my necklace whenever you want," Megan said. It was the only one of her designs she'd brought with her, except for her turquoise studs and coral earrings. Everything else remained at home. The school had suggested barn clothes only, although she wished she'd been better dressed when she met Scott. A girl didn't mind taking a little extra time for a guy like that.

"I can borrow your necklace? Sweet!" Tami's sharp squeal made Megan wince. She felt ancient around her roommate. Of course, designing jewelry was a solitary career, and she hadn't let many people into her life. Seemed she felt old around everyone.

"Maybe I'll borrow it tonight," Tami went on, giving her hips a happy wiggle. "No, you'll need it for your meeting. You better look your best, just in case. And don't tell Lydia you have an evening appointment. She doesn't like girls and she's only mean keeping you in the field. Everyone knows you're a better rider than me."

"She didn't like the guy who disappeared least month either," Megan said, grabbing the opening. "Jamie? Or was it Joey?" It seemed sacrilege to mangle her brother's name, and she stooped to tighten her bootlace, hiding her distress.

"Joey," Tami said. "Joey Collins. And Lydia liked him well enough. But one of the grooms said Joey had hooked up with Eve, and Lydia wants every good-looking guy for herself."

Megan forgot her bootlace and stared up at Tami. This was exactly the type of information she needed and even though a roommate cut into her cherished privacy, Tami was always full of gossip.

"Joey and Eve?" Megan straightened. "Is Eve the girl with the dark hair, the feisty one? You'd think they'd have talked to her..."

"Who? Who would have talked?"

Megan shrugged off the question, but found it puzzling that neither the police nor the school had bothered to question Eve. "Lydia acts like she knows so much about Joey," Megan said slowly, "when obviously she doesn't know anything at all. Eve said Joey wasn't involved with drugs. And she'd know, especially if she was sleeping with him."

Tami giggled. "But people don't talk much during sex. I sure wouldn't mind hooking up with a guy. It'd be easier to have a single room though. More private, you know." She eyed Megan hopefully. "I don't suppose you're a sound sleeper?"

"I can hear a pin drop," Megan said, keeping a straight face.

Tami shrugged but looked disappointed. "By the way, thanks for making another chocolate run today. Too bad it made you late but we have enough bars to last the week now. I think we should raise the price to three bucks though. We'd make more money."

"No," Megan said, shaking her head. "We'll sell for two. Everyone needs chocolate. I don't mind covering the gas." And today had been well worth the drive. If she hadn't gone to the store, she'd never have met Scott.

She pictured his intelligent eyes, those lethal cheekbones. Men who looked like that always had plenty of girlfriends. It was probably a good thing she avoided messy relationships. But a day at Santa Anita would be fun. Lots of fun.

Tami tilted her head. "You look rather happy for someone who strolled into class late and was reamed out by Lydia. I'm glad you went to the store though. You're one of the few students with a vehicle, and selling chocolate is a great way to meet people." She snickered. "Lydia's going to freak out wondering why the grooms and exercise riders are gaining weight."

But not the jockeys, Megan thought ruefully. She hadn't met any jockeys yet. They must have amazing willpower. She'd already chatted with most of the grooms and exercise riders—many had dropped by her room and bought a chocolate bar or two. However, the jocks stayed away, despite the limited cafeteria menu.

Grooms ate like normal people and the diet of an exercise rider wasn't too restrictive, but the jockeys had it tough. Lydia made them stand on the scales everyday, constantly preaching about how racing meant a lifetime of vigilance. Jock students always squeezed into the sauna before morning weigh-in.

Joey probably hadn't visited the sauna much. Like her, he was naturally slim. He probably hadn't liked Lydia much either. Nor would he have been enthralled with the school cafeteria and its sugar-free Jello. When he was little, she'd made him Jello, the real stuff with whipped cream. Raspberry had been his favorite. She would have made it for him more often, but her dad had called it fairy food.

Her chest tightened in a familiar vise. Joey had been so cute and later so resentful. How could a father desert a kid like that? Their dad had taught her how to ride but he hadn't had any time for Joey. Didn't matter though. She'd taught her brother, and since Joey was a better rider than her, obviously she was a better teacher than her dad.

If not for her, Joey wouldn't even have considered jockey school. She'd encouraged his love for horses. Even paid his tuition...so his disappearance was her fault.

Tami was still rambling about junk food and misunderstood Megan's anguished sigh. "Hey, you don't have to worry about chocolate," Tami said. "Weigh-ins are for jocks only. They're competitive about everything, especially since the top student gets to go to Mexico."

Megan made an encouraging sound, hoping Tami would keep talking. Joey had mentioned the Baja Tinda, a ranch in the Baja where students were sometimes invited. He'd even worried about his passport, afraid his record might ban entry. He'd been so excited, definitely not sounding like a student ready to quit.

"The school nearly lost the travel perk though," Tami went on. "The government almost blocked foreign students too. That Joey guy caused a real mess."

"But no one seems to be thinking of Joey," Megan said. "His family must be worried—" She clamped her mouth, nearly biting her lip in the process. It wasn't Tami's fault. She was only parroting the crazy tales.

The police confirmed Joey had accompanied Ramon, head instructor, to Mexico along with four horses. Joey had never returned. Apparently he'd deserted the truck and trailer at a small town ten miles north of the Baja Tinda Ranch, claiming he was sick of jockey school.

Megan didn't believe it.

He was only three months away from graduating. He'd already applied to several race stables. One trainer had even offered a job galloping at Santa Anita. Besides, Joey would never abandon anyone. Would never abandon horses... Not if he were clean.

She fought a traitorous prick of doubt. Joey *was* clean. His texts had been upbeat. There'd been no sign he was using again. Clearly he'd been enjoying the classes, the riding, the people.

"Does Ramon decide who goes to Mexico?" Megan asked. "Or is it Garrett?"

"Who knows." Tami shrugged. "But they need two people to haul. Usually it's the Mexicans that go but if they're short, Ramon invites one of his better students. It's a reward."

"So Joey must have been doing well or he wouldn't have been asked by Ramon. He couldn't have been that wasted."

Tami shrugged again, clearly bored with the topic. "Don't know. But if you're trying to wrangle a trip to Mexico, forget it. You can't even two-point on the Equicizer."

The Equicizer. Megan jammed her hands in her pockets. The mechanical horse was physically demanding, and she wasn't accustomed to a tiny saddle with stunted stirrups. Her background was pure western. Plus she wasn't in top shape.

She'd come from her jewelry studio with only a daily jog for exercise. Her cardiovascular fitness didn't match the other students, most of whom had been riding daily.

She'd never imagined she'd be at the back of the class, but after six days on the Equicizer she still lost her balance at speed—she, who had galloped stock horses since she was four. It was frustrating.

At first, being limited to trotting hadn't bothered her. She didn't want to exercise horses for a living anyway, had only wanted admission to the school so she could find her brother. But if riding was critical to meet the jockeys—and perhaps earn a trip to Mexico—she'd have to pick up the pace.

Ironically, she'd always been considered an excellent rider in Western disciplines. However, the exercise saddles were different and so tiny, weighing only five pounds. She'd been taught to sit straight and keep her butt in the saddle. Leaning forward and standing in the stirrups was a precarious position, and one she hadn't yet mastered.

Joey would have laughed at her difficulties. Clearly, he hadn't struggled, but he was a superb athlete with excellent balance and reflexes. He could ride anything. He probably would have made it as a jockey too—she gulped back a wave of grief and turned her head from Tami, hating how she always thought of Joey in the past tense.

Was it her subconscious saying something terrible had happened? And where was her positive thinking when she needed it most?

Ramon stalked from the grooms' barn, sweeping both of them with an enigmatic stare. He inspected their barn every afternoon but spent most of his day teaching the jockeys. He was also the liaison with the Mexican students and the Baja Tinda. The police report stated he'd been the last person to see Joey, that he'd been the instructor Joey had abandoned. So either Joey was back on drugs...or Ramon was lying.

An odd expression flashed across Ramon's face and for a moment, Megan feared he'd sensed her simmering hostility.

"Hurry it up," he said. Ramon always talked in a low voice, yet even Lydia listened when he spoke. "Horses are hungry. And the outside water tubs need scrubbing."

"Why us?" Tami asked. "Isn't that grooms' work?" She pushed back her shoulders and gave her hair a flirtatious swish.

"Why not you?" Ramon asked, unaffected by her posturing. "Exercise riders need to learn a groom's job too. Makes for better horsemen."

Megan forced an agreeable smile. Ramon gave her a curt nod but certainly not one that qualified as friendly. Of all the staff, he was the most difficult to approach. He was a retired jockey and a national hero in Mexico but spent the bulk of his time with the elite jock students.

It would be easier to poke around if she were in his class. Yet for jockey admission, students had to weigh less than one hundred and fifteen pounds, and there was also a height restriction of five foot six inches. At five foot seven, one hundred and twenty-two pounds, her application had been rejected.

She'd have to get to know Ramon some other way.

"I'll clean the tubs," she said brightly.

His eyes narrowed. "Is your name Megan? The one who just started the groom program?"

"Exercise program," she corrected, feeling exposed beneath his hard stare. She and Joey didn't really look alike but there was some resemblance, especially in the nose and mouth. Everyone said they had the same shaped mouth.

"Why haven't I seen you on the track?" Ramon's eyes locked on her face.

"I'm still riding in the field," she admitted.

"Well, if your name is Megan," he said, "forget the tubs. Tami can do them. You need to see Garrett now. He has a friend arriving tonight so he moved up your interview." Ramon cast her another penetrating stare before turning away. He walked with a faint limp and a not-so-faint swagger... a swagger that most of the jock students emulated.

Megan looked at Tami's dismayed face. "Don't worry," she said. "I'll help you clean the tubs when I get back."

"I just hope you come back." Tami pressed her knuckles against her mouth, her voice mournful. "You're a cool roommate, but he was looking at you kind of weird. Maybe he knows Garrett's going to kick you out."

"It'll be fine. They want my tuition money as much as anyone else's." She gave Tami a reassuring smile because after all, she was ten years older and supposed to be confident. But her heart hammered against her ribs because Tami was right; Ramon had been looking at her very strangely.

CHAPTER FOUR

Megan trudged up Garrett's cobblestone drive, pulling in deep breaths, trying to boost her confidence. Ramon's dark expression might have been related to dirty water tubs, a sick horse or any number of things. It didn't necessarily mean she'd flunked out. Joey had never worried about lasting the trial period, although he probably hadn't been stuck trotting in the field with the grooms either.

She fought another grinding fear. Had Garrett and Ramon discovered she was Joey's sister? She'd assumed they wouldn't make the connection since her name and address were different. She also was taller than Joey...and obviously didn't ride like him. But her mother and step-dad were filing a lawsuit. Maybe her name had popped up on the legal papers.

She rubbed damp hands on her jeans, trying to quell her paralyzing thoughts. She'd find out soon enough.

At least it was a lovely evening. A pastel sky colored the ridge and stately elms shaded the long drive. A sprinkler whirred. She slowed her steps, absorbing the smell of budding eucalyptus, the refreshing silence. It was utterly serene, like her studio. No students hollering, no instructors criticizing. If she weren't so apprehensive, she would have enjoyed the walk.

This was her first visit to the restricted section of the grounds. Her entrance interview with Garrett had been off campus. The property was much larger than she'd anticipated and obviously, the school was prospering. This section was like an oasis, far removed from the dust and parched grass that marked the stable area. An ornate brass sign pointed directions to the track, the dorms, and the cowshed.

Cowshed? She'd never even seen that building. It must be behind one of the imposing grilled gates. Judging from the prices on the school website, the cattle clinics targeted an elite clientele. She took an experimental sniff but couldn't catch a whiff of cow.

There were no signs pointing to Garrett's house or to the luxurious villa settled to the right of the drive. This must be the back entrance, the student route. She wondered what Joey had thought when he'd made this all-important walk. Maybe he hadn't noticed the contrast between the stark dorms and Garrett's private property.

Joey hadn't stressed about anything but horses, not since he'd straightened out his life. So, where the hell was he? And what had happened to him? It was as if he'd fallen into a black hole. And no one cared.

Her fists tightened, her steps lengthening. She strode up the driveway and rapped on the thick door. Wondered what the mighty Garrett Baldwin would think if she just blurted out, 'Where's my brother!'

A muffled bark sounded, followed by a sharp command. The door swung open. Garrett was tall, blond and just as tanned as he'd been last month. "Come in, Megan," he said. "Sorry I had to switch your time."

"No problem." She stepped into the spacious entry, her gaze shooting to the magnificent German Shepherd sitting on the cool tiles. He didn't move but his watchful eyes and ears were locked on her face.

"Do you mind dogs?" Garrett asked. "Rex is very obedient but I can lock him up, if you prefer."

"I love dogs," she said, "but thanks for asking." Twice in the last year she'd almost brought home a puppy, then decided she wasn't ready for the commitment. Besides, a dog's life span was short and it hurt too much when loved ones left.

Garrett shot her a relaxed smile, looking like a surfer with his golden skin and rumpled bronzed hair. "I usually do these interviews in the office but let's sit in the den. I've been at my desk all day."

She nodded, trying to settle her jangling nerves, and followed him down the cool hall. Rex's nails clicked behind them. She scrambled to remember all the Internet details about Garrett: divorced, no kids, passionate about the race industry. But he'd sent two students home yesterday so clearly he wasn't a pushover.

The thin lady who'd been uncomfortable with horses had been booted out as well as the curly haired teenager who chain smoked behind the barn. Surely the school couldn't afford to lose three students in one week? She knew of no way to hunt down Joey other than to start at the place where he'd disappeared.

Garrett gestured at the sofa. She sat, keeping her arms loose, hoping he wouldn't sense her desperation. He lowered himself on a chair and thumbed through several files, obviously searching for her progress report. Rex sniffed curiously at her jeans and she patted his big head, grateful for the diversion.

"You initially applied for the jockey program," Garrett finally said, "but didn't meet the physical requirements." He lifted his head, his eyes narrowing. "Now that you've been here a week, do you think you'll be happy galloping horses for a living?"

"Oh, yes," she said. "I love being around horses. I'm not used to the short stirrups but it's getting a lot better." She crossed her fingers at the blatant lie. She didn't feel as if her riding was improving, not one bit.

He smiled, but not unkindly. "Lydia tells me you're having difficulty with the position. A lot of experienced riders have trouble, especially dressage and some of the western disciplines."

"That's good to know." She let out a cautious breath. "I feel like I've never been on a horse before. Lydia says I'm the worst she's ever seen."

Garrett's face flashed with amusement. "Lydia tends to exaggerate, but she does a heck of a job teaching. A bit of fear is often good for the younger students."

The tension in Megan's shoulders eased another notch. She leaned forward and scratched the base of Rex's left ear. It didn't sound as if Garrett intended to kick her out. In fact, he seemed rather friendly. Too friendly? His warm gaze lingered on her breasts, and she wished she hadn't followed Tami's suggestion about wearing a low-cut shirt.

"Remember race riding is about balance, not grip," he added, glancing back down at her resume. "I see you finished high school ten years ago and have been working at your family ranch. Have you thought about building on your program? Our courses are recognized at Bay University. A degree would open up more opportunities in the equine field."

His voice rang with sincerity and she swallowed, hating to lie. She'd neglected to list her fine arts degree from Berkeley. Garrett may have earned his reputation as a womanizer, but he seemed to genuinely care about the future of his students.

"I can't afford to go to school for longer than six months," she said, scratching harder at Rex's ear and avoiding Garrett's gaze. "I just need to finish the exercise rider program and find a job."

"But money shouldn't be the deciding factor," he said. "Not when you're mapping out your future. Scholarships are available. I can help with your application. Many opportunities exist now, especially for the grooms and exercise riders."

"But not for the jockeys?"

He smiled, such a dazzling smile she couldn't help but smile back. No doubt about it, this man knew how to charm. "The jockeys are convinced they're going to make the big leagues," he said, "despite Ramon's warnings. They don't consider a backup plan. A few will make a living of course, but most won't. And many will never even ride at a public track. They'll just disappear."

Like Joey. She tried to control her despair but Rex sensed her tension. He cocked his head, staring up at her with soulful brown eyes. "Do you have many quit your jockey program?" she managed.

"If they do, it's usually the first month. Some riders don't have the ability or courage. And that's something that can't be taught."

"I heard one guy recently quit, after seven months of riding." She willed her voice not to crack.

Garrett shrugged. "A very unusual incident. That particular student has been trouble since he was a kid. A convicted felon who enrolled under false pretenses, trying to establish drug runners at the track. As you know, we have zero tolerance here. All students sign a form to that effect."

Rex whined, nudging her hand with his nose, and she automatically resumed scratching. But her mind whirled. Joey's juvenile record was sealed. Garrett and Lydia shouldn't know his complete background, not unless the police had spilled it during the investigation. Not totally surprising though. Many cops had big mouths.

"Don't you check for a record during the admission process?" she asked.

"Guess we didn't look into his background closely enough," he said, his tone rueful. "And that was unfortunate since the student was very talented. Ramon said he had more potential than anybody he's ever seen. Now enough of that, Megan." His smile was slightly apologetic. "Lydia suggested you need more practice on the Equicizer. She says you're still trotting in the field."

"Yes, that's right. But I'm close to getting the hang of it."

"Really?" He rose and walked toward a mahogany cabinet. The diamonds in his Rolex watch flashed as he reached for two wine glasses. "Red or white?"

She'd intended to refuse any drink, but her heart thumped with panic. He looked amused but also disbelieving about her assurance that she was getting better. Apparently she wasn't over the hump, but dammit, she couldn't leave the school. Not yet. She hadn't learned anything of value, hadn't had a single meaningful conversation with the jockeys.

She swallowed, wetting her throat. "Red wine would be lovely," she said.

An hour later, she leaned back on the sofa, smiling as Garrett told another joke about his university football team. Some of their escapades had bordered on insane but he had a very persuasive personality, and his tales were definitely entertaining. He moved the wine bottle to a side table—she was surprised to see it was empty.

"Sounds like you weren't very nice to your rookies," she said.

"I probably wasn't, but our quarterback looked after everyone. He didn't tolerate much razzing."

At some point, Garrett had joined her on the sofa and his warm leg now grazed her knee. She inched away, careful not to jostle Rex whose big head rested on her ankle. However, she'd reached the edge of the sofa and there was simply nowhere left to go.

"Some guard dog." Garrett leaned down, his arm brushing her thigh as he patted Rex. "I've never seen him act like that. But I approve. Clearly he has excellent taste."

He gave her a look full of such blatant appreciation,

she considered rising and darting to the bathroom. He must have sensed her unease and leaned back.

"So keep up the hard work," he added smoothly. "The first week is the toughest, but you're through that now. If you ever need to talk, just let me know. I'm meeting someone in half an hour, but usually I'm available...any time."

"Thank you." She rose so quickly Rex's head bumped the floor. He gave a reproachful grunt but thumped his tail to indicate no hard feelings. She stooped and gave the dog an apologetic pat. However, it was clear Garrett wasn't talking about student interviews, and she didn't feel the least spark of attraction. He was the shallow flirty type she always avoided.

Still, Garrett headed the school. If he didn't know the truth about Joey, he was acquainted with people who did.

"Great," she said, straightening and edging toward the door. "I'm sure I'll need your advice sometime." She forced a smile, but it felt fake and she didn't like the way his satisfied gaze lingered on her breasts.

CHAPTER FIVE

"How was your interview with Garrett?" Tami asked. She leaned over the table, trying to be heard over the jangle of cafeteria trays and cutlery.

"It went fine," Megan said, reaching for the jug of iced tea and topping up her glass. "I'm not being kicked out yet, although he'd heard about my trouble with the two-pointing."

"I'm not talking about the interview." Tami rolled her eyes and grabbed an apple from the fruit bowl. She took a crunching bite, her eyes inquisitive. "How did you get along with Garrett? Isn't he gorgeous?"

"Yes, he's nice. He talked about the degree program. Told me which courses are transferable. That new addictions course is worth a full credit."

"But did you sit in the office or the living room? Did he give you anything besides water? That's a big indicator, where you sit and what he gives you to drink." Tami swept Megan with an objective once-over. "You're definitely his type."

"What type is that?"

"Pretty, but not tiny like the jocks. Rumor is he prefers long legs and lots of curves. His wife recently left him. So, you know, I'm really curious if he hit on you?"

Megan busied herself with her tea. Tami generally leaped to another question if her first one was ignored, and Megan hoped this time wouldn't be any different.

How far would I go to find news of Joey? Garrett had seemed attracted although it was clear the nature of their relationship would be her decision. He probably wasn't enamored enough to pursue her so if she kept things at a business level, all would be fine. No big deal.

He probably wouldn't be so amiable if she pretended interest and then shut him down. But while Garrett was okay, he definitely didn't make her pulse kick. His divorce was also recent, never an ideal situation.

Maybe she wouldn't be so reluctant if she hadn't met Scott earlier today. Now that guy was the real deal. And she'd see him the end of April. She sighed and folded her palms over the table, accepting she wasn't capable of faking interest with someone like Garrett, no matter what the reason. Undercover work definitely wasn't her strength.

"Sheesh, this apple isn't much bigger than a cherry." Tami waved the fruit disdainfully. "Bet Lydia measures them. At least we have more than vegan. Look at what the jockeys are stuck eating. Their plates are tinier too."

Tami had already jumped to a different subject and Megan nodded, relieved her roommate had forgotten the questions about Garrett. She followed Tami's gaze to the jockeys, happy to encourage this new topic.

Generally the students ate in groups. Grooms sat closest to the kitchen, exercise riders hung out in the middle of the dining hall and the jockeys claimed the far end, furthest from the kitchen, probably so they weren't tempted by second helpings.

And their plates were smaller. Megan had noticed the difference in size the very first day. She wondered where Joey had sat. There was an empty chair by Eve, the pretty dark-haired girl. It was precisely the location he would have chosen, back against the wall and slightly removed from the others. Joey was always a little reserved. Like her, he avoided meaningless chatter and shallow relations. He must have liked Eve though, a lot.

Eve abruptly turned, catching her appraisal. Megan flashed the girl a friendly smile. But Eve looked away. Reserved, shy or a snob? Hard to tell. Megan did know it was frustratingly difficult to make friends with any of the jockeys.

Tami followed her gaze, switching topics without missing a beat. "Jockeys prefer to stick together but they're a special breed. Imagine having your weight a public record, every extra pound announced. Not for me. They are cool though. Any one of those twenty could be the next superstar."

"Nineteen," Megan said absently. "Unless they already replaced Joey."

Tami's lips moved as she counted the people at the far table. "There are twenty now but that cute guy by the aisle is new. He showed up a few days ago. I heard he stays with Ramon. They're always talking in Spanish." She blew out a frustrated sigh. "I've never seen such a cliquey bunch."

Megan nodded. They were a clique, and that was the problem. Joey had spent most of his time on the track, yet she couldn't ride there until she was approved to gallop. And because the jock program was longer and more specialized, the jockeys had already molded into a cohesive group.

Megan had one class with Eve, but so far they'd barely exchanged pleasantries. Most of the jocks' horses were stabled in a different barn. Almost eight full days here and she still knew nothing about Joey's life. Her idea of selling chocolate bars to the students hadn't helped—the grooms and exercise riders were enthusiastic customers, but the jockeys hadn't come knocking on her door.

"Don't look now," Tami whispered, still eying the jock table. "But that new guy is staring. Do you think I'm taller than him?"

"Wish I could get close enough to tell," Megan said ruefully.

"He's still looking. Hide the napkins. I'll make a reason for him to come over." Tami abruptly dropped the napkin dispenser out of sight on Megan's lap, then fumbled for her water glass.

Splash!

Tami's squeal sounded so shocked Megan jerked back, her flinch genuine as water drops splattered her arm. Tami scrambled to her feet, blue eyes wide with dismay. Her white T-shirt was soaked, the thin fabric hugging her breasts. She clearly had bigger boobs than any girl at the jock table.

Tami glanced around helplessly, as though searching for something to absorb the water. Three jockey students rushed over, including the new one, with napkins bunched in their hands.

"Thank you *so* much," Tami said, even letting the new guy blot the front of her shirt. He lingered, chatting up Tami while Megan sat at the table, feeling old, clueless and invisible.

The new jockey was the last to swagger away, shooting Tami a smoldering look over his shoulder.

"He's definitely taller than me," Tami whispered triumphantly as she sat down on her newly dried chair. "His name's Miguel and he's going to give me a tour of the jock barn tomorrow night."

Megan scooped up the soggy napkins, trying to remember if she'd ever been that young. Tami was only nineteen and no doubt resented being saddled with a roommate who was a decade older. She'd already confided she'd broken up with her last boyfriend and was searching for a replacement.

"I really love an accent," Tami went on. "Did you see the muscles in his arms?"

Megan's attention had been more focused on his colorful tattoos, but Tami leaned closer, still bubbling with enthusiasm. "If you don't like Garrett, what about Ramon? He's older but he definitely noticed you. He has his own villa, and he and Miguel are friends. Wouldn't that be cool!"

"No, I'm just here to get my license as an exercise rider," Megan said, afraid Tami would try to hook her up with Ramon if given any sort of encouragement.

"Fine," Tami muttered, hurt shadowing her eyes. "But you sure were interested in the jockeys earlier. I'm only trying to help."

"Sorry for the misunderstanding. Mine was more of a professional interest." Megan took a sip of tea, feeling rather guilty. She had asked a lot of questions, especially the first couple of days. Unfortunately Ramon wasn't a big talker and she hadn't been able to encourage much conversation. Little wonder her young but big-hearted roommate was confused.

"I'm going to do some laundry this weekend," Megan added meekly. "I can do yours at the same time if you'd like."

"Sweet!" Tami's smile returned. "And could I borrow your truck to run into town tomorrow? I want some new jeans, maybe some sexy underwear. I'll need a little cash too, just a few bucks. We can call it an advance on our chocolate bar sales."

Tami definitely considered Megan a softie. However, Megan had learned a lot from dealings with her younger brother so she tilted her head, pretending to frown.

"Of course," Tami added, "I'll also clean our bathroom for the next week."

"Three weeks," Megan said, already aware her roommate's idea of cleaning was much different from her own. She'd definitely be scrubbing the toilet when Tami wasn't looking, but a little negotiation was healthy. And if she couldn't find any news of Joey in another three weeks, it probably wasn't going to happen. At least they'd have a clean bathroom.

Garrett smiled at Scott, then gestured toward the spacious kitchen filled with shiny appliances. "The fridge and bar will be restocked every day," Garrett said. "And meals delivered from the cafeteria. Leave a list if there's anything special you want. You saved my ass again, buddy, just by coming here."

"No problem," Scott said. "I'm banned from my office anyway."

Garrett leaned forward, his eyes gleaming. "You finally did something illegal?"

Scott tapped his forehead. "Just a little headache. Doctor wants me to relax a bit."

"You seem fine. Women will love the scar. Besides, that's what you get for always trying to save the world." Garrett gave a dry chuckle. "I only want to save a jockey school."

Scott flipped through the stack of brochures Garrett had dropped on the coffee table. "Looks like more than a school for jockeys. There's something here for everyone."

"Yes. We offer programs for grooms and exercise riders but the jocks are high profile. Longer terms, bigger money and of course, the exchange students pay almost triple."

"How many kids am I teaching tomorrow?"

"Thirty," Garrett said. "And there's a waitlist. The course is fully accredited at Bay University so everyone is clamoring for a seat. And these students aren't all kids. Ages run from eighteen to late sixties."

Scott studied the class list and the range of ages. Naturally the jockeys were the youngest since that was so physically demanding and they also had weight restrictions. He shook his head, realizing the last time he'd made jockey weight was back in the sixth grade. Jocks were also the ones most prone to drug and alcohol dependency.

"You want just the basic info?" he asked. "Stick to the outline we discussed?"

"No," Garrett said. "I want you to scare the hell out of them. Can't afford to have any more shit rats sneaking in. That trouble last month almost lost me the business."

"Lost the business? You mean the school?"

"The school, yes," Garrett said quickly. "The kid was a damn good rider too. Could handle the toughest horses. But it was only a front. He planned to set up drug runners at the tracks and was targeting my students."

"What happened to him?"

Garrett's lip curled in disgust. "He knew we were onto him. Ramon asked some tough questions when they were in Mexico and the kid bailed. He's still down there unless he managed to get a fake passport."

"What were they doing there?"

"Hauling horses. The owner sponsors all our Mexican students and is trying to rejuvenate Baja racing. He has plenty of resources and is doing things right."

Scott glanced around at the luxurious villa complete with pool, Jacuzzi and an inner and outer bar. Clearly, Garrett was doing things right too. This place was like a five star vacation condo. "Sure swanky digs for a school," he said.

Garrett looked mildly embarrassed. "Staff bungalows aren't like this. Or the dorms. But the Baja Tinda people expect luxury when they come, and this is the villa they use. Since your secretary insisted you have a place of your own, we put you here. She made it a deal breaker."

Scott grinned. Garrett still had a faintly dazed look when he spoke of Belinda who, unlike Scott, had proved impervious to Garrett's powers of persuasion. But it was Scott's habit to help, ever since the day they'd met when the neighbor's bull cornered Garrett in the back pasture.

"She also insisted you have a good horse to ride," Garrett went on, "so tomorrow I'll show you my roping horse. He's stabled in the cowshed but you can ride on the private grounds or join Ramon and the students on the track. Maybe help some of the beginners. Whatever you want.

"There's not much else to do here," he added, giving a dismissive shrug. "The closest town is thirty minutes away, and the campus shuts down early. It's not like our old Friday frat nights."

"Thank God," Scott said, but he dragged a restless hand over his jaw. A couple hours in the classroom and some riding time would still leave endless hours to fill. He'd already left Snake four messages. It was surprising Garrett had chosen this kind of life. The man had always been a high roller. So had his wives.

"What about Shelley?" Scott asked. "How does she like living here?"

"Apparently not much, since we've separated." Garrett smiled with complete unconcern. His third failed marriage, yet the man seemed as carefree ever.

"I'm sorry," Scott said.

"Don't be. It's fine. You should try this marriage thing someday." Garrett cleared his throat. "Or should I say, consider it again."

Scott gave a lazy stretch and faked a yawn. It had been nine years and he still didn't like to talk about Amanda. Even with Garrett. Besides his head was throbbing again.

"All right, Professor. I get the hint." Garrett rose with an amiable grin. "Your class is at eight. Put the fear of God into them." He paused, no longer smiling. "And I owe you, again. I won't forget this."

He shook Scott's hand, looking uncharacteristically solemn, then turned and strode across the marble floor. The door closed, leaving Scott alone.

Alone with nothing to do but admire the posh accommodations. No wonder Belinda had been grinning. A made-to-order vacation with only four classes a week—he'd either learn to relax or go crazy trying. He grabbed his phone and called Snake again. The man still didn't answer. Scott left another voice mail, much more forceful than his message an hour earlier.

Bored, he scrolled down his short list of names. He couldn't call Belinda who was taking some well-deserved time off. It was too late in England to call his dad. Snake wasn't responding. His finger lingered over the latest addition... Megan, his beautiful and intriguing savior who made jewelry, boldly crawled under cars and liked horse racing. Maybe he should text her that the local police intended to call for a statement. Yeah, that was definitely appropriate.

He pressed out a quick text, before he could change his mind. *Thanks again for your help today. Police might call.*

Five minutes later, his phone chirped and Megan Spence's name appeared on the display. *They already did. How's your car?*

He texted back with fingers clumsier than usual. *Works fine. How's jewelry biz?*

Good. Do you give massages?

He paused. Odd question but promising, very promising. Anticipation swept him at the memory of those long legs, encased in tight jeans, the cotton shirt that couldn't quite hide her curves. He'd always loved a country girl. So if she wanted a massage, hell, yes, he did massages.

Sure do. See you Apr 30, SA paddock, race one?

Ok, she texted. *See you Apr 30.*

He checked his calendar. Nine weeks. It couldn't come fast enough. He was looking forward to getting to know Megan. And strangely enough, his headache had disappeared.

He stacked his course notes, no longer cursing the idiots who'd forced him off the road. Instead he pictured her elegant profile, that smile with the hint of reserve, the endearing piece of hay stuck in her gleaming braid of chestnut hair. A woman who wore jeans like she was born in them. Someone who preferred to go to the track instead of a tedious restaurant... she was his dream date.

Buzz. He grabbed his phone, hoping it was her, but the display showed Snake. Finally. He'd left five messages.

"I haven't heard from you all day," Scott said, slightly aggrieved. "What's happening with the Dexter surveillance?"

"Nothing yet, boss. It's only been six hours." Snake's voice rumbled with amusement. "You lonely? Maybe finding people slow to answer your calls?"

Scott stalked into the kitchen, his good mood vanishing. "I need to know what's going on at the office," he said. "Why don't you answer your damn phone?"

"Oh, I will...now." Snake chuckled. "I just didn't expect a massage expert to be calling me, that's all."

Scott groaned in sudden comprehension. Belinda had fixed him up with one of the office phones and the company had many public facades, depending on their investigation. He should have been alerted by her mischievous smile when she handed over the new phone. "What's my display name?" he asked.

"Scottie's Massage Services."

He winced, remembering Megan's question about massages. To compensate for his embarrassment, he bit off a list of rapid-fire instructions. However, it didn't subdue Snake in the least, and the man was still laughing when Scott cut the connection.

CHAPTER SIX

Megan filled her bucket with a spray of water, surprised by the rush of people. The aisle was bustling, unusual for so early in the morning. Feeding started at six, followed by breakfast and muck out, with first class at eight. Students usually trailed back from the cafeteria, yawning and in no hurry to clean their stalls and then cram into a stuffy classroom.

Today though, even Tami whipped through her chores, monopolizing the two best wheelbarrows, while the gray-haired lady three stalls down had been in such a rush she'd almost poked Megan's eye with a pitchfork.

"What's the hurry today, Tami?" Megan called, lingering to give Jake, one of the two horses she'd been assigned, an affectionate pat. She liked both geldings under her care, but Jake was everyone's favorite. She'd never ridden him—only top students earned that honor—but she always saved a few extra minutes for the friendly horse.

"Sheesh, Megan. Weren't you listening to announcements?" Tami rubbed a piece of straw off her boot than jammed the overloaded wheelbarrow against the wall. "The alcohol and addictions class starts today. Everyone is hurrying so they can grab a seat. Sometimes I wonder what you're even doing here."

I wonder too. Megan's shoulders slumped in defeat. At this point, she was just wasting time. The students who knew her brother were galloping on the track while she was stuck far away, trotting baby circles in a field. She'd accused the police of incompetence, yet she'd been here an entire week and uncovered nothing new. It was time to step outside her comfort zone and do some serious sleuthing.

Besides, she didn't care about lectures and diplomas, and certainly wasn't interested in this new class. She'd already experienced Joey's desperate struggle against drug addiction. No need to relive the experience.

"I might skip that class," she said. "Spend some more time on the Equicizer."

Tami's eyes widened. "Are you crazy? This new course is full credit. We're lucky Garrett gave us a spot. Most of the grooms are on the wait list."

"But I'm not going for a degree. I just want to ride on the track...that is, qualify as an exercise rider so I can ride at other tracks."

Tami didn't even notice Megan's blunder. In fact, she'd already turned away, pulling her hair from its ponytail and fluffing it around her face. "Then do you mind emptying my wheelbarrow? I want to go and get a good seat. This class is mandatory for the jockeys so Miguel should be there."

"Really?" Megan asked. "All the jockeys are going?" She peered out the end door at the adjacent barn and dorms. The jockey barn had restricted access. But if everyone was busy with the new class, she'd finally have a chance to poke around Joey's room. If the jock dorms were like hers, no one ever locked their door.

Joey had been in room thirteen, something he'd joked about as being bad luck. He'd even paid extra for a single room, preferring privacy. The police assumed he'd wanted to hide his drug activities.

"Sure, I'll finish up for you," Megan said, trying to keep the excitement from her voice. "You can just go to the class now."

She brushed off Tami's exuberant thanks and waved goodbye, eager to be alone. No doubt, Joey's room was still vacant as new jockeys were generally accepted in September. Maybe she'd find something. The school had shipped back his riding helmet and clothes, but his phone and iPod had never surfaced.

She rolled Tami's wheelbarrow to the manure pile, in a hurry now to finish her chores. Jake stuck his head over the stall door, watching intently, as though suspicious she might sneak a rival horse a peppermint. All the students looked after two horses, not necessarily the ones they rode. Jake was always in huge demand but her second horse, Rambo, was never ridden so needed to be turned out in his paddock.

Rambo was an incorrigible bucker and several students had broken bones when they tried to gallop him. A crude 'DO NOT RIDE' sign was nailed to his door. Luckily, the horse was fairly manageable on the ground. After three days, she no longer needed a chain over his nose.

"Let's hurry today, fellow," she said, grabbing Rambo's halter and lead line. The quicker she finished here, the quicker she could sneak into Joey's room.

Rambo flattened his ears. The haughty gelding had an excellent deal—daily turnout and no work, but it didn't help his disposition. Most of the school horses had only one day off a week and the fact that Rambo was such a badass made his care easier. She only had to muck out one stall during the day and had already scrubbed and filled his outdoor water tub.

She led Rambo to his paddock. The pen was brown and bare, stripped of grass. But it was close to the jockey barn so she lingered by the rail, watching the building and hoping it would empty.

Clearly someone was still working in the aisle. A bucket rattled and stall doors banged shut. Obviously not all the jockeys were attending the new class. Disappointed, she sagged against the rail. Rambo flattened his ears, annoyed by her presence. Seemed she couldn't even befriend a horse.

Grass grew eight inches from the bottom rail, just beyond his reach. She picked up a handful, tossing it over the fence as a peace offering. He blinked in surprise then stepped forward and slowly picked it up.

She shaded her eyes against the morning sun and checked the time. Almost eight. If the jockeys were going to class, they'd have to leave soon. At least Rambo no longer resented her presence. In fact, he watched her rather hopefully. She picked more grass, killing time while she waited.

Finally two laughing students swaggered from the jockey barn, leaving the building silent. She tossed one last handful of grass to Rambo, pulled in a fortifying breath and hurried toward the forbidden barn.

She stepped inside. The aisle was wide and cool, and she paused, letting her eyes adjust to the interior light.

Horses contentedly munched hay, clearly accustomed to their morning routine: breakfast at six, another flake of hay at eight, groomed and saddled by ten fifteen, then on the track for an hour. Most of the exercise riders had advanced to riding with the jockeys, but she still didn't know any of the students in this barn.

Her mouth flattened. Joey would have chuckled if he'd known she'd been assigned to the lowest riding group. Heck, she'd taught him to ride, hauled him to his first show, even coached him to a ribbon in the State barrel racing. But he wasn't here to tease her now. Her stomach clenched with despair, the same gut-wrenching ache she'd experienced when her father had left.

What the hell happened to you, bro?

She crept down the aisle and climbed the stairs to the dorms on the second floor. Pushed open the door and scanned the corridor. It was wide and well lit, with a similar layout to her dorm. But she passed a large kitchen near the steps, complete with a fridge and coffee maker. There was no kitchen in her residence. If grooms or exercise riders missed meals, they were out of luck.

No wonder the jocks always strutted as though superior. They were.

She tiptoed to room thirteen and paused outside the door. It seemed utterly still. She knocked softly, praying no one would poke their head out. But there was only silence. She tried the knob. Unlocked. She pushed open the door and slipped inside.

Joey's room.

She stood unmoving, trying to feel his presence. But no matter how hard she tried, she felt nothing. The room looked and felt deserted. The bed was stripped. The tile floor gleamed. It was hard to imagine he'd ever slept here.

She crossed the room and pulled open the desk drawers. Empty but not scrubbed. The wood was stained and several cracker crumbs were visible, along with a twisted paper clip. Good. The cleaning staff had rushed this job. Maybe she'd find something.

She dropped to her knees and peered beneath the bed. The ridged end of a magazine, dusty and dog-eared, was pressed between the corner bed leg and the wall. She yanked it out. *Racing in California*, last month's edition.

She blew out a satisfied sigh. Strung-out druggies didn't buy horse magazines. The last time Joey was using, he'd lost interest in everything.

She flipped through the pages, scanning the articles, desperate to find any type of connection. Joey had read this and now she would too. Every single page.

She shoved the magazine into her back pocket and renewed her search. The police had been here but it was doubtful they'd looked very hard. After interviewing Ramon and Garrett, the official conclusion was that Joey had chosen to remain in Mexico, the nirvana of drugs.

A groan escaped from deep in her throat, a helpless sound that surprised her. She wasn't usually a pessimist, but Joey's bank accounts hadn't been touched. Not a good sign. Even worse was her aching sense of loss, a feeling she simply couldn't shake.

She hoped he'd stayed in Mexico. Wished he were using drugs. It would be much better than this wrenching fear that she'd never see him again.

She stepped into the bathroom and opened the medicine cabinet. Empty. Not spotless but certainly there was no sign of drugs, prescription or otherwise. And now there wasn't anywhere else to look. On impulse, she raised the top from the back of the toilet tank but found nothing, only murky water and green mineral stains.

She wandered back to his bed and stared out the window. He hadn't enjoyed much of a view. No horses, merely a small hayfield, recently cut. If she pressed her face against the glass pane, she could see the back of Rambo's paddock. The rooms on the other side of the hall would look over the training track.

Booted feet thudded up the steps, and for a second she quit breathing. Then she bolted across the room and pushed the center on the doorknob. It was only a cheap lock, but now it would need a key before opening.

She stared at the thin door, her mouth drying with fear. It wasn't such a big deal that she was here. There was no reason to be so scared. If caught, she'd simply claim she needed a single room and heard this one was empty. Or that Tami snored—which she did—or that she was meeting a jockey here. Heck, any number of excuses should work. But her heart hammered and swallowing didn't help her dry throat.

The footsteps drummed closer. A man spoke in Spanish, talking much too fast for her rudimentary knowledge. It sounded like he was by the kitchen, likely just wanted a drink.

Her heart steadied. It was ridiculous to be so jumpy. Probably no one had entered this room since they'd packed up Joey's things. But she had to leave before the new class ended. Jockey students would hurry to their rooms, drop off their notes, and change their clothes before going downstairs to saddle. She didn't have much time, so hopefully this guy wasn't planning to hang around the kitchen.

Her ride time was ten-thirty, and her horse wasn't even groomed. She wished there was a peek hole in the door so she could see this guy with the aggressive walk. He obviously was cutting class too. Rather odd since most students were keen about the new class.

She pressed her ear against the thin door, straining to understand the rapid-fire Spanish. The man was walking down the hall toward the stairs now, still talking. She caught the word *caballo*, not surprising since they were surrounded by horses.

She tiptoed back to the window, craning for a glimpse of the barn entrance, but all she could see was the hayfield. It was impossible to tell where he was heading—back to class or had he remained below in the barn aisle? If so, there was no way she could escape unseen. If he asked what she was doing, she'd need some sort of excuse.

One thing for sure, she wasn't leaving Joey's magazine. She pulled it from her pocket and tucked it into the front waistband of her jeans, glad she'd worn a loose shirt. The cover poked her skin, but didn't stick out too much. If she folded an arm over her stomach, no one should notice.

She cracked open the door. There was nobody in sight and no sound from the stairs. Flattening her palm over the magazine, she stepped into the aisle. It was impossible to walk silently on the wooden floor, not with boots, but she definitely was quieter than the thumping student.

She ducked into the kitchen and filled a Styrofoam cup with black coffee, wryly noting the row of washers and dryers squatted in an alcove. Exercise riders and grooms were restricted to a single coin-operated machine by the cafeteria. These jock students were definitely pampered.

Cradling the warm cup, she descended the steps. The aisle was empty, the barn devoid of humans. Relieved, she hurried toward the doorway and out into the bright sunlight. She didn't even need the coffee as an excuse.

"*Hola.*"

She whirled toward the greeting, so quickly the coffee splashed her wrist.

Miguel, the new student, leaned against the outside wall, phone in his hand. "I thought everyone was in that new class," he said, arching an eyebrow.

"I slept in." She made a rueful face and took a sip of coffee. It was black and much too strong. Probably had been sitting for hours. If she'd known she'd really be drinking it, she would have added milk. "I heard you guys had a coffee machine," she added. "Hope you don't mind me popping in, but your barn was closer than the cafeteria."

"I can tell you're not a jockey." His dark eyes swept over her in bold assessment. "Isn't there a coffee machine in your dorm?"

"No," she said. "We don't have washers or dryers either." She folded her free arm over her stomach, praying Joey's magazine wasn't showing.

"That's probably why they posted the 'JOCKS ONLY' sign," he said, jabbing his thumb at the red-lettered sign on the door. "To keep out riffraff. But pretty girls like you can come and visit anytime."

Riffraff. It was quite clear he wouldn't notice the magazine beneath her shirt, not the way he was staring at her breasts. For that matter, she doubted he'd even recognize her face. In fact, he was rather insolent for a new student. "We riffraff aren't the only ones cutting classes," she said. "Guess at least one jockey student is playing hooky too."

He had straight white teeth, but his smile didn't reach his eyes. "I don't need the addictions class. I'm almost finished the program."

"How did you do that?" she asked. "I only noticed you last night."

His eyes flashed and he stepped closer, surrounding her with the smell of liberally applied cologne. "I'm glad you noticed me, *querida*," he said. "I noticed you too. But

I'm not new. I'm from the Baja Tinda. Are you a groom?"

"No, exercise rider." Her mouth tightened. It was clear she'd never be mistaken for a tiny jockey, but his question brought back the grim reality that she was still riding with the grooms.

"Good," he said. "Then I'll see you later on the track. Maybe I will choose you as my riding partner."

He clearly had a high opinion of himself but at least he was friendlier than the other jockeys. It was unfortunate he hadn't known Joey...or had he? Joey had mentioned that only he and a Mexican student were able to ride the tough horses. And no horse was tougher than Rambo.

Her gaze drifted over Miguel's sinewy forearms. Extensive tats wrapped around them, the green and black ink edging below his neck. "You look like you can handle a horse," she said.

"Definitely." He flexed his biceps, his voice lowering suggestively. "Believe me, I can ride anything."

She edged back, trying to keep it light. "But can you ride Rambo? He's one of the horses I groom."

Miguel dropped his arms, his leer changing to a frown. "That horse is loco. I tried him once. No one can ride him."

"Not anybody?" she asked, breathing a little easier now that she had more space.

Miguel shook his head. "He isn't safe for students. Don't put your saddle on him."

"I won't. But there must have been someone who could ride him. A lot of riders pass through here."

"One student did okay," Miguel said grudgingly. "But he's gone now."

"He must have been a good rider," she said, sensing Miguel was talking about Joey. "Is he working at a track now?"

"I don't know where the guy is," Miguel said. But his gaze darted to the left, as if searching for another topic.

Her hand shook with pent-up emotion. He was lying. It was obvious. She wanted to demand answers but he kept talking, oblivious to the coffee sloshing against the side of her cup.

"All the best horses are in this barn," he was saying. "Come back sometime and I'll give you a private tour. Maybe I'll even make you a special coffee."

She gave a curt nod, knowing she had to humor this guy.

"I have liquor hidden in my tack box," he went on. "For you, I'd share."

She swallowed, needing to wet her throat before attempting to talk. "That would be nice, Miguel," she finally managed. "Let's do that sometime."

And surprisingly, her voice barely quivered.

CHAPTER SEVEN

"Get your ass up, Megan," Lydia snapped. "Why is that so difficult?"

Megan stuck her rear another inch in the air, but the position felt totally wrong. All her life she'd been told to keep her seat in the saddle. To sit straight. Maybe she was too old to learn such a different riding style.

She circled the field, following a line of nine riders. Her horse, Barney, was lazy and lacked impulsion, stumbling over each clump of grass. Every ten feet he tried to stop and she had to sit back in the saddle and use her legs to push him forward.

Peter, on the energetic gray, was lapping her now. He chuckled as he passed. "I had to ride Barney my first day here. It's impossible to lean forward on that plug. Just tell Lydia you want a different horse or else ask permission to carry a whip."

She grimaced. Lydia would bite her head off if she made any requests. It was fine for Peter to ask, but he was one of Lydia's favorites. Actually all the guys were the instructor's favorites. And despite her waspishness toward the girls, Megan had to admit that Lydia looked unusually attractive today with flashing red and silver hoop earrings that matched her shirt.

Barney stepped out a few strides, briefly energized by Peter's horse, a narrow-chested gray with an arched neck and white-rimmed eyes. For a glorious moment, they trotted in tandem.

"Is Lydia dressed up for you?" she teased, careful to keep her voice low. It was okay for Peter to talk, but Lydia always snapped at the girls if they 'disrupted' the class.

"Not for me," Peter said. "It's because of the new addictions prof. All the girls were drooling this morning.

Not a bad dude actually. Didn't you notice him?"

"I missed that class. But I'll catch the next one."

"Better not miss any more or you'll lose your spot. It's a full credit so there's a wait list."

She nodded absently, tired of hearing about full credits and half credits and no credits. She didn't want the course anyway. Besides, she knew enough about addictions to last a lifetime. But a good-looking instructor explained why Tami had lingered after class and been too rushed to answer any of Megan's questions about Miguel.

Peter's horse drew away, and she glanced wistfully at the big track where more than twenty riders cantered in pairs. They all looked so capable from this distance, leaning forward and standing in their stirrups like real jockeys.

Tami was among them and no doubt Peter would join their ranks soon. He actually looked good on his gray. Once he left, she'd be the only exercise rider still stuck with the grooms—grooms who weren't expected to ride and only needed to understand the basic concepts.

At this rate, she'd never be able to buddy up with anyone from Joey's class. They'd all have graduated by the time she joined them. Ramon might be her only hope, and he was like a stone wall. Of course, now there was Miguel. But she stiffened with distaste. For a moment Barney responded to her tension, stepping out for three jerky strides.

"Congratulations, Peter!" Lydia called, her smile vivid beneath shiny red lipstick. "Tomorrow you can ride out with the jockeys. I like how you're two-pointing, and only making contact with your legs.

"This class is over for the day," she added. "I'll see the rest of you tomorrow."

Lydia hurried away, in such a rush she forgot to deliver her usual warning about walking back to the barn in single file.

Students and horses milled, confused by her abrupt departure. She was already a hundred feet away, bee lining toward the building that housed the classroom, cafeteria and fitness center.

"Bet she's looking for the new instructor," a stout lady snickered. "Did you see her makeup? Poor Garrett has totally lost her affections."

"Garrett doesn't care," Peter said. "And do you realize we only had a twenty-minute lesson? Waste of time to even tack up."

"At least you'll be riding with the big boys tomorrow," a gray-haired woman called. "Well done, Peter. Now I'm going back to the barn to practice my bandaging."

The rest of the riders turned and straggled toward the barn. However, Barney stretched his neck and didn't move, pleased with this unexpected chance to nap.

"At least I won't have to put up with Lydia anymore," Peter said, "other than in the classroom. I don't know why she's so rough on you." He circled his gray around Megan's dozing horse. "Everyone knows it's impossible to look good on Barney."

Megan gave Barney's neck a rueful pat. Everyone else had ridden at least three horses, but so far, she'd only been assigned one mount. Maybe Peter was right and she would be able to two-point on a different horse.

"Would you switch horses?" she asked impulsively. "We still have an hour before lunch. And Lydia didn't give us any instructions."

"That's because we already know it's taboo to switch." Peter peered over his shoulder as though afraid the instructor might reappear.

"But she's gone now. No one will know. Besides, she likes you. She even lets you carry a whip."

Peter flipped his reins and looked smug.

"I'll give you two chocolate bars," Megan added, watching his expression. She could tell he was almost swayed. Peter had a real sweet tooth. "Plus I'll groom both your horse and Barney after the ride."

"All right," Peter said, blowing out a sigh. "Just make sure you're back before the jockeys return. I don't think Ramon talks to Lydia much, but she seems to hear everything." His voice softened. "And I would have switched without the chocolate. You know I'm glad to help, especially when it's you."

She dismounted, pretending not to hear. Peter was always helpful, especially to her and Tami, but he was too nice to lead on. Giving him something in exchange made her feel she wasn't taking advantage.

"Look at Barney," she said, trying to lighten the conversation. The horse's lower lip was slack, his eyes drooping. He seemed oblivious to the rider change, and when she legged Peter onto his back, he didn't move.

However, Peter's gray circled and yanked at the reins, upset by this unusual procedure in the middle of the field. He called to his receding line of stablemates, his shrill neighs blasting her eardrums.

"Maybe we shouldn't have swapped." Peter's eyes widened with alarm. "He's going crazy. And how are you going to mount?"

"Like this." She grabbed the gray's mane, hopped once and vaulted into the saddle.

"Damn, Megan. You really can ride." Peter gave a relieved smile. "You'll be fine then. Want me to stick around?"

"No, go on back to the barn. I'm just going to trot some circles and practice standing in the stirrups. No problem."

But two minutes later, it was a problem. Peter's gray—Megan couldn't even remember his name—was panicky at being deserted, and his half-hearted crow hops had turned into aggressive bucks.

She pulled her feet from the short stirrups, clamped her legs around his barrel and pushed him forward, trying to keep his head up. Clearly he wasn't used to being without his buddies, and even more clearly, she wasn't going to be able to practice her two-pointing. It took most of her energy just to stay on.

The gray's attention swiveled, tracking movement below the ridge, and he suddenly relaxed. Another horse, a confident-striding bay, was at the far end of the trail. She hoped the new horse and rider would stay in the field. The gray was obviously fearful when separated from other horses.

Luckily the bay's rider seemed to understand her predicament and stopped thirty feet away, watching her from beneath the brim of his cowboy hat.

"Thanks," she called. "My horse doesn't like to be alone."

"Megan?"

She swung around. *Scott?* The gray took advantage of her attention lapse and sidled toward the muscled bay, eager for company.

She was too stunned to do anything but stare at the

rider—and wow, it really was Scott, looking every bit as good on a horse as he did standing by the ditch. He rode in a western saddle, and his obedient bay appeared chiseled from a Quarter Horse model.

"Hello, Megan." Scott's deep smile made something kick in her chest. "I'm surprised to see you here. Not making jewelry today?"

"No...actually, I'm taking a riding program here. What about you?"

"I'm teaching here."

Her gray was already bored with the new horse and began to sidestep. She turned him in small circles, wishing he'd remain still so she could talk. Scott, here at the school? This was too good to be true.

"Are you teaching massage?" she asked.

"No massage." His voice rippled with amusement. "That phone ID was my assistant's idea of a joke. I'm supposed to be taking it easy for a month."

She remembered the mark on his head, hidden now beneath his hat or maybe not. Darn. The gray wouldn't stand still long enough for her to see, although Scott didn't appear to have a similar problem. His horse stood on a loose rein, as relaxed as his rider.

"But your name really is Scott?" she asked, still circling her horse.

"Yes. Scott Taylor."

The gray snapped out a sneaky buck. She pushed him forward, glad at least she had something to do and Scott wouldn't see how flustered she was. She simply couldn't believe he was here. Couldn't believe how her heart was hammering.

"Your horse is definitely herd bound," Scott said. "I noticed him from the ridge and wondered if I could help."

"Thanks for coming." Her voice was breathless and it wasn't entirely from trying to control the gray. "I need to work on my two-pointing, but he's too upset to listen."

"I'll pony you," Scott said, reaching over and slipping a loop over her bit. And suddenly they were trotting, the gray happy to be moving forward.

"Stand up," Scott said. "Keep all your weight in your heels. That's it." His voice was confident and encouraging, and he clearly had control of her horse. She bounced for a few strides, concentrating on her position, then suddenly nailed it.

She was actually balancing in the stirrups, butt in the air, head up! It wasn't hard at all. Now the horse's impulsion was working to her advantage. She looked at Scott. "Thanks so much. I've been trying all week to get this."

"Often it's harder for experienced riders."

She grinned in triumph. The gray moved freely, head arched, as she balanced over his neck in perfect rhythm. It was a different sort of riding but definitely exhilarating. No wonder Joey had loved it.

Scott moved his horse into a canter, and her gray stretched out gleefully. Lydia had never let Megan go faster than a trot. Her poor horse must have been so frustrated. And holy shit, Scott was leading her toward the track.

She scanned the oval but Ramon and his class were at the far end, obviously finishing up. And she was having too much fun to tell Scott she was restricted to the grooms' field. Besides, he seemed to know what he was doing.

They slowed to a walk as they approached the gap. "We'll do our fast work on the track," he said. "The ground's safer. Do you want a rest first. Are your legs tired?"

"No, they're good. But I can see why they want us fit." Her breath came in short gasps. "My horse is in better shape than me."

His warm gaze slid over her, and she was suddenly glad she hadn't indulged in too many chocolate bars. "You'll still pony me," she asked, "when we're on the track?" Her breath was still ragged but she wasn't sure if it was from her lack of fitness or because of his obvious interest. Even the air seemed to be crackling.

"Megan," he said softly, "I don't intend to let you go."

She glanced sideways, but his hat shaded his expression. She didn't see the signal, but both horses moved into a ground-covering trot, making further conversation difficult.

She pulled her attention back to her riding. At first, she was too conscious of Scott's presence but he didn't say anything more, and she was able to concentrate on the track.

Trotting was easier on the smoothly harrowed oval. Her horse didn't stumble and moved straight, seeming to know his job and utterly accepting of the composed bay at his side. Obviously racehorses were accustomed to being escorted, and it was a big help to be able to concentrate on her position and let Scott control their speed.

A speed he was gradually increasing. And, wow, the horses were galloping now. She was doing it. She was actually galloping on the track. She felt like a real jockey, balancing in the stirrups, moving in quiet rhythm with her horse.

They slowed much too quickly. But her legs felt like rubber and her breath was labored so maybe it wasn't too soon, even though her eager horse felt like he wanted to gallop another mile.

"This is great, thanks. Before, I was putting too much weight on my knees." She shot him a delighted smile. "I don't really want to stop."

"Me neither," he said, his eyes locked on her face.

She swallowed. Her face felt warm but that could easily be blamed on exertion. He wasn't even doing anything, just looking at her, but he was so damn attractive it left her unsettled.

"Guess my horse is ready for lunch," she said.

"Why don't you take him back to your barn and have lunch with me?" And then he smiled, so slow and intimate she thought she might hyper-ventilate.

"I'd like that," she managed. *Boy, would I.* "But there's not enough time," she added, unable to hide her disappointment. "The cafeteria closes at one-thirty and I have a class right after that."

"Dinner tonight then," he said, so easily she could only nod. "What program are you in?"

"Exercise rider."

"That explains why you wanted to meet at Santa Anita. But you said you make jewelry?"

"I do. I'm just here for a while...to improve my riding."

He tilted his head and she caught a hint of puzzlement in his intelligent eyes. Even to her, the reason for being at the school sounded lame. "Thanks for helping me," she added quickly. "I have to get back to the barn. Maybe now I'll be approved to ride on the track."

"I'm sure you will." He gestured at the dirt trail winding over the ridge. "My horse is stabled in the cowshed. Is my number on your phone?"

"Scottie's Massage? It sure is." She smiled, and even though it was late, she wanted to linger. "I was expecting a massage."

"Then I won't dash your expectations," he said. "Call me when you're ready to eat, and we'll go from there."

The undercurrent in his voice made her hands tighten around the reins, but she wasn't quite ready to leave. She had more questions, like where they would meet and when. But he just reached over, gently squeezed her shoulder, then turned and trotted toward the ridge.

Her horse tried to follow, and she completely understood the feeling. She wanted to follow too. Her skin still tingled from the touch of Scott's warm fingers.

Sighing, she headed back to the barn. At least, she'd see him tonight, and they wouldn't have to wait until April. She hoped he knew the cafeteria hours. It was obvious they both might miss lunch, and she didn't want to skip supper too. However, 'call when you're ready to eat' sounded rather vague.

She adjusted her reins, trying to keep her horse from trotting, but the gray was alone again and desperate for company. He gave several ear-ringing neighs, and they both glanced toward the ridge. She thought Scott's horse called back. But her mount remained distraught and despite his hour of exercise, he pranced the entire way home.

By the time they reached the barn, his neck was coated with a white lather. There definitely wouldn't be time for lunch. It would take at least half an hour to cool him out and she had to look after Barney too. Still, the long morning had most definitely been worth it.

Smiling, she dismounted and gave her horse's sweaty neck a pat. Poor fellow. If she were his groom, she'd take him for daily walks. Teach him that his world wouldn't collapse when he was alone. It must be horrible to always need buddies. That was the good thing about a solitary life—it didn't hurt so much when people left.

"Is this the despicable way you treat animals when I'm gone?"

Megan wheeled toward her instructor's angry voice. Lydia's eyes flashed and her mouth was clenched so tightly that white marks dotted the edges.

"It's more of an emotional sweat," Megan said. "He's

nervous when he's alone. I'm going to bathe and walk him now."

Lydia jammed her hands on her hips and stalked closer. "And who gave you permission to ride him?"

Peter hurried from the barn, stepping between Lydia and Megan. "I wanted to switch," he said. "Edzo has so much energy and with the short lesson today he needed more trotting. Megan was kind enough to help."

"Were you both present a few weeks ago," Lydia asked, "when I stressed no switching horses?"

Megan actually wasn't present, but she didn't think 'no' was the answer Lydia was looking for, and it wasn't fair to let Peter shoulder the blame.

"The switch was all my fault," Megan said. "I needed to practice two-pointing, and wanted to work on some of the other things."

"But you stayed out by yourself," Lydia said. "Edzo is difficult to ride alone. And the school can't afford any more bad publicity. Not after last month's awkward incident."

"Awkward?" Megan's head jerked up. She forgot about looking contrite, forgot about everything but her mother's anguish. "You mean Joey disappearing? You call that an awkward incident?"

"He didn't disappear," Lydia said, her voice icy. "He chose to stay in Mexico. And you're suspended from my class the remainder of the week. That should give you plenty of time to practice on the Equicizer. Now go cool out that poor horse."

Lydia jerked away, her back ramrod stiff.

Peter groaned. "She came back about twenty minutes ago in a very bad mood. I knew we were in deep shit."

"I'm so sorry," Megan said.

"It's all right." He gave a crooked smile and helped remove the saddle. "Lydia likes me. And I'm sorry too. I didn't realize Edzo was such a psycho when he was alone. I've only ridden him in a group."

"It wasn't your fault. Besides I wasn't alone. Someone ponied me."

"Why didn't you tell her that? She might not have been so pissed."

Megan shrugged and led the gray into the barn. She didn't want to cause trouble for Scott. If Lydia knew they'd both been on the track without permission, she would have been doubly mad. Besides, Lydia was clearly touchy about Joey's disappearance and that knowledge alone was worth the price of punishment.

Still, four days on the mechanical horse would be torture. Just thinking of the Equicizer made her muscles groan. Lydia had installed surveillance cameras in the fitness room too so there'd be no slacking.

"The cafeteria closes in ten minutes," Peter said, angling toward the door. "You're not going to make lunch. Want me grab you something?"

"Thanks," Megan said. "An apple will keep me going until supper." And then she'd see Scott again. Despite being banished to the fitness room, anticipation left her smiling.

Edzo nudged her shoulder, as though reminding that his nervousness was the real reason Scott had even appeared in the field.

Megan gave the gray an appreciative pat and turned to Peter. "And please bring a second apple for your lovely horse," she said.

CHAPTER EIGHT

Megan lingered in the cafeteria entrance, scanning the boisterous supper crowd. The smell of chicken thickened the air and her stomach rumbled, protesting at going all afternoon with only an apple. She waved at Peter who was chewing and talking to tablemates with equal enthusiasm. There were lots of familiar faces, but no Tami, who was probably still shopping in town.

And there was no sign of Scott.

She dug out her phone and pulled up his number, hoping he'd arrive soon. She was famished.

He answered on the second ring.

"Hi," she said. "Are you ready to eat soon? I'm in the cafeteria."

"Good," Scott said, his deep voice making her stomach kick with another type of hunger. "Wait outside. I'll pick you up."

Puzzled, she stepped back outside. *I'll pick you up?* She was already at the cafeteria.

Two minutes later, he cruised up in his silver Mercedes. The cracked bumper and broken headlight looked out of place against the elegant lines of his car.

He leaned over the passenger's seat and pushed open the door. "Hop in," he said. "It's not far but directions are complicated."

The car was immaculate, smelling of leather, spice and man. She hid her confusion and settled into the buttery soft seat. His forearm rested on the center console, only inches from her leg. Dark hairs dusted the muscled ridges. He wore a rugged looking sports watch and old scars crisscrossed his knuckles. He had beautiful fingers. No rings.

She pulled her gaze away. "Is there another place to

eat?" she asked, her voice slightly husky.

He smiled. "Same cafeteria food but different location."

They passed a rectangular gatehouse, empty but still imposing with its black grilled windows. The drive wound behind Garrett's house and led to a beautiful Spanish-style villa with ornate gates.

She slipped from the car and followed him up the cobbled walkway, her eyes widening. This place was like an oasis after the dust and dirt of the barns. Colorful bougainvillea lined the grass, kept lush by an elaborate sprinkler system. Lemon and kumquat trees grew in bright ceramic pots. A soothing waterfall babbled in the background, accompanied by the faint tinkle of wind chimes.

"Wow," she finally said. "This is almost as nice as my dorm."

He chuckled, pressed a remote entry pad and pushed open the front door. "You'll have to show me your room sometime."

The intimacy in his voice made her gulp. "Sure." And that was all she could manage. Her mouth was so dry her brain seemed disconnected to her tongue.

She swallowed, pretending to admire the Spanish tiles. The villa was beautiful, but right now she was too aware of his proximity, and his masculine intent. He was making no effort to hide his interest. Heat radiated from him in waves, turning her hyper-conscious.

"How long is this cow program?" she managed. "I don't know much about it."

"Me neither. I'm teaching a new course at the jock school."

She blinked with sudden comprehension. "The addictions course?"

"That's right." He shut the door, but remained close, his voice softening. "And I'm very relieved you're not taking my class."

"Why?"

He reached out and tilted her chin, his gray eyes darkening as he studied her mouth. Her heart hammered. He was going to kiss her. And she wanted him to. Maybe. And then his mouth slanted over hers, and she stopped thinking.

His lips were hard and firm, persuasive but patient, as though they had all the time in the world and he was willing to wait. But she didn't make him wait long. She arched upward, and his arms tightened. She rose higher on her toes, her mouth opening. Oh, wow. She loved his feel, his taste, his smell, how he seemed to be memorizing her mouth.

He raised his head way too soon. "Because an instructor shouldn't be doing *this* with a student," he murmured.

Her breath came out in a shuddery sigh and she couldn't even remember her question. She wanted to drag his head back to her mouth. Didn't want his kiss to stop. His eyes were on her face now and he wasn't even doing anything, just trailing his thumb along her collarbone, turning her entire body quivery.

She didn't care about the instructor thing. She wasn't even a real student. But of course, he'd be concerned about his job. She didn't want Lydia giving him a hard time. Maybe he wouldn't have invited her for supper if he knew she was in his class.

And that was a shame because their bodies molded together so well. She liked being in his arms, liked the possessive feel of his hand against the hollow of her back, the slight roughness of his fingers. Already tiny sparks of electricity sensitized her skin. But students shouldn't date instructors. A few more kisses like this and who knew where they'd end up. She certainly didn't want him to lose his job.

"I am in your class though," she admitted. "I missed the first day."

"You're in my class? Damn." But he didn't sound at all concerned. He slid his hand beneath her hair, that big thumb stroking the hollow below her ear. He tilted her head, his eyes so dark now they seemed a different shade of gray.

His head swooped again and this time he didn't deliver a restrained parlor kiss. His hungry mouth covered hers, inhaling and drinking her in.

Her arms tightened over his shoulders, her nipples prickling against the hard ridges of his chest as his tongue did a slow erotic dance, mating with hers and making her sizzle.

She could feel his belt buckle, his zipper, his obvious erection. Her heart thumped and she fought to stay cool. Relationships only caused pain, and one-night stands weren't her style. But her body was clamoring for one now. And maybe it wouldn't only be for one night.

Heck, it wasn't even night yet. The sun still shone. They were supposed to be having a simple supper, and she'd barely made it two feet past his door. In another minute, she was going to hook an ankle around his long leg, pull him even closer...and tomorrow she'd cringe from embarrassment.

I can't do this.

He immediately lifted his mouth, as though sensing her ambivalence. "Food's in the kitchen," he said. "Hungry?"

"Starving," she said, but her voice sounded unfamiliar, and she couldn't meet his eyes. He probably sensed she was starving for something else. "I can't wait to eat," she added, trying to salvage a shred of dignity.

He eased back a few inches but kept an arm looped around her waist, so relaxed that her self-consciousness eased. Maybe he didn't realize how out of control she'd been. Her heart still raced but, then again, so did his. He'd tucked her against the left side of his chest and she could hear its drumming, although his hand on her neck was still slow. Still assured. And very nice.

She let out a little sigh, relaxing enough to splay her fingers over his arm and enjoy the rumble of his voice.

"We have chicken marsala or fettuccine," he was saying. "Both fresh from the cafeteria."

"I didn't see either of those on the whiteboard." She cleared her throat. "You must have a special menu."

"Luckily I do because it's a weight watchers' paradise over there." His easy chuckle restored her feelings of normalcy. He seemed as relaxed now as he'd been when they were riding. "I turned down the no-sugar Jello," he added with a grin.

She and Tami always joked about the tasteless desserts, and she smiled back. His gaze settled on her mouth then jerked away. He wrapped her hand in his, guiding her beneath the gracious archway and into a bright kitchen that hinted of chicken and basil.

He lifted the cover from a silver serving tray while

keeping such an easy discourse about the menu, she felt more at ease. There was succulent chicken and fluffy rice, complete with a colorful Greek salad, enough for ten people. It was hard to believe this feast came from the cafeteria.

She settled into the tall chair he'd pulled out, relieved they were eating in the kitchen and not his formal dining room. She wasn't prepared for an elegant dinner. Had been expecting the cafeteria, not this luxurious villa. It was very apparent the school held him in high esteem.

"How long have you known Garrett?" she asked, as he poured two glasses of wine.

"Since first grade, when his parents bought the ranch next to us."

She nodded but glanced around the gourmet kitchen with its state-of-the art appliances and six-burner stove. Beyond the patio door, a pool glistened. A hot tub sat on the far right, next to a bar and an intimate fire pit. One class for all this? It didn't make sense.

She studied him over the rim of her glass, trying to remember Tami's comments about the addictions class. She hadn't paid much attention to instructors and courses. At the time, it simply hadn't mattered. She was almost certain Addictions 101 was a new class, but maybe Scott taught something else. Maybe he'd taught Joey. Did he know something about her brother's ill-fated trip?

She set her glass on the table, her fingers clutching the stem. "Did you teach here over the last nine months?" she asked, trying to keep her voice level.

"No, this is my first visit." His gaze flickered over her restless hand, and it was clear he didn't miss much. "Would you like a different wine?"

"Oh, no. This is great." She picked up her glass again, relief tempered with disappointment. He didn't know anything about Joey, although maybe her brother wouldn't have disappeared if Scott had been around. He seemed so level, so trustworthy, so...capable.

"You came here just to teach one course?" she asked, still confused about his role at the school.

"That's right. I had some surgery and have to take it easy for a bit. Let's eat."

Clearly, he was reserved, but in a polite way. And the food was superb. She couldn't remember when she had enjoyed a meal so much. Or relaxed so quickly with such an attractive man. He moved competently in the kitchen too, even surprising her with a dessert loaded with chocolate and pecans.

Her eyes widened. "Gosh. My roommate and I drive thirty miles for forbidden stuff like this."

"Yes, fortunately for me." His grin flashed. "Not only did you haul me out of the ditch, but I seem to recall you offered me one of your chocolate bars. I owe you."

She shot him a cautious smile. Perhaps this meal was really about payback and she'd overestimated their attraction. But even that concern faded as the chocolate melted in her mouth. "This is probably contraband," she said, savoring the delicious sweetness, "but it's wonderful. How'd you get it?"

"I knew you liked chocolate. And the cook offered to whip up something special."

She almost choked. It was hard to imagine the sullen cook making that offer. Only yesterday the woman had yelled at Tami for requesting a second bowl of soup. Still, if anyone was likely to receive favors, it would be Scott. He was exceedingly likeable. However, he must have gone to considerable effort to obtain this gourmet meal.

"It's a wise man who understands women and chocolate." She dipped her fork back into the dessert, keeping her tone deliberately light.

He didn't say a word but his eyes flashed with amusement. He definitely knew his way around women, probably had a girlfriend or two. Maybe even a wife? Kids who needed him? His fingers were bare, but lots of people didn't wear rings.

"You're not married, are you?" she asked abruptly.

"No."

He didn't return the question so she pretended to be absorbed in the dessert. He was very private, but then so was she. And either he was the type of guy who didn't care if she were married, or he really intended this as a thank-you-for-the-tow meal. Her cheeks heated at the memory of how she'd responded in the hall.

She shot him a cautious peek. He didn't look uncomfortable, more like he was thinking. And he was drop dead gorgeous. Already yesterday's pallor had disappeared. Riding had left those lean cheeks tanned and lethal, although the pink scar was still visible. He looked like he was feeling fine. She certainly hoped so. "Did you have a bad injury?" she asked.

"It was touch and go for a while. But the headaches are fading."

"Galloping this morning didn't hurt?"

"Surprisingly not," he said. "Are you riding at the same time tomorrow?"

"Unfortunately I'm grounded the rest of the week," she admitted. "I wasn't supposed to stay in the field alone. So Lydia, my instructor, assigned dry training."

"Why didn't you say you were with me?"

"And get you in trouble too. No way." She twisted to face him. "Besides, it was worth it. I learned more today than in the past week. Hopefully she'll move me up to Ramon's class soon. That's the reason I came."

His eyes narrowed. "That's why you came? To ride with Ramon?"

"Yes, well, I mean...to learn from Ramon on the track. So I can get a job as an exercise rider." She paused, remembering that earlier she'd claimed she just wanted to improve her riding and was only taking a break from jewelry. She fingered her wine glass, uneasy with the deception. Far safer to change the subject.

"I'm not sure what I want to do," she added with a smile. "What about you? You're a good rider. That's a nice horse you rode."

"Garrett's finest," Scott said. "A Quarter Horse named Braun's Little Lena." He studied her for a moment as though making a decision, rose and grabbed the dessert plate. "Come on. We'll wrap the leftovers up for you and your roommate. Then I'll show you Braun and the other side of the property."

"They call this the cowshed?" Megan asked, staring around the indoor arena in awe.

Scott chuckled. "Garrett has a sense of humor. I doubt there's been many cows here. It doesn't seem to be used for anything now except dumping hay."

It was a waste of a beautiful building, Megan thought. The only tracks in the arena were from a vehicle, not animals, and a mound of forgotten hay sat next to a green hay baler. A dusty roping dummy had been shoved in the corner. Their neighbor had owned a similar model, and she'd always wanted one of her own. Her father had taught her to rope on a tree stump and when he hadn't been watching, she'd roped their dog. And then Joey— much to her little brother's dismay. Those had been good times.

"You ever use one of those?" Scott asked, following her gaze.

"Yes. My dad and I tossed ropes every Sunday at our neighbor's ranch, back when I was about ten. I didn't realize I missed it until now." She shrugged away her nostalgia. "I don't miss the baler though. We used to cut a lot of alfalfa. Now my mom leases out the land so there's nowhere to rope."

"I haven't roped in a while either," Scott said. "Got too caught up in work. Come see the horses."

They walked through a shadowed doorway and into the attached barn. The stocky horse he'd ridden earlier was familiar, but not the other three.

"Braun is a Quarter Horse, a longtime resident," he said. "The other three are Thoroughbreds. They're heading to Mexico next month. Some friend of Garrett's is trying to restart racing in the Baja."

Her breath quickened. So this was the holding barn for Mexico. Joey had probably been here, helping Ramon load. Or perhaps jockey students worked here?

"Who looks after these horses?" she asked. "Students?"

"No, I don't think so." His gaze lingered on her mouth as he scratched the top of Braun's neck. "Ramon is the only one I've ever seen working here."

Ramon? She couldn't imagine the instructor stooping to clean a stall, but someone was obviously taking good care of the animals. The barn was spotless, although the stack of hay in the middle of the arena was sloppy, if not downright wasteful. It looked like expensive alfalfa that someone had neglected to bale. Jake and Rambo would love an armful.

She raised on her toes and checked Braun's stall. He had plenty of night hay but it wasn't alfalfa. It looked like timothy blend, similar to the hay in her barn.

Scott raised an eyebrow.

"Just checking his hay." She gave a sheepish grin. "I

wonder why they don't use that nice alfalfa. The horses I look after would love it."

"Throw some in a feedbag and take it to them."

"Really? No one will mind?"

"Can't see why they would." He reached up and snagged an empty feedbag from a wooden shelf. "Come on. We can put it in the trunk of my car."

He was a man of action and didn't seem to worry about rules. It probably didn't hurt that he was good friends with Garrett and his easy assurance was contagious.

He slid a hand over her hip and they walked back to the hay stack. Alfalfa was richer than other hay and a sudden change in diet was never good for horses. However, a little treat wouldn't hurt. Grumpy old Rambo would surely be delighted.

She held the feedbag open while Scott stuffed in armfuls of the hay.

"It looks like nice stuff," he said. "Your horses will be happy..." His voice trailed off as an iPod dropped into the dirt, its headphones still entwined with stalks of hay. "And someone else will be happy to get that back," he added, scooping it up.

Her breath caught as she gaped at the iPod. It was achingly familiar. She'd given it to Joey this past Christmas. Could picture his lopsided smile as he carved his initials with a pocketknife.

"May I see it?" she asked, her voice shaky.

Scott passed it over, his eyes on her face. "Something wrong?"

"No," she said quickly. "But I think this belongs to my roommate, Tami. I'm not sure how it ended up here but those are her initials." She held her thumb over the bottom curl of the J.

"Well, I'm glad it resurfaced," he said. "At least it was safe inside."

"Yes," she said. "It seems fine." She pressed the 'play' button and the cover of Joey's favorite album hit her like a sucker punch. Two thousand, one hundred and ninety-six songs. He'd loved his music. The last time she'd seen him, he'd been working beneath her truck, unaware of her presence until she'd teasingly pulled out his earphones.

She slipped the iPod into her pocket and forced a

smile, conscious of Scott's astute gaze. Tonight she'd listen to Joey's music, read his magazine and indulge in private memories of her missing brother.

"Guess that's enough hay for tonight," Scott said. He picked up the bag, still studying her face. "Don't want them to colic. But you can take back a little hay every day."

"Thank you for this. For everything." She pressed a hand over the precious iPod in her pocket. If he hadn't been such a good sport about the hay, she never would have found it. Never would have had this link to Joey. She rose on her toes and brushed his mouth with a grateful kiss.

His hands remained on the bag of hay, but his entire body seemed to still. "Do you have more time," he asked, his voice gruff. "Or is there some sort of curfew you have to follow?"

"Definitely there's a curfew," she said. "Ten o'clock. And it's strictly enforced." Despite her fragile emotions, she couldn't contain a bubble of laughter. "You're the most easy-going instructor here. But you better learn the rules or you might be demoted to the Equicizer too."

"I'm thinking that wouldn't be a bad thing." He gave a slow, curling smile. "Let's get you back to the dorm on time. And you can fill me in on your schedule tomorrow."

CHAPTER NINE

Megan waved goodbye to Scott and walked down the barn aisle, happily swinging the alfalfa bag. She'd offered to walk back but Scott insisted he'd drive. He hadn't even flinched at tossing the hay into the spotless trunk of his car.

And he was meeting her tomorrow in the exercise room. Suddenly the Equicizer no longer felt like punishment.

She tossed an armful of alfalfa to Jake and Rambo. Barney had treat radar and gave a hopeful nicker. She pulled out a handful of hay for him and then couldn't resist Edzo's wistful eyes. She ended up giving every horse in the barn a bite. They seemed to enjoy the special hay as much as apples or peppermints. It was a shame the alfalfa stack was wasted in the cowshed.

Rambo stuck his head in the hay bag and lipped off the last stalks. "I'll bring you some more tomorrow, Grumpy," she said.

There was probably no longer any reason to call him grumpy. He liked her well enough now, ever since she'd picked him the grass outside. He didn't even pin his ears.

Someone giggled, a teasing flirtatious sound, and she glanced toward the end door. Seconds later, Tami and Miguel appeared in the aisle.

"Oh, you're here," Tami said. "Thanks for lending your truck." She tossed Megan the keys and shot a conspiratorial smile at Miguel. "We almost missed curfew and had to speed since your muffler is way too loud to sneak in. Miguel, this is Megan, my roommate."

"We met this morning," Miguel said, his gaze sweeping over Megan with blatant approval. "How fortunate for me. The prettiest girls at the school and they're both in one room."

"We have a chocolate bar stash too," Tami said, gazing at Miguel with adoration in her baby-blue eyes. Megan hoped she hadn't looked at Scott like that, but feared she probably had. Love was definitely in the air tonight.

"Then let's go upstairs and eat some forbidden chocolate, girls." Miguel looped his sinewy arms around both their waists. He reeked of strong cigarettes and even stronger cologne, but she sucked in her breath and accompanied them, relieved curfew would prevent him from staying too long. It was almost ten o'clock and she wanted to listen to Joey's music undisturbed.

They climbed the stairs while she tried to ignore Miguel's too-familiar hand on her hip.

Tami pushed open the door to their room and tugged Miguel toward her cluttered desk. "We have five kinds of chocolate bars," she said, opening the bottom drawer. "Better than any dessert at the cafeteria. We usually sell them but you can have any one you want."

Miguel grabbed a Snickers bar and ripped it open. The torn wrapper drifted to the floor. He didn't bother to pick it up but instead stretched out on Tami's bed, leaving dirt smudges beneath the heels of his snakeskin boots.

"These are my favorite," he said, his mouth full of chocolate. "I eat a lot of these back home."

Megan dragged her gaze off the wrapper on the floor. "Where do you live?" she asked, struggling to be polite. "Near the Baja Tinda?"

"Of course," Miguel said, his words muffled by the wad of food crammed in his mouth. "My father owns it."

Megan blinked, momentarily at a loss for words. She'd thought he was a simple student, saving money to come to the States and finish his jockey course. No wonder he was so arrogant. No wonder he stayed with Ramon. Still, this was a great opportunity to ask questions.

"Is there a racetrack there?" she asked, watching him now with genuine interest.

"A training track." Miguel stuffed another piece of chocolate into his mouth and smacked his lips. "Mainly we race Quarter Horses."

"But I thought your father was trying to start Thoroughbred racing?"

"Yes, that too." He shrugged and hauled a giggling Tami onto his chest. "But he needs more staff as well as horses. We have some riders but they're only experienced at short dashes."

Tami slipped her arm around his neck, her eyelashes fluttering. "Maybe your dad would hire me," she said.

"Probably he would, *querida*. If I ask him." His gaze lowered. He lifted the silver necklace Tami had borrowed from Megan and dragged his thumb along the swell of her breast. Megan turned away. She didn't like the way he touched her jewelry, but the casual way he fingered Tami bothered her more.

Miguel's voice lowered. "It's frustrating Ramon doesn't allow me to have guests. You and I, we could have a very good time."

Despite her aversion, Megan couldn't resist another peek. When Miguel wasn't smiling, he looked older, almost jaded. He also looked much too tall for a jockey and the way he shifted his eyes when he spoke of racing was interesting. Perhaps Joey had been lured to the Baja Tinda for a job. But then what?

"Does your father often hire students from here?" At Megan's sudden question, both Tami and Miguel turned, as though they'd forgotten her presence.

"No," Miguel said. "There are too many of my countrymen who need jobs. But he will listen to my recommendations."

He dismissed Megan and turned back to Tami, splaying a bold hand over her breast. His voice lowered. "It's ten o'clock and I must leave. Ramon doesn't like me spending time with beautiful American women. But with you, I can't help myself." His left hand slid beneath Tami's shirt, his head blotting out her face in a noisy kiss.

Megan yanked her gaze away and retreated into the bathroom.

Five minutes later, footsteps thumped. A door opened and closed amidst the murmur of whispered goodbyes.

She cautiously opened the bathroom door and checked the room. Tami was alone on the bed, smiling dreamily and clasping a pillow to her chest. "Isn't he wonderful?"

"I guess," Megan said, hiding her concern. It wasn't any of her business but if Tami were her little sister, she definitely wouldn't want the girl hanging out with a player like Miguel. "Did he give you the barn tour before you went to town?" Megan asked.

"Yes, it's really nice there. The jockeys have their own washer and dryer, and there's even a kitchen. Miguel gave me a cup of coffee and added some alcohol. He's wicked fun."

Megan swallowed, realizing she hadn't seen her roommate all day. She wanted to ask what Scott's class had been like, but Tami clearly wanted to talk about Miguel.

"Wouldn't it be awesome if he found me a job?" Tami went on, her arms tightening around the pillow. "Moving to Mexico and being with Miguel. That would be so romantic. And the Baja Tinda is beautiful."

"How do you know?" Megan asked. "It might be a dump." She hated her cynicism but Tami was a sweet girl and while it was nice to see her happy, there was definitely an unsavory element about Miguel.

"It's not a dump. Look." Tami tossed the pillow aside and grabbed her phone. She jabbed at the screen. "I bookmarked it. The barns and track are brand new. And they have one of those straight race strips with a fence down the middle." She shoved the screen in front of Megan's face.

Megan had studied the school website, checking every link after Joey disappeared. But this was an entirely different site. The Baja Tinda did look impressive. There was even a narrow track, separated by a rail, where two horses broke from a starting gate to race in a straight line. She'd heard of that type of racing before but had never seen it.

"Look at all the little houses," Tami said, scrolling down the screen with proprietary pride. "There's no picture of Miguel's mansion but he said it's very big. It's hidden behind that high wall. Wouldn't it be cool if he could get me a job?" She clutched the phone to her chest and bounced on her bed, making the mattress squeak. "I wouldn't mind moving to Mexico. Miguel is almost twenty-six. He probably wants to settle down."

"You hardly know him," Megan said. "And men are always keen at the beginning. It never lasts."

"Who cares. It's fun for a while, especially when it's totally unexpected and you can't think of anything but him. Surely you remember that feeling?"

It was amusing that Tammy viewed Megan as old. But an image of Scott's face flashed, so distractingly handsome Megan quit smiling and had to accept that she'd been hit just as hard as Tami.

"Yes," she said softly. "I remember that feeling."

CHAPTER TEN

Scott sipped his coffee, waiting as Garrett filled their plates with scrambled eggs and bacon. "A few more breakfasts like this," Scott said, "and I'll have to ride much harder than I did yesterday."

"We have a nice fitness room and sauna." Garrett passed Scott a heaping plate. "Not the range of equipment you're used to, but by midmorning it's generally empty."

The dog edged closer, hopeful eyes on the bacon. Garrett gestured and Rex immediately turned and dropped on the colorful mat by the back door.

"You trained him well," Scott said.

"Not me. I bought him like that, from one of those security places."

"You bought a guard dog? Why?"

Garrett shrugged. "There's a lot of students around. We had that drug dealer last month who had criminal connections. I have to be careful." Garrett forked a mouthful of egg into his mouth. "So, how did you like your first full day? Did Lydia ever stop chasing you?"

"She was just trying to be helpful." Scott picked up his fork. "Does she start all the riders?"

"No, only the exercise riders and grooms. She's a stickler for detail." Garrett gave a wry smile. "Actually she's a first-class bitch, but she's a hard worker and gets results. Two of her grads won Groom of the Month at Del Mar. She also looks after most of the lectures."

"So she's busy," Scott said. "Then is it okay if I work with a student from her riding class?"

"Sure. Take as many as you want." Garrett chuckled. "The girls will thank you for it. Lydia can be tough on them."

"Can't you make sure she's fair?"

"She's not that bad," Garrett said. "And students need to deal with that kind of shit. They'll run into bosses much worse. She toughens them up for the real world. But if you feel the need to rescue someone, knock yourself out." He paused for a moment then added, "Just don't make waves."

Scott shot him a glance but Garrett was concentrating on his eggs again, and Scott didn't care anyway. They'd always held different opinions—on everything from how to treat a woman, to football and politics—but had still remained good friends. At least, he'd be able to help Megan. He'd seen her ride yesterday. She deserved to be on the track, not stuck trotting in the field.

But he didn't want to sour Lydia against Megan, especially if Lydia was already tough on the girls. He took a thoughtful bite, considering the most diplomatic approach.

Rap, rap.

Rex scrambled to his feet and bolted toward the front door, his claws rattling on the marble tiles.

Garrett frowned. "Students aren't supposed to come here unless they have an appointment. Excuse me a second. I'll get rid of them." He wiped his mouth, rose from the table and disappeared down the hall.

The door opened to a flurry of Spanish. Scott tried to concentrate on his spicy eggs. The cafeteria staff was efficient, delivering delicious food with minimal notice. Garrett had always liked to surround himself with luxury.

The conversation lowered, muffled but still excited. This visitor wasn't leaving as quickly as Garrett had anticipated. And now the voices raised a notch, bleeding back and forth between English and Spanish.

It was definitely a male at the door. The voice was too aggressive for an employee so it probably wasn't Ramon. A disgruntled student maybe? Apparently two had been sent home last week. But Scott was too far away to distinguish the words and besides, he didn't want to eavesdrop.

And then Rex exploded with such a threatening bark, it echoed in the foyer and couldn't be ignored. Scott rose and strode down the hall.

Garrett glanced over his shoulder and raised his palm. His other hand gripped Rex's leather collar. "It's okay, Scott. Finish your breakfast. I'll be right there."

Scott glanced past him, checking out the man at the door. Dark hair, insolent eyes, loaded with tats and testosterone. He looked like a gangbanger. God, Scott hated them.

"Fine," Scott said. But he lingered. "Want me to take the dog into the kitchen?"

Garrett's eyes met his. "Great. I'm sure he'll go quietly."

Scott was quite sure Rex wouldn't. The dog quivered with rage, hackles raised, growls rumbling deep in his throat. But 'go quietly' had always been their code that everything was fine. He and Garrett had used it on parents, girlfriends and coaches, as well as the occasional cop.

"Come on, Rex," Scott said, relieved when the dog ignored him. At least Garrett had formidable backup.

He walked back into the kitchen. A minute later, the front door slammed, and Rex and Garrett reappeared.

Scott sipped his coffee but didn't ask any questions, aware Garrett disliked silence. Besides, usually the easiest way to learn anything was to stay quiet and wait. Most people rushed to fill the gap.

"Just another student," Garrett finally said. He dumped more salsa on his eggs, swearing as half the jar poured out, leaving his eggs drenched in a river of red.

Scott kept his mouth shut, watching his friend over the rim of his mug. Garrett poked his fork in the reddened eggs but didn't take a bite. "Actually Miguel's from the Baja Tinda... he's the owner's son."

That explained it. The kid looked far more aggressive than the average student. Megan hadn't stormed up to Garrett's door to complain, even though Lydia was clearly holding her back. She was a cool girl. Their brief kiss had rocked him. He definitely wanted to get to know her better.

"They want more horses."

Scott blinked, realizing he'd been staring at Garrett but thinking of Megan. He forced his attention back to his friend. "More Thoroughbreds?"

"Yeah, I sent four down last month but they want more. They're getting a little impatient for another shipment."

Scott nodded but thought the guy at the door had looked more threatening than impatient.

"How's your head?" Garrett asked abruptly.

"Not bad at all." He'd felt a brief twinge when he talked to Snake last night but that was it. And oddly, he'd spent as much energy figuring out how to free Megan from Lydia's clutches as he had worrying about the LA office.

"You realize the school has been approved?" Garrett asked. "They pushed it through when I advised of your involvement. So if you want to get back to your business, someone else can teach the course. There's no need for you to stay...much as I like having you around."

Scott dragged a hand over his jaw, imagining Belinda's consternation if he showed up at the office. "It's no problem. I agreed to the month. Besides, I don't mind sticking around."

His thoughts jumped to Megan's extremely kissable mouth.

"I don't mind at all," he said.

CHAPTER ELEVEN

"Good morning!"

Scott pulled in a bracing breath and turned toward Lydia's exuberant greeting. The woman rushed down the cafeteria steps, her boots rapping on the wood. In addition to being an expert with horse grooming, she clearly spent a lot of time in front of the mirror. After Megan's wholesome beauty, the woman's makeup seemed garish.

"I didn't see you at supper last night," Lydia said, filling the air with a pungent cloud of perfume. "And I wanted to offer my help. The first days of teaching can be so lonely. With only one course, you probably have a lot of spare time."

The perfect opening. Scott gave a solemn nod. "Garrett and I were just discussing my time over breakfast. He told me about the great job you're doing with the grooms but said you still have some exercise riders with the class."

"Yes. The riders are extremely inexperienced this session, and the groom class is at capacity. It's taxing since some of the students are incredibly difficult. Perhaps we should compare notes?" Her fingers fluttered over her hair. "Did Garrett tell you about the national recognition my grads have received?"

"He certainly did." Scott tried to smile but the floral smell of her hair battled with the reek of perfume, and the spot behind his left eye began to throb. He'd assumed stress triggered the headaches but maybe it was odors. Or possibly shrill voices. Lydia certainly had both. He edged back a step. "That's why I've offered to look after the exercise riders still left in the groom class."

"Okay," she said. "But there's only one."

"What's her name?"

"Megan Spence." Lydia's forehead creased in thought. "But wouldn't it be better if we worked together—"

"Great, that's settled then," Scott said. "I'll look after Megan and her riding." He gestured at the cafeteria. He was still full from breakfast with Garrett but for Megan's sake, he wanted to make sure Lydia didn't hold a grudge. "Do you have time for coffee? I understand you're one of the school's most experienced lecturers. Garrett said your grooms have won a lot of awards."

It was a half hour of numbing babble in the cafeteria before Lydia glanced at her watch. "I hate to leave but the students are almost ready for the field. I do appreciate your help."

"Should I walk over to the barn with you and meet up with Megan?" he asked innocently.

Lydia's smile faded. "Actually I told her to work on the Equicizer so she'll be in the fitness center. But of course that extra ground training isn't really necessary. Just let her know it's okay to ride today and you can join me—us—in the field."

"Fine," Scott said, careful to keep a straight face. "And naturally we'll want her on an experienced Thoroughbred. One who knows the job so she can concentrate on her position."

"She can ride Jake." Lydia's head pumped, all helpful eagerness now. "He's one of our best horses, reserved for advanced students. But since Megan is our first joint project, this is a special occasion."

"Definitely," Scott said. And Megan would be thrilled. She liked Jake, even caring enough to bring him armfuls of alfalfa. The horse would be a much better mount than the hyper gray she'd ridden yesterday.

He smiled at Lydia. She was the type who craved recognition and unfortunately wasn't attractive enough to warrant much attention from Garrett. "Thank you," he said. "And if Megan's riding improves so that she can gallop on the track, it'll be to your credit. It's proactive to assign her such a good horse. No wonder Garrett thinks highly of you."

Lydia flushed with pleasure and rose from the table. He waited until she left before he walked down the hall to the fitness center.

He pushed open the door and stepped into the cool

room. An air conditioner hummed and somewhere a machine thumped. He walked past the line of gleaming equipment toward the back of the room where five mechanical horses squatted in a row. Megan rode the Equicizer at the end, a larger, more deluxe model than the others. It was painted a dappled bay, and the name 'Zenyatta' was written in pink on the bridle.

She stood in the stirrups, her forehead glistening as she pumped her arms into the machine's neck. He hadn't realized the exercise horses weren't motorized but clearly the cardiovascular benefits were impressive. At the speed she was going, it definitely simulated a galloping horse.

Megan spotted him and the Equicizer slowed. She shot a look at the far corner where a surveillance cam was bolted to the wall then sped up. "Good morning," she called. "Are you ready to grab a machine and race?"

"Not a chance. Not if you're riding Zenyatta." Grinning, he circled the machine and studied the overhead monitor. "You can stop working so hard too," he said over his shoulder. "This cam is fake."

Her mouth dropped and the Equicizer slowed again. "You're kidding? How can you tell?"

"I just know." His gaze drifted over her in open appreciation. Jeans, T-shirt, hair tamed in a thick braid. Not a speck of makeup but still stunning. He'd always preferred wholesome girls and she even liked racing. A simple country girl who'd probably never swallowed an Aspirin. Different in every way from Amanda and the type of women he seemed to attract.

The mechanical horse slowed to a standstill and the room turned quiet. Megan remained silent, perched on the machine, waiting for him to speak. Another great thing about her. She didn't babble, was comfortable with silence. She was like a breath of fresh mountain air.

He walked over, leaned down and grazed her mouth with a swift kiss. "Want to go riding with me?" he asked.

"I'd love to but Lydia wouldn't allow it."

"She already agreed that I should take over the riding portion of your training."

"What?" Megan jerked back so fast the Equicizer moved.

"Is that okay?" he asked. Maybe he'd interfered too much. Maybe she liked riding under Lydia.

"Are you kidding!" She leaped off the machine. "That's absolutely okay. Fantastic. Nothing could be better."

"And from now on your horse is Jake," he said.

"Well, that is better." She laughed, a musical tinkling laugh that definitely didn't hurt his head. "But no one gets to ride Jake," she said. "Not unless they're good enough to ride on the track."

"You are good enough, and Jake was Lydia's suggestion."

"So she's not mad?" Megan's eyes widened, her chest still heaving from the exercise. "Wow. Thank you."

He pulled his gaze off the curve of her breasts. "No doubt, I'll be tougher than Lydia so save your gratitude...although I may feel compelled to remind you of it later." He made no effort to hide his desire because riding, though pleasurable, was a distant second to what now filled his thoughts. And judging by the way she'd responded to his kiss last night, the attraction was mutual.

At least, he hoped it was mutual.

But she glanced past him, as if worried about an audience.

"I'm not really an instructor here," he said. "Not a permanent one. So we don't have to hide anything."

"Do you usually do this?" She looked back at him, her eyes wary.

"I've never taught a class before. Never will again. So no, I don't usually do *this*." He leaned down and brushed her cheek with his mouth, careful to keep his hands by his side, conscious of her concern.

"And you're sure that's not a working cam?" she asked.

"Absolutely." A tendril of hair had escaped from her braid and he itched to touch it. But he jammed his hands in his pockets.

"You must have taught before though," she said. "Lydia claimed you had a sixty percent failure rate."

His lip twitched. His background was summarized on the school website—all police and PI work. No mention of any teaching experience. "Clearly Lydia was exaggerating," he said.

Megan still looked troubled so he added, "She probably wanted students to take the class seriously. Especially since they had that dealer skulking around."

"He wasn't skulking." She stepped back, her eyes flashing, and there was no mistaking the frostiness in her voice.

"Did you know him?"

"I've only been here nine days," she said.

"Luckily you missed him then. He was bad news. Trying to set up dealers at the school."

"Want me to saddle Jake now?" she asked, turning toward the exit.

"Sure," he said. "I'll get Braun and meet you by the barn. Don't ride without me."

"Of course not. That would be against *school* rules." She spoke with a bite of disdain, and he understood now why she had trouble with Lydia. Lydia required stroking and Megan had too much backbone. She definitely wouldn't brown-nose either, another admirable trait.

But it might be nice if she brown-nosed a bit. Maybe treat him to a little smile. But when she glanced over her shoulder, her mouth was set in a flat line, her beautiful eyes almost wounded. She muttered goodbye and rushed out the door, obviously keen to escape his company.

What the hell did I say? He rubbed his forehead, trying to remember. Something about the druggie? Or maybe she was just in a bad mood from being stuck inside.

But that didn't make sense. She'd been happy to see him, glad to be sprung from the week of ground training. He glanced at the Equicizer, but the mechanical horse remained regal and unmoving, offering no clues to Megan's sudden mood swing.

CHAPTER TWELVE

Megan tightened Jake's saddle and led him from the barn, relieved she was ready before Scott arrived. Rambo shoved his head over the paddock rail and nickered at his stablemate. He always looked imposing with his high head and pricked ears. The big gelding didn't care much for people, not unless they were carrying treats, but he definitely liked Jake.

In the distant field, riders jogged around Lydia and her pink blouse. Megan blew out a little sigh. If not for Scott, she'd be stuck trotting circles. She wasn't sure how he'd managed to pull her from the grooms' class, but she was grateful.

However, she wasn't going to sleep with him, no matter how much he helped. It would be foolhardy to become involved with an instructor. Besides, his crack about Joey skulking around the school had dampened her ardor. Well...almost dampened. She wasn't naive enough to think she could hold out long against his expert kissing. That quick embrace in the fitness center had left her filled her with an odd restlessness, a yearning to be held. To touch and be touched.

She gave her head an impatient shake. This was not the time to be thinking about sex. It was important to concentrate on her riding. After a few more lessons, she might be able to move into Ramon's class and get closer with the students who'd known Joey best. The jockeys were the only people who were important here.

Hooves thudded from the hilltop, and Scott and Braun jogged over the ridge, an impressive partnership of man and horse. For a moment she indulged in admiring his deep seat, those long legs, the easy way he fit his horse.

Obviously, her ardor hadn't been dampened much.

But he shouldn't talk about Joey like that. Her mouth clamped and she stroked Jake's neck, resenting the attraction and feeling like a traitor.

Scott stopped Braun a few feet away. "Did you check everything?" he asked, his eyes inscrutable. "Safety vest? Helmet? Girth?"

"Girth is tight," she said. "And my helmet and vest are good."

His gaze narrowed on the bridle. "Your bit is a little low. Tighten it a hole and lower the noseband an inch."

"But this bridle is used on him every day," she said. "I assume it's the way Lydia wants it."

"Never assume anything. Always check your tack." The steely rebuke in his voice made her cheeks flush.

"Okay," she said. "But it's already late so I'll do it for the next ride."

"Do it now. I'll wait." His jaw turned rigid. He sat unmoving on Braun who seemed as disapproving as his rider.

"Right," she said meekly.

But it wasn't easy to make the adjustments. Jake was impatient to go to work, tossing his head and fussing, and the leather was stiff. Scott was no help either, just watching from high on his horse, looking rather formidable and not at all like the smiling man in the exercise room.

She tugged at her lip, trying to hurry, but it seemed endless minutes before she managed to shove the buckle in its keeper. "There," she said. "Is it okay to mount now?"

"Yes. But lead him back inside. You'll always mount in the shedrow at the track."

"But there's a mounting block outside."

"Where does Lydia have you mount?"

"Inside," she said.

Sighing, she led Jake back into the barn then glanced around in dismay. Lydia always legged them up, and the stirrups on the exercise saddle were too short to reach. It was probably safe to vault up but that wasn't good for the horse's back.

Still, she'd done it hundreds of times before. No one was watching and she didn't want to push Scott's patience by making him wait any longer. He was already being very generous with his time. She grabbed mane, took a little hop—

"Don't even think about it." Scott's low growl sounded behind her and the authority in his voice was so startling, she stumbled.

"I'll leg you up," he said, his voice softening.

She gave a humble nod, bending her knee so he could boost her into the saddle. "Where's your horse," she asked, once she settled safely in the saddle.

"Ground tied." He paused, keeping a restraining hand on Jake's reins. "You have to listen to me, Megan. Or it will be hot dogs for supper tonight."

"I'm invited for supper again?"

"Of course. Bring your swimsuit because you'll need the hot tub."

"Why will I need that?"

His sudden grin softened the angles of his face, making him look much more approachable. "Because you're going to be very stiff," he said.

He was much too confident, assuming she'd even want to join him for dinner. It was probably prudent to play a little hard to get, but that was impossible considering the way he smiled. "Why will I be stiff?" she asked, smiling back.

"You want to join Ramon's group? That's your goal?"

"Yes."

"Then we're playing catch-up so you will be stiff. And next time adjust your bridle inside. Don't frustrate your horse. Or me."

"That was a mistake," she said. "I'm sorry to make you wait."

"I don't mind." His expression turned enigmatic. "Take as much time as you need." He gave her knee a gentle squeeze, stepped outside and mounted Braun.

Her emotions felt jumbled but at least he wasn't the type to nurse an annoyance. And the thought of a hot tub at the end of the day was very appealing.

They headed to the far end of the track, away from Ramon's group that clustered around the starting gate.

Once they moved into a trot, she temporarily forgot her reservations about Scott and even her fears about Joey. Problems blew away. It was always like that when she was on a horse. And Jake was a real pleasure to ride.

Businesslike, with a beautiful floating stride, keen to move forward but not fighting her control.

"Keep your weight balanced in the stirrups," Scott said. "Don't push on his neck. Save that for when you want speed."

He was an excellent teacher, patient but firm, and soon it was hard to remember that she'd ever found this position hard. A jockey's crouch was almost second nature now, easy to do, easy on her horse. And she couldn't contain her smile.

"You're ready to learn how to switch your whip hand," Scott said. "But you can practice that while watching TV."

"I don't have a TV."

"I do," he said.

He spoke so naturally she nodded, somewhat overwhelmed at the easy way he linked them. But she didn't have time to worry because already they were increasing speed.

"The track is clear so we're going to gallop around once," he said, his voice rising so she could hear his instructions over their thudding hooves. "I'll stay on the rail. Don't let Jake run off. He'll be eager, especially going down the lane."

Jake was eager and she didn't think she'd ever galloped so fast. Tears blurred her eyes, and it was obvious why Ramon's top students always wore goggles. But her hands moved automatically with Jake's pounding stride, her seat was secure and she thanked her time on the mechanical horse for helping with the rhythm.

She wasn't so good with her whip though and at the quarter pole, she almost dropped it. Switching hands was a whole new skill set, but Jake galloped straight and she was able to keep the whip clutched in her fist. Still, it took every ounce of her strength to prevent him from charging down the stretch.

Scott and Braun were a reassuring presence and she glanced over twice, sharing her exhilaration. She was panting but grinning when they finally pulled up just past the finish line.

"My legs feel like jelly," she admitted, her breath escaping in gasps as they slowed to a bouncy trot. "If there were horses in front of us, the kickback would really sting. But it was great. Thanks so much."

"You did well," Scott said. "Tomorrow you can move on to gate work. You might want to use a different horse though. Jake will break like a rocket."

"He sure acts like a racehorse." She gave his sweaty neck an approving pat. "After some gate work, I'll be caught up to Ramon's class. Think I'll be ready to join them soon?"

"Sure," he said. "Or you can stay with me."

She glanced over her shoulder at the riders milling around the starting gate. Part of her wanted to stay with Scott, wished they had met under different circumstances, but she'd never meet Joey's friends that way. "I'd like to join the jockey class as soon as I can," she said.

He nodded, his eyes hooded. "Certainly. I'll speak with Ramon. Let's ride around the ridge and cool out these horses."

Jake followed Braun off the track, his ears pricking with interest once they turned away from the barn and headed toward the ridge. She was just as eager, aware she'd never be allowed to ride the trails unchaperoned. Even the cowbarn was forbidden territory.

Knowing Scott certainly simplified checking out the campus, although so far she hadn't unearthed much about Joey—only his iPod and one dog-eared magazine. She shoved away the depressing thought, determined to enjoy this unexpected trail ride, along with Scott's easy company.

They passed a rusty starting gate that was stripped of doors, then climbed the steep hill, following an erosion cut lined with sagebrush. They paused at the top of the ridge, enjoying a panoramic view of the school.

"Wow, this place is beautiful," she said, absorbing the property and enjoying the rare freedom. "It's wonderful to have the chance to ride up here. I really appreciate it."

"Definitely beautiful," he said, but he wasn't looking at the view and the way his eyes drank in her face made her melt. He simply exuded pheromones, drawing her like a magnet. She'd thought her sex drive was safely dormant, but he filled her with an unsettling awareness.

She jerked her head away, glad she was sitting on Jake. She was still embarrassed about last night's embrace in the hall, how she'd wrapped her arms around his neck as if she didn't ever want to let go. "That must be Garrett and his dog," she said, gesturing at the figures by the cowshed.

Scott had subtly moved his horse closer, his long leg brushing hers, but his attention shifted to the building below. "There's someone in the doorway talking to Garrett," he said. "Do you recognize the man?"

She tilted her helmet, shading her eyes against the sun. "Not sure. Looks like he has dark hair."

Scott remained unmoving, his gaze fixed on the men below. However, when Rex gave a sharp bark, he turned Braun toward the lower trail. "Let's ride down there," he said over his shoulder.

He pushed Braun into a lope, which seemed to defeat the purpose of cooling out the horses, but it was exhilarating to be riding again, not stuck in a field or circling on a track. And she and Jake gleefully followed.

It didn't take long to reach the back of the arena. A horse nickered a greeting and Braun answered, muffling the low voices in the cowshed.

"Let's get off and stretch our legs," Scott said, speaking so loudly it was obvious he wanted the men inside to hear.

"Sure, that'll be nice." She followed his lead and answered just as loudly, warmed by his approving wink.

They dismounted. Seconds later, Garrett appeared in the doorway, his hand gripped around Rex's collar. At least, she assumed it was Rex. The dog looked far different than he had during her interview. His hackles were raised, fangs bared and angry growls rumbled deep in his throat.

She inched closer to Scott, wishing they had remained mounted. Rex looked ferocious, more like a guard dog than a house pet.

"It's all right," Garrett said, noticing her movement. "Rex is okay. You're not the reason he's upset."

In fact, the dog looked at Megan and wagged his tail, seeming to recognize her. Garrett glanced back in the cowshed, then released his grip on Rex's collar. The dog trotted to Megan's side and shoved his wet nose into her hand.

"Hey, boy," she said, kneeling down and scratching him in his favorite spot. Jake kept his hooves planted but stretched his neck and gave the dog's head a cautious sniff.

"Rex is a sucker for a pretty face," Garrett said,

shooting Scott a tight smile. "How did you meet *her* so quickly?"

"Megan kindly rescued me on the road," Scott said, leading Braun closer to Garrett. "What was the dog upset about?"

"He wasn't upset."

"He's not the type of dog to act like that, without a clear threat."

"Yes, but it's okay now," Garrett said. "Just a visitor."

"Same visitor as this morning?" Scott's voice lowered. Megan pretended absorption with Rex who now sprawled at her feet, paws in the air, shamelessly begging for a belly rub.

"Yes, but it's no problem." Garrett glanced over his shoulder at the dark interior of the cowshed. "We sorted it out."

"Good," Scott said. But there was something hard in his voice and she peeked at his face, glad he wasn't looking at her with that unrelenting expression. Sometimes he was easy—other times, not so much.

"I'm going to ride with Megan back to her barn," he added. "I'll see you in a bit."

"It's fine." Megan rose, sensing the men had something more to discuss. "I can ride back by myself."

"I'm sure you can," Scott said. "But students aren't allowed to ride without an instructor. Isn't that right, Garrett?"

"That's the rule," Garrett said, but he wasn't smiling. "Are you two going to be riding around the cowshed a lot?" he asked. "Together like this?"

"Yes, we are," Scott said, boosting Megan into the saddle. He stepped into the longer stirrups of his western saddle and glanced at Garrett. "I'll see you back here in half an hour."

Megan followed Scott's horse, gripping her reins a little too tightly, hiding her discomfort. Scott was Garrett's employee, yet it had almost sounded like Scott had been the one giving the orders. He seemed preoccupied too, his mouth set in a grim line.

"You obviously know Garrett well," she said, once she was certain they were out of earshot. "But I wonder if he minds me riding over here?"

"Braun is stabled in the cowshed. Obviously I have to

ride here," Scott said, although she noticed he didn't really answer her question. "Do you know anyone called Miguel?"

"Yes," she said. "He's a part-time jockey student. His dad owns the Baja Tinda." She paused, doubting Scott wanted to hear about her roommate's infatuation. "He's cocky, but okay, I guess. I don't know why Rex would growl at him."

"Rex is a very smart dog," Scott said.

CHAPTER THIRTEEN

"Too bad you missed lunch again," Tami whispered, her face glowing with excitement. "Miguel sat with me. He even gave me some of his soup."

Megan nodded, careful to keep her eyes pinned to the front of the classroom. Lydia wheeled from the whiteboard, still talking but searching the classroom for the origin of the whispers.

"Injuries can occur at any time," Lydia said. "As riders, you need to be able to feel when a horse is moving differently. The quicker you can pull up, the safer it is for both horses and humans." Her eyes narrowed. "Do you have something to contribute to the lesson, Tami?"

Tami hunched her shoulders, shaking her head.

"Then that's it for today," Lydia said. "Next class we'll be looking at video clips of breakdowns and catastrophic falls. You all need to understand that riding is an extremely dangerous career."

Odd, Megan thought, rising and packing up her notes. Normally she would have been Lydia's target, not Tami. Yet today, the instructor had left her alone. It seemed she hadn't angered Lydia by leaving her riding class.

Relieved, she pulled the headphones from her bag. Whatever Scott had said to Lydia, he'd obviously been diplomatic. He'd also been correct about her stiffness. Her muscles ached from their long morning ride, and she slowly followed Tami toward the exit.

"Where the hell did you get that iPod?"

Both Megan and Tami wheeled toward the accusing voice.

Eve stood behind them, hands on her hips, flashing eyes as dark as her short raven hair. Tami looked at

Megan, obviously expecting her to admit that she'd found it in the cowshed. But Megan's hand tightened around the iPod. She didn't want to give it up. Listening to Joey's music provided a sense of connection, a connection she was determined to keep.

"Where'd you get it?" Eve repeated, stalking closer. She was slight and at least five inches shorter than Megan, but at that moment she radiated a tiger-like ferocity.

Megan glanced toward the front of the room. Luckily Lydia seemed busy stacking papers and except for Tami the classroom had cleared.

"It's Joey's," Megan said quietly, wishing the other girl would lower her voice.

"I know it's Joey's. I see his initials." Eve's voice sharpened. "But you didn't answer my question. Where'd you get it?"

Lydia closed her briefcase and turned around. "Is there a problem, ladies?"

"Yes," Eve said. "There's a big problem. Either this new student stole Joey's iPod or else she found it and intends to keep it. She clearly didn't report it to Lost and Found." Eve gave a contemptuous snort. "I'm sure his family would love to have it returned. Especially under the circumstances."

Megan's eyes widened. Finally, someone who empathized. Joey's family would indeed treasure the iPod. Lying in bed last night, listening to his songs, had been bittersweet. Even learning about his music preferences had been comforting. He'd always teased her about liking Taylor Swift. Yet, he had downloaded several of her songs—many of them Megan's favorites.

"That iPod belongs to Joey Collins?" Lydia asked. "Give it to me."

Megan opened her mouth to protest.

"Now." Lydia circled the desk and thrust out her hand.

Megan hesitated then reluctantly dropped the iPod into Lydia's grasping palm. "Eve's right," Megan said. "This should be forwarded to Joey's family. I think they'd really want it."

Her gaze caught Eve's and for a moment she spotted the other girl's expression, a blend of wistfulness and sorrow that mirrored her own.

"I'm sure Mr. Baldwin is capable of deciding what to do with it," Lydia said. "However, there's a bigger issue here—this item wasn't voluntarily turned in. And theft is cause for immediate dismissal."

"I didn't steal it," Megan said. "I found it in the cowshed."

"An area which is strictly off limits to students." Lydia's mouth thinned. "I'll be filing an incident report but I believe you're in a great deal of trouble. Thank you, Eve, for bringing this to my attention."

Eve strode from the room. Megan followed more slowly with an ashen-faced Tami trudging beside her.

"You planned to turn the iPod in at suppertime," Tami said, after a minute of silence. "That's what I remember. And I'll make sure that goes in Lydia's stupid report. I don't mind lying for my friends if it doesn't hurt anyone. But you should have guessed someone would notice." Tami sounded troubled. "That's an expensive model."

Three hundred and twenty-two dollars. Megan's fingers curved into her palms. She hadn't been thinking. It would have been wiser to leave the iPod in her room. Now it would be even more difficult to befriend Eve, who obviously had shared something special with Joey.

"Don't worry," Tami went on. "It hasn't even been twenty-four hours. Last year at high school I was caught in a situation like this, and there was a twenty-four hour rule. But I think if Garrett is mad, tears would definitely help. So be sure to cry a little. Maybe then he'll let you stay."

Megan's breath escaped in a shuddery sigh, half amusement, half despair. She reached out and squeezed Tami's hand. "I'm glad you're my roommate," she said. "I really appreciate you."

Tami gave a flippant shrug. "Great, but could you show your appreciation by staying away from our room for a while tonight? I invited Miguel over. Ramon doesn't let him invite people to the villa so we have nowhere else to go."

Megan gave a distracted nod, still picturing the anguish on Eve's face when she spotted the iPod. Maybe she should tell Eve that she was Joey's sister. Drop by the jock dorms and talk.

"Be sure to knock," Tami said.

"What?" Megan yanked her attention back to Tami. For a moment, she feared she'd been thinking out loud.

"Be sure to knock," Tami repeated. "You know, when you come back tonight. In case, Miguel is still there."

"Okay," Megan said. "I'll knock first." Besides, it wouldn't be a chore to stay away. Scott had already invited her for supper.

"I saw you riding with the hunky professor," Tami said. She seemed to have perked up thinking of men and no longer looked so troubled over the iPod. "Next to Miguel, he's the hottest guy on campus."

"I suppose," Megan said, astonished Tami considered Miguel more attractive than Scott. "You really like Miguel?"

"Oh, yeah." Tami's expression turned dreamy. "You should see him ride. Yesterday one of the horses was giving a student trouble, and Ramon asked Miguel to switch. Miguel sure made that horse sorry."

"Sorry?"

"Yes, Miguel showed the horse who was boss. He'll be a great jockey someday. Bet he'll be as famous as Ramon."

Infatuation seemed to have clouded Tami's judgment, and Megan shot her a cautious look. Miguel had too much spit and swagger for her liking. And the tractable lesson horses might listen, but she doubted a racehorse would give Miguel any extra effort, not if he were in the habit of roughing them up.

"I wonder how a horse would respond at the end of a race?" she asked mildly. "When they're exhausted and the jockey is pleading for every last drop of energy? When they need to work as a team to reach the wire first?"

"Don't know if they were much of a team," Tami said, scrunching her nose in thought. "The horse was really pissed. His ears were back and he was wringing his tail. Like he was listening but not really trying."

"Guess that's why we take horse psychology next month," Megan said. She wouldn't be here for that particular course, but Tami would and the girl was going to make a good exercise rider. Despite her obsession with Miguel, it was clear Tami was open to a wide range of training strategies.

"Miguel lost his temper a little," Tami admitted. "Ramon yelled at him for being too aggressive with his whip. But Miguel can stick to a horse better than anyone else, except maybe Eve. Both Peter and I fell off again this morning. Breaking from the starting gate is hard work, especially if your horse comes out fast. My ass is black and blue."

Megan smiled, realizing both she and Tami were walking stiffly. Her legs ached and the thought of Scott's bubbling hot tub was appealing. So was the prospect of seeing him tonight.

She gave a tiny bounce of anticipation but it only aggravated the muscle ache so she resumed her sedate walk, glad Tami was too absorbed with Miguel to ask any further questions about their sexy new instructor.

CHAPTER FOURTEEN

Rap, rap. Scott pressed the phone to his ear and walked toward the front door. Garrett wouldn't knock and the food had already been delivered from the cafeteria. Must be Megan.

"Okay, Snake," he said, trying to finish up the call. "Sounds good. We can review the rest of the cases tomorrow."

"But guess who the husband's banging." Snake chuckled. "T-Bone bet it was the insurance agent. You wouldn't believe—"

"Probably not," Scott said. "But you can tell me tomorrow."

"Don't you remember the lawyer with the big ass? And you wanted updates. Are you feeling okay?"

"Yeah," Scott said. Actually he was more than okay. Megan and the horses were like a tonic, and he didn't want to think about insurance scams or surveillance jobs. Belinda had been right. It was time for a vacation. Maybe even a lifestyle change. His business was established. He could cut back on work, hire a few more ex-cops.

"Want me to call back later?" Snake asked.

"Tomorrow," Scott said. "No earlier than mid morning."

"Oh, man." Snake's voice rippled with amusement. "I should have guessed. You met a hot woman—"

Scott cut the connection, silencing Snake's snicker. He pulled open the door. Then blinked in surprise, his smile freezing. "Hello, Lydia," he said.

She stepped in, carrying a bottle of red wine and a whiff of flowery perfume. "A little housewarming gift," she said.

"Thank you. That's very kind."

"Should we drink it now?" she asked. "I wasn't sure if your kitchen had a corkscrew so I brought one along, just in case." Her throaty laugh sounded forced and it didn't take a trained investigator to realize she was nervous.

"I'm busy now," he said gently. "But we can drink it tomorrow. With lunch," he added. The wine was a nice gesture and she was obviously lonely, but he didn't want to be close to her when the sun came down.

"Are you busy tonight?" Her disappointed gaze darted over his shoulder. "I guess tomorrow would be fine. But we can't drink wine in the cafeteria, not around the students."

"Of course. We'll eat here. Garrett can join us as well."

"But he never eats lunch. So it'll just be the two of us although you can always ask him...that is, if you're seeing Garrett tonight?"

"All right. I'll ask him." He stepped back, ignoring her clumsy attempt to probe, and pushed the door wider. "See you tomorrow."

"Tomorrow then," Lydia said.

He closed the door, relieved Megan hadn't arrived yet. Garrett had admitted Lydia was tough on pretty girls, and he didn't want to make Megan's situation worse. And Garrett would definitely be joining them for lunch tomorrow. He'd insist.

He carried the wine into the kitchen, debating about calling Snake back and finishing their conversation. His money had been on the insurance agent too, not the lawyer.

But he really wasn't that interested in who the sleazy husband was banging and Snake could handle everything at the office. Besides, Belinda would be back tomorrow. His time would be better spent removing the cover from the hot tub and getting ready for Megan.

"Do you want dessert now or after?" Scott asked as Megan finished her last bite of steak.

"After?" She raised an eyebrow, looking very poised. But he noticed that her index finger tapped at the base of the wine glass.

"After the hot tub," he said. She'd walked stiffly when she arrived and he'd already decided to make tomorrow's riding session a little easier. Of course, she'd still have to do some gate work, especially if she were moving into Ramon's class.

Those jocks were flying from the gate, although some of the exercise riders looked very inept, much greener than Megan. But he wanted to make sure she was prepared, while he was around to help.

"Maybe you should stay with the private lessons until next week," he said thoughtfully. "Get used to galloping with the shorter stirrups. Toughen up your legs."

"No, I'm fine," she said quickly. "I'm not sore at all."

"All right. Then we'll do three long sessions tomorrow so you're good and ready for Ramon."

Her eyes flared with such panic, he chuckled and tugged her from the chair and onto his lap. "I'm teasing, sweetheart," he said. "But breaking from the gate is challenging. I don't want you to get hurt."

And he was a little chagrined she didn't want to ride with him, that she preferred to move to Ramon's class. But she was in his arms now, and for tonight that would have to be enough. He adjusted her against his hips, enjoying the feel of her soft curves. "Did you bring a swimsuit?" he asked, reluctant to let her go.

"Yes. It's in my purse."

"Good. Sounds like it's tiny."

"It's my grandmother's old one-piece." But she looped her arms around his neck, her mouth curved in a teasing smile. This was the first time she'd looked at him like that, deep and full of such promise it made his breath stall.

He slid his hand along her hip, pressing her between his thighs. Her breasts brushed his chest and she fit against him perfectly. He held her for a moment, simply savoring her closeness and anticipating the remainder of the evening.

She was the first to pull away, looking up at him with steady eyes. "I have to leave at nine."

"Nine? I thought it was ten."

"Curfew is at ten but Lydia just asked me to feed the hay tonight."

He almost winced, his sharp disappointment surprising. However, he'd hoped for a little more time. A lot more time. "When did you see Lydia?" he asked.

"Just before I came. On the walkway, between the

cafeteria and your villa."

Damn. So that meant Lydia knew who his visitor was. Weird. Had she hung around to check? His arms tightened protectively, but Megan was already looking outside at the bubbling hot tub.

"Guess we should get moving then," he said, checking the kitchen clock. "There's a bathroom by the side door...or you can change in my bedroom."

Unfortunately she didn't choose his bedroom but instead slipped into the bathroom and closed the door. Still, it was only seven. They had until nine. She probably should stay awhile in the hot tub. It had been a hard session today. He'd never admit it but his muscles were tight too, and he'd been riding with long stirrups and a western saddle.

He walked into the bedroom, yanked off his shirt and jeans, and quickly changed. Time was wasting and it was clear from his response to Megan that he was going to want much more than a kiss.

He lingered in the kitchen, waiting until the bathroom door clicked open. Glanced over his shoulder and gave a hard gulp. It might be a problem making it out of the hot tub. Already his body flagged at the sight. His wholesome little ranch girl had the body of a Vegas dancer.

He dragged his gaze back to her face, but a muscle ticked in his jaw as visuals of raunchy sex flooded his brain. Hell. He was going to need a lot more than two hours.

She paused, alerted by his stillness. "Is something wrong?"

"Why don't I help you feed hay tonight?" he asked, his voice husky. "And then you can come back and sleep here."

She laughed as though he'd made a joke. "No, I'm just getting to know the other students. And I've hardly talked to Ramon yet. It wouldn't be good for people to know we're too chummy."

Chummy? He paused, watching her face, trying to understand her rationale. She worried about the students and Ramon, but hadn't mentioned Lydia. Yet Lydia was the authority figure for the exercise riders. And Megan seemed much too confident to care what the other students thought.

"You don't worry about Lydia?" he asked.

"Certainly," Megan said. "But she already doesn't like me."

And that could get worse, he thought, with a spike of guilt.

"Besides," she added, "it's the other students and Ramon I'll be riding with. They're the ones I want to get to know better."

How much better? He wheeled and grabbed the closest bottle of wine, surprised by his spurt of jealousy. Of course, she wanted the camaraderie of other riders. And it was probably because he was bored that he wanted to monopolize her attention...not because she was anything special. *Yeah, right.*

"You could bring some of your student friends here," he heard himself say as he splashed wine into two glasses. "You could all use the hot tub."

"Really? Tami would love that. She had another fall today."

"Well then, invite her over." He sucked in a resolute breath. Normally he wouldn't want a bunch of students squealing in his pool, annoying him with their chatter. It had been an impulsive offer, made because Megan put him in an incredibly fine mood. And her company was worth a little inconvenience.

He stuck the open bottle under his arm, balanced the two glasses in one hand, and switched on the deck lights. She followed him onto the patio. The sky had darkened, and a half moon glowed beyond the hedge. Garrett's mansion was barely visible, shaded by the darker outline of a magnolia tree.

Megan padded past him, all shapely legs and voluptuous curves, and stepped into the bubbling tub. Seconds later, water concealed everything but the swell of her breasts. He'd never have guessed her faded jeans and T-shirt hid such a hot body. Most women would be flaunting it.

"Here." He cleared the gruffness from his voice and pressed a glass into her hand then lowered himself into the water beside her.

"Wine, food, hot tub." She gave an appreciative sigh and closed her eyes, resting her head against the back of the tub. Her hair was pinned up, exposing her elegant neck, her flawless profile. "This must really impress the students," she said, oblivious to his scrutiny.

"I don't want to impress students...just you."

She opened her eyes and smiled. "But you've already impressed me."

Relief swept him. He slipped his arm around her waist and tugged her off the ledge and onto his lap. He wasn't usually uncertain with women, but there was a reserve about her, something that didn't quite jive. A wall that popped up at the oddest times.

But hopefully not tonight.

She balanced the wineglass on his forearm and relaxed against his chest. "This Jacuzzi would really help my roommate. Tami's only nineteen and quite resilient, but she's been banged up by the gate. She has some big bruises."

"Your roommate's only nineteen? How's that going?" A strand of her hair tumbled from its restraint and he tucked it behind her ear, trying to imagine sharing a tiny room again. In university, he and Garrett had constantly bickered until they moved out of residence and into an apartment. Admittedly, a bounty of fun-loving girls had played a big part in their desire for separate rooms.

"Sharing with Tami is great," Megan said. But light from the patio shadowed her face and he felt her hesitation. "I've lived alone for six years though. I miss my solitude."

"You can come here for quiet," he said. "Anytime." He skimmed his thumb along her collarbone. She stared up, eyes luminous. "I'm not a big chatterbox," he added, dipping his head and dragging his mouth along the side of her neck, following the trail of his thumb.

The peachy smell of her hair blended with night-blooming jasmine, and every one of his senses heightened. He had no headaches now, just a burning desire to know this woman. "Actually you're welcome to come for other things too," he said. "Food, sleep...sex."

She laughed but it was a nice laugh, an inviting laugh.

He slid his hand higher, grazing his thumb over the underside of her breast.

"That's tempting," she said, covering his hand and stilling his progress. "But is there another woman somewhere that might be hurt by that type of offer?"

"If there was," he said, "I wouldn't have made it."

She linked her fingers through his, raising his hand to her mouth in a poignant gesture that made his heart kick. "All right then," she said.

And that was it. So sweet, so honest, so refreshingly uncomplicated.

He tucked her close to his pounding chest, savoring the bubbling water, the darkening night, this special woman in his arms. She still held his hand, tracing his knuckles before running her fingers over his wrist and along his forearm. Her touch was light, but exploratory, and already he stiffened with eagerness.

"How did you do this?" She lingered over a scar on his wrist.

"Football."

She twisted, raising her hand to the side of his head, and gently kissed the raised scar. "Are your headaches better?"

"Much," he said gruffly, too conscious of her roving hand to consider long answers.

He unhooked the back of her swimsuit with a flick and tossed it over the wine bottle. Her skin felt warm and slick and smooth. He cupped her breast, thumbing her nipple, watching as her eyes darkened. "You're beautiful, Megan," he whispered.

"Not as beautiful as you." She gave a rueful smile and skimmed her fingers over his chest. "I thought you were an athlete or Special Forces or something when we first met. You must work out a lot."

He grunted, fascinated with her breasts, both accessible now, lying just below the erotic bubbling water. Light illuminated the side of the tub, shadowing her face but he could feel her, feel her everywhere. Her breasts rubbed against his chest, skin on skin, and a hungry heat pulsed through him.

He plucked the glass from her hand and set it beside his, then turned back, nibbling at her lip, teasing with teeth and tongue, coaxing her mouth wider. He couldn't get enough, not of her lips or her tongue or the way that slick body pressed against his. She tasted so good, and she was moving against him now.

He slid his hand higher. Her eyes turned dark and slumberous, her lower lip thick.

A dog's bark cut the night.

She twisted, glancing over his shoulder.

"It's just Garrett's dog," he murmured, tugging her back into position. He nibbled her lower lip then slid his mouth along the swell of her breast, finding her nipple. She gave a throaty groan, her breasts thrusting up. He palmed the smooth mound, exploring the firm weight, the satiny skin, just perfect for his hand.

Rex barked again, an explosion of furious noise, so stark they both flinched. "Damn," he said. "Let's go inside." He scooped her up, spraying water over the side as he carried her from the tub. "It'll be quieter—"

A yelp sliced the night, rising into a string of painful cries. He jerked to a stop, his grip tightening around her. Clearly something was in horrible pain. Thank God, she was beside him. And safe.

But the cries continued, razoring the night, calling him like a siren. He dragged his mouth over her forehead in an apologetic kiss and set her down.

"Some animal needs help, sweetheart. Wait here. I'll be right back."

He jogged around the back lawn, vaulted over the hedge and cut across the divider, ignoring the rocks biting his feet. Air chilled his skin and he wasn't sure if the goose bumps were a result of the night air, shockingly cold against the contrast of the hot tub, or because of the eerie cries, subdued now but still gut wrenching.

Garrett's dog? Or a coyote? Maybe something had been hit in the driveway, although coyotes were generally more stoic about pain. His stride quickened as he reached the smooth concrete.

"Oh, damn!" He jerked to a stop beside a stunned Garrett.

Rex lurched in panicked circles, crying and biting at his mangled leg. Bone protruded from the dog's skin, gleaming whitely beneath the driveway light.

"What the hell happened?" Scott asked, checking the driveway. But both Garrett's vehicles were parked benignly in the carport.

"You'll have to shoot him." Garrett's voice cracked as he grabbed Scott's arm. "Rex won't let me near him. He bit me when I tried."

"What happened?"

Garrett gave a helpless shrug. "I don't know. He was outside barking. I didn't think too much of it, then...Jesus, the noise. I can't stand it. He's hurting."

Rex lurched into a hedge and began another series of aching cries. Scott edged forward and tried to grab his collar but the dog twisted, teeth snapping.

"Easy, Rex." Scott glanced back at Garrett. "How close is your vet? Maybe we can throw a blanket over him. Get him in the car."

"Here, use this." Megan stepped from the dark and pressed a pool towel into his hands. She'd yanked his T-shirt on but her curves were visible beneath the damp cotton.

"I'll get a blanket." Garrett turned and rushed toward his door.

"And warn your vet we're coming," Scott called, wrapping the towel around his left hand.

Rex seemed oblivious to his approach, but when Scott tried to touch him the dog twisted, grabbing his hand in a lightening fast reflex. The towel proved much too thin, but then Megan was beside him with a thick blanket, promising Rex that everything would be fine, and the dog appeared to believe her.

"Bring the car as close as you can, Garrett," Scott said, watching as Rex let Megan touch his head. "He might bite," Scott warned, but all the fight seemed to have drained from the dog. He was quiet now, his eyes glazed with shock.

They wrapped him in the blanket and three pairs of hands gently eased him onto the back seat. Rex didn't complain. His head was on Megan's lap, his mouth half open, his gums pale.

Scott noted Garrett's white face, his uncharacteristic silence. "I'll drive," Scott said, sliding behind the wheel of the BMW. "We can stop by the tack room. Give him a shot for pain. How far is the vet?"

"Fifteen minutes," Garrett said.

Not worth the extra time, Scott decided. He wheeled the car out of the driveway and directly onto the main road. "Did you tell him we're coming?"

Garrett gave a wordless nod.

Scott checked the rearview mirror. Megan still murmured assurances to the dog but her face was pale.

Pieces of hair tangled around her cheeks, the ends still dripping. He cranked up the heat, letting in a rush of warm air.

Her eyes met his and he managed a reassuring smile but damn, the dog was badly hurt. It looked like some bastard had smashed him with a club.

He turned to Garrett, keeping his voice low. "Who hurt him? Was it Miguel?"

Garrett shook his head and glanced meaningfully over his shoulder at Megan.

"We're going to talk about this," Scott said, pressing his bare foot on the accelerator, hoping there was no traffic.

The narrow road was twisted but empty. He winced every time they hit a bump although Rex remained scarily silent. They only passed one slow-moving van before the road lightened with a sprinkle of houses and finally they spotted the town's glowing streetlamps.

"Turn right after the car dealer," Garrett said. "Four blocks."

They pulled up to the front door of the vet clinic. A short lady in a green gown rushed to the car. Her mouth tightened as she appraised the damage. "Bring him inside," she said. "Follow me."

They walked through an empty waiting room carrying a dull-eyed Rex, he and Garrett at either end with Megan stroking the dog's head.

"Do whatever you need to patch him up, Doc," Garrett said.

"I'll try. Sign those forms." The vet motioned to an assistant who led Garrett toward a desk.

Scott turned with a sense of relief, and guided Megan from the clinic and out to the car. Garrett sometimes made ruthless decisions, but luckily for Rex, that wasn't the case tonight. Garrett clearly valued his dog.

"Do you think he'll be okay?" Megan asked, her teeth chattering. He closed the passenger door and joined her in the warm car.

"I think Garrett is committed to doing everything he can," Scott said cautiously. "If money can fix him, Rex will be fine."

He blasted up the heat, leaned over and gave her a grateful kiss. "You were a huge help, but I thought I told you to wait. How's this going to work for us if you don't listen to every stupid thing I say?"

She forced a half smile, as though aware he was trying to cheer her up. However, she clutched his fingers, her voice shaking. "What kind of horrible person could do that?"

"I don't know." He slid a hand beneath her damp hair and rubbed the base of her neck, trying to warm her up. "But I'll find out."

"Good," she said. Her grip on his fingers relaxed, and she lowered her head onto his chest while he massaged her neck. "You must be cold too. You don't even have a shirt." Her lips brushed against his bare skin. "What now?"

"I'll drive you home," he said. "Help you hay the horses. Then come back for Garrett."

She straightened far too soon, leaving an empty spot where her body had been. "You're not going to wait? Shouldn't you tell him we're leaving?"

"Garrett will figure it out. You need to get home." He wheeled the car around the circular driveway and back onto the highway. "Besides, he might want to leave with us. And I figure a man should stay with his dog."

Her smile was tremulous but it was an improvement over the horror that had clouded her face.

"It looks like a nice clinic." She glanced back at the vet building. "They can do a lot nowadays," she added, as though reassuring herself.

"I've seen worse." He reached over and gave her hand a comforting squeeze. "Did you ever have a dog that broke a leg?"

"Our Lab was hit by a car, broke some bones, but my father shot her. Said it was for the best. That was the last dog that my brother...that my mom and I had."

Something odd sounded in her voice and he shot her a swift look, but darkness cloaked her expression. "Your parents are divorced?" he asked.

He felt her nod.

"My mom remarried," she said, after a slight hesitation. "It's just her and Steven now."

No doubt about it, her voice was definitely strained.

Chirp. Garrett's cell phone sounded, forgotten on the console. Scott checked the display. Unknown caller.

Probably Garrett calling about his car since Scott's own phone was back in the kitchen. He gave Megan an apologetic smile, regretting the interruption, and pressed the green button.

"I'll pick you up later, Garrett," he said firmly. "Megan has to feed."

No one spoke. There was only the sound of breathing. Then utter silence.

"Not Garrett," Scott said, disconnecting. "Guess it was a wrong number." But he automatically scanned the rearview mirror because his instincts told him it hadn't been a misdial.

CHAPTER FIFTEEN

Megan rushed into the barn, praying Lydia wasn't patrolling. Night hay was scheduled for nine and already they were forty-five minutes late. It had taken extra time to stop at Scott's villa to grab her clothes, but he'd noticed her shivers and insisted she couldn't feed in a damp bathing suit.

Hopefully it was Ramon's turn for barn check. The other instructor was taciturn but not as fussy as Lydia. Sometimes he didn't even walk inside the barn. But it would be difficult for anyone to ignore a bunch of loud and hungry horses.

She skidded to a stop, so quickly Scott's hand reached out to steady her. But something was wrong. It was much too quiet. Not a single horse whinnied or pawed. In fact, only Jake bothered to stick his head over the stall door. He studied them with mild curiosity while contentedly chewing a mouthful of hay.

"Guess someone already fed," she said, glancing around. "Swept the floor too."

She peered into Jake's stall. As usual, he'd nosed his hay all around the stall, but it appeared there was at least one flake left. And he wasn't acting ravenous which meant he'd been eating for a while.

She shot Scott a relieved nod. "Yes. Someone definitely fed them."

"Good," he said. "Where's your room?"

She gestured, then realized he was waiting to walk her upstairs. Unnecessary but rather sweet. His chivalry and sheer competence seemed to extend to everything he did.

Maybe I should ask his help in finding Joey?

She hesitated then pressed her mouth tight, accepting he was far too close to Garrett—and there was no doubt who would command his loyalty. Someone at the school was a treacherous liar. And now someone had viciously attacked Rex.

Her shiver was slight but Scott immediately wrapped his arm around her waist and guided her to the stairs. "Get some sleep," he said. "You've been yawning the entire drive back. I apologize for the shitty night."

"The first part was great. My aches are gone so the hot tub worked. It was after that—" She swallowed, didn't want to relive the horror of Rex and his pitiful cries. "Guess it's a good thing you were around," she added. "Garrett seems to depend on you."

"It's a good thing you were there too. Rex trusts you." He raised his hand and traced his finger along her cheek, such a casual, intimate gesture that she forgot her exhaustion and truly regretted the student curfew.

"Do you think he'll be all right?" she asked, looking up into Scott's steady gray eyes, knowing he wasn't the type to lie.

Scott nodded. "Garrett made the decision to save him. And he has the means to make it happen."

"But you pushed him into it. I heard him ask you to shoot Rex. It seemed rather cold. And why did he think you were hard hearted enough to kill—"

Scott pressed his finger against her lips, his eyes hooding. "It's past curfew and you need your sleep."

He tugged her up the rest of the narrow steps and checked the empty hall. Light spilled beneath the door of room twenty-three. All the other doorways were dark.

"Is that your room?" he asked. "Looks like your roommate is still awake."

"She might have company," Megan said, giving a cautious knock. Tami called a muffled 'come in' and Megan eased open the door.

"Finally!" Tami said. "You're late and Lydia was asking all kinds of questions." Her eyes widened when she spotted Scott.

"This is my roommate, Tami," Megan said.

"I love your class, sir," Tami said, rushing across the room and pumping Scott's hand. "And don't worry about the horses. Miguel and I fed them."

"Miguel?" Scott spoke so sharply Tami stiffened.

"Yes," she said. "It was his idea to help. We didn't

break curfew or anything," she added.

"What time did you feed?" Scott's voice was casual now but Megan could feel the intensity radiating from his body. Even Tami straightened, her expression wary.

"They're supposed to be fed at nine," Tami said. "But I could see that Megan wasn't around. Lydia was checking the jock barn so Miguel and I decided to give them their night hay and just pretend Megan had been there. I thought you'd be happy." Tami glanced at Megan, hurt shadowing her eyes, and she suddenly looked much younger than nineteen.

"I am happy," Megan said, edging between Tami and Scott. "Thanks for covering for me."

"Yes. I appreciate it too," Scott said, his hand splaying protectively over Megan's hip.

Tami's eyes widened and Megan guessed hers probably had too. She'd assumed they'd remain discreet. Of course, Tami was her roommate and it would be hard to hide anything from her. And Garrett had already seen Megan come from Scott's villa, still dripping from his Jacuzzi.

"So Miguel was with you tonight?" Scott asked Tami, his voice much gentler now. "What time did he come by?"

"After supper." Tami nodded, happy again. "We had coffee and watched TV in the jock barn. Probably why I can't sleep now. They have six different kinds of coffee. I probably should have gone for the decaffeinated. Or maybe the herbal tea."

Scott's hand tightened around Megan's hip and she felt his impatience. "How long were you and Miguel watching television?" she asked, trying to nudge Tami back on track.

"A few hours. We walked back from the cafeteria together. Did you know Ramon gives them video to watch every night? They have way more homework than us." Tami turned away and sat on her narrow bed, suddenly engrossed with her nails.

So it couldn't have been Miguel who attacked Rex, not if he'd been with Tami. Megan's breath escaped in a whoosh of relief. "Garrett's dog was hurt tonight," she said. "That's why we wondered—"

Scott gave her hip a warning squeeze, and she quit talking.

But Tami's head shot up. "What are you talking about?" she asked. "Miguel wouldn't hurt an animal. Wouldn't hurt anything." She crossed her arms, a mutinous set to her chin. "Like I said, he was with me the entire night. And we had a great time," she added.

Megan glanced at Scott in apology, realizing she should have kept her suspicions hidden. But he gave her a reassuring smile.

"Garrett and I will find the guy," he said softly, "but let's not talk about it around campus." He brushed her mouth with a swift kiss. "Try not to worry about Rex. I'll see you tomorrow." And the raw promise in his voice made her pulse kick.

His gaze lifted over her head. "Good night, Tami," he said politely, before turning and striding down the hall.

Tami rose from the bed and peeked past the door, watching until he disappeared in the stairwell. She turned around with an excited squeal. "Score! I knew you were riding with him but didn't know you'd hooked up. An instructor! That's even better than a jockey."

She followed Megan to the bathroom door, still bouncing. "Guess that means Peter's wrong," she said.

Megan brushed her teeth and stepped back out.

"What's Peter wrong about?" she asked, yawning and heading toward her bed. She needed sleep. Hopefully she wouldn't agonize over Joey and Rex and shattered bones. There'd be time to talk to Tami in the morning. But right now she was drained.

"Peter saw Lydia draped over Scott in the cafeteria," Tami said. "Later he saw her leaving Scott's place."

"I saw her too." Megan adjusted her pillow and slipped between the sheets. "They're both instructors. Obviously they're friends."

"Yeah," Tami said quickly. "Peter always jumps to conclusions. He's so desperate to get laid, he can't think of anything but sex. Are you going to sleep now? Because I want to show you my new phone. It has every app in the world."

Megan pried her eyes open and glanced across the room. "You already have a nice phone," she said. It was a mystery how Tami could function on so little sleep.

"Not like this one. Miguel gave it to me. It's loaded and the service is prepaid. It's brand new and way faster than my old one."

"That's nice of him," Megan said. It was strange Miguel would give away a new phone but she was too tired to rouse much interest. "I'll look at it tomorrow," she added, her words lost in another yawn. Her brother was missing, an innocent dog had been brutalized and even the suspicion that the incidents might be related couldn't keep her awake.

Tami was still droning on about all the apps on her new phone when Megan fell asleep.

CHAPTER SIXTEEN

"I want a good seat for this class," Tami said. She pushed past a slower student and bolted toward the sole chair left in the front row.

Megan studied the crammed room. She'd never seen so many students in one class—grooms, exercise riders and jockeys. Front seats were in huge demand, unlike Lydia's classes where everyone scrambled to sit at the back. Scott's class didn't start for another five minutes but if she didn't hurry, she wasn't going to find a seat.

She edged along the back row, carefully balancing her coffee, and slid into a vacant chair. "Good morning," she said, glancing at the student on her right. Her smile froze when she recognized Eve.

"No iPod today?" Eve snapped.

Megan's mouth tightened. "As you know, Lydia took it."

"Don't worry," Eve said, raking her with a contemptuous stare. "I'm sure you can steal another."

"Maybe. After all, the day is young." Megan immediately regretted her flippant words. She didn't want to goad the jockey, but the fiery girl had cost her Joey's iPod and Megan harbored a little resentment of her own. "I wasn't trying to steal it," she added.

"What did you say?" Eve was staring with an odd expression.

"I wasn't trying to steal it."

"No, that expression," Eve said. "About the day being young." She tilted her head, her eyes widening as they studied Megan's face. "Oh my God. I see it now. You have the same mouth. You're Megan, his sister."

"Joey mentioned me?"

"All the time. He showed me pictures too. You taught him to ride, taught him to rope. You helped him...with everything." Eve leaned closer, her voice lowering. "What the hell are you doing here?"

"Trying to find out what happened, and if he was really back on crack. Heroin would be his second choice," Megan said wryly.

"He wasn't using." Eve's head whipped back and forth. "He really wasn't. And he wouldn't have dumped me like that. I don't care what Ramon said."

"What exactly did he say?"

"That Joey stayed for some girl in Mexico." Eve's voice rose. "But I know him. He wouldn't have done that. No way!"

The room turned silent. Someone muttered 'shush.' Students turned in their seats, shooting frowns in their direction. Megan looked up and met Scott's enigmatic gaze.

"Good morning," he said, turning his head and addressing the rest of the class. "Today we're going to talk about weight loss drugs—the pros and cons, and why it's important to exercise caution."

Megan stared blankly at his face, struggling to absorb Eve's words. There had never been any mention of Joey taking off with a girl. Would he do that? Maybe. After all, their father had deserted his family. Walked out on a wife and two kids. Perhaps it ran in the family.

"Joey wouldn't do that," Eve repeated, her voice fierce.

The stout lady in front of them turned around and glared.

"But why would Ramon say that?" Megan whispered. Scott's eyes narrowed so she waited a moment, then covered her mouth and leaned closer to Eve. "The police report didn't mention any girl in Mexico. They made it sound like heroin. Why—"

"Because I was Joey's girlfriend and they knew I didn't believe Ramon." Eve wrung her hands. "Joey wasn't doing drugs. Not anymore—"

Scott quit talking. Heads swiveled, following his steely gaze. He definitely knew how to use silence. Every student in the room twisted, staring at Megan and Eve with shared censure. He hadn't said a word, didn't have to. The entire classroom crackled with disapproval. Even Tami turned and rolled her eyes. Someone's nervous cough punctuated the quiet.

Megan pressed against the back of her seat, cheeks warming with embarrassment.

Eve rose to her feet, her pen dropping to the floor with a clatter. She brushed past Megan's chair and rushed from the room.

"If anyone else wants to leave," Scott said, staring at Megan, "now's the time."

She picked up her notes, her coffee and Eve's deserted bag, rose and walked toward the exit, studiously avoiding the shocked expressions. Fifteen feet but it felt like fifty. The back of her neck didn't stop prickling until the door closed behind her.

Eve swung around in the deserted hall, her pretty face flushed with temper, continuing as though the conversation had never stopped. "Ramon's lying. He knew Joey wasn't into drugs, but he didn't want me to make trouble. Something's up, but I can't figure it out."

"You hung out with Joey?"

Eve nodded. "For the last ten weeks we were really tight. Honestly, Megan, he wasn't using." She checked over her shoulder, but they seemed to be the only people in the hall. "I have no idea what's going on," she added. "I have to ride with Ramon every morning and I hate his guts. He's looking for a chance to kick me out. If they know you're Joey's sister, you'll never be allowed to stay. They'll find some excuse—"

"But they can't know," Megan said, wishing Eve would lower her voice. "No one knows but you. And I intend to get close to Ramon. And find out the truth."

"You're a lot like him." Eve smiled for the first time. It was weak and wobbly, but it was a smile. "Joey was so brave, always asking questions. He never let Lydia get away with bullying the girls. I just wish he hadn't helped Ramon so much. Once they found out Joey was a mechanic, he was always fixing stuff. That new baler had a lot of glitches."

"The baler in the cowshed?"

Eve nodded. "Ramon was desperate. He couldn't get it

to work, and they needed to send alfalfa down with the Baja Tinda horses. That trip was Joey's reward for helping."

"So it wasn't for riding?"

"No. Joey was top in the class but the trip happened because of the baler. Joey only texted me once that day. Said he was going to help Ramon deliver some horses...I never saw him again."

The anguish in Eve's voice was so genuine, Megan gave her an impulsive hug. "Let's go for a drive. I'd love to talk more. But we better go someplace private, where nobody can hear."

Eve shot a wary look down the hall. "That's probably safer," she said.

CHAPTER SEVENTEEN

Scott led Braun back into the cowshed, his mouth clenched with annoyance. He yanked off the heavy saddle. It had been an easy day for the patient horse. Megan hadn't shown up for her riding lesson, wasn't answering her phone, and in fact, had been AWOL since she'd waltzed from his class that morning.

"Goddammit."

Braun flicked his ears at the low curse, and Scott gave him an apologetic pat. The horse was great but the little lady was turning difficult. Two unexplained absences. *And I thought we were getting along so well.*

Someone had placed hay and water in Braun's stall and the gelding stuck his nose in the pile of hay, dismissing the frustration of his rider.

Buzz. Scott grabbed his phone, disappointed when he saw Snake's name on the display.

"Hey, boss," Snake said. "Think I'll put two guys on the husband for another week and then make a final report. That job is getting boring."

Scott pushed open the tack room door and tossed the saddle onto the rack, his mind still wrapped around Megan. Her phone was ancient. Maybe it wouldn't hold a charge. Perhaps she wasn't getting his messages. Maybe he should check her room.

He gave his head a shake. He certainly wasn't going to go knocking on her door, hunting her down. Students were supposed to attend class without a special invitation. And she'd chosen to walk out of his lecture.

"Boss?"

"That sounds good," he said quickly. "But check the credit card receipts at the restaurant. See who owns the company. It's not necessary to update me on all the details."

Snake didn't answer. Silence stretched as Scott hung Braun's bridle on the hook, replacing it among the line of neat tack.

"How are you really feeling?" Snake finally asked.

Scott slammed the tack room door shut. "Fine. I'm fine." The only headache he'd had today was when Megan had blown him off.

But Snake sounded skeptical and it was another ten minutes before Scott was able to finish the call and hurry back to his villa.

He had important things to do. He had a girl to track down and Lydia was coming for lunch. He fervently hoped she didn't ask any questions about Megan's missed riding lesson. Because as much as he liked Megan, he didn't intend to lie for her.

Garrett stepped through the back door and gave Scott a wry smile. "I considered staying away and leaving you to lunch alone with Lydia, but didn't want to rouse your anger."

Scott gave a nod of acknowledgement and tossed Garrett a can of beer. "How's Rex?"

"Stable. There's a cast on his leg and he'll be at the clinic awhile. He might walk with a limp but at least he'll walk... Thanks."

"I know you saw who did it." Scott kept his eyes pinned on Garrett's face.

"Yeah," Garrett admitted. "I saw the guy." He took a swig of beer, wiped his mouth with the back of his hand and blew out a resigned sigh. "It was Joey Collins. The student who ran off last month. We thought he stayed in Mexico but obviously he's back now."

"Why pretend you didn't see him? That you were in the house?"

Garrett shook his head. "I couldn't talk in front of Megan. The school's reputation has already suffered. If people hear we have someone like Joey hanging around..." His voice turned slightly accusing. "That's the downside of staff dating students."

Scott cracked open his can and took a pensive drink. Garrett had a point. He wasn't quite sure how to handle Megan's insubordination today. Walking out of class, not showing up for a private riding lesson. If it was anyone else, he'd skin them alive.

A knock sounded at the front door and Garrett's grin returned. "That will be the lovesick Lydia. Girls never were your problem, were they, buddy?"

Garrett had always cut a wider swathe with the women, but this didn't seem the time to debate quality over quantity. Scott merely shot his friend a warning look then walked down the hall and swung open the door.

Today Lydia wore a red silk blouse and black pants that looked out of place for a casual lunch at a riding school. Nothing wrong with her figure though, if you liked skinny. He didn't.

"Come in, Lydia," he said. "Garrett's already in the kitchen."

"Really?" Her forehead creased with puzzlement. "Garrett told me he never ate lunch."

"Not usually," Scott said, as she followed him down the hall. "But he missed breakfast this morning."

He scanned the wine rack, searching for Lydia's gift bottle from last night, then realized it was half gone. He'd grabbed it last night by mistake, when he'd been so distracted by Megan in her sexy bikini. Couldn't even remember the wine except that the lingering flavor had tasted damn good on Megan's lips. She obviously hadn't been as affected.

Lydia followed his gaze and gave a moue of disappointment. "I see you opened the wine without me."

"Guess I did," Scott said, his frustration with Megan leaving him in no mood to stroke Lydia's fragile ego. He poured her a glass of wine and dropped three plates on the table, ignoring Garrett's amused grin.

"Direct from the cafeteria," Scott said. "Enjoy."

Lydia flashed a bright lipstick smile and pulled her chair so close he could smell her perfume. It was apparent she'd selected him as her new best buddy. "Afterwards," he added, "I'll come back to your place, Garrett, and we can review those numbers."

"What numbers?" Garrett's eyes twinkled with mock innocence.

"The proposed salary raise for your fulltime instructors," Scott snapped.

"Oh, yeah," Garrett said, "those numbers."

"A raise?" Lydia said. "How lovely. I had no idea that was being considered." She beamed and was quiet for a blessed moment then leaned forward. "Working lunches are very time efficient, don't you think? We should make lunch part of our daily routine. It's a good chance to discuss important matters."

"Probably not necessary." Both men spoke at the same time.

"But I have a few confidential things I'd like to discuss." She gave a dramatic pause. "Did you know Megan Spence had Joey Collins' iPod?"

Scott stilled. Garrett set down his beer can.

Lydia nodded, delighted she'd captured their attention. "She stole it. I caught her with it yesterday."

"Was there anything else found?" Garrett asked. "Any more of Joey's things?"

"No, but in addition to possessing someone else's property," Lydia's voice rose in triumph, "Megan neglected to feed the horses last night."

"Neglected to feed the horses?" Garrett frowned. "But she was helping us—" He caught Scott's warning look, closed his mouth, then gave a grave nod. "Don't worry about it. I'll put Scott in charge of Megan Spence."

"But shouldn't she be sent home?" Lydia asked.

"No," Garrett said. "But Scott will look into it. He's experienced at undercover work. And the best man to handle any...probing."

"All right," Lydia said. "But remember it's wise to take a firm hand with these students."

"A firm hand indeed," Garrett said, his mouth twitching.

Megan rushed down the walkway to Scott's villa, dismayed she and Eve hadn't returned in time for their riding lessons. But time had rushed past and it had been cathartic to drive around in her truck, swapping stories about Joey, talking with someone else who'd loved him.

She'd learned so much. He had been happy here, had

loved riding and Eve confirmed he'd been offered a job galloping at Santa Anita. Megan didn't understand why Ramon was lying about the drugs, but now her resolve had strengthened. First though, she had to apologize to Scott.

She reached up but his door swung open before she could knock. Lydia stared, two slight lines angling between her perfectly plucked eyebrows.

"Oh, hi," Megan said, scrambling for an excuse. Scott had no doubt told Lydia she'd missed her riding lesson as well as the class. The two instructors had clearly just spent the lunch hour together. But if by some stroke of luck, he hadn't reported it, she certainly wanted to keep it secret. "I just wondered how Garrett's dog is," she said lamely.

"He's doing okay," Scott said, appearing behind Lydia.

"Great, that's good." Megan backed up a step, studying his mouth. She could have sworn there was a speck of lipstick on the left corner. She stared at him, uncertain, but he remained silent, arms crossed.

"Okay, well that's good," she repeated. But he wasn't helping her out and her cheeks turned warm in the prickly silence.

"I have to go to class now," she said. "Sorry to bother you." She turned away and for the second time that day, felt hostile stares raking her back.

By the time she rushed into the classroom, she was alternating between curses and gratitude, relieved he hadn't reported her absence but hurt by his quick defection to Lydia. Thank God she hadn't slept with the guy.

"Are you ready for Lydia's class?" Tami asked. "Catastrophic accidents. It's going to be gruesome." She wrinkled her nose. "What were you thinking this morning? You and Eve were so rude, walking out of Scott's lecture this morning."

"We didn't mean anything. Eve felt sick and I was trying to help."

"Well, you better explain that to Scott. He was in a bad mood the rest of the class."

"I saw him since," Megan said, pulling out her pen and paper. "Lydia's cheering him up."

Minutes later, Lydia swept into the room. Peter rolled his eyes behind Lydia's back, pantomiming at her inappropriate outfit. But as soon as Lydia turned around, he flashed her a deferential smile. That boy was going to go far, Megan decided bleakly. He sure knew how to suck up.

The next two hours were interminable as they watched a series of gut wrenching accidents. Some horses and riders walked away; others weren't so fortunate. Megan repeatedly wiped her eyes but almost everyone else in the class was crying too. Even the guys.

"And that," Lydia said, blowing her nose and switching off the video, "is why an ambulance follows the race riders. It's a demanding and dangerous profession. Consider it carefully."

"Megan Spence," she added. "Please remain after class."

She was using Megan's last name now. Not good. Tami shot Megan a sympathetic look then bolted with the other students from the room.

Megan squared her shoulders and stopped in front of Lydia's desk, trying to recall school policy on skipping class.

Missing a riding lesson was the biggest infraction, much worse than skipping a lecture. Eve feared Ramon's reaction too but thought they were permitted one absence, with a medical excuse. Megan hadn't even thought about rules, had been too consumed with talking to Eve and hearing about Joey. She didn't have a reason for her absence and prayed she wouldn't be expelled, especially now that she'd met Eve and was finally making headway.

"Your behavior is unacceptable," Lydia snapped.

Megan gulped. She couldn't be kicked out before she talked to Ramon. She had to follow Peter's lead and suck up. Lowering her head, she forced a humble nod. "I'm sorry," she said.

"Chasing after instructors is embarrassing for everyone," Lydia went on. "It's also strictly against the rules. You will not visit Mr. Taylor's villa again."

Relief swept her. Scott hadn't turned her in. Hadn't breathed a word. And Lydia was so zealous. No doubt, she was the one chasing Scott. "Of course not," Megan said meekly. "I'm sorry for any embarrassment. It was very rash of me to...visit. To knock on his door."

Lydia nodded, oblivious to the sarcasm. "Yes, it was unacceptable. You can go now. But remember what I said." She gestured toward the door, her mouth pinched.

Megan rushed from the building, pulled out her phone and pressed Scott's number. He answered on the first ring.

"Sorry I had to leave your class this morning," she said quickly. "And miss the riding. I was really busy with something."

"You need a better excuse than that," he said. "Are you coming over?"

"No." She lowered her voice. "I just left Lydia's class. She warned me about seeing instructors."

"Meet me at the cowshed," he said. "I'll be there in ten minutes."

Lydia stepped outside, only a few feet away, so Megan pressed the phone against her ear and raised her voice. "Okay, Tami," she said. "See you in ten minutes."

Scott sighed and cut the connection.

A narrow footpath circled the back of the cafeteria. She followed the trail around the building, through the parking lot scattered with cars and past a dumpster that reeked of rotting food. An old golf cart and a stock trailer with a 'FOR SALE' sign were squeezed into a graveled parking lot. And then the trail joined a beautiful private drive lined with white stucco fences so blindingly bright they seemed to mark entry into a different world.

She hurried along the deserted drive to the cowshed. Braun and the other three horses stood in neatly railed paddocks. They pricked their ears as she approached, clearly anticipating an early supper. Scott's car wasn't in the parking lot but Braun stared over her head at the barn, tossing his head and hopeful for hay, too impatient to accept her pat.

She entered the cowshed through the side door, straining to see through the gloom. Maybe Scott had walked from his villa.

But he wasn't in the little barn or the tack room. She stepped into the cool arena. The haystack was still there, untouched. Hopefully he'd let her bag some more alfalfa. Jake and Rambo had appreciated the treat, and it was a shame to let such nice hay go to waste.

Movement flashed—a man's arm. His back was bent over the hay baler. She skidded to a stop, her mouth drying. Students weren't allowed in the cowshed, and she was here without Scott. Best to slip out the back door and hope he arrived soon.

But the man turned and lifted his head.

"Good afternoon," Ramon said, his eyes narrowing. "Do you have another riding lesson today?"

"No...I don't think so."

"Then you shouldn't be here." He bent down and selected a wrench from a shiny red toolbox. He didn't look too mad but wore that closed expression that was always hard to read. However, this was a rare opportunity to talk to him.

"I'm supposed to meet Scott here," she said. "I'm not sure if there's time for a lesson before supper but I'm hoping to work hard and be ready to join your class soon."

"I saw you galloping yesterday. You're ready now."

She blinked, surprised he'd noticed her riding with Scott. They'd been at opposite ends of the track, and Ramon would have been busy with his large group of students.

"Really?" she asked, stepping closer. "I can join your class?"

"Yes. You're ready."

"Well...that's great." She'd expected to feel more satisfaction but after talking to Eve, the only emotion she felt for Ramon was resentment. The man may have been a great jockey and a good teacher, but for some reason he'd lied about Joey. She itched to pry the truth from those thin lips, but sensed Ramon would be able to see through any bullshit.

"I've wanted to join your class since I came," she said, knowing that statement, at least, was true. "I've been over a week trotting in the field with the grooms."

He lifted his head over the side of the baler. His mouth cracked in a smile and for a moment, he looked a little more approachable. "Some people take longer to balance in the stirrups," he said. "But once they get it, they're often my best riders. I think you're one of those people."

Despite her distrust of Ramon, she enjoyed a little rush of pleasure. It had been demoralizing to be the last student promoted, especially since she'd always been considered an excellent rider.

"Can I help while I'm waiting?" she asked. "Are you

baling hay?" She glanced at the loose pile of alfalfa. She hoped he wasn't going to bale it all today, at least not until she had a few more bags for Jake and Rambo.

"No," Ramon said. "I'm just making some adjustments. This machine is new but cranky. If you want to help, you can bring the horses in for the night. I didn't know Scott would be riding so much. Now the grain schedule is screwed up." His voice thickened with disapproval.

He didn't look so happy now and she nodded, turned and walked out the end doors.

Leather halters hung by each paddock so she slipped on Braun's halter.

"Stealing horses now?" Scott's voice sounded behind her. "In addition to cutting class?"

She turned, surprised she hadn't heard his approach. He'd swapped his sports jacket for a black T-shirt and jeans but looked just as reserved, and there was a definite edge to his voice. His arms were folded over his chest, the edge of his shirt banding formidable biceps. He didn't look like anyone in need of recuperating, just a gorgeous hunk of man who was rightly annoyed. And unfortunately she couldn't offer much explanation.

"Ramon asked me to lead in the horses," she said cautiously.

Scott said nothing more. He just walked toward the second paddock and picked up a halter.

Braun shoved his nose against her arm, impatient with the delay. She pushed the gate open and led him from the paddock into the barn.

By the time she closed his stall door, Scott was walking down the aisle with the remaining horses clip clopping behind him. She wouldn't have tried leading three strange Thoroughbreds at the same time, but they seemed perfectly behaved. Maybe they'd noticed his powerful physique too.

He latched their stall doors. "Does Ramon want them grained?" he asked.

"I'm not sure. He's working on the baler."

Scott strode down the aisle and scanned the arena. He called Ramon's name but the arena was empty. He turned back to her, crossed those big arms again, and part of her wished Ramon had stuck around.

"I'm sorry about disturbing your class," she said softly. "And that I left early. My friend was upset."

He raised an eyebrow but didn't speak.

"And I'm sorry I missing my riding lesson," she said. "I know that was even worse but I was with her, and we both lost track of time and it was thoughtless but it really was important." Her voice quivered with thoughts of Joey. "Please. You have to know it was important."

"Okay," he said.

"I can't even say why..." She blinked in surprise. "What? It's okay?"

"Yes." He dropped his arms and walked closer, surprising her with a hard kiss. Seconds later, it softened, becoming tender. She'd been prepared for a grilling but now she was melting. He deepened the kiss, his tongue turning teasing, tantalizing with its exploration until every nerve in her body woke. She wrapped her arms around his neck and pressed closer.

He slipped his hand beneath her shirt, running it along her back, slow and assured and confident. She sighed when he lifted his head, a throaty sound of disappointment, but now his mouth trailed along her neck and that felt good too, his teeth and lips jolting her with sensations.

His hand drifted higher, moving just below her breast, fingers teasing as they stroked her skin, lingering when he found a sensitive spot until she wiggled and thrust up with impatience.

He obligingly palmed her breast then honed in with unerring certainty, squeezing her nipple beneath the bra, his mouth returning to hers, hungry now, hungry and possessive.

He lifted his head but kept her centered against his thick erection. "I want you," he said, his voice husky. "And it doesn't matter how many classes you skip, sweetheart. Come home with me."

"I have to feed my horses first." She gave a throaty sigh as his thumb brushed her nipple. "And I have to hide from Lydia."

"There's no need to sneak around." He dipped his head, his breath warm and insistent. "Just pack your bag and move in."

Move in? She shook her head but it was tough to

rationalize under the ministrations of that persuasive mouth, the erotic way his hand stroked her breast. She sucked in a quivery sigh, her mind and body turning pliable beneath his touch.

"I think Lydia would make my life miserable if I did that," she managed. "Don't you?"

His hand lowered an inch, settling over her ribs, and she almost groaned with disappointment.

"I'll look after you," he said. "Garrett's a good friend."

"But I still don't want people to see us together. Not even Garrett." A sense of unease filled her and she glanced over her shoulder, certain she heard the shuffle of feet. "I need to feed Jake and Rambo," she added. "And wash some clothes. Maybe I'll come over later."

"Later?"

"When it's dark," she said.

He lowered his arms and stepped back, leaving a coldness where his body had been. "The parts for my car arrived," he said, "so I won't be home when it's dark. I was hoping you'd drive into town with me and have dinner."

She hesitated far too long for such an astute man.

"Some other time then," he said. "I'll see you tomorrow. We'll do some gate work."

"Oh, I just found out." Her words came in a rush. "Ramon is letting me join his class tomorrow. He says I'm ready."

Scott nodded but his jaw looked like granite. "Congratulations," he said.

CHAPTER EIGHTEEN

"Why are you drinking rum with me," Garrett asked, "when you could be doing more pleasurable things with the school hottie?"

Scott pressed his mouth shut but Garrett only chuckled and propped his feet on the coffee table. "I had my eye on her, you know," he admitted. "But as usual, women prefer your scowling mug."

Scott frowned. The idea of Garrett with Megan was irritating. "Is that why your wife left?" he asked. "You were dipping into the student body?"

Garrett reached over and sloshed more rum into his glass. "I've always had a hard time resisting temptation," he said, totally unabashed. "But there were other factors too. I love my life here, Lord of the Manor, so to speak."

"Lords don't usually have their dog's legs bashed in."

"No." Garrett gave a negligible shrug. "And once in a while we run into a dangerous student like Joey Collins."

"Is he ganged up?"

Garrett nodded. "Working with a group out of L.A."

"Was?"

"Is," Garrett said. "So tell me where's the luscious Megan tonight? I need to thank her for helping out with Rex."

Scott reached for the remote. He pointed it at the huge TV then tossed it aside in frustration. Eleven o'clock. Megan would be in bed. She might have been in his bed if he hadn't been so pissed, but it rankled she thought he wouldn't protect her from Lydia.

And he also had the feeling she'd been scrambling for an excuse. He didn't expect women to fall all over him, but admittedly they were usually more eager. Something was holding her back.

He turned to Garrett. "Do you have some sort of rule that instructors can't date students?" he asked. "If so, I want it changed."

"All right." Garrett gave another of his irritating shrugs. "Tomorrow I'll announce that students are free to bang their instructors."

"Don't be an asshole," Scott said. "Or I'll quit."

"You've never quit anything in your life." Garrett twirled his glass, studying the melting ice. "But everything's been renewed so maybe you should go. This was all your battle-ax of a secretary's idea anyway. There's no real reason for you to stay."

Scott rubbed his temple, out of habit now. He didn't have a headache, just a nagging sense he was missing something.

"Belinda's my assistant, not a secretary," he said slowly. "And we have to find that punk who hurt your dog. That's the reason I can't go."

Garrett just laughed.

Megan flipped through Joey's magazine, staring despairingly at more ads of racing studs, rugged trucks and details about farm tractors. Just the usual stuff. Any hope Joey had jotted down a Mexican address or name in the margins had been dashed. If there was a clue to his whereabouts in these pages, she couldn't see it.

Tami sprawled on her bed, eating chocolate and commenting with animated detail about her new phone's functions. Megan closed the magazine, deciding it was more fun to listen to Tami than stare any longer at Joey's boring reading material.

"Hey, look," Tami said. "I googled our school and I can see everything." She groped for another piece of chocolate bar, not taking her eyes off the screen. "The track looks tiny from an aerial shot but when you're galloping and your legs turn to jelly, it feels like a marathon."

"Garrett sure has a big house," she added, almost in the same breath. "There's even a tennis court. And the villa next to him is really nice too."

Megan padded across the room and plunked down

beside Tami. Garrett's pool looked immense, a kidney-shape of blue. She recognized the front driveway where Rex had been brutalized and then Scott's villa with its own hot tub and pool.

"Who lives in those two smaller units on the other side?" Megan asked.

Tami pointed at the screen. "Ramon is in that one. Miguel is pissed because it doesn't have a pool." She snickered. "Lydia has the tiniest one, stuck way off in the trees. Serves her right for being such a bitch."

Megan leaned forward, craning to see. Judging from the size of the villas, Ramon had more status on campus than Lydia. So did Scott, although that was probably because of his friendship with Garrett.

"Can you google Scott?"

"I already did," Tami said. "I checked out the Taylor Investigative Agency too."

"Taylor Investigative Agency?" Megan asked. "That's the name of his company?"

"Yes. Remember when Garrett introduced him on the first day, and droned on about all his accomplishments."

"I missed that class," Megan said, her eyes glued to Tami's phone. Scott had mentioned working in L.A., but she hadn't asked details. Hadn't wanted to spark any return questions about why she'd left a thriving jewelry business to attend jockey school. But a private investigator? That was wonderful.

"What kind of cases does he take?" She strained to read the tiny writing. "Things like missing persons?"

Tami shrugged. "It says fraud, asset searches, child custody, protective services. Boring stuff. And there are no good pictures. Do you want to see the Baja Tinda's pool? The diving board is so high—"

"Wait, Tami. Please. May I see your phone for a sec?"

"It's cool, isn't it?" Tami passed it over with a satisfied smile. "Way better than my old one. I can't believe Miguel gave it to me."

Megan thumbed down the screen, engrossed in the material. There was plenty to read—Scott had been an L.A. cop with numerous citations, including a medal of valor, but had switched to private practice. Some rough stuff too. She followed a recent link, skimming quickly:

The frantic search for Robbie Stevens finally ended last night when authorities trapped his kidnappers in a remote section of Wheeler Ridge. Robbie had been celebrating his third birthday and was on his way to Disneyland when he was abducted from his parents' limo. The family engaged private investigative services after rumored dissatisfaction with the FBI.

Reports of last night's daring raid are still scanty. However, it is believed there were several fatalities, and one of the rescuers is in serious condition. John and Mary Stevens appeared briefly on camera to thank the public for their support, but both were visibly shaken in the wake of the shootout. "Scott Taylor is our son's guardian angel," Mary Stevens said. "He pushed Robbie to the ground, shielding him from the gunfire. I pray Mr. Taylor recovers."

Megan's breath caught. She remembered the newscasts, the heroic agent who had taken a bullet to save a child's life. Not an FBI agent, but Scott. Thank God he'd been able to bring that little boy safely home. She brushed away a tear, fighting the lump that clogged her throat.

Tami tugged the phone back and resumed her scrolling, oblivious to Megan's distress. "Let's look at the Baja Tinda now," she said. "Their diving board is amazing."

Megan swallowed, gathering her emotions. Now she understood why she'd been instantly attracted to Scott. Why he was the school's golden boy. He was a good man. He found people, and rescued them.

She pressed her hands over her chest, buoyed with hope. Tomorrow she'd tell Scott the truth about her presence at the school. About her, about Joey. And then she'd hire him.

CHAPTER NINETEEN

Megan followed Tami into the classroom, smiling when she saw Eve already seated in the front row. "You're early too," Megan said, grabbing the adjacent seat.

Eve grimaced. "Ramon was wild about me missing his riding lesson yesterday. He'd flip if he discovered I also missed the addictions class." She shot a wary look at Tami who seemed engrossed with texting. Her voice lowered. "Did you get in much trouble?"

"A little," Megan said. "But it'll be okay." At least she hoped so. Scott hadn't been happy yesterday. Her gaze drifted to the side door, willing him to appear. This morning she intended to act like a model student, take copious notes and nod respectfully at everything he said.

And after the lecture, she'd explain the real reason why she didn't want to draw attention to their relationship, and then hire him to find her brother. Scott's elite agency probably charged hefty fees, but he was obviously the best. And she wanted him.

In more ways than one.

She blocked that thought, determined to focus on Scott, the professional. "I have an idea about finding Joey," she whispered to Eve.

"Make Ramon and Lydia take a lie detector test." Eve sounded absolutely serious.

Tami put away her phone and shot them a worried look. "I don't want you two sitting beside me," she said, "if you're going to talk again. Addictions is my favorite class."

"We'll be quiet as soon as he walks in," Megan said. "Promise."

"Which means right now." Tami elbowed her in the ribs as the door clicked open. Scott strode to the front of the room. Megan gave him a welcoming smile, but his businesslike gaze covered every student.

"Good morning," he said, without a trace of a smile.

Wow, he looked surly. He didn't have his usual jacket on either, just worn Levis and a faded shirt that picked up the gray in his eyes. He didn't need clothes to project his power though. The room was so quiet she could hear Peter breathing two rows back.

Every female watched intently as Scott turned and walked to the whiteboard. Were they really listening or just admiring his body, the way the denim tightened around his butt? When he pivoted, Tami's head jerked up and Megan realized at least one other person had been checking him out.

Not me though. She kept her gaze focused on Scott's face, trying to be the picture of an attentive student. He hadn't shaved this morning and the dark stubble was rather intimidating. Rough...but kind of sexy. She pressed a finger to her lips, imagining the feel.

The sound of pens on paper yanked back her attention. Oh no, everyone was writing while she hadn't absorbed a word.

She ducked her head and scribbled her name. Couldn't think of anything else to write so jotted it again. At least she was writing. She doubted Scott would be able to read upside down. On the other hand, he was multi-talented.

She wiggled in the chair. It had been a mistake to sit this close. She felt like a groupie and it was impossible to concentrate, not with him scant feet away. He looked like a cop today, an undercover cop with a sexy voice and a sexier body. Her cheeks turned hot. She shifted again, trying to focus on his words.

"Some states have mandatory breathalyzers," he was saying. "Not only jockeys can be tested but also grooms who lead a horse to the paddock. And exercise riders. You may be asked to provide urine. Be prepared for random screening and hair follicle testing." His gaze seemed to settle on her and she pressed back, her shoulder blades digging into the chair.

Why was he staring? She hadn't used drugs in years. Not even a joint.

"For most," he went on, "it will be a constant battle to maintain riding weight. Learn your triggers so you can deal with them. Substance abuse can start with a simple weight loss drug and continue because of emotional dependency."

She put down her pen, her face stiff. None of this stuff applied to her. She'd never had much trouble with her weight, and emotional dependency was an overused expression. They'd used that phrase in every stage of her ten-step counseling. She was sick of it. Her dad leaving hadn't been that big a deal. It hadn't affected her much. Her mom was good, she was good, Joey...

Joey wasn't so good.

She realized she'd stopped breathing and sucked in a ragged gulp of air. But persistent voices kept whispering that her brother was dead. She sensed it in every fiber of her being, the way an iron weight cramped her chest, and how she always thought of him in the past tense. Even his girlfriend, Eve, had lost hope.

Her eyes itched and she glanced at the exit. The air was stifling now, almost impossible to breathe. And all these people were around. She didn't want them to see her cry. She had to get out. Now. But it was twenty endless feet to the door.

And she couldn't walk out on Scott. Not a second time. Her fists clenched and she blinked frantically, afraid if she looked at Eve her grief would erupt. Scott's gaze caught hers. She jerked her head away, feigning a cough, and swiping at her eyes.

"We'll stop a few minutes early today," he said.

She rose so fast, her pen and paper dropped to the floor. She bent down, but her eyes were too blurry to find the pen.

"Here it is," Eve said, reaching under Megan's chair. "Want to grab a coffee before our riding lesson? That was a crazy short lecture so we have time."

Megan turned her head, still blinking. She really wanted to be alone. Curl up in a private spot and grieve. However, Eve sounded so sad and was obviously hurting too.

"Sure." Megan kept her head bent as she pretended to reorganize her notes. "Want to come with us, Tami?"

"No, thanks," Tami said, already scooting toward the door. "I just texted Miguel. We're meeting at the jock barn.

See you later."

Megan glanced toward Scott but he was already surrounded by a group of fawning students, all females. Besides, she had to escape. She turned and hurried toward the fresh air, conscious of Eve at her heels.

Outside, the glaring sun stung and she paused to rub her eyes again.

"Are you okay?" Eve whispered.

"Yes," Megan said. "It's just that the sun's so bright."

Eve slipped her hand around Megan's wrist and gave a quick squeeze. "It's hard not to think of him," she said. "It hits me out of the blue too." Her quiet empathy made Megan's eyes prick again.

"He wasn't doing drugs," Eve added, her voice low. "You have to believe that and never doubt it. He had a single room so I was with him almost every minute. He was riding great too. Top of the class. We were on the list to ride at Santa Anita...and then Ramon took him to Mexico.

"I wish he hadn't gone." Eve's voice cracked. "The trailer left so fast he didn't take his helmet. I never even said good bye."

This time it was Megan who squeezed Eve's hand. Usually Megan liked to deal with her pain in private—she hadn't had many close friends since her teenage brush with the courts—but it helped to share this crushing sorrow. And soon they'd have Scott's help.

She shot a cautious glance over Eve's shoulder. Peter sauntered toward the barns, walking alongside a petite brunette, but he was well out of earshot.

"I'm going to hire Scott," Megan said, dipping her head closer to Eve. "Maybe he can find out what really happened."

"Is that wise?" Eve asked. "You realize he's a good friend of Garrett's?"

"Yes. But he's not a good friend of Lydia's. Or Ramon."

"But they all work here. And Garrett owns the school. Scott's allegiance will be to him."

"I know." Megan tugged at her lip. "I keep playing that out in my head. But I'm kind of seeing Scott and it would be nice to explain why I want to be discreet. He doesn't understand—"

"Understand? You mean it would be easier for your relationship?"

Megan nodded, remembering Scott's shuttered expression in the cowshed yesterday. "A lot easier," she said.

"Sounds like you're worrying about yourself, not Joey." Eve turned and yanked at the cafeteria door. "I saw you riding with Scott yesterday. You looked happy. Not exactly the picture of a grieving sister. And what's your mother doing to help? Both of you seem to believe this drug bullshit. And what about some redemption for Joey? It's like you're okay with having his name smeared."

Megan charged forward, flattening her palm against the door. "Listen," she said. "I left my business to come here so lay off. I'm sorry you lost a boyfriend you dated for seven whole weeks, but my mother lost her son. So don't you say another word about her. And Joey did have a drug history."

"Sorry," Eve muttered. But her voice was flat and she didn't sound very apologetic. "But the drug accusations are crazy. Surely you don't believe them?"

"The police and school were very convincing." Megan dropped her hand from the door. Of course, she didn't swallow the official line, but Eve's statement about her feelings for Scott rankled. Because there was a bite of truth. She was getting too close, falling too fast. Maybe not thinking clearly. She hadn't come here to indulge in a superficial affair.

"I'm sorry for what I said." Eve gave a tight smile. "But I don't trust the staff one bit. It could be Lydia who really has the drug problem. Her moods change every hour."

"Maybe we should sneak over there," Megan said. "Check out her villa."

"Good idea," Eve said, and this time her smile was genuine. "And we should check out Ramon's place too. Or you could do it, while he teaches my riding class."

"But I'm in his class too. Starting today."

Megan stepped back, pulled open the door and followed Eve to the coffee dispenser.

"That's great you finally graduated from the field riders," Eve said. "Bad timing though. I'm not sure about

Ramon's schedule other than he teaches in the morning. At least it's quiet here," she added, glancing around the room. "Safe to talk."

Except for a few students straggling in from Scott's class, the cafeteria was deserted. They poured their coffee and chose a table in a secluded corner.

"I know Ramon goes to the cowshed at suppertime." Megan pulled her chair closer to Eve, keeping her voice low. "Looks like he's going to start baling too, so he might be busy with that."

"Joey helped modify the baler the last week he was here," Eve said. "Are they adjusting it again? That could take hours, give us more time."

Megan nodded and fiddled with her coffee cup, but the idea of sneaking into Ramon's villa without knowing his routine made her stomach lurch. And Miguel also slept there so that meant two schedules needed to be checked. It was clear Eve was brave and loyal but also rather impulsive.

"Maybe we should do Lydia's villa first," Megan said. "She always eats in the cafeteria, so we'd have at least an hour. She's not as scary as Ramon."

"You really will do this? Sneak in?" Eve leaned forward, clearly eager. "But what if she locks her door?"

Megan took a thoughtful sip of coffee. No one locked their doors in residence. However, Scott always locked his villa. Maybe that was because he kept work papers inside or perhaps it was just PI habit.

"If Lydia locks her villa, then we don't get in," Megan said. "And we'll give it up. Do you want any milk?"

Eve had barely touched her coffee. In fact, her face looked oddly white against her dark hair. It *was* scary thinking of sneaking into someone's house. If caught, they'd both be kicked out. Worse, Eve's career as a jockey would be finished.

"Look, don't worry," Megan added. "You don't have to go inside. You don't even have to come—"

Eve's nostrils flared. She pressed a hand over her mouth and bolted to the bathroom, almost toppling the chair in her haste.

She was really scared. Little wonder. Eve had so much more to lose if she were caught. Megan straightened the chair, then walked to the bathroom door and pushed it open. Eve's worn boots peeked out from below the stall door.

"I have a better idea," Megan said. "You can just wait down the road. Call me if anyone comes. It's safer to have a lookout."

The toilet flushed and Eve stepped out. "Whatever works," she said, running the tap and rinsing her mouth. "I'm good with anything. I'm just glad you're here."

Megan blinked. Clearly she'd jumped to the wrong conclusion. Eve wasn't scared at all. In fact, the color in her cheeks had completely returned—it hadn't been fear that sent her racing to the bathroom. Joey had spoken about fellow students who were desperate to keep their weight down. And that bulimia was common.

She blew out an empathetic sigh, tore off a piece of paper towel, and handed it to Eve. "Maybe you should rethink this profession if it means flipping food."

Eve wiped her mouth, wadded the paper in a ball and fired it into the garbage can.

"Unfortunately," she said, her voice clipped, "it's much too late to rethink anything."

CHAPTER TWENTY

Megan gaped at the whiteboard, her heart pounding in a mixture of nervousness and delight. *Megan & Jake.* Finally her name was posted with the other exercise riders. And Ramon had assigned her a wonderful horse.

"Glad you're here, slowpoke," a grinning Peter said. "They can laugh at you today, instead of me. All the exercise riders are flunking gate training. The jocks think we're hilarious. Ramon doesn't think it's quite so funny."

"Is he a good teacher?" she asked, tightening her safety vest another notch.

"I haven't decided if he's a genius or a prick." Peter's smile faded. "But sometimes when I'm spitting dirt, I'd prefer to be back in the field with Lydia. Come on. Get your horse ready. He gets mad if we're late."

Megan saddled and bridled Jake then led him into the aisle where Ramon was already boosting up riders.

"At the track," he said, looking at Megan, "we mount inside. And no showboating and leaping on without help. You can hurt a horse's back that way."

She nodded, keeping her face impassive but enjoying a rush of confidence. Thank you, Scott, she thought gratefully. Already he'd taught her so much.

"We're doing gate work today," Ramon added, his eyes narrowing on Jake. "And that horse breaks like a rocket. You'll need to hang on."

She nodded, her confidence deflating. Scott had also warned Jake would break hard, and she'd never ridden from a starting gate before. There wouldn't be a practice walk-through either. Perhaps she should have stayed with Scott another day.

But there was no time to worry. Ramon legged her into the saddle and Jake charged from the barn, head high and keen to get to work. The horse's confidence was infectious. Besides, this was different, almost liberating. There was no Lydia around, scowling and sniping at her every step. Ramon seemed the type to issue instructions and then let riders sink or swim.

The eager horses pranced toward the track, the experienced jock students in front, led by Miguel. Megan fell into line, relishing the positive energy.

Tami edged up beside her on a narrow-chested bay with a leather breast collar. "You'll finally be able to see Miguel ride," she said, gesturing toward the front of the line. "He's awesome. Sometimes Ramon lets the jocks work from the gate and they blister around the track. It's like a real race."

She paused for a moment, eyeing Megan's horse with concern. "I'm surprised you're on such an experienced racehorse. It would be safer if Ramon switched you to another one. Miguel rode Jake last week and that horse can really motor."

Megan nodded. "Scott already warned me that Jake would come out fast." She checked the trail from the cowshed, but no horse and rider appeared on the ridge. She straightened in the saddle, fighting her stab of disappointment. Of course, Scott wouldn't ride over to watch but she sure would have appreciated his presence. "I guess Ramon knows how to assign horses," she added, trying to reassure Tami. And herself.

"I don't know," Tami said, her brow still furrowed. "Miguel said the school is short of horses since two pulled up lame last week. And Ramon needs four racehorses to send to the Baja Tinda. But they only have three."

"Didn't they just send some last month?" Megan asked. "How many do they give them?"

"Not sure. I only know the school is short of horses." Tami straightened in the saddle, her attention shifting. "Look at that girl flirting with Miguel. She's such a skank."

Megan studied the line of riders. The exercise riders were familiar but other than Eve and Miguel, she only knew the jock students by sight. Everyone looked different beneath helmets too, especially from the rear. However, if anyone was flirting, it was probably Miguel.

"They're just talking," Megan said. "I doubt he gave her a new phone."

"Guess you're right," Tami said. "Besides, Miguel has to be nice. He owes me."

"Why does he owe you?"

"What I meant is that he wants to get in my pants so he has to be nice." Tami fiddled with her helmet, oddly subdued. "I want a new boyfriend," she added, "but I'll be the first to admit you can't trust them."

"You can't trust anyone," Megan said. "Only yourself." Friends vanished at the first hint of trouble. And dates and sex were fine, but why would anyone want to invite heartache with a steady boyfriend?

Tami still stared at Miguel, silent and strangely pensive. Megan shifted in the saddle, hating to see her roommate so troubled, especially over a sketchy guy like Miguel. It was a relief when they reached the gap and Ramon began barking instructions. Even Tami had to stop moping and pay attention.

"Okay, everyone," Ramon said, his critical eyes sweeping over each horse and rider. "I want you to warm up by trotting in pairs on the outside rail. Jocks pair up with the green riders. Watch for any runaways. Miguel, you go first."

Tami pushed her horse to the front of the line, grabbing the chance to ride with Miguel. Jake pawed, eager to follow. Megan turned him in a circle as riders called out names. Pairs formed and stepped onto the track. But no one looked her way.

She sat taller, trying to pretend it didn't matter. No big deal. She was used to being alone. Understandably, no one wanted to be stuck with the new rider. Even Peter had chosen the red-haired girl who always slumped in the saddle. At least, he made eye contact, shooting her a sheepish look before turning away.

"Hey, let's go, partner."

Megan blinked, then grinned as Eve called to her from the back of a dark bay. Jake shot forward, seemingly as relieved as Megan to finally have a partner. The two horses trotted in tandem onto the track.

"Loosen the reins, Peter," Ramon called. "You're cranked up way too tight. Eyes up, Tami."

Ramon shot out a string of rapid-fire comments but didn't mention Megan's name, and her tension eased as they passed by his eagle eye. They followed the three pairs of riders already cleared to trot along the rail. Eve's bay was a big striding gelding who matched Jake perfectly.

"Thanks for buddying up with me," Megan said, giving Eve a grateful smile. "I felt like I was back in school and stuck on the sidelines."

Eve tilted her head. "Did you go to juvie too?"

"No. But word got out that I was a bad influence. I lost a lot of friends." Megan shrugged. It hadn't mattered. Small towns were tough but she'd learned to like her own company. "You look ready for a real track," she added.

"I'm talking to some trainers at Santa Anita," Eve said. "But I need a reference from Ramon and Garrett, and so far they've refused to give me one."

It was hard to imagine Eve having trouble earning a reference. She looked like a natural extension of her horse, with ability far beyond that of the other students. Megan adjusted her legs, trying to mirror Eve. Scott had given valuable tips, but it was easier to follow his instructions when there was a jockey to copy. She felt comfortable too, and Jake trotted out beautifully, not fighting her hold.

"Your horse will be tougher when we go the other way," Eve warned, as they slowed to a walk and turned around. "All the experienced racehorses wake up when they run to the left, especially if they get close to the inner rail."

Megan nodded, remembering how Scott had kept Jake to the outside. He really had been looking out for her—and he was the only reason she'd escaped Lydia's clutches. She checked the ridge again. But nothing moved except a solitary tumbleweed.

"Jake only left the track six months ago," Eve added, pulling back Megan's attention. "Everyone likes him because he's so honest. But you need to be alert in the gate. He tends to think it's a real race."

"Everyone warns to be careful in the gate," Megan said. "But how exactly do you do that?"

Eve gave a mischievous grin. "Not much you can do. Just grab mane and pray. It's like jumping, when your horse stops then gives that crazy leap and your heart jams in your throat. It's a real adrenaline rush."

Megan gulped. She'd never jumped anything but logs and streams. But she knew the heart-in-her-throat feeling extremely well, and it usually came with pain, right before she hit the dirt.

"If we gallop well," Eve went on, "Ramon might let us run from the gate to the finish line. But I can find a more experienced partner to race."

Race? Megan gave another gulp. Of course, she didn't expect Jake to break from the gate and then immediately slow to a sedate canter. After all, he'd been bred and trained to run. But now that she'd made it into Ramon's jockey class, she wondered if she belonged. Already her hands were hot and sweaty, her stomach flipping with fear. It had been years since she'd chased after cattle, and this would be an entirely different dimension of fast.

But she pulled in deep breaths, determined to steady her nerves. She'd always loved speed, and thanks to Scott, at least she could balance in an exercise saddle. She scratched Jake's neck, silently promising more alfalfa if he just kept her safe. And on his back. Maybe it was sucking up, but it never hurt if a horse liked its rider.

"You're a lot like Joey," Eve said. "He was always communicating with his horse. In fact, when you're in the saddle, you remind me of him. Why is your last name different?"

"After my father split, I took Mom's maiden name," Megan said. "Joey was six years younger...and more forgiving."

"He never talked much about his dad."

"Not much to say." Megan squeezed the reins a little tighter. Her father wasn't much of a man. He'd hugged her goodbye, claiming he'd met another woman, one he couldn't live without. But she knew the truth—he hadn't wanted the hassle of teenagers and police and problems. The last she heard he was living in New Zealand. She'd made many tearful phone calls in the middle of the night, promising to behave. Had sent countless texts pleading for him to come home. He never replied. And now she no longer cared.

"It wasn't a big deal," she added. "Mom missed him and money was tight. But Joey and I barely noticed he was gone."

"But I thought his leaving caused all your problems? Oh, never mind." Eve paused, her expressive eyes dark with empathy.

"Scott said I should make the knot higher," Megan said, pointing at her reins. "What do you think?"

"Yes, that'll help. Better shorten them now. It's our turn to gallop next. Ramon will signal and then we pick it up at the quarter pole. If we look good, we go to the gate."

The pair in front of them broke away and Megan quickly knotted her reins several inches higher, trying not to stress about the next few minutes. Already Jake pushed at the bit, aware of what was coming next. She wished she could share his excitement, but her hands felt sticky against the rubber-backed reins.

"Great. Our turn now," Eve said, clearly not sharing her apprehension.

They moved off together. Jake gave a happy buck and then he was galloping. Megan clamped her mouth shut, automatically balancing in the stirrups. Eve stayed on the inner rail, Jake to the outside.

Wind stung Megan's eyes, and she had no idea where the quarter pole was. There were a bunch of black and white poles, but the other riders had started at the red and white post in the backstretch. Jake rammed at the bit, trying to stretch out but she kept a tight hold and simply maintained Eve's speed. It was actually kind of fun.

They rounded the turn and shot down the backstretch, and Megan couldn't stop her whoop of delight. This was definitely exhilarating, far better than any carnival ride.

Jake loved it too and she wasn't sure she'd be able to stop him. But Eve veered out, floating Jake to the middle of the track. The horse flattened his ears in protest but soon tucked his head and slowed.

"You did great," Eve called, her voice splintering as they slowed to a bouncy trot. "Jake ran off with Miguel just last week."

"But you helped slow him." Megan's words came out ragged but happy. "If he'd been on the rail, I would have been cooked."

"Nah, you're a natural, just like your brother. Look at Miguel's face." Eve gave a triumphant smile. "He never likes to be upstaged. And you're fresh from field riding. He'll hate that."

Miguel twisted in the saddle, sneering at Eve as they

trotted past. "You gallop like an old woman," he said. "Can't even beat an exercise rider. My dad has a donkey that can run faster."

"That explains why you can't ride Thoroughbreds," Eve called. "Better go home and ride Daddy's little donkeys."

Miguel's face darkened. "*Puta*."

Eve flipped him the bird, then turned to Megan, still grinning. "He hates to have his riding ability questioned. Joey told me that's the easiest way to get under his skin. I don't know what everyone sees in that jerk. Even Ramon thinks he walks on water."

Not Scott though, Megan thought. He was tough and shrewd and certainly had been quick to question Tami about Miguel's whereabouts. Like Eve, he hadn't seemed to like Miguel one bit. And now Miguel was glowering at them both.

"What did we do to set him off?" Megan whispered, surprised by Miguel's open hostility.

"He's just a spoiled prick," Eve said. "Acts like he owns the school and is jealous when any rider upstages him. That's why he hated Joey."

"Hated?"

"Yes," Eve said. "So I love rattling him. For Joey's sake."

Megan studied Eve's face, the fiery glint in her eyes. It was clear the girl was a fighter. She would have been good for Joey. And while Megan knew she should make nice to Miguel, it was suddenly more important to support Eve. "Then let's blast out of the gate today," Megan said, squaring her shoulders. "And really piss him off."

"Really? Are you ready to race?" Eve's gaze shot back to Miguel. "He thinks he's number one student now that Joey's gone. I'd love to fire it up, but I don't want you to get hurt."

"I'll be fine," Megan said, shoving away her fear.

They approached the gate, then circled, awaiting their turn.

An assistant led an ashen-faced exercise rider through the open doors. The horse looked half-asleep but even so, the rider leaned forward, gripping the reins in a stranglehold.

"Stop him there," Ramon said to his assistant. "Let

them both stand."

Megan kept Jake twenty feet behind the gate, simply watching the action. This was the closest she'd ever been to a starting gate. This one only had four slots and the openings were very narrow, barely wide enough for a horse. No wonder some animals feared the gate.

Some riders feared it too.

"That guy, Skip," Eve whispered, "slammed his knee against the steel frame last week. He's only been walking through with both doors open. But it hasn't helped his confidence. He's not a great rider. I think Ramon wants him to quit before he hurts himself—or someone else."

Jake stopped fidgeting. His ears pricked as though curious about the solitary horse standing in the open gate. Megan glanced from the rider to Ramon, seizing this opportunity to study the instructor's face. Usually Ramon was contained, but today he seemed frustrated, his lips thinned in a tight line.

He climbed into the slot beside the horse and rider, and deliberately rattled the bars. The horse didn't move. But the rider flinched. "You have to get used to this," Ramon snapped. "That's how they start races in this country."

"I'm fine," Skip mumbled. "I'm relaxed."

Ramon jumped to the ground. "Really? You're relaxed? Enough to ride from the gate today?"

"Yes, sir," Skip said.

Ramon pulled a whip from the loop of his back pocket and abruptly cracked the horse on the rump. The gray leaped forward, then settled in a ragged canter, more irritated than afraid. Skip bounced on his neck, then clumsily regained his balance as the horse slowed to a trot.

Ramon turned to the circle of watching riders. "You see? Never relax in the gate. The doors can open at any time. Now that horse," he thumbed over his shoulder in disdain, "can barely trot. That's not the case with animals fresh off the track." His eyes narrowed on Megan. "You're looking good out there. Are you okay busting Jake from the gate or do you want a horse with less engine?"

"I'm okay," Megan said. Some of the track terminology was confusing, but she didn't want to be on a deadhead like the gray and have Ramon swat him on the rump. She'd rather take her chances on Jake. Besides, she wanted to prove something to Miguel. It was like she was riding for Joey.

"All right," Ramon said. "You can bust out with Eve." He gestured to his assistant. "Close the front doors."

The assistant pressed the control button and the front doors clanged shut. Jake flinched then sidled sideways, quivering with eagerness. She turned him in a circle, trying to keep him calm, then noticed Eve was lowering her goggles.

Heck, she didn't even have goggles. Had never been assigned any.

Ramon opened the back doors to gate two and four as Megan fought her panic.

"Eve in two," Ramon said. "The new girl in four." He looked at the assistant. "Stay in there with Jake."

Ramon doesn't even remember my name. Then the assistant grabbed Jake's bridle, led him into the slot, and the door banged behind her. Jake jerked forward, but could barely move. It was like being in jail. Except that in a few seconds the door was going to slam open and her horse would charge out.

"Grab the mane. Look up," the assistant said, keeping Jake's head pointed in the vee of the gate. She was tempted to look sideways at Eve but kept her head straight. It didn't sound like anyone else was beside her. Not yet. At least she hadn't heard a second gate slam.

Jake was poised, every muscle tense, but the assistant remained relaxed and talkative. "No goggles?" He laughed, but not unkindly. "You better hope you're in front," he said.

A second door slammed and the entire structure rattled, the noise loud in the still morning.

"Look up," Ramon called. "Don't jerk your horse in the mouth. He'll do his job. You just do yours."

Megan stared straight ahead, peering through the grill at the expanse of dirt, her heart pounding, not entirely sure what her job was except to go fast.

Clang.

The gate whipped open. Jake shot forward.

For a moment, she quit breathing and simply tried to stay on his back. It was a good thing she'd grabbed mane. She felt awkward, like a passenger, not a rider. But Ramon had said not to yank Jake in the mouth, and she was determined not to interfere. After the horse's first burst of speed, he moved fluidly, carrying her with him in a natural rhythm. It wasn't so hard, not after Scott's instruction.

And she was in front. No dirt smashed her in the face. Only the wind stung, blinding her eyes with tears. But she chirped at Jake, asking for more speed, and encouraging him to run down the long stretch.

A tall pole whipped by in a blur of white. Someone hollered to pull up, and she rose in the stirrups, grabbing mane again, just in case. Jake seemed to know where the finish line was and obligingly slowed as Eve and her bay inched alongside.

"You sandbagger!" Eve called as they slowed to a canter. "You ride like Joey!"

"What do you mean?" Megan asked, her breath escaping in gasps.

"Just that I was riding to win, and you still beat me."

"It was all Jake," Megan said. "I was only the passenger."

"Well you stayed out of his way." Eve tugged her dirt-smeared goggles off her face, dropping them around her neck. "I even had a stick. Miguel is definitely going to whine today." She gave Megan a jubilant grin.

Both horses were cantering now and they pulled over to the far rail and slowed to a trot.

"What do we do now?" Megan asked, still breathing hard but unable to stop smiling. This was way more exciting than designing jewelry, and Jake deserved a big armful of alfalfa. He'd been an absolute pro.

"We go back to the gate. Listen to Ramon's criticisms. Cool out our horses while we wait around for the other riders. We'll be here at least another forty-five minutes."

Two horses shot past as they walked along the outer rail. Miguel was crouched over his horse's neck, flailing with his whip while the second rider trailed four lengths back. Both riders wore goggles.

"Were we going that fast?" Megan asked, staring in awe.

"Probably faster. Miguel is a bully. Always using his whip. I don't understand why Ramon and Garrett let him come back." She rolled her eyes. "Look, he dropped his whip. Serves him right. He'll have to walk back and find it."

Or maybe he has so many whips, he doesn't care, Megan thought. Judging from Tami's pictures of the Baja Tinda, Miguel's family was grossly rich.

They were only fifty feet from the gate now and Eve's voice lowered. "Lydia is usually in the cafeteria between five and six. Are we still going to check out her villa?"

"Yes, but you're staying outside. Joey wouldn't want you kicked out."

"I'm not afraid to go in," Eve said staunchly.

"No. It doesn't matter so much if I'm kicked out. But riding is your career."

Eve shook her head but quit protesting when she saw Megan's face. "Okay, I'll stay outside. But only if you do me a favor. You and Tami are the girls who sell the chocolate bars, right? Do you have a vehicle? I need to go to town and pick up some things."

"Sure," Megan said. "I can drive you tonight. Maybe we can even buy a hamburger for supper?"

"That would be great." Eve's smile lit up her face. "I've been craving fast food all week."

They were still grinning, discussing their favorite burger joints and the carb/calorie content, when they reached the starting gate.

Ramon gave a rare smile. "Both you riders did well. Eve, you need to hustle your horse out of the gate a little faster. Jake's rider, don't throw away your reins. It was a few jumps before you had any control. Fortunately your horse stayed straight." He nodded. "But it was very impressive. Don't bother to wait around. Cool out your horses. You two can take the rest of the morning off."

Eve reached out and gave Megan a delighted fist bump. Tami and Peter called out congratulations. But Miguel slouched in the saddle, a scowl darkening his face.

"Hey," Ramon called to Megan. "You need to start carrying a whip. I want to see it in your hand. You need goggles too."

Megan nodded and gave Jake a grateful pat. Peter and Tami didn't have goggles yet or carry a whip. Despite her slow start at the school, she'd already passed them. Of course, it was mainly because of Scott, and she needed to thank him. She also wanted to hire his investigative services. But obviously he wasn't riding Braun this morning, at least not anywhere near the track. The ridge was deserted.

"I wish we were allowed to ride over the hill," Eve said, following Megan's gaze. "There's a lot of land here. But Joey was never impressed with how the hay crop was managed."

"Yes, there's still some loose alfalfa in the arena," Megan said as they walked toward the barn. "It's not even baled. That's where I found his iPod."

Eve fiddled with her horse's mane, flipping it to one side and back again. Then she looked at Megan and sighed. "I'm sorry about that iPod. I was way too impulsive. If I'd known who you were, I never would have said anything to Lydia."

Megan gave a forgiving smile. "But that's what started us talking, so it's all good. And I'll get his iPod back. It's being mailed to Mom. See you at five? When Lydia goes for supper?"

"Five sharp," Eve said, nodding and turning her horse on the path to the jock barn.

Jake lowered his head and blew out a sigh, not seeming to care that he was now alone. Megan loosened her reins, sharing his relaxed mood. It was reassuring to be able to confide in someone, to know that Eve would be watching her back tonight. But it was going to be even better to have Scott.

She'd hire him today. Granted, he was good friends with Garrett but if he accepted the job, he'd be working for her. Not the school. He'd know how to find a missing person. And with both Scott and Eve on her side, the mystery surrounding Joey's disappearance might finally be solved.

CHAPTER TWENTY-ONE

Scott checked his watch and edged toward Garrett's front door. "Okay. If Joey Collins is on the property, I'll find him."

"Ramon will look after the cowshed," Garrett said, following Scott down the hall. "It's the dorms that need protecting, although the punk probably bolted by now. I can't imagine why he hates me so much that he'd hurt my dog. All we ever did was teach him to ride."

"He's an addict," Scott said. "He's not thinking straight." There was no accounting for a druggie's thought process. And it was impossible to help someone who didn't want help. *Like beating your head against a brick wall but twice the pain.*

"Twice the pain?" Garrett raised an eyebrow, and Scott realized he'd spoken aloud. "Is that the reason you left the police and went private? Because you didn't want to deal with drug users?"

Scott shrugged. Not exactly. But he preferred to believe his work made a difference, not wasted arresting addicts whose hopeless eyes only reminded him of Amanda. "I have to go," he said. "It's Megan's first day with Ramon. I want to see how she's doing. And I need to stop by the cowshed and bag some alfalfa. If she does as well as I expect, she'll want something special for her horse."

"You're taking alfalfa from the cowshed?" Garrett asked.

"Just from the loose pile in the arena, stuff no one bothered to bale. It's good hay going to waste."

Garrett dragged a hand over his jaw. His eyes looked tired, not surprising since the two of them had spent much of the night drinking rum, talking football and arguing about the ten all-time best quarterbacks.

"If students want treats for their horses," Garrett said, "I'll have a truck dump off a load of carrots. We're switching Braun over to the school barn too. It'll be more convenient for you, not having to ride over the ridge. It'll also free up a stall for the Baja Tinda horses."

"Do you have four to send? I thought you wanted to wait until next month?"

"Well, they're very insistent." Garrett gave a strained smile. "I just need to find a fourth Thoroughbred."

Scott shrugged, his mind already on Megan. In class this morning, her beautiful face had looked almost tragic, and it had been tough to hide his concern. The tiny girl to her right had been twitchy too. Weird. Those same two girls had bolted from his class yesterday.

"I have to go," he said, pushing open the door. "And Braun is fine at the cowshed."

"No. We'll move him. It'll be easier for you to watch for Joey...and I'm sure Megan will be happy too." Garrett gave a teasing smile.

Scott closed the door behind him and walked to his car. Garrett might think he was doing Scott a favor but Megan might not be so happy about the barn switch. In fact, she was damn confusing. Half the time she was hot as hell, seemingly as eager as he was to pursue their attraction. Unfortunately the other half, she seemed ambivalent, like he was the driving force in the relationship. He never knew what she was thinking, and usually his woman radar was bang on.

He did know she'd be happy to have more alfalfa. At least he could please her with the hay.

He pulled into the cowshed parking lot, filled a feedbag with alfalfa and tossed it into his trunk. The interior was already littered with green stalks, and the company car was beginning to look like a hay wagon. Belinda would be mortified.

He pressed Belinda's number as he drove. She answered on the first ring.

"Welcome back, Belinda," he said. "How was your trip?"

"Wonderful. Thanks for the hotel upgrade. But I was glad to get back to the office. A lot has been going on." Her voice rose with satisfaction. "Did Snake tell you about the

Tupper case, that the insurance company finally agreed to pay?"

"Yes. He mentioned something this morning. That's good, great in fact."

He eased his car to a stop in front of the student barn and adjusted his sunglasses. Lydia's hapless students ambled circles in the field, and it appeared Ramon's group was still working with the starting gate. The parking lot held a couple vehicles, including Megan's Ford truck, but the barn itself seemed deserted.

"Scott?" Belinda hesitated a moment. "Is your head all right? I made a list of doctors within an hour radius. I can make an appointment."

Something flashed behind the barn and he leaned forward, alerted by the unexpected movement. He'd love to catch that Joey prick. Give the asshole a special hello from Rex.

But a horse's head appeared—Jake, recently bathed and looking relaxed and happy. Megan walked beside the horse. Her ponytail was slightly lopsided. Her helmet had left an imprint on her hair and dirt smudged her right cheek. She looked beautiful.

She spotted him, gave a brilliant smile, and something kicked deep in his chest. "I'm okay, Belinda," he said, reaching for the door handle. "Wonderful, in fact. I'll call you next week."

"Wait," she said. "This isn't like you. When you're away, you always want to know everything."

"Belinda," he said. "I've never been away from the office before."

She turned silent and he stepped from the car, still smiling at Megan.

"I suppose not." Belinda's voice lifted with concern. "But you're not acting at all like Snake and I expected."

"Everything's great," he said. "I haven't had a headache in days and I'm enjoying the time off. It was a great idea. Thank you, sweetie." He cut the connection and walked toward Megan.

"How was your first day riding with the jockeys?" He grinned. "Fall off much?"

"Not once," she said, stopping Jake. "And that's because you're the best teacher ever. Ramon let Eve and I leave early. Even Miguel is still out there riding. And you're right. Jake is the best horse in the barn. I didn't have to do anything coming from the gate except stay on. Tomorrow Ramon wants me to go for less mane and more rein, and I need to practice with my whip but it was the most fun I've had since I was a kid."

She looked up at him with shining eyes, and she looked so damn sweet, he impulsively dipped his head and kissed her. She didn't seem to have any walls up today, thank God.

"Are you finished with Jake?" he asked, dragging his head up but keeping a hand around her slim hip. If she was in a receptive mood, he intended to stay close. Very close.

"Yes. I was just putting him in his paddock. Everyone else is still riding."

"I brought you some alfalfa."

"Thank you! Jake deserves it. He was so good today. I'm too tall to be a jockey, but now I think it might be fun to be an exercise rider."

"That's reassuring," he said. "Especially since that's the program you're enrolled in."

She stepped back, holding onto Jake's lead, her face turning serious. "Yes, well about my enrollment, I'd like to ask you something privately. Can you come to my room for a minute?"

"Sure," he said, checking over her head. Lydia's group still bumped around in crooked circles while Ramon addressed his string of riders. "We can get the alfalfa later."

She nodded and led Jake into his paddock, next to a big bay with a scar on his left cheek and an arrogant eye. "You'll get some alfalfa too," she called. But the big horse merely stared over her head, as though absorbed with something far more important than mere humans.

"That's my other horse, Rambo," she said, with an affectionate smile. "I've been picking grass so he expects it. When I first came he barely tolerated me, but now I can lead him without a chain."

Scott shot another glance at the horse. Rambo had an imperious head and a stubborn glint in his eye, and if the gelding had been at the track, he definitely would have been worth a bet.

"That horse has a high opinion of himself," he said,

eying Rambo's deep chest and powerful hindquarters. "He probably won some money in his younger days and is used to special treatment."

"That's what I heard," Megan said. "But everyone here just thinks he's a pain. No one can ride him. It would be nice to know more of his history."

"We can check his race record." Scott slipped his hand around her waist and urged her back to the dorms. "But not now."

She seemed oblivious to the fact that his mind was on more enjoyable pursuits and talked animatedly about the morning ride. They climbed the stairs and stopped in front of her door. He pushed it open, checking the tiny room, then turned and locked the door.

"Tami will be back soon," she said. "And I wanted to ask you something."

"Ask me anything," he said, coaxing her closer. "But after staring at Garrett's ugly mug last night, I need a little loving first."

"Okay." She smiled up at him then curved into his chest as though made to fit. "I thought you were getting your car fixed? Did you end up drinking with Garrett? You looked a little grumpy in class this morning."

And she'd looked a little emotional. So much that he'd shortened the lecture. But he didn't want to get into serious talking now. She smelled of sunshine and peaches, and it seemed like a week since he'd seen her.

He inhaled her scent then covered her mouth with his, drinking deeply, savoring her taste. She wrapped her arms around his neck and arched against him, leaving him glad he'd locked the door. He tugged her shirt from the waistband of her jeans and slid his hand along the hollow of her back. She was sweet and soft and receptive, and his blood heated as he caressed the flare of her hip, the curve of her ass. He palmed her breast, enjoying her soft sighs, then backed her purposely to the bed.

Clip, clop. A horse nickered and voices drifted up the stairwell. Someone thumped up the steps. The entire building vibrated with activity. Obviously Lydia's class had returned.

Groaning, he lifted his head and whispered into her neck, "This would be easier if you just dropped my class and moved into my place."

"I'll drop your class. I don't need it anyway."

Something nibbled at the back of his brain—she was oddly quick to give up a university credit—but he was too absorbed by the feel of her silky breast, how it fit perfectly in his hand. "It's not in your best interest to drop it," he said thickly. "But we can talk about it tonight. What do you want for supper?"

"Oh, but I can't come for supper." She pressed an apologetic kiss into the hollow of his throat. "I'm driving Eve into town. We're going to eat there. She's part of what I wanted to talk to you about."

"Eve? Isn't she the jockey who hung out with Joey Collins?"

Megan shifted back a step.

"Garrett asked me to hunt down the guy," Scott went on. "He filled me in on all the details and the students Joey's most likely to approach. Eve is at the top of his list."

Megan's eyes widened. "You mean...Garrett hired you? You're working for him now? As an investigator?"

Her voice quavered and he dropped his hand to her hip, rushing to reassure her. "Don't worry. Joey is the guy who hurt Rex, but there's little danger. Small time dealers don't generally hang around once it gets hot."

"J-Joey hurt Rex?" She stiffened, her body rigid.

"Yes. Garrett saw Joey that night. He wants me to catch him. Keep an eye on the dorms and pump up safety."

She shook her head. "But that doesn't make sense. Garrett *saw* Joey?"

"Yes. He didn't want to scare you but that kid is definitely bad news. Obviously he left Mexico under a different passport."

She backed away so abruptly her legs pressed against the bed. "You're sure of this? Garrett saw him?"

"Yes. Kid must have a vendetta against the school. Rex may have scared him or he might have been trying to hurt Garrett."

She pulled away and walked into the bathroom. Water splashed. She reappeared, blotting her face with a towel. Another good thing about country girls. They didn't waste much time with hair and makeup. Hell, when you looked like Megan you didn't need help.

But when she lowered the towel from her face, he could only gape. He didn't know what she'd done in the bathroom but she looked different. She always looked beautiful but now she was radiant with happiness. Her eyes, even her skin, simply glowed.

"I have to see Eve now," she said, tossing the towel on the bed. "To ah...warn her."

He blinked and lowered his arm. Hiding that he'd been reaching for her. Wanting her. While she was hurrying off to see Eve. Again. "Good idea," he said, keeping his voice level. "But let's get the hay from my car first."

She gave him such a brilliant smile, he smiled back despite his disappointment that the room visit was already over. "Wait. What did you want to ask me?" he asked, hoping to wring out a few more minutes of her company.

But she'd already flung open the door and stepped into the hall.

"Hey," he called. "Students need to lock their rooms now."

She glanced over her shoulder, staring for a moment as though she'd forgotten he was around. But she didn't stop walking.

"Come back and lock your door," he said. "Junkies are unpredictable and dangerous. You don't want to surprise him in your room."

"I'm not worried about Joey," she said. "And I can't lock it now. Tami doesn't have her key. Come on. We have to get the hay from your car so you can go."

"Megan..." His protest trailed off. She was almost skipping now, had already reached the top of the stairwell. Damn, that woman was hard on the ego. It was brutally clear he was the more interested party, and he didn't like the feeling. Physically she seemed willing enough, but emotionally she shut him out at the most inconvenient times. Now normally a woman who preferred to keep things casual was a definite bonus, but with Megan, it only gave him a headache.

He sighed and followed her back down the steps and into the busy barn aisle. Sweaty horses clomped past, swishing their tails, eager for lunch. He slipped on his sunglasses and stepped outside, ignoring the students' curious looks and hoping to discourage any conversation.

Megan was already halfway across the parking lot, her shiny ponytail bouncing. It looked like she'd received a happy drug. She simply radiated joy, a polar opposite to her anguished look in his classroom earlier this morning. He liked to see her happy—but he didn't understand this type of mood shift.

He'd certainly check out this Eve girl and wished Megan would chum around with someone safer. If Joey was looking for his girlfriend, he didn't want Megan caught in any blowback. Especially after seeing the brutal way Joey had dealt with the dog.

"Scott," a woman called.

Lydia's voice. He blanked his face and turned.

"I see you've already been checking the dorms." Lydia flashed an approving smile. "Garrett said you need a list of students and room numbers. I'll have it to you within the hour. Let me know if there's any other way I can help."

"Thanks." He glanced over his shoulder and couldn't stop his mouth from twitching. Megan was poking ineffectually at his car lock, trying to open the trunk. When it didn't open, she threw her hands up in frustration. Rambo had already trotted to the adjacent fence, head high and expectant. And now Jake decided treats were imminent and began to paw.

She couldn't hurry off to see Eve now, not with both her horses wheeling in anticipation. She'd have to return and ask for his car keys. Maybe then he could entice her with lunch.

"I also need a list of empty rooms," he said, looking back at Lydia. "Just in case Joey's holed up here. Tell everyone to lock their doors, even when the rooms are unoccupied. Let's not make it easy for him."

He shifted, watching his car over Lydia's head. Megan was in a real quandary now. She couldn't approach him with Lydia around—Megan's desire to stay low-key, not his. But she couldn't leave without getting the alfalfa for her impatient horses. They really should have lingered a few minutes in her room and waited out Lydia.

Her eyes held his and it was apparent she knew exactly what he was thinking. But her imploring look was impossible to ignore.

Lydia was still talking, completely unaware of his communication with Megan. He shifted his arm behind his back, aimed his remote at the car, and the trunk opened.

"Thank you," Megan mouthed. She pulled out the hay bag, splitting the alfalfa between Rambo and Jake. Then tossed the empty bag back into the trunk, blew him a grateful kiss, turned and starting running. She didn't look back, didn't stop until those lovely long legs disappeared into the jock barn.

The day instantly turned duller. He'd hoped to see her longer, maybe squeeze in lunch before her next class. Hadn't anticipated she might have plans. And why the hell was she so eager to visit the girlfriend of a drug trafficker? If Eve was hiding Joey, Megan really should keep a prudent distance.

He dragged a hand over his jaw and turned to Lydia, waiting for her to finish her spiel about how eager she was to help.

"There is one thing you can do for me," he said.

Her head bobbed. "Anything."

"I'd like a complete copy of the school file on Joey Collins," he said. "As well as the file on a jockey student named Eve."

CHAPTER TWENTY-TWO

"He's alive!" Megan burst into Eve's room, her heart pounding with joy. "Joey's alive!"

A hairbrush dropped from Eve's fingers, falling to the floor with a clatter. "Where is he? Did he call?"

Megan shook her head, still pumped with adrenaline. "He's here though, right here. Garrett saw him. He thinks Joey hurt his dog but of course, we know that can't be true."

"What are you saying?" Eve pressed a hand over her mouth, her eyes clinging to Megan's face.

"I tried to hire Scott," Megan said, her words tumbling out with eagerness. "But I couldn't because Garrett already asked him to find Joey. That's when he told me that Garrett saw Joey."

A little line appeared between Eve's eyebrows. "But that's crazy. If Joey were here, he wouldn't be sneaking around. He'd want everyone to know those accusations were false."

"Well, maybe he's acting a little weird," Megan said, her voice faltering. "But at least he's alive. I had my doubts before. And no matter what kind of trouble he's in, I can help. I'd rather him doing drugs than be dead."

"Listen." Eve stepped forward and gripped her wrists. "They didn't see Joey. Maybe they saw someone who looked like Joey but it wasn't him. He would have called me, especially since...well, believe me, he would have called. And what's this about a dog?"

"Someone clubbed Rex, Garrett's dog. Broke his leg. It was horrible."

"Well, there. That's proof enough." Eve shook her head. "You know Joey wouldn't go around clubbing dogs. He loved animals."

"Loves. He *loves* animals."

"Megan." Eve's grip tightened, her eyes turning a sorrowful black. "I'd like to believe it too, but Joey isn't coming back. Something terrible happened down in Mexico."

Megan pulled away and sank onto the bed. She dropped her head in her hands, her earlier euphoria replaced by a numbing pain. She'd wanted to believe so badly. For fifteen wonderful minutes, she'd been ecstatic.

But this was worse. To be given hope, and then have it wrenched away. Replaced by the stark and brutal truth. "You're right," she said, her voice cracking. "Joey wouldn't hide. He always faced things head on. Oh, God. I was so excited I almost called Mom."

"At least the school is finally doing something, hiring Scott." Eve dropped on the bed beside her. "He has a good reputation. If he digs up something, Garrett will have to listen."

"But Scott thinks Joey is a dangerous drug dealer." Megan squeezed her eyes shut. "He won't be too keen to clear his name. Besides, he's looking in the wrong place."

"Then hopefully we'll find something in Lydia's villa," Eve said. "So we can subtly point him in the right direction."

"Aren't you eating supper?" Tami asked, as Megan veered from the cafeteria door and headed toward the exercise room.

"Not yet," Megan said, trying to act casual. The plan had been to meet Eve in the exercise room at five o'clock but she was already a few minutes late. Rambo had kicked a stall board loose and it had taken time to find a hammer and remove the dangerous nails. She was hot and edgy, and her stomach rolled at the prospect of sneaking into Lydia's villa.

"I'll save you a seat," Tami said.

"Thanks but no need," Megan said, avoiding Tami's gaze. "I'm not that hungry. And I need to practice switching my stick on the Equicizer."

"You rode well today." Tami lingered by the step. "Ramon said you were a natural, that you reminded him of someone. He asked your last name."

"Really." Megan forced a casual shrug but her breath caught.

"I couldn't remember it though," Tami went on. "Nobody uses last names much. What is it again?"

"Spence."

"Oh, right." Tami's head pumped in recognition. "Anyway, he said you reminded him of Joey Collins. My last name is Tomlin. Pretty cool, right? Tami Tomlin. Just like a movie star."

"Yes, that's a nice name." Megan swallowed, her gaze shooting toward the open door of the exercise room. Eve sat on a stationary bike, barely moving the pedals and clearly waiting. She'd made a similar comment about Megan's resemblance to Joey. Was it really that obvious?

"Look, I need to ask you a favor," Tami said. "Could you find something to do this evening? You know, so Miguel and I can have a little privacy. We can't go to Ramon's, and Miguel's getting...impatient." Her smile looked strained.

"Don't let him push you into anything," Megan said, lowering her voice so a passing student couldn't hear. "You shouldn't sleep with him. Not unless you want to."

"Sleep?" Tami gave an exasperated eye roll. "You're such a dinosaur. It's called sex. And of course I want to. Every girl here is hot for him. I just want you to stay away for a while. That shouldn't be such a biggie. It sucks to have a roommate."

She wheeled and flounced into the cafeteria.

Megan sighed. Miguel was a manipulative asshole. No doubt, he'd deliberately hit on that other jockey, just to yank Tami's chain. It was sad that his pathetic ploy was working. Maybe girls did like him—they certainly flocked around him—but she couldn't understand the attraction.

He was spoiled, arrogant and rough. *Rough with horses, rough with women.* Many of those old sayings were grounded in truth.

Eve swung off the exercise bike and gestured impatiently at the back exit. Megan pushed aside her misgivings and hurried around the building. She had enough to worry about right now, and they were losing precious time. Lydia always left the cafeteria following announcements. That gave forty-five minutes, max.

Plenty of time to check out the isolated villa. But a trickle of perspiration slid between her breasts and her forehead felt clammy. She swiped at it with the back of her hand, but it was impossible to wipe away her nervousness.

Sneaking into Lydia's villa had sounded simple earlier in the day. However, the reality was daunting.

She squeaked in surprise when Eve popped up in front of her.

"Let's hurry," Eve said, giving a determined smile. "Ramon's in the cafeteria too so we should be good."

"Great," Megan managed, marveling at Eve's rock-solid nerves.

They rushed down the dirt path that cut behind the cafeteria, their steps quickening until they were almost running.

Eve patted her pocket. "Make sure you put your phone on vibrate."

"I already did," Megan whispered, even though it was suppertime and the winding path was empty of listeners. Garrett and Scott were the only two who didn't dine at the cafeteria...the two buddies at the top of the food chain.

And now Scott was hunting Joey. For Garrett.

She squashed her pang of betrayal and concentrated instead on Lydia's villa. She had to be alert, not distracted by thoughts of Scott. "You wait by this tree," she said, "where you can watch the path. If you see Lydia, text me."

"But I want to go in."

"No," Megan said. "There's no reason for both of us to get caught. And I'm not the one who desperately wants a riding career."

She turned and followed the graveled walkway, leaving Eve no time to argue. Pebbles rattled beneath her boots so she slowed to a creeping walk, trying to control the noise. And her nerves.

On second thought, maybe it was best to act natural. Squaring her shoulders, she stepped boldly up the pathway and rapped on the door. No answer, of course. She glanced over her shoulder, reassured by Eve's encouraging nod. There was no security panel, unlike the elaborate system at Scott's villa. She pulled in a resolute breath and turned the knob.

The door didn't open.

She twisted harder, then pressed her shoulder against

it and shoved. It still didn't budge. Damn. She'd assumed it wouldn't be locked. Lydia must be following Scott's crazy edict about securing doors.

Eve was barely visible now, leaning against a giant avocado tree, alert and watchful. She was a good person to have guarding one's back. Megan gestured at the side of the villa then eased around the corner.

The rear door backed onto a brick patio with a yard vastly different from Scott's. There was no pool or hot tub, only a scraggly patch of uninviting grass and a barbecue with a ripped cover. She stepped over some fallen palm leaves, curled and brown with decay, and pulled at the sliding door.

It didn't move.

She groaned. Trust Lydia to follow Scott's every order. But it must be inconvenient. No one liked a sharp key stuck in their pocket, and Lydia always wore tourniquet-tight pants. The students in Megan's dorm had shrugged and simply tossed their keys in the large planter at the end of the hall. It was much simpler to hide a key than carry it around the barn and risk losing it.

Brightening, she rushed back to the front of the villa and lifted the doormat. And there it was, a silver key glinting by her foot. She gave Eve a triumphant thumbs-up, pushed the key in the lock and opened the front door.

She paused, bent down to pull off her boots, then gave her head a shake. Intruders didn't remove footwear. However, she brushed them off on the inside mat, relieved they weren't too dirty.

She began her search in the bathroom, pulling open drawers and checking the medicine cabinet. There were some expired antidepressants, two types of diuretics and a guaranteed tooth whitener. But nothing odd or illegal.

She moved into the TV room, checking the coffee table and lifting the sofa cushions, not even sure what she was looking for. The stack of notes and magazines were related to horses and education. But there was nothing specific about Mexico. Or Joey.

Lydia was meticulously neat although there were some redeeming dust bunnies beneath the sofa. Her life seemed boring, but a well-stocked wine rack suggested she did enjoy her wine.

Megan checked the time. She'd been inside for seven

minutes. This wasn't so scary.

More confident now, she strolled down the hall and into the main bedroom. The double bed was made as tightly as a marine's, and she fought the urge to check it with a coin toss. She scanned the closet and the bedside table but balked at rifling through Lydia's underwear.

She moved through the door and into the spare bedroom. Lydia obviously didn't anticipate any guests. The room had been converted to an office, stark and bare except for a cheap computer desk. The walls, however, were plastered with pictures. Megan edged closer, her eyes widening.

'Groom of the Week at Del Mar.' 'Apprentice Jockey Scores First Win,' 'Fighting the Odds.' The coverage was extensive. Lydia obviously followed the careers of every student, even the man who'd ended up as a pari-mutuel clerk. Five students had written thank you notes, pitifully few considering the number of grads, but those were tacked on the wall in a place of honor.

Nothing about Joey. He hadn't had time to make the grad wall.

A bag of golf clubs sat in the corner. Megan inspected the shafts. There was no sign of blood. She dragged her finger over the ends. Dust or hair? She wasn't certain. It seemed inconceivable that Lydia could club a dog, not considering how much she loved horses. But still...

Squaring her shoulders, Megan turned toward the computer.

Sonofabitch.

She stiffened, then charged forward and yanked off the cord that connected Joey's iPod to the computer. Unbelievable. Lydia had raised such a stink about the iPod going to his family but hadn't even bothered to return it. Instead she was callously enjoying his music.

Megan shoved the iPod into her pocket, shaking her head with annoyance. At least this visit had produced something worthwhile.

She stomped back down the hall and checked the path through the living room window. Eve sat on the ground, her lower back resting against the tree, arms clutched around her knees. She looked stoic and alert, but wasn't using her phone. Not yet.

Megan opened the front door, locked it, then replaced

the key beneath the mat. She jogged back to Eve.

"Find anything?" Eve rose to her feet, her eyes hopeful.

"No sign of drugs. Nothing about Mexico or the Baja Tinda." Megan patted her pocket. "But I did get Joey's iPod back."

"His iPod was there?" Eve's mouth tightened. "Thought she was going to mail it."

"Guess it had some music she really liked," Megan said, comforted by Eve's disgust. "So, what should we do now? Still want to go to town?"

"Definitely," Eve said. "I need to buy some stuff and I'm tired of tofu. Just thinking of a hamburger makes me drool."

Megan glanced sideways, unable to block the visual of Eve gripping the toilet bowl and barfing her burger. It must be hell for jockeys, knowing over-weights were announced to the world. Maybe Scott's class would really help people like Eve.

"Did Joey battle his weight while he was here?" Megan asked, struggling to keep the empathy from her voice, sensing Eve was too proud to want sympathy.

"No." Eve gave a wistful smile. "He could consume way more calories than me. He spent a lot of time in the exercise room though, and jogged every evening. He tried to get me to join him, but he ran too fast."

"He was on the school cross country team," Megan said. She paused. Joey had also been a star on the juvie soccer team. But he never talked about his time at the institution so out of respect, she didn't want to mention it either.

"He told me how the juvies beat the local cops," Eve said. "And how he scored a hat trick that day. He claimed the food at reform school was way better than jockey school."

"Wow." Megan blinked in surprise. "He told you all that?"

Eve nodded, her eyes luminous. "He also said that through his drug troubles, you never gave up on him. You were his sister, but also his best friend."

Megan's throat thickened, realizing this girl had been exceedingly important to Joey too.

She reached out and linked Eve's arm with hers. And

they continued down the twisting path, sharing their stories and emotion, talking about the special young man who they had both loved.

Megan shifted in the driver's seat, her discomfort growing. She wasn't used to greasy food, and the fries and hamburger, though delicious an hour ago, now sat in her stomach like an oversized brick. Despite feeling slightly ill, it had been a lovely evening, sharing memories of Joey with someone else who cared.

But now she was eager to return to the school. She'd told Scott she'd be back by nine, and it was already eight-thirty.

She peered through the window, trying to see into the drugstore. A customer, much too tall to be Eve, stood in the checkout line. Eve had said she wanted to stop and pick up a few things, but probably she was searching for a bathroom.

A private place to purge.

Megan sighed, grateful Tami wasn't a jockey. Rooming with someone who enjoyed chocolate was much easier than agonizing about the real reason behind Eve's frequent bathroom trips. Although she did worry about Tami and her quest to find a boyfriend. At least Tami would be happy that Megan was giving her the privacy she'd requested.

Tami might be happy to have more chocolate bars too. Sales had been steady and their current stash was running low. It could take her mind off Miguel and his little mind games. Megan didn't intend to poke her nose into Tami's affairs, no way, but it wouldn't hurt to cheer her up with a little gift. She grabbed her purse and slid from the truck.

A bell jangled above the doorway announcing her entry in the store. She grabbed a plastic basket, filling it with an assortment of chocolate bars. Tami liked Crispy Crunch, Peter preferred Mars Bars. She didn't pick up any Snickers for Miguel.

She walked to the front with her basket, relieved Eve was the only person in line. They'd be able to pay quickly and be home in twenty minutes.

Eve spotted Megan and flinched, her gaze shifting to a

pink box lying on the check-out counter.

"I just wanted—" Megan's words mired in her throat when she recognized the pregnancy kit.

Eve squared her shoulders and paid the cashier without looking again at Megan.

"Anything else?"

Megan blinked, realizing the cashier was talking to her. She fumbled in her purse and somehow paid for the chocolate.

She followed Eve to the truck, her legs wooden. Neither of them spoke until they settled in their seats.

"So that's why you threw up," Megan said. "I thought you were bulimic. Oh, Eve." She leaned over and hugged her, feeling Eve's struggle for composure.

"I think I'm p-pregnant," Eve choked. "But I need to know for sure. That's why I had to go to town."

"What are you going to do?"

"I don't know."

The misery in her voice made Megan's eyes prick, and she averted her gaze. Eve needed someone strong, not a blubbering idiot. "I can help," Megan said. "Whatever way you want. I have some money too. Just let me know—" But her throat constricted and she gripped the wheel, struggling to find some semblance of control.

Joey's baby. God, she wanted it in her world. She wanted it badly.

"I want to ride," Eve said, her voice so low it was barely discernable. "Not take time off for a pregnancy. And Joey's gone. So I'm leaning towards...well, you know."

Megan gripped the steering wheel. "I guess the first step is to take the test," she said, her voice surprisingly calm. "Find out for sure. Did Joey know?"

"We knew I was late, but we weren't certain. That's why, well I knew he wasn't the type to run off."

"No." Megan pried her hands off the wheel. "Of course he wouldn't. Do you need a bottle of water? Some juice?" She scanned the stores. "Let's find a bathroom so you can take the test."

"No." Eve's voice firmed. "I want to go back to my room."

"But don't you want to know?"

"What I want is to be alone."

It was a quiet drive. Eve spoke in monosyllables, her

face shadowed while Megan drove on autopilot, battered by a flood of emotions, teetering from despair to the optimistic hope of new life.

They turned into the driveway leading to the school. Megan eased to a stop in front of the jockey barn.

"Will you at least let me know what you find out," she asked, struggling to keep her voice from cracking.

"Yes. And thanks for the hamburger and the drive to town." But Eve said no more. She just pushed open the door and bolted inside.

Megan jerked the truck into the parking lot, then dropped her forehead on the steering wheel. Her mother would be delirious with joy. If, if, if...so many ifs. She sucked in several breaths, cast a last wistful glance at the lights shining from the second floor of Eve's dorm, then turned and walked into the barn.

"Hey, Megan," Peter called, his voice hopeful. "Can you help me with night hay?"

Megan dropped the bag of chocolate bars and slumped onto the nearest bale of hay, too drained to walk further. "Sure," she said. "But I didn't know it was your turn tonight."

"Yeah, only guys are allowed to feed at night now. Joey Collins broke into Lydia's villa so all the girls are terrified."

"What!" Megan tilted forward on the bale.

"Lydia's okay," Peter said, "but Garrett and Scott were here an hour ago. Garrett made some more rules. And his expensive Quarter Horse is moving into this barn." Peter's eyes narrowed on the bag at her feet. "Wow. Did you get more chocolate?"

"Help yourself," Megan said, still absorbing this new development. Joey was being blamed for their visit to Lydia's? It was all too staggering, especially after Eve's possible pregnancy.

She picked up a whip, gripping it in her hands, seeking stability in something. Anything. "But nobody saw Joey," she finally managed. "At Lydia's. Why is he being blamed for everything?"

Peter shrugged. "Who else could it be? And apparently they know from what was taken." He pulled out a Mars Bar and gave a conspiratorial wink. "Tami won't want hers for a while. She's still upstairs, holed up with Miguel."

Pain spiked behind Megan's eyes, and she pressed a palm against her forehead. Pregnancy, break-ins, Joey. She wanted to crawl into bed, and pray and cry, and pray some more. Unfortunately her room was off limits right now. Besides, Scott was expecting her.

She stared down at the whip. He wanted her to practice using it on the ground, but her fingers felt numb and the idea of being able to switch whip hands while galloping seemed ludicrous.

"Hey, move your ass." Peter's boots shuffled in front of her. "I need that hay."

She looked up, blinking.

"Never mind," he said, studying her face. "You look weird. Just stay there. I'll grab another bale."

Stall doors clanged open and shut as Peter tossed hay, but her thoughts remained wrapped around pregnancy. She was older. Single. She didn't want to ride for a living. Maybe Eve would let her raise the baby—if Eve would only carry it to full term. But was Eve actually pregnant? She crossed her fingers and made a fervent prayer.

"Almost finished." Peter materialized in front of her, his kind face concerned. "I just need to check their water." He cocked his head. "I'm assuming you didn't go to your room because Tami and Miguel are there. Want to hang out with me and Skip?"

"No, thanks," she said. "But I appreciate the offer. Miguel will probably go soon."

"Don't know about that." Peter gave a wistful sigh. "I sure wouldn't leave if I were him."

CHAPTER TWENTY-THREE

"I won't be able to sleep a wink." Lydia gave an exaggerated shudder. "Knowing Joey Collins was creeping around my bedroom."

"What makes you think he was in your bedroom?" Scott asked. "You said the iPod was on the kitchen table, ready to go in the mail."

Garrett raised an amused eyebrow but blanked his face when Lydia looked at the two men.

"I just know," she said, "that I don't feel safe." She fluttered her eyelashes at Scott. "Is there another place I could stay?"

"Sure." Garrett's voice rippled with mischief. "Scott's villa is big enough—"

"Garrett has seven empty bedrooms," Scott broke in, "so if you really think safety is an issue, that's the logical alternative."

"But there's no need to panic," Garrett said quickly. "The measures Scott suggested will be enough. I don't think Joey is a big threat."

Scott leaned forward. It was hard to get an accurate gauge of Joey Collins. He ranged from a violent kid to a gang dealer and then to a hopeless addict. Now he was harmless? Even Garrett waffled.

"But he was certainly a threat to Rex," Scott said.

Garrett shrugged. "Yes, but with this last incident he took nothing but his own iPod. That's not exactly stealing."

Scott rubbed his forehead in frustration. According to Ramon and Lydia, Joey was a hard-core dealer with an expensive habit and gang affiliations. It was difficult to understand Garrett's ambivalence, especially with a group of students on the grounds.

"Do you want to catch this guy or not?" Scott asked, crossing his arms. "I can run a check. Find the area he works. Snake knows most of the gangs—"

Garrett shook his head. "I don't want you to spend any extra time with this. There's no need to scare the students. Just concentrate on teaching your course. But if you see Joey hanging around, grab him." Garrett turned to Lydia. "About that other matter, can you spare me a racehorse?"

"Not this month." Her brow furrowed. "The grooms need the quiet ones. Sphinx is out with a tendon, Cody pulled his stifle. We don't have any extra mounts."

"Then we'll have to ship Rambo."

"Not Rambo!" She jerked forward but quelled under Garrett's hard stare. "I hate to send Rambo to Mexico," she said, settling back in her chair. "You know what will happen to him down there. He deserves better."

Scott had been scanning his phone, hoping for a message from Megan, but glanced up, drawn by the passion in Lydia's voice. She wasn't pulling any helpless act now. She seemed to really care about the horse.

"What's Rambo's story?" he asked, remembering the horse Megan cared for and the animal's regal appearance.

"He's an old stakes horse," Lydia said. "Won almost a million dollars. He was donated to the school. Supposed to be semi-retired." She shot an accusing look at Garrett.

"He's supposed to be teaching students to gallop," Garrett said. "Not how to hit the ground. And if he isn't any use, he's going on the trailer next week."

Scott's phone vibrated. He didn't want to get his hopes up. It was probably Snake again. But the screen showed 'Megan Spence.' He rose to his feet and walked into Garrett's office.

"Sorry I'm late," she said, her voice subdued. "I just have to grab some stuff from my room, and I'll be right over."

He wished she'd grab her suitcase and move in, but at least she was coming. "Don't walk," he said. "There's been another incident. I'll pick you up."

"Okay, but I need to wait a few minutes. To get in my room."

"Yeah, fine," he said. "I'll be right there."

Garrett and Lydia were in deep discussion about the scarcity of usable horses, and it sounded like Ramon had now joined in, via speaker phone. Scott poked his head in the kitchen, gave a quick wave and escaped out Garrett's back door

He strode back to his villa and slid into his car. He drove slowly, keeping a watchful eye on the shadows. Both barns and adjoining dorms were well lit, but he circled the parking lot, relieved Megan's truck was parked close to the door. He didn't like the idea of her hanging out with Joey's girlfriend. Lydia claimed it had been a transient affair. However, if Joey was looking for Eve, Scott wanted Megan a safe distance away.

He parked by the end door and walked in, passing a bright-eyed student with hay sticking to his chest and a dark smear on the side of his mouth. "Good evening, sir," the student said as he headed toward the stairs.

Scott nodded but his gaze swept the aisle. Megan sat on a bale of hay, practicing switching her whip hand.

"Peter told me Braun is moving here tomorrow," she said, rising to her feet.

He'd been eager to see her, to touch her, but paused. There was something strained in her expression, a darkness to her eyes, and her voice held an accusatory note. "That's right," he said, keeping his hands at his side. "Garrett is rounding up some horses for Mexico. He wants to use the cowshed as a base and needs Braun's stall."

"I understand you think Joey broke into Lydia's villa."

"That's also correct," he said, absorbing the agitated way she twirled the whip, almost brushing him in the chest. Clearly something was bothering her, but he had no idea what it was. He only knew he wanted to help. He reached out and stilled her hand, guiding it gently to her side. "Which is why you shouldn't be sitting in the aisle alone," he added.

"I'm not worried. And Peter stayed until he heard your car." Her throat moved, then her words escaped in a rush. "Do you really think Joey is doing all this stuff? That he was into drugs? Eve knew him better than anyone else and she's not the type to lie. She swears he was clean."

"I think Garrett and Lydia know his history best," Scott said cautiously.

"But all these accusations. Whenever anything happens, it's blamed on him." She waved the whip again. "It's not fair."

"What's really bothering you?" he asked, studying her face. She'd gone to town with Eve. Had Joey already made contact?

"Not a thing," she said. "We had a great night. From beginning to end."

It didn't look as though she'd enjoyed the evening. Tension radiated from her, and she still fiddled with the whip. He remained silent, waiting.

"Most of the night was good," she finally said, tugging at her lip. "But Miguel and Tami are upstairs. I'm not sure when I can get into the room, and I really wanted my toothbrush and stuff. Guess I'm just tired."

He gave her a comforting hug, appalled at how cold she felt. Obviously she'd been sitting in the barn aisle a while. "Let's go home." He turned her toward the door. "Garrett keeps my villa well stocked. There are extra toothbrushes in the bathroom."

"What about chocolate?" she asked. "Do you have any of that?"

He almost groaned, aware his cupboards were empty of anything but liquor. But he could drive like hell to town, if necessary. "Is that a deal breaker?" he asked.

"Not at all." She flicked the whip and even gave a glimmer of a smile. "I'm only offering because I bought a bunch of chocolate bars. You can have your pick except I want to save a Crispy Crunch for Tami."

"Thank you," he said solemnly, suppressing his flare of annoyance that a self-centered teenager monopolized the double room while Megan shivered in a damp barn aisle. Even worse was the painful realization that she might only be going home with him because she needed a place to stay. He wanted her, badly. But not that way.

"I can wait here until Miguel leaves, if you're tired and want your own bed. Or if you want to keep practicing with that whip?"

"No, I want to go with you." She flushed and tossed the whip on the hay. "I was practicing switching hands and didn't mean to be waving it so much. Did I scare you?"

"Oh, sweetheart." He blew out a sigh of relief, pressed

a hand against the small of her back and urged her to his car. If she only knew how scared he was.

He sped along the curving driveway. The ornamental lamps cast some light but he didn't bother checking the shadows. He just wanted her in his bed. If Joey Collins stepped in front of his bumper now, he'd give the guy a free pass.

He jammed the car close to his front door.

"When does Rex come home?" she asked, sliding from the car and glancing in the direction of Garrett's house.

"Not sure. Apparently he has a cast now and needs some rehab."

A few lights glowed over the tree tops, but all was silent, and he prayed it would remain that way. He didn't want any interruptions. Not tonight. He entered the code on the security pad and pushed the door back.

The light was on in the kitchen and he didn't flip any more switches. Just kicked the door shut and tugged her close, before she could feel uncomfortable, before that wariness crept back into her eyes.

He dipped his head and her lips met his, her mouth soft and inviting. His hands splayed over her back, pressing her close as heat shot to his groin. He'd intended to offer a drink, but the taste and feel of her blew that idea from his head. "I want you in my bed," he said thickly. "But maybe you want something else? Wine, food, Jacuzzi? Or just to talk?"

Her arms tightened around his neck. "I don't need anything," she said. And the husky invitation in her voice made him stiff with eagerness.

He scooped her up and rushed into his bedroom. Laid her on the bed and removed her boots then tugged off their shirts. Her bra gleamed whitely, but he concentrated on her mouth, sucking in her sweetness until her tongue was mating with his, sharing his urgency.

He trailed his mouth down her neck, kissed her fluttering pulse, then palmed her breasts until her nipples tightened beneath the thin fabric of the bra. He tugged it aside, took a nipple in his mouth, and her soft moan nearly blew away his control.

He tossed the bra on the floor, caressing her breasts until she arched against him. Jeans rustled, the sound of zippers erotic in the darkness. Finally it was skin against skin, and the air was thick with feverish exploration and their breathy whispers.

There was no dog yelping, no other interruptions. But he grabbed a condom, driven by a sense of urgency, a feeling she could be snatched from his arms if he wasn't careful.

He scooped his hands over her hips, adjusting himself between her legs. She clung to his shoulders, eyes closed as he entered. Sweat beaded his forehead but he kept it slow, not thrusting all the way, not until she hooked her legs around his and wiggled with impatience.

He gave a last fierce, possessive kiss then drove hard and deep, moving faster, until her soft shudders undid him and he found his own release.

In that final moment of intimacy, she opened her eyes. And their gazes locked, gripping each other as if unwilling to ever let go.

CHAPTER TWENTY-FOUR

Megan snuggled into Scott's chest. It was still dark and she didn't want to wake up, relaxed from their lovemaking and the feeling of being safe and cherished. But something nagged at her, prodding her from a luxurious sleep.

Eve. She jolted awake, flooded with memory. Was Eve pregnant? Would she even keep the baby?

Scott's hard arms banded around her. "We don't have to get up yet," he said, his mouth tickling her neck.

"What time is it?" She tried to find a clock but his hand was already stroking her breast, his mouth trailing a suggestive line along her collarbone. She quivered. Damn, he was talented. Her mind needed to dissect baby options, but her traitorous body wanted other things. His hand drifted to the inside of her thigh, coaxing her legs apart.

He positioned himself over her, pushing in with the familiarity of a longtime lover. She closed her eyes and arched to meet him, wanting to keep reality at bay a bit longer.

However, he slowed his strokes. His hand cupped her face until she opened her eyes. "What's wrong?" he asked, his alertness apparent even in the darkened room. "It's only five. Want me to stop?"

"Don't you dare." She hooked her legs around him. "Or I'll tell everyone at school that you're a lousy lover."

He chuckled, but she could feel him studying her face and then she didn't feel anything more but his sweet kisses...and his hard body.

She must have dozed off, but woke to the feel of his hand stroking her back.

"Time to get up," he said.

"What time is it?"

"Almost six."

"Oh, no!" She jackknifed out of bed, grabbed her clothes and rushed into the bathroom. Yanked her hair in a ponytail and splashed water on her face. She borrowed his toothbrush. No time to check the guest bathroom. Besides, after the night they'd shared, it seemed pointless.

When she returned, the light was on in the bedroom and he was pulling jeans up over his tapered waist, all gorgeous naked male. She felt rather self-conscious, but he gave her such a tender smile, her chest kicked.

"It's okay," she said. "Go back to sleep. I can walk back."

"You're not walking." He tugged on a T-shirt, crossed the room and gave her a quick kiss. "Let's go."

"How long does it take to feed and muck out?" he asked as they walked to the car.

"About forty minutes. Then we shower and have breakfast." She looked up at him, waiting while he opened the car door. "Guess I'll see you at class."

"It's Saturday, sweetheart. No lectures today, only the weekly update."

"Oh, perfect." She eased onto the seat, relaxing against the headrest. The weekend meant a little more leisure time. Maybe she and Eve could go for a drive tonight. They could talk about beautiful new babies and the joy of keeping the little one—if Eve really were pregnant, that is—although then Eve's riding career would be put on hold, and Megan really had no say in the matter. It wasn't her place to interfere, but the prospect of Joey's baby filled her with a deep and bittersweet longing.

And then there was Scott. Naturally he was bored at the school and wanted a playmate but she was falling far too hard, too fast, and this was the point where it was prudent to step back. She'd think up a few excuses, maybe see him again on Tuesday. That would give her a couple days to regroup, forget the feel of his mouth and hands, at least until the next time.

Of course, he'd need more diplomacy than her previous sex partners, simply because she'd see him daily. But it shouldn't be a problem. Especially if she dropped his class. He might even be relieved. A guy was always keen until they'd taken you to bed. After that their ardor cooled considerably.

She faked a yawn. "I'm going to catch up on my rest

tonight. How much sleep did we have, a couple hours maybe?"

He threaded the powerful car along the twisting drive and didn't respond. Didn't make the usual trite reply after a hookup. She glanced at his rugged profile but couldn't read his expression, despite the muted glow from the road lights.

"Three hours maybe?" she asked. "It was quite a session." She kept her voice light, careful to show it was no big deal. Not to him. Not to her. She shot him another swift look, wondering why her throat felt so tight. He definitely was silent. Had to mean something. Probably that she shouldn't talk anymore.

"Anyway I had fun," she added lamely.

He reached over and squeezed her hand, but that simple gesture made her feel better.

"I'm going to see Rex tonight," he said. "Come with me. We can eat in town."

"Oh, but I have to wash clothes and sleep and—"

"I heard the dog is depressed," Scott said smoothly. "Not showing much interest in Garrett. A visit from you might help."

She clasped her hands, picturing Rex and the last time she'd seen him. That poor dog. "Yes, of course," she said. "If you think it will help. What time are you going?"

"I'll pick you up at five. Bring your laundry. You can throw it in my machine on the way."

"Okay," she said. But she absolutely wasn't sleeping over, even if he invited her. She shot him a sideways look, wondering if she should make that clear right now. But it didn't seem necessary. His stubbled jaw looked rock hard under the shadowed light, not at all like an eager lover.

Of course, that was a good thing.

They bumped into the parking lot and she leaned forward, checking the activity. Shadowy figures drifted between the stalls, but luckily neither Ramon's nor Lydia's cars were in the lot. "I think I beat them," she said, her voice thick with relief.

"You did." Scott reached over and opened her door, his arm brushing her thigh. "Garrett's having a breakfast meeting with the instructors so you can relax and clean stalls at your leisure."

"Oh, good." She paused, checking his expression. "I

imagine you'll be talking about Joey? At that meeting?"

His face remained inscrutable.

"Because," she swallowed, grabbing her courage, "Eve and I think he got a bum rap. And someone with your experience would probably discover he wasn't doing drugs, or selling them. So that means his disappearance was very odd. I know Garrett wants you to catch him but maybe Joey's not here. Maybe he's even...dead." She grabbed for the door, her fragile control crumbling.

"Hey, wait." Scott leaned forward, sliding a hand over her shoulder. "Is that what's bothering you? Is it important to you?"

His concern was shredding her composure and she averted her head, desperate to hold back her tears. Didn't want to break down in his car.

He leaned over and pulled the door shut then wrapped her in his arms. His hand slid beneath her hair, stroking the back of her neck. "Don't worry," he said. "I'll do some digging. See what I can find." She let him tuck her head against his chest, temporarily soothed by the comforting rumble of his voice. "I gather your friend, Eve, is pretty tore up about this?"

She nodded into his chest but a tiny sob leaked out, spurred by his empathy. "I'll pay you. I mean...I'm sure Eve will pay."

"No need. I'm happy to do it." He still rubbed the back of her neck, but his voice lowered in warning. "She might not like what I find though. And I don't sugarcoat."

"It'll be a relief though," Megan said. "To finally know the truth. The police haven't been any help."

The glove compartment clicked. She didn't realize she was crying until he pulled out a tissue and gently dabbed it against her cheek. She waited a moment, then sucked in a breath and reached once again for the door handle. She wanted to escape his sharp gaze, his pointed questions, but wasn't ready to walk into the barn and have all the students stare. She just needed a moment to regroup.

His hand covered hers, stopping the door from opening. "Braun's moving to your barn today," he said. "Sure hope he doesn't get that dark stall by the wash rack."

"Yes," she managed, seizing the change of topic. "That's not a very nice stall."

"He's used to a window and a big paddock," Scott

said, his tone thoughtful. "I wonder what horses think. If they miss their old stall or wonder why their water bucket is in a different corner. Or maybe they're really happy when they luck out and get a thoughtful groom who brings them alfalfa."

She sniffed, even managing a wobbly smile as he filled her head with horse talk, stuff she'd often wondered about but never imagined a tough guy like him would even consider, much less ponder aloud. She released her grip on the door handle, letting her fingers entwine companionably with his.

"It would be hard to be a horse," she said. "Having no control when people come and go in your life."

"Yes, and imagine when your best buddy is sold." Scott rubbed the pad of his thumb gently over her palm. "And the guy you played halter tag with every day just disappears."

"And you wait and wait," she said, "wondering if he's ever coming back."

"Dogs have it much better than horses," he said. "People make a lifetime commitment to a dog."

She impulsively leaned over and kissed his cheek. "Thank you," she said. "I'm good to go inside now."

"Scram then," he said, his voice amazingly gentle as he pushed open her door.

She walked across the parking lot and into the barn, feeling much lighter. The aisle was empty now. But she winced with guilt when Jake and Rambo thrust their hungry heads over their doors.

Jake nickered, but Rambo kicked the wall in displeasure, irritated his breakfast was late. She grabbed their grain and hay from the feed room and hurried to their stalls, afraid Rambo might splinter another board. They clearly felt ill-used. But they weren't the only animals not fed. Both Tami's horses swung their heads over their doors, their eyes anxious. She returned to the feed room and fed them as well.

It was odd Tami hadn't grained yet. Had Miguel stayed the entire night?

She climbed the stairs to her room, praying he was gone. She needed more sleep before mucking the stalls, showering and listening to the weekly update. She was emotionally and physically drained. Breakfast wasn't worth the trek to the cafeteria. Joey, Scott, Eve, Rex—it was all overwhelming.

She groped in the planter for her room key, frowning at the new lock-up rules. Joey wouldn't hurt anyone and he definitely wasn't responsible for the iPod disappearing from Lydia's villa. It was bizarre how the stories mushroomed.

She knocked then unlocked the door. The room was dark, but clearly there was only one person in Tami's bed. And Megan had fed her horses so Tami could just keep sleeping.

Megan blew out a sigh of relief, stripped and slipped beneath the covers. For a moment she wished Scott's arms were still around her, but she banished that thought. She was used to sleeping alone, preferred it.

"Megan?"

"Go back to sleep," Megan said. "I fed your horses. As long as we clean their stalls before ten, we're good."

"Did Ramon or Lydia notice I wasn't up?"

"No. They're in a meeting so we can sleep in." Megan rolled over and wrapped her arms around her pillow. Maybe there was no harm in pretending the pillow was Scott, just this once.

"Sorry about hogging the room last night."

"It's okay," Megan said.

"Where did you sleep?"

"At Scott's." Megan rolled over on her back, keeping her eyes shut.

"He's a big guy."

Megan cracked open her eyes and glanced toward Tami's bed. Dawn's colorless light crept through the curtain, but the room was too shadowed to see Tami's face. But she sounded in a weird mood. *Big?* What the hell was she asking?

"About six two, I think," Megan said cautiously.

"I heard cops like to use cuffs. Probably normal, right? Guys always want to do that stuff?"

Megan opened her eyes and stared at the ceiling. Scott certainly hadn't needed cuffs. "He's not a cop," she said. "Not anymore."

"So you've never let anyone tie you up?" Tami sounded troubled. "Maybe some of the other guys you slept with? Other boyfriends maybe?"

It was a relief the room was dark. Megan had never talked candidly like this with anyone and she knew she was blushing. "I haven't had many boyfriends," she admitted. "Certainly not anyone I'd trust, to do that." *Although I would trust Scott.*

"But you and Scott are old. I'm sure younger people do it all the time." Tami's voice wobbled.

"Hey, what's wrong?" Megan sat up, fumbling for the light switch. Turned it on and gaped.

Tami's eyes were swollen, her face distorted from tears. Even her hair was tangled.

"I look awful, don't I?" Tami mumbled. "My eyes get puffy when I cry."

She must have been crying all night, Megan thought. She hurried across the room and dropped to her knees by the bed. "What happened?" she asked, keeping her voice gentle even as she raged inside at Miguel.

"I don't think Miguel likes me, not as much as I like him. He was a little...frustrated and his phone rang, and I think it was that girl who rides the gray. He left. Walked out." Her voice quivered. "It was like he didn't even care."

"I'm sorry," Megan said. "But sometimes we have to accept that. The trick is not to get involved. Don't let yourself care too much."

Tami jackknifed up, her jaw mutinous. "Well, I'm already involved. And I like him, a lot, so I'm going to make him like me."

Megan squeezed her eyes shut, remembering all her efforts, her mother's efforts, even Joey's attempts. They hadn't swayed her father one bit. "Unfortunately it doesn't work like that," she said. "You can try—try real hard—but men still leave. And then it hurts even more when they go." She paused, certain something else was bothering Tami. "Can I help with anything? Did Miguel want to tie you up? Maybe get mad when you refused?"

"You wouldn't understand," Tami said dismissively. She grabbed her brush, yanking it through her hair with single-minded determination. "But if you really want to help," she added, "please go get some ice for my eyes. So I don't look like a hag when I see Miguel again."

CHAPTER TWENTY-FIVE

Students gathered in a ragged circle outside the barn, listening to the instructors' weekly update. Megan couldn't concentrate. She peeked again at Eve's flat stomach. "I can't believe you're pregnant," she said, unable to contain her delight.

"That's what the test said," Eve whispered. "But promise not to tell anyone. I'm not sure what I'm going to do. It'd be different if Joey were around. Now quit talking. Ramon is watching, and he's already looking for a reason to get rid of me."

Megan nodded, still grinning. Eve was pregnant! She tried to blank her face and listen to Ramon. One student had dropped out, the guy who had struggled in the starting gate yesterday, and Braun was now stabled in the big stall next to Jake. Fairly routine stuff but it was the horses' day off and listening to the instructors was easier than riding.

And this was such a glorious day. Eve was pregnant! Joy leaked from the corners of her mouth, and she couldn't stop it. Scott stood on Garrett's right and she averted her gaze. He was too astute. He'd know something was up if he saw her grinning like a fool. But Joey's baby... She only prayed Eve would keep it.

"And now we'll have Scott's update on the anticipated apprehension of Joey Collins," Ramon said.

She jerked to attention, no longer merely pretending to listen. If they could find Joey, it would help Eve. And aid her in making such an important decision.

"Thanks, Ramon," Scott said. He went on to talk about locking doors and simple vigilance. Spoke with such easy authority that everyone stopped fidgeting. He was so damn cool, and the students recognized it. All the males, even Garrett, copied his body language. The girls simply stuck out their chests and flipped their hair, staring with rapt expressions.

"In closing," Scott said, "I need to remind everyone that Joey is not formally accused of anything. We just want to talk. He may be completely innocent. So we all should keep an open mind."

Megan's breath stalled. She heard Eve's relieved gasp but could only stare at Scott in grateful silence. Garrett shrugged, as if in agreement, but Ramon's eyes flashed with anger. After his big preamble about apprehension, Scott had made the man look rather foolish.

And then Garrett wished them all an enjoyable day, and the meeting was over.

"Eve," Ramon called, stalking toward them with Lydia scurrying at his heels. "You'll be switching horses on Monday. I want you to ride Rambo."

"Rambo?" Eve asked, her eyes widening.

"Lydia feels the horse can be of some value to the school," Ramon said. "You're one of our best riders, after Miguel. But clearly if you're afraid to ride him, he's no use here and should be shipped out."

"What about Miguel?" Eve asked, feisty as ever. "Since you think he's the best rider and all."

"He already refused," Ramon said. "The horse has thrown him a couple times."

"Okay, then," Eve said. "Rambo certainly deserves another chance." But her hand dipped protectively over her stomach before she turned and walked away.

Megan gaped at Ramon. The man knew Eve would never turn down a challenge like that. But this wasn't fair, or safe.

"No, I'll ride him," she said impulsively. "Rambo knows me. He likes me." I hope he likes me, she thought, lifting her head and trying to sound brave. Other students were listening now, and she hoped no one caught the quaver in her voice.

"You do it then," Ramon said. "Work with the horse over the weekend. Just be sure to have him on the track, ready to gallop on Monday."

She nodded, relieved Eve wouldn't have to risk a fall. But a blast of disapproval chilled her neck. She glanced sideways. Scott stood to her right, only ten feet away, his face stony.

"What the hell are you thinking?" he asked. "You're not a good enough rider." A muscle ticked in his jaw and his eyes had that contemptuous cop look. The kind of look that always made her feel worthless.

Her throat balled and for a moment she couldn't speak. Could only stare in hurt dismay. He'd been so kind earlier and she'd planned to thank him for his public defense of Joey. But now he was belittling her riding ability. In front of the entire school.

Her cheeks felt hot. Peter hunched his shoulders and kicked at a rock, his sympathy obvious. But two female jockeys snickered and moved closer to Scott, as if agreeing with his assessment.

Lydia gave a nervous cough. "We appreciate your kind offer," she said. "And you are a competent rider. But it would be better if Eve does it."

Megan raised her head. "No, it wouldn't," she said. "I'll start working with Rambo this afternoon."

She nodded at Lydia, then strode past Scott and into the barn, her back ramrod straight.

His thoughtlessness cut even more when contrasted to Lydia. She expected criticism from Lydia, was prepared for it even, but to have Scott turn on her so unexpectedly left her blindsided. Worse, she'd just slept with the man.

She fled up the stairs to her room and collapsed on the bed, hoping Tami wouldn't ask for any more advice. Clearly, she sucked at relationships.

Tami lifted the ice from her face. "Thanks for mucking out my stalls. Did Lydia notice that I missed the meeting?"

"No one noticed," Megan said, wishing her eyes weren't so itchy. "It was quick and informal."

"Did Miguel ask where I was?"

"I didn't even see him." Megan grabbed a pillow and pressed it over her face, hiding her expression.

"Do you think he felt bad about last night?" Tami asked.

"He's a guy. So probably not."

Tami paused for a second. "Did you have trouble with Scott too?"

"A little," Megan said, her voice cracking.

Tami gave a sympathetic sigh and rose from the bed. "I'll get some ice for your eyes," she said.

***

Megan groaned and lifted the bag of melting ice from her eyes. It was impossible to sleep. Boots thudded down the aisle, voices echoed excitedly in the stairwell and the paper-thin walls did little to muffle the noise.

"This is our only day to nap," Tami complained, propping on an elbow and scowling at the door. "Why is everyone being so loud?"

"I don't know," Megan said. "But I'm going to find out."

She tugged on her boots and shot an assessing look at Tami who looked much better now, her eyes no longer red and swollen. "You have to see Miguel sometime," Megan said. "Let's find out what's happening, then walk over to the cafeteria.

"I'm going to ride Rambo today," she added, trying to sound nonchalant. "Will you help me lunge him? See if we can get him to stop bucking."

"Rambo?" Tami jerked to a sitting position. "Are you nuts? Even Miguel won't go near him. That horse belongs in a rodeo."

"Probably just rumors. He seems quite normal on the ground."

"It's not rumors." Tami kicked off the sheet, swinging her feet to the floor. "Miguel told me the horse is loco. And smart. Like he thinks he's too good for us."

"Then he's too good for Mexico," Megan said.

"Of course, he's too good for Mexico. If a horse isn't useful there, he's sent to the slaughter house."

"That explains why Lydia doesn't want Rambo to go," Megan said. "At least she's trying to save him."

"Yes, but she isn't the poor sucker getting on his back." Tami's voice muffled as she yanked a T-shirt over her head. "Let someone else do it," she added, tucking in her shirt. "Eve is the best rider here, even though it kills Miguel to admit it."

Megan bent down and tightened her bootlaces. She wasn't going to stand back and watch Eve risk a dangerous fall. If Joey were around, he wouldn't let his baby's safety be jeopardized either. This was the least she could do. Besides, she'd trained young horses before, and her barrel racer had routinely crow hopped on cold mornings.

"I can ride a buck or two," she said, heading to the door.

"It's more than a backyard buck," Tami said. "It's YouTube worthy. Wait a sec." She pulled a compact red camera from her drawer. "Some websites pay for spectacular wrecks so if you're really going to climb on, this camera will take better video of your fall than my phone. Maybe I'll make some money. Of course," she added sheepishly, "I really hope you don't fall off."

Megan shook her head and continued down the hall. She didn't want to listen to any more talk about Rambo and how he was such a renegade. She was frightened enough just thinking about it.

There was no way she'd be able to eat lunch today, not the way her stomach churned. While Tami's warning didn't help, it was Scott's comment that she wasn't a good enough rider that had completely shattered her confidence.

He could have given her some advice. Instructors were supposed to be supportive, not knock you down. According to rumors, Rambo had run bravely for many years. He'd put his heart on the line every race and didn't deserve to end up in a dog dish. Maybe she wouldn't be able to stay on, but at least she intended to try.

Better her than Joey's pregnant girlfriend.

Squaring her shoulders, she trudged down the steps with Tami pounding behind. The barn aisle was empty so maybe now was a good time to start the groundwork. She didn't want a snickering and skeptical audience further shredding her courage.

"Would you mind skipping lunch so we can get Rambo out now?" she asked. "While no one is around to watch."

Tami nodded, her eyes wide but determined. Jake stuck his head over the stall door and sniffed Megan's hands. She gave him a pat then resolutely moved on to Rambo.

But his stall was empty. She jerked to a stop, so surprised her stomach momentarily stopped its flipping. He hadn't finished his hay, wasn't due for paddock turnout until one. She glanced up and down the aisle. Had they shipped him out already? Was she too late?

"Don't worry," Tami said. "Miguel said the trailer isn't going to Mexico until Sunday. Rambo must be around."

Hooves thudded beyond the barn, the sound sharp

and unexpected.

"Maybe he got loose," Megan said.

They both rushed out the end door.

Rambo wasn't loose. However, a cluster of people circled the round pen—Miguel with a sullen expression, Lydia with a nervous smile and about ten transfixed students—all gaping as Scott trotted Rambo in easy circles. The horse had a beautiful floating trot, but it was the rider who grabbed Megan's attention. Scott sat deep in the saddle, two hands on the reins, looking as assured as when he was driving his car.

And Rambo was behaving perfectly, his big body collected. His ears tilted back, attuned to his rider and alert to his cues. No wonder he'd been a stakes winner. He had lovely movement.

She and Tami cautiously approached the rail. Scott's gaze flickered over her, a mere second of distraction, but Rambo's eye flashed and he suddenly leaped into the air, trying to fishtail. Now she understood why Scott was riding with his hands so wide. He straightened the horse virtually in midair.

Rambo jarred back to the ground, stiff legged and resentful. He tried to stop, but Scott nudged him forward with his spurs. The horse trotted an obedient circle, as though the earlier leap had been a misunderstanding, then abruptly flattened his ears and kicked out with a wicked twisting buck.

Scott yanked Rambo's head up, pushing him forward but the horse snapped out with another violent kick. Megan gripped the rail, her knuckles white. It didn't seem possible Rambo could still buck, not with Scott keeping his head up, keeping him moving forward, but the horse was incredibly athletic.

Someone edged closer. Megan pulled her eyes off the horse and rider and saw Eve standing next to her.

"It's been like that for the last ten minutes," Eve whispered. "Rambo pretends everything's cool but as soon as Scott gives him an inch, he's in the air. He's okay on the track when galloping flat out, but it's the before and after when he plays with his rider."

That was playing? Megan gulped.

Eve touched her arm. "I heard about what you did earlier. Volunteering to take my place. You're very brave."

Megan shrugged but knew the color had leached from her face. She wasn't brave at all, had only offered because of the baby. It was obvious she wouldn't have lasted eight seconds on a horse like Rambo—and Scott had known. She wanted to slink back to her room and hide.

Scott trotted for another ten minutes without incident then stopped Rambo in the middle of the pen, loosened the reins and let the horse stretch his neck. Rambo blinked, turned and eyed his audience, then rested a hind leg. He looked like a benign trail horse. Megan would have laughed if she didn't feel like such a fool.

"Megan," Scott said, "would you saddle Braun and escort me on the track."

She felt her eyes widen. Only instructors were allowed to pony horses. And Braun was Garrett's expensive cow horse. Students did not ride Braun. Everyone was looking at her now, their expressions mirroring her confusion.

Maybe he just wanted her to admit that she'd been wrong, to say in public that she wouldn't have been able to handle Rambo. And she could do that. It was only fair.

"Braun prefers a quiet rider like you," Scott added. "And I really would appreciate your help. Please."

She stared into his steady gray eyes, not understanding.

"I'll saddle Braun for you," Lydia said.

"I'll help." Eve and Tami spoke together.

Megan nodded mutely and walked into the barn. By the time, she gathered her helmet and vest, Braun was saddled and waiting in the aisle.

"I adjusted the stirrups," Lydia said, passing Megan a leather lead line, "but they won't go any shorter. Students don't usually ride Braun, but this is for a good cause. I'll have the cafeteria staff save you some lunch."

"Thank you," Megan said. She could get used to service like this.

She mounted, avoiding eye contact with Eve and Tami who both looked rather astounded, and walked Braun from the barn. It was comforting to be back in a western saddle, riding a horse who neck reined, a horse that moved off the slightest leg pressure.

Rambo still stood in the middle of the round pen but students were already drifting away, deciding the show was over. Good. She hoped they wouldn't follow them to the track. Who knew what Rambo might do out there? Besides, she wasn't accustomed to ponying horses. Didn't know if she'd be any help at all.

Peter swung open the gate, giving a respectful salute to Scott as he rode Rambo from the round pen.

"Just link the lead line through the bit and we'll walk over to the gap," Scott said, moving Rambo alongside Braun. "Rambo knows the drill."

Megan leaned forward, slipped on the lead, and the two horses walked to the track like veterans.

"How do you think he'll act?" she asked, keeping a wary eye on Rambo. "He looks happy to be out. But if he starts bucking, do you want me to turn to the left or just choke up on his head? Or maybe get him galloping?"

Scott remained silent.

"Get him galloping then?" she asked. "Is that best? Because I want to do this right." She noted Scott's taut jaw and hesitated. Maybe he intended to switch horses. Make her ride Rambo as punishment. Her father had done that too, set her up for a fall whenever he thought she needed to learn some humility.

"Do you want me to ride Rambo now?" she asked, "If so, I totally understand."

His eyes flashed with an odd glint. "Megan, I don't want any student to ride him. But especially not you. He's not an easy horse."

Warmth filled her chest. It seemed Scott really was looking out for her. She wasn't used to anyone doing that. It was an odd feeling, nice but a little unsettling. "He would have dumped me the first buck," she admitted. "I can't understand how Joey stayed on. I always thought I was the better rider."

"But you just came here. You didn't know Joey."

"That's right," she said quickly. "Eve knew Joey though, so that's just based on what she said."

"I see." But his eyes narrowed. "My office ran a background check. They found nothing on him, not since his last rehab when he was twenty-one."

"See. Like Eve said, he wasn't here to sell drugs."

"Maybe not. But an addict is always an addict. If someone doesn't want to be helped, it's impossible. Eve should forget the guy. He'll only drag her down."

She pressed her lips together and stared over Braun's

ears, appalled by Scott's quick dismissal. If she'd given up like that, hadn't supported Joey through those dark days, he wouldn't be here right now.

Of course, Joey wasn't here right now.

"Some people successfully fight addictions," she said, her voice strained.

"And many more don't," Scott said. "A bunch of stories are floating around. Possibly they're exaggerated, but the truth is undeniable. Joey Collins was an addict. He may have turned to a gang to support his habit so it's possible he's somewhere with a needle shoved in his arm. There are lots of bodies between here and Tijuana. He may not be the big drug dealer Ramon thinks, but he's undoubtedly bad news."

Bodies? Joey's? It suddenly hurt to breathe. Braun slowed as though sensing her distress but Rambo charged forward, impatient with the tortoise-slow pace.

"Dammit." Scott tightened the reins as Rambo snaked his head and tried to buck. "Get your horse moving, Megan," he said. "Or we'll have a rodeo here."

She squeezed her legs, and Braun instantly moved alongside Rambo.

"Don't go to sleep on me, sweetheart," Scott added, shooting her a smile. But she couldn't return it, and at that moment resented not only his easy way with a horse but also his easy way with her.

Clearly he didn't know what it was like to love someone, in spite of a few failings. Her school friends had written her off too, no doubt influenced by their parents. But she couldn't just write off Joey. Couldn't stop caring because of a mistake or two. What kind of person did that?

She adjusted her grip on the lead, grateful Braun, at least, was dependable. In fact, he was an awesome horse. Any other day she would have been thrilled to ride him. But today she was too tangled with misery.

Lots of bodies between here and Tijuana. She tried to banish the bloody image, but it was difficult. And Scott was right about one thing. Joey had been an addict. Maybe he'd chosen to remain in Mexico. Maybe she should just drive in the direction of the Baja Tinda and check every town on the way. She'd helped him with rehab before. She could do it again. She certainly wasn't going to give up, no matter what Scott thought.

She shot him a dark look, too resentful to speak. Even pictured him flat on his intolerant ass, smack in the dirt.

"Why do I get the feeling you want Rambo to buck me off?" Scott asked.

She yanked her gaze away but still didn't speak, aghast he could read her thoughts so well.

"But you didn't want to risk your friend, Eve," he added thoughtfully. "You're a complicated woman, Megan."

He glanced at the white BMW cruising along the lane beside the track. "We've got company," he added. "Probably Garrett checking that you're not abusing another horse."

"I wouldn't abuse Braun," she said. "Or any horse. And that day Edzo was all sweaty, you were with me. You know I didn't ride him too hard." She spotted Scott's smile and realized he was only trying to tease her into talking. And his ploy had worked. She flattened her mouth in annoyance.

"I don't know why you're sulking," he said, reaching over and patting her knee. "But let's ride over and give Garrett a report."

She felt the warmth of his palm through her jeans, knew how magical those hands were, and a tingle shot up her leg. Unfortunately, it seemed her body operated independently from her brain and didn't resent his nasty comments about Joey.

She sniffed and turned Braun toward the parked car, dismayed by her reaction.

Garrett leaned over the rail. "Thanks for tuning that horse up for us, buddy," he called, his sunglasses reflecting a warped image of Rambo's head.

"A tune-up isn't going to be enough," Scott said. "He may have been a quality racehorse once but he's not suitable for the school. He'll only hurt someone."

Garrett nodded. "Then he can't stay, but at least we gave him a chance. And that solves another problem. We need a fourth horse for the Baja Tinda. He can fill the trailer."

"Are they better riders down there?" Megan asked, tilting her head in confusion. Miguel had refused to ride Rambo, and apparently he was the top rider at the Baja Tinda. It didn't make sense to send Rambo to another riding school.

Garrett shrugged but didn't look at her.

"I think what's happening," Scott said, glancing at Megan, "is that Rambo will be someone else's problem. Their decision." His voice hardened when he looked back at Garrett. "That's a heartless thing to do with a horse who's won a million dollars."

"But I can't keep him," Garrett said. "He's dangerous under saddle, difficult on the ground. Lydia doesn't even let her grooms work on him. Yet she's the one making the biggest stink."

"Did you check his papers?" Scott asked. "Maybe someone offered a home after he's...used up."

Garrett flinched at Scott's tone but didn't back down. "I run a business. And I'm not the one who made the big bucks. He's been nothing to me but hospital bills."

"I could call his past owners," Megan said tentatively. "My brother did that once and placed our old Quarter Horse. The breeder was happy to get him back—"

"That's just plain stupid." Garrett's head snapped around, and the anger in his voice made her recoil. "The horse is going to Mexico."

"After she's tried calling," Scott said, pushing Rambo forward. "And I don't think it's stupid."

The steel in his voice was unmistakable. Laughter sounded from the jock barn and a horse called from a paddock, but around them the air was taut. She could definitely picture Scott as a cop—a tough and formidable one.

A flush climbed Garrett's neck. She looked down, pretending to straighten Braun's mane, guessing he wouldn't like a student to see him challenged. But surely Rambo deserved a chance? It wouldn't even cost anything. Most people would rather have their horse placed in a home, not dead-ended at a meat plant.

"You're right," Garrett said, stepping back and raising his palms in surrender. "I'll wait and give Megan a chance to place him."

She blew out a pent-up breath, her tension easing. It was fortunate Scott had backed her up. Now she only prayed a previous owner would be generous enough to provide a home. If not, Rambo would still be shipped out and Garrett would be doubly annoyed.

Scott gave a reassuring nod as though sensing her doubts. "It's worth a shot, Megan. Let's put these horses away and you can start calling previous owners."

"And I'll bring over the horse's papers," Garrett said. He adjusted his sunglasses, sweeping them both with an agreeable smile—a smile that was big and white, but somehow seemed forced.

CHAPTER TWENTY-SIX

"Rambo's not suitable for a beginner rider or even an intermediate," Megan said into the phone. "But he's sound, after sixty-two races. What a testimonial to your breeding program."

Scott tore his gaze away and glanced back at his laptop, trying not to eavesdrop. However, Megan looked so beautiful, so passionate. He loved her generous nature and how gamely she was trying to save a battle-scarred horse. Her conversation was much more entertaining than analyzing Snake's report, but what the hell, he liked looking at her, even when she was sleeping. It had been a long time since he'd been so attracted to a woman—not since Amanda.

Of course, that had ended badly.

He tossed his pen on the table, walked into the kitchen and refilled his coffee cup. Megan wasn't like Amanda, other than he sometimes didn't understand her moods. Now she sat at the kitchen table, oblivious to his scrutiny, fielding questions from someone on the phone while at the same time loyally defending Rambo.

"No, he doesn't bite," she said. "He just pretends to be grumpy. People don't matter a whole lot to him."

And that's exactly my problem, Scott thought.

I don't matter much to Megan. It was apparent she hadn't wanted to see him tonight but he'd lured her out with talk of Rex. And she was here this afternoon, but only because of Rambo.

Sure, she was willing enough once his hands and mouth were on her but if not for Rambo, she'd be hanging out with her friends today. She viewed him as temporary, never asking questions about his past or dropping hints about their future.

Now normally a beautiful woman who was satisfied with simple sack time made him very happy. Grateful even. But Megan was holding back when he wanted to charge forward. It was frustrating.

"Okay then," she said. "Bye."

"Are they interested?" He propped his hip against the counter, studying her bright eyes as she cut the connection.

She leaped from the chair, surprising him with a hug. "They're going to think about it. Rambo was foaled there. Sold as a weanling but they were very open and appreciated the call. They might take him."

He curved his arm around her waist. If she was giving away hugs, he intended to take full advantage. "Where's their farm?" he asked.

"Kentucky." She peered up at him, her eyes shining with gratitude. "Thank you so much. For making Garrett agree. That's two no's, one maybe, and I have another number to call. Cross your fingers for this last one. They owned him when he raced at Del Mar."

She looked so sweet, so happy about saving an old warhorse, that he couldn't resist dipping his head. "We need a kiss for luck," he said, finding her mouth, but keeping it brief.

Damn, he couldn't keep his hands off her. Maybe he scared her. Maybe that was the problem. He straightened and turned for the coffee. "Want a refill?" he asked.

"No more coffee for me. I'm going home after we see Rex. Catch up on the sleep we didn't get last night." She flashed him a teasing smile.

There it was again, a reminder she wasn't staying and despite her pretty smile, it was pissing him off. He wanted to know everything about her, from her first horse to her last boyfriend.

She didn't even care how he liked his coffee. Preferred to be in a cramped dorm with a giggly girl fresh out of high school.

"Well," he said, "if your roommate locks you out again, or wants to stay up late—what is she, ten years younger?—you can always use one of my spare rooms."

She gave a distracted nod, not even reacting to the little dig. She wasn't at all insecure about her looks, her age or maybe she simply didn't care. But she did care about her friends, certainly about Tami and Eve, and that gave him another angle.

"And we could set up the back room," he said, watching her expression, "as the Joey Collins op center."

Her head shot up, and he knew he had her. "Where we'll maintain charts of the last sightings," he added smoothly. "Map where he's been. Figure out his territory." He kept a straight face, trying to remember what the TV shows did so he could throw out the terms that clients loved to hear. "Get in Joey's mind," he went on. "Understand his psych. Draw up a profile of drug dealers."

"Eve swears he's not a drug dealer," she said.

"Maybe, maybe not." It was understandable Eve wouldn't believe anything bad about her boyfriend, but Garrett and Ramon were more objective.

"Could you look into the Baja Tinda too?" she asked. "That's where Joey was going. And I was thinking, maybe you and I could go to Mexico. Retrace his steps." She tilted her head, studying him thoughtfully. "Do you speak much Spanish?"

Jesus. He jerked in surprise. She clearly was expecting much more than a few colorful posters. "I'm fluent," he said cautiously. "But I don't think a trip to Mexico is necessary. Especially since Joey's been spotted around here. A lot can be done with a computer. But I'll look into the Baja Tinda."

She nodded, her face glowing with eagerness. "I was thinking we should check out Miguel and Ramon too. Miguel has a tattoo on his left arm, some sort of cross with weird symbols. Would it help if I took a picture?"

He picked up his coffee mug, studying her over the rim. "How long have you known Eve? You seem very eager to find her ex-boyfriend."

"He's not ex," she said, fingering her phone. "They never even broke up. He just disappeared. And she needs him."

"Why?"

Megan stared at her phone, but her fingers wouldn't remain still and he caught the way she tugged at her lip. Definitely evasive.

"Is Eve missing her supplier?" he asked, unable to keep the distaste from his voice. "Garrett said—"

Her head shot up. "Did Garrett accuse Eve of using drugs too? You're just like everyone else. If that's your attitude, forget it. I can do this myself."

He set the mug down, trying to control his impatience. "Just make sure you're telling me everything, Megan. Because I've never condoned drugs. If anything shakes out from this, all parties will be turned over to the police. Garrett feels just as strongly."

"I'd hoped you'd be able to think a little independently of your buddy, Garrett."

"And I hoped you'd be a little more honest." His coffee tasted bitter now, and he dumped it into the sink. "Why don't you make that last call and then we'll drive to the vet clinic. Where we can visit Rex and see Joey's handiwork up close."

Her face whitened and he immediately regretted his words. He wasn't a cruel man, but that had been unkind. Hell, maybe he was jealous of her interest in Joey Collins. He opened his mouth to apologize but she stopped him with such a look of disdain, he snapped it shut.

She picked up the phone.

He wheeled and walked into the second bedroom on the left. Shoved the bed against the wall. Opened up a card table and placed it in the middle of the floor. He slapped Joey's file on the center of the table. The file was thin now, but in a few days it would be bulging. He'd make sure of it.

He removed three framed pictures from the wall and jammed them into the closet. Maps of Mexico and California would replace them. And he'd nail up anything else that might please her. He'd have to compensate Garrett for the wall holes, but if she wanted a real investigation, she'd damn well get one.

When he returned to the kitchen, she was talking on the phone.

"Yes, Rambo's still like that," she said into the mouthpiece. "He's extremely confident. Has a very high opinion of himself." She glanced up and for a moment, Scott thought she was talking about him.

"I'm so glad you want him," she went on. "I'm his groom and he's definitely a very cool horse."

She shot Scott a wary smile, and he forgot his frustration and smiled back. Obviously she'd found Rambo a home. Five minutes later, she pressed the button to disconnect and gave a delighted fist pump.

"That lady owned Rambo six years ago," she said. "Once he dropped into the claiming ranks, she lost track of him. Apparently he was always tough to gallop but very professional in a race. He won almost a quarter million dollars for her family. They have a field set aside for their retirees and even made a little pond so older horses can stay cool." Her smile widened. "He's welcome anytime."

"Good work," Scott said. "You saved him. If he bucked riders off in Mexico, he wouldn't have lasted long."

Her face shadowed at the mention of Mexico, and he reached out and took her hand. "Come with me."

He led her down the hall and into the newly created investigative office.

"My assistant, Belinda, did some checking," he said, flipping open Joey's file. "There's no evidence Joey ever crossed the border back into California. But Garrett is fairly certain he saw Joey club Rex."

She started to protest, but he pressed a gentle finger over her mouth.

"There was also a break-in at Lydia's villa," he went on, "where the only item stolen was Joey's iPod. So he either crossed the border illegally or is operating under some other ID. I want to question your friend, Eve. See if she knows any of Joey's contacts. And I'm also going to call his parents."

"I can talk to his parents," she said quickly, her fingers tightening around his hand. "Please, let me do that. I want to help."

He paused. Often it was how people spoke or what they didn't say, but she was squeezing his hand like a lifeline, and they'd probably catch Joey creeping around Eve's dorm anyway. Besides, when Megan looked at him with those glowing eyes, how could he refuse?

"All right," he said. "But you'll have to work with me from this office. All paperwork and files remain here. This villa has excellent security."

"Okay." She gave a grave nod. "And I'll try to get a picture of Miguel's tattoos. I don't know if I can see Ramon without a shirt though."

"No, sweetheart. Stay away from Miguel and Ramon." His hand tightened protectively. Her enthusiasm scared him. Ramon was too taciturn for an easy read but Miguel eyeballed girls like they were candy. Cheap disposable candy.

"But Ramon said Joey deserted the horses," she said. "So it's important to find out if he's lying. There must be ways of checking Ramon's background, if someone knew what they were doing...someone like you." She stared up at him with those beautiful eyes, blowing away his plan of throwing up a few colorful maps.

He gave a rueful sigh. Like it or not, the Joey Collins' investigation had begun in earnest.

Belinda was going to be livid.

CHAPTER TWENTY-SEVEN

Rex whined and licked Megan's hand, his tail thumping with delight.

"That's the happiest I've seen him," the technician said, smiling at Scott. "He's doing well though. He may have a tiny limp, but Dr. MacLeod says there's so much callus forming, he'll never break his leg in that spot again. It's unfortunate she didn't know you were coming tonight. She would have demonstrated the infrared treatment."

"We'll come again," Scott said. "It's obvious the dog likes to see Megan."

Rex was certainly happy to see her, but Megan doubted the technician noticed. The shapely blonde hadn't pulled her eyes off Scott and was practically rubbing her boobs in his chest.

"Here's my number," the technician said, pressing a card in Scott's hand. "If you're driving through after hours, call me at home and I'll be happy to meet you at the clinic. You too, Mrs. Baldwin," she added, although Megan noted the woman didn't pass her a business card.

"This is Megan Spence." Scott curved his palm around Megan's waist. "And she's certainly not married to Garrett."

It was rather insulting how emphatic he spoke, as though she wasn't good enough for his highbrow friend.

"Sorry," the technician said, glancing at Rex's chart and then back at Scott. "I thought she was the owner since the dog likes her so much."

"Everyone likes her," Scott said. He kept his hand on Megan's hip and shot her one of his intimate smiles, the kind that crinkled the corners of his eyes and filled her with a rush of confidence.

And then she understood. He wasn't trying to belittle her. He was merely marking his territory. And he wasn't a flirt. He'd blocked the technician's advances as effectively as he always did Lydia's and the other fawning students. Likely he wasn't the type to desert a family either.

On the other hand if he did leave, he'd be hard to forget. Maybe impossible. It had taken her mother ten years to recover when her dad had walked out, and her father hadn't been much of a man. Losing someone like Scott would really leave a woman shattered.

He was studying her, as usual picking up on her misgivings. Megan turned her attention back to Rex. "When will he be able to go home?" she asked the technician.

"Oh, he's ready now. But Garrett requested that he stay so he can receive the light and magnet treatment. It's expensive but will speed the healing."

Rex pressed his nose over Megan's arm, his eyes imploring. She scratched behind his ear, torn by his heart-rending plea. She didn't want to walk away and leave him in this sterile clinic with the artificial lights and stinky disinfectant and crying cats.

"We can come back tomorrow," Scott said. "If you're free."

It was unwise to spend too much time with Scott, but Rex clearly enjoyed her visit and she hated to leave the dog. He seemed to think she was deserting him—and that was a horrible feeling. However, she had one more thing to check. Still rubbing the base of his ear, she pulled Joey's shirt from her purse.

She waited, afraid to breathe, but Rex didn't react. He simply stared up at her with liquid brown eyes, as though realizing she was going but he still loved her anyway. And her heart cracked.

"See you soon, fellow," she whispered, stuffing the shirt back into her purse then turning and leaving the room. Rex whined in protest, but she wasn't tough enough to look back.

She trudged to the car, waiting while Scott unlocked the door.

"Okay super sleuth," he said, after he eased the vehicle from the curb. "Whose shirt did you have?"

"Joey's. It was an old one Eve gave me. Don't you

think Rex would have reacted if it had been Joey who hurt him?"

"Maybe the scent was too faint."

"There would have been some reaction. Eve said she hadn't washed it. And Rex didn't even twitch. He just wanted me to take him home."

"I imagine you're used to that," Scott said.

She shot him a sideways look. He was the one who had women passing out their home numbers, and she expected more credit for thinking of the shirt. "Admit it," she said. "Rex didn't react to Joey's shirt. No growl, no whine, no flinch. Nothing."

"Sure, he didn't do anything," Scott said. "But that doesn't prove much. Animals are notoriously unpredictable."

"But if he growled at a shirt, that would mean something, right?"

"It would give an indication, yes." He reached over and tucked her hand in his. "But I don't want you running around collecting men's shirts. Or taking pictures of chest tats. Let me look after the investigation while you concentrate on your riding program."

He went on to speak about legalities and court issues and a bunch of other stuff but his thumb was rubbing the underside of her wrist, and she always found it hard to concentrate when he touched her like that. Soon she'd be panting like one of his lovestruck groupies.

"Where would you like to eat?" He released her hand and turned down the town's main street. "Garrett said there're a couple nice restaurants here."

"It doesn't matter," she said, trying to summon up some enthusiasm. She was more exhausted than hungry and never much liked sitting in stuffy restaurants. However, he seemed determined to keep her close. He was probably angling for another marathon sex session, while she just wanted to escape his dynamic presence and re-erect her defenses.

The horses couldn't be used as an excuse either, since Tami had offered to feed them in exchange for Megan washing her clothes. One thing for sure, she was sleeping in her own bed tonight. Her emotions were too fragile, and she needed to regroup. There wasn't any room for Scott, no matter how intense their attraction. The problem was she owed him...and she hated owing people.

"You pick the restaurant," she said, as they passed an attractive seafood house with stained glass windows and a statue of a giant marlin. "Any place you want," she added. "I'll pay, in exchange for your time."

"Absolutely not."

His words came out clipped and she glanced sideways. His eyes had narrowed and his mouth was clamped in a line. She hadn't meant to insult him, but clearly she had.

She folded her hands on her lap. "I just thought that since you're helping find Joey that I should buy dinner."

"Really? I don't think that's what this is about." He raised an eyebrow and whipped the car in a sharp left, then glanced back at her with those intelligent gray eyes.

He was far too savvy, and she blew out a sigh. "And then I thought you could drive me home and I wouldn't feel like we needed to have sex," she said. "I'm sorry, but I'm really tired tonight."

His jaw still looked like it was carved from granite, and her throat felt just as tight.

"You've never slept with someone," he asked, "and not had sex?"

No. However, she crossed her arms and gave a worldly sniff. "Well, of course...probably. But we both know sex is the main reason people sleep together. And I'm really tired."

He picked up the phone and ordered a pizza but didn't ask what she wanted on it, so she guessed he was truly annoyed. He stopped at a pizza joint next to a secondhand car dealer and ten minutes later reappeared with a large white box.

He dropped it on her lap but it was much too hot, so she moved it to the floor.

The drive back was silent but not uncomfortable. He didn't turn the music on and neither of them spoke. The smell from the pizza filled the car, leaving her mouth watering, and she realized she was rather hungry after all.

It made sense to eat a slice or two before she went home, although maybe he was too disgruntled to give her any. Guys often turned sulky when things didn't go their way.

He pulled into the driveway of his villa. "You can pay

for half," he said. "Ten bucks. Dry your clothes, eat, and then I'll take you home."

She nodded, relieved he was going to share the pizza. Her stomach rumbled now and there was certainly more than enough for two.

She followed him into his villa, detouring to the washing machine where her clothes waited in a soggy clump. She tossed them in the dryer and walked into the kitchen, following the mouthwatering smell.

She climbed up on a stool. He slid a slice of pizza in front of her, a thick piece loaded with cheese and meat and vegetables, and it was clear he hadn't skimped on the ingredients.

Two glasses sat on the counter, filled with Coke and ice, and she took a big swallow. Then slammed down the glass, sputtering with shock.

"What's in this?" she asked, coughing and wiping her mouth. "Rum?"

"You're acting like a guy," he said, "so tonight you get a guy's drink."

Fair enough. She shrugged and took another sip before biting into the pizza. It was only lukewarm now but still delicious. They chewed silently with Scott topping up their drinks while she cut them both another slice.

"I didn't know I was so hungry until I smelled the pizza," she said.

"You missed a few meals today."

He didn't sound quite so chilly and she gave a cautious smile. "So did you. And you had to deal with Rambo, not the most relaxing ride." She studied him over the rim of her glass. "Eve might be able to handle that horse," she said, "but I definitely can't."

"Then why did you offer to take her place?"

His incisive gaze drilled into hers and she shifted on the stool. However, the pizza, the alcohol and her bone deep weariness bogged down her brain, and she couldn't think of a plausible reason that wasn't a lie. "That's really between Eve and me," she said. "And her friendship is important. Could I have a little more rum?"

He obligingly poured a generous amount of amber fluid into her glass, followed up with a splash of Coke then rinsed the dishes, brushing off her attempts to help. Finally she gave up and simply propped her elbows on the counter, sipping her drink and trying not to yawn.

He studied her face, then tossed the dishcloth in the sink. "Come on," he said, snagging his glass and the bottle.

She followed him into the living room, pausing to listen for the dryer. It was still whirring, stuffed with three pairs of Tami's jeans, two of hers, and a motley bunch of shirts and underwear. Drying would probably take another twenty minutes and then she'd leave, despite what Scott wanted.

Actually, he didn't seem to care now that she wasn't staying. He'd turned on the television, watching intently as a massive guy with no neck explained to a pretty interviewer why he was retiring. She hesitated, wondering if she should just leave and pick up the clothes in the morning.

"Sit down." He patted the sofa beside him. "Ever watch much football?"

"No." She hit the coffee table with her knee and dropped onto the sofa, feeling unusually clumsy.

"Ever had a boyfriend who watched it?" he asked, managing to refill their drinks without shifting his attention from the screen.

She held her glass up against the light, studying the ice cubes and the prints her fingers left on the condensation. "I never had much time for television or sports." *Or boyfriends.* "It's been really busy, trying to get the jewelry established," she added.

"Really busy," he asked, "but you left it for jock school?"

She shot him a wary look but he seemed engrossed in the screen, not paying her much attention. "Yes, well I heard a lot of good things about this riding school." She took another sip, surprised the rum was going down so easily. Normally she preferred wine. "And it's good to do that kind of stuff, you know...when you can."

"When you can?" He glanced sideways, his eyes gliding over her face. "What do you mean?"

"It's good to go away and do things before you have other commitments, like kids and stuff." She waved a hand, almost spilling her drink. "You know, people shouldn't take off when they have commitments. It's important to be dependable."

He looked away from the television, even though the

people seemed to be sharing a hilarious joke. "So that's why you're so skittish," he said, prying the glass from her hand.

"Skittish? You make me sound like a horse. And I'm not skittish."

His smile was deep and gentle. "I think you had a boyfriend and he was crazy enough to treat you badly."

She shook her head but the motion made her dizzy so she stopped and pressed a finger against her lip, realizing they were slightly numb. "No boyfriend," she muttered. "They aren't dependable."

He slipped his arm over her shoulders. "I'm dependable, sweetheart. And when you're finished your riding program here, I'm going to visit you in L.A. See the little earrings you make, lie on your sofa and drink beer, and when you let me, watch some football."

She tilted her head, imagining him squeezed into her bungalow. He was a man who took up a lot of space and there was hardly any open floor. When she'd first started her business it had been more organized, with everything contained to one room. Now the studio bulged and her creations covered every horizontal space. Her sofa was tiny too. There'd be no room for him there. She could afford a bigger place but it was too much trouble to move. Besides, she loved her private location, nestled in the foothills but still close to the city.

"And sometimes we'll have sex," Scott went on, his voice a soothing rumble. "And sometimes we won't. But we'll still sleep together." He tilted her chin. "We have a good thing here. Don't fight it." His eyes locked on her face and for a moment he looked uncertain, which was odd because she doubted he'd ever been uncertain in his life. "So...how's that sound to you?"

"The sex part sounds okay," she said, trying to lighten the mood. But he was scowling now and she didn't want to admit that even a dog was too much of a commitment. Although dogs were loyal, especially ones like Rex. Maybe she *should* get a dog.

She was even starting to like being around people more, even though Tami's constant chatter sometimes hurt her head. And she'd definitely miss Scott. He was dependable and if he said he'd do something—like help find Joey—he'd do it. It was unfortunate he was Garrett's close friend.

"You're missing the point here, sweetheart," Scott said, sighing as she rattled the ice in her empty glass. "And you don't need any more to drink."

Her thoughts were skipping and she couldn't remember what points they were discussing. Her fuzziness couldn't all be blamed on exhaustion. Their last few drinks had been less Coke and more rum, and she'd matched him glass for glass.

"You're the one who wanted me to drink rum," she said, "and I'm not used to it." She tried to sound indignant. However, it had been excellent rum. In fact, it had been the smoothest drink she'd ever enjoyed.

"A common investigative technique," he said, tucking her head against his shoulder, a spot that was oddly comfortable despite its hardness. "I'm thinking you were married before?" He lifted her hair and rubbed the skin on her neck. "Obviously, unhappily."

His fingers felt good and she didn't want to dislodge them, so she was careful not to shake her head.

"I've never been married," she said, her face pressed into his shirt. "I started the jewelry business right out of university. It's been really, really busy. Much too busy to let bossy men lie on my sofa and drink beer."

"I see." His voice softened as if he were smiling. "Then why did you leave such a booming career? Why did you choose jockey school?"

She tilted her head, studying his aggressive cheekbones, the stubborn line of his jaw. He wasn't the type to give up easily—that was obvious from all she'd read on the Internet. And it would be comforting to tell him the truth. To admit why she was really here. And to share her suspicions about the school.

About Garrett's school.

She traced the raised abrasion on the side of Scott's forehead. When they'd first met, he'd refused to talk about it. But they were definitely much closer now. And if he could confide a little, maybe she would too. "How did this happen?" she asked.

"A kidnapping case. The money was paid, but they never intended to let the kid go."

She knew it was the Stevens case, knew his role in it, but he wasn't the type to brag. If she admitted she was

Joey's sister, he'd probably keep his mouth shut. Although maybe not around Garrett.

Her finger drifted over the tiny mark on his cheek, a scar, not a dimple, and something that made him look oddly vulnerable. He remained still, as though aware she was deciding something.

"Garrett and I were target shooting," he said, his eyes on her face. "A piece of rock cut me."

"You've been friends a long time," she said. "Do you trust him?"

"With my life."

"That's a very good friend." *Too good a friend. Obviously he'd side with Garrett.* She flattened her lips and turned away, listening for the dryer. "I have to go now," she said. "Do you think my clothes are ready?"

He tilted her chin, pulling her attention back. "Who do you trust?" he asked. "Quick. Don't think."

"Eve," she said.

"Interesting. You've only known her a few weeks. That's it?"

"You made me hurry." She frowned. "There're all kinds of other people. Besides, you only said one. You say two names quickly. See how hard it is."

"Snake, T-Bone."

"Too weird. You're making those people up." She lurched to her feet. "And I really have to go. I'll pick up the clothes tomorrow."

He rose, much more gracefully than she, and strode down the hall. "I'll walk you back," he said. "But first I need a jacket. It's cold tonight."

She tagged along beside him, disappointed at the prospect of a fifteen-minute hike. "Wouldn't it be easier to take your car?" she asked. "Since we're both sleepy." She studied his face but he didn't look tired. In fact, his expression looked almost mischievous.

"I'm not driving," he said, pulling on a jacket. "Not after I've been drinking."

"But it's private property," she said weakly. "And there are no other cars."

He shook his head and swung open the door, letting in a rush of night air so chilly it blasted her face.

"Do you have an extra jacket I could borrow?" she asked, stepping back from the onslaught of cold air.

"No. But if your roommate has company and you have to wait in the barn, I can unlock the tack room. Maybe find you a horse blanket." He adjusted the sheepskin collar on his jacket then reached back in the closet and made a show of pulling on gloves.

"Never mind looking for a scarf and hat." She rolled her eyes at his theatrics. "Guess it would be easier if I just slept here tonight."

"Good idea," he said, his mouth twitching. "But we both need our sleep. So no sex. No matter how much you beg."

"Fine." She was keen to climb into bed, any bed, but she didn't like to be outmaneuvered. "I need to get up early though, so please set the alarm for five. Bet you'll wish then I hadn't stayed."

"I'll take that bet," he said.

CHAPTER TWENTY-EIGHT

Clothes rustled from the side of the room, and Megan guessed it was time to get up, especially if Tami was rising. However, neither her body nor brain seemed inclined to listen. Her mouth felt parched but not so dry she wanted to lose those last precious minutes of sleep.

The mattress sagged and a hand curved around her hip. She stiffened, then memories flooded back. She remembered the pizza, the rum. And where she'd slept last night. She cracked open her eyes and peered at Scott's face.

"Did I sleep in?" she whispered.

"Yes." He tugged her into his warm body. "But your horses are fed. Go back to sleep."

"But who did it? Were you at the barn?" She leaned over his chest, straining to see the bedside clock, guessing it must be after six based on the light beyond the curtain.

"You need to catch up on your sleep, sweetheart," he said. "So better quit wiggling."

She could feel his growing hardness but was still confused. "You fed Rambo and Jake? But I still have to clean their stalls. And you don't even know what they eat."

"No problem. I just offered an 'A' to anyone who'd look after them. When I left, Tami and a bunch of other students were fighting for the job."

"Scott, that's not even funny. And I really have to go." But his hand was caressing her breast now, his mouth nuzzling her neck, and her voice lacked conviction.

"Actually I told Lydia how busy you were finding a home for Rambo and she said you should take the day off."

"But I already found him a home."

"She doesn't know that." He chuckled, his breath

warm against her skin. "And she's extremely grateful for your efforts. Now do you want more sleep? Because I'm trying to prove how dependable I am. And I don't want to blow it."

She blew out an exaggerated sigh but tilted her head, giving his mouth more room to explore. "I'm not sure if I need more sleep or not," she said. "It's a hard decision."

"Well, let me know what you decide," he said, skimming his mouth along her collarbone and using his fingers to tease her nipple to a taut point.

"Maybe if you could just..." She guided his head to her breast, wiggling as sensations rippled from her breasts to the suddenly damp spot between her legs. He was wonderfully thorough, paying attention to every hollow and curve and then he was too thorough, and she reached down, trying to grab him.

"I'm ready," she said, arching impatiently.

He chuckled and pinned her hand against the pillow. "What's your hurry? We have all morning, that is, if you've finished sleeping." He fanned a thumb over her nipple. "I'm thinking I need to go slow. Show you my best work."

"I'm fine with mediocre work," she said, reaching for him with her other hand and hooking a leg over his calf.

He gave a low laugh but flattened both hands above her head, and moved back to her mouth, plundering her in a deep kiss, exploring her face, her neck, her breasts, until she quivered with need.

She hooked both legs over his calves, but he pulled back, releasing her hands and sweeping her with his gaze.

"You're damn gorgeous," he said, and the way his eyes caressed her body made her feel beautiful. "But so impatient." His hand slipped to the inside of her thigh, stroking her with the pad of his thumb, so slow she wiggled with pleasure, the throb inside her building.

She grabbed his shoulders, trying to hurry him along, but his hands parted her legs, his head dipped and it felt so good. She tried to scoot away, knew she'd climax too fast, but he flattened a big hand over her stomach, holding her in place, and then she didn't want to escape any longer.

The orgasm left her weak and quivery.

"You shouldn't have done that," she said. "Now sleep just moved back to my priority list."

"Not for long."

"You're always so sure of yourself." She cracked open her eyelids, feeling marvelously languid. "But that was great."

He unrolled a condom and positioned himself over her. "You can sleep if you want, sweetheart. Or spread your legs a little wider. You decide."

She waited a beat, then gave a tender smile, unable to hide how he made her feel. "That's never a tough decision," she said.

"Here's the video you requested." Garrett dropped several labeled discs on the kitchen counter in front of Scott. "Joey Collins should be in some of them, although it's hit and miss. Lydia films the students more than Ramon, so most of these riders were in her class."

Megan glanced at the discs Garrett had delivered, then gave Scott a grateful smile. She hadn't even thought of school video. Already he was pursuing angles she hadn't considered, or been able to access. She wasn't sure what they might show, but the chance to see Joey made her inch forward on the stool.

Scott seemed to sense her eagerness and gave a quick wink before turning and pouring Garrett only half a cup of coffee.

"Not sure why you asked for that stuff," Garrett said, accepting the coffee and propping his hip against the counter. "You must be bored." He looked at Megan. "Maybe Scott should head back to L.A. since he always feels the need to hunt down criminals."

Megan wrapped her toes around the rung of the stool, resenting Garrett's reference to criminals. But she was determined not to say anything about Joey. Luckily, she and Scott had showered and finished breakfast before Garrett arrived. But the speculative look on the man's face showed that he guessed she'd stayed the night.

"Scott can't leave," she said, keeping her voice light. "The students love his course."

"Of course they do," Garrett said. "Especially the distaff portion of the class. Since we were little kids, he's always had to beat off the women. It always pissed me off." He gave a dismissive shrug but the way his eyes swept

Megan was almost demeaning.

She picked up her coffee mug and peeked at Scott. He'd stepped closer to her side. His expression hadn't changed but his displeasure was obvious in the way his shirt tightened over his shoulders.

"What's wrong, Garrett?" he asked, his voice flinty cold, almost unrecognizable from the tender one he'd used in the shower only an hour earlier.

"It's just that a tech from the vet clinic called," Garrett said, frowning at Megan. "Ostensibly to give an update on Rex, but she slid in some loaded questions. Trying to find out if Scott was single. Rather amusing. But as director of the school, I need to be aware of any relations, especially ones between students and instructors."

"Temporary instructor," Scott said, wrapping his hand around hers. "What's the problem? You knew we were seeing each other."

"I didn't know it was this serious. I thought, since Amanda, you know..." Garrett's eyes flickered over their linked hands. "Guess I'll have to file a consensual relationship form. But this is a complication."

"File whatever is necessary," Scott said. "But don't worry. I promise to mark her extra hard."

"Not necessary," she said. "I'm dropping his course."

"No." Both men protested at the same time.

She nodded, straightening on the stool. Garrett was clearly unhappy with the situation, and the addictions course didn't even matter. Not to her. Dropping it was the ethical thing to do. She didn't want to cause tension between the two men.

"My worries are with the other instructors," Garrett said. "I have no qualms about Scott's professionalism. Although this explains why he supported you with Rambo. But what I don't understand is why you're so interested in Joey?" Garrett's voice was calm but the blue eyes that drilled into her face were surprisingly icy.

"I, um..." she paused, struggling for words.

"Eve is her friend," Scott said. "Naturally Eve wants to know where Joey is, and why he left the school. Megan just wants to help."

Garrett's attention swung back to Scott. "So that explains why Joey and Eve were always together. So your interest in this stems from the Eve girl." He took a thoughtful sip of coffee. "I doubt the police even talked to her. Guess that's the reason I'm supposed to pay more attention to these little school flings."

Little school flings. Megan pressed her arms closer to her sides, wondering if Garrett knew how much his words hurt.

"No problem." Scott gave Megan's hand a reassuring squeeze. "I'll be talking to Eve later today. I'm hoping she can give me a better picture of Joey. Right now, it's still murky."

"Well, we didn't have a PI on it before," Garrett said dryly. "Let me know if you need anything else... Maybe you'll catch Joey in time to pay Rex's vet bill."

Megan set her mug down on the counter, the sound jarringly loud. But she was no longer able to ignore Garrett's snide comments. "Are you sure it was Joey you saw that night?" she asked.

"Without a doubt," Garrett said, pushing away from the counter. "Don't drop the course, Megan. It's not necessary. And I want to thank you for finding a home for Rambo. And for visiting my dog. Rex ate all his food this morning, and the cast is coming off in four weeks." He gestured at the front door and raised an eyebrow. "Walk me out, Scott?"

Megan remained at the counter, sipping her coffee as the two men walked down the hall. But their voices drifted, not from the front door but from the other side of the villa, and it was apparent Scott was showing Garrett the new office. They lingered there, laughing about something.

She rinsed the breakfast dishes and placed them in the dishwasher, the mundane tasks easing her annoyance. Garrett had made some pointed remarks about Scott's old girlfriend—sometime she'd have to drum up the nerve to ask Scott about Amanda—and Garrett's comment about flings had definitely been disparaging. But the bond between the two men was obvious.

She didn't have a single friend like that. Her school buddies had scattered after her drug bust, and she'd chosen to be a loner at university.

Scott seemed to think she was a hermit, and granted, maybe she was. But she intended to change that. She'd definitely keep in touch with Eve and Tami, and there might possibly be a baby in her life, and everything was going to be different. Maybe she'd even get a dog, and hopefully she'd keep seeing Scott, and she was going to work harder at building relationships.

She was so distracted by the fresh possibilities, she didn't realize Scott had returned to the kitchen.

"Sorry about that, sweetheart." He brushed a gentle kiss over the top of her head. "Garrett can be a bit of a pain. But aside from his big mouth, he only wants to help."

"We should have been more discreet," she said. Garrett had tried to mask his reaction, but his displeasure had been obvious. He'd actually looked stunned to see Scott holding her hand. Or was it her presence in Scott's villa so early on a Sunday morning?

"And we probably shouldn't have said anything about looking for Joey," she adding, fighting a growing sense of unease.

"But Garrett's already helped by bringing the DVDs," Scott said. "I can tell you're interested in watching those."

She nodded, shaking off her concern. Scott was right. Garrett didn't seem to mind their relationship, only the administrative hassle it created. And it was worth telling Garrett that they were searching for Joey, if only to get the video.

She slid her hands beneath Scott's shirt, rather surprised she still needed to touch him. It was amazing some lucky woman hadn't snagged him. She was just grateful he wasn't married. Obviously he'd been close to the altar and something had happened. Something he didn't want to talk about.

He was silent for a moment, just holding her close. "About what Garrett said..." Scott cleared his throat. "Amanda was my fiancée. She died of a heroin overdose."

Megan groaned and reached for his hand.

"I tried to help." His voice sounded rusty. "I was a cop then. You'd think I could have helped...but I didn't do enough."

The pain in his voice made her ache. There was nothing worse than watching a loved one self-destruct. And feeling helpless. Twice Joey had left rehab. The third time he'd stayed.

"She sold her engagement ring," Scott said slowly. "Sold everything. Nothing mattered but her next fix. She died on the street." He had a distant look in his eyes but still held her hand. "After that, it was too hard to deal with druggies in the alley. They weren't faceless anymore."

"That's why you left the police force?" A lump constricted her throat. "I'm sorry, Scott."

"Private work lets me choose my own jobs. Avoid the ones I hate."

"So my asking you to look for Joey...a possible drug dealer. That's why Garrett was so surprised." She winced then pressed her forehead against his chest.

"Now he realizes how important you are to me," Scott said.

Her emotions swirled—pain and empathy but also joy. She was important to him. This wasn't temporary. He wasn't going to leave. Her breath leaked in soft surrender. "You're important to me too," she whispered.

"Good," he said. "I wouldn't want to be in this alone."

They remained silent for a long moment, his arms wrapped around her, their hands clasped. "It's not any woman I fold clothes for," he added after another minute, or perhaps it was ten. But her chest was bursting with such happiness that time was immeasurable.

She glanced up, savoring their closeness, the comfortable silence that said so much. "You folded my clothes?"

"Yes," he said. "And there were some very interesting items."

"Probably Tami's." She tried to look composed but the idea of his big hands sliding over her underwear made her breath quicken.

"Really," he said. "I could have sworn that sexy black lace would be a perfect fit. Maybe we should check it out." His voice lowered and his fingers were doing erotic things to her neck. She quivered and glanced toward his bedroom. He could turn her on faster than any man she'd ever known, but they weren't going to find Joey by jumping back into bed.

"We need to get to work," she said.

She slipped from his arms, scooped the discs off the counter and walked into the den. "What are we looking for?"

She inserted the first disc into the slot and clicked the remote.

"Not sure," Scott said, following her into the room. "But we definitely can't start watching yet."

Images of hopeful students flashed on the screen and she didn't want to press the pause button. Despite Eve's protests, Megan still wasn't certain Joey had been clean. But once she saw his face, she'd know. His eyes had always been a dead giveaway.

"Why can't we start?" she asked, still studying the screen. "Oh look, this must be the first time the class broke from the gate. I don't see him though." She dropped on the sofa and leaned forward, watching intently

"Megan."

Something in Scott's voice made her swing around.

"How do you know what Joey looks like?" he asked.

She stared into his narrowed eyes, appalled at her mistake. There were grad pictures in the cafeteria but certainly none of Joey. And Scott hadn't shown her any files yet. How would she know what he looked like?

"I saw his picture on Facebook," she said quickly.

"Anywhere else?"

She gave a weak headshake. "No. And they were a little grainy so if you have a better one it would help."

"Anywhere else?" he repeated. Scott's eyes had turned a gunmetal gray and he looked scarily imposing, a stark contrast to her tender lover.

"Of course." She copied his crisp tone. "His picture is on Eve's phone."

Scott studied her for a moment then jabbed his thumb at the screen. "Pause the video. Get his file from the office, some pads and a couple pens." His voice softened. "We need a good picture, Megan. We need something in front of us."

"Okay," she said. She pressed the pause button and hurried down the hall and into the new office.

It looked very professional. Scott must have been working this morning while she slept. A detailed map of Mexico hung on one wall. The Baja Tinda was circled in red. And the little town where Joey had apparently quit was also marked.

Another map showed Southern California and Joey's last known permanent residence—her family home. She stepped closer to the wall, studying the notations. The ranch looked closer to the ocean than it actually was and the road appeared much straighter. She'd loved that place, at least until her father grew tired of being a dad. Her mother always claimed it wasn't Megan's fault, but she knew differently. He'd left nine days after her brush with the law.

She picked up the file from the table and slowly opened it. Joey's face smiled back. She couldn't remember when the picture was taken, or how Scott had obtained it, but Joey's grin was as confident as ever. He would have been a daring jockey.

She dragged a finger over his cheek, staring with a well of longing. The back of her neck tickled. She turned. Scott stood in the doorway, his gaze on her face.

"Looks like a cocky kid," he said. "Most dealers are."

"As are most jockeys, farriers and cops," she said. She closed the file and glanced at the wall, trying to harness her emotion. The constant disparaging comments ripped at her heart, but she was still appreciative of his efforts. And soon he'd discover that Joey was innocent.

"This room looks great," she added. "I really like the maps. It looks like the big investigations they show on crime shows."

Amusement softened Scott's voice. "Exactly the look I was going for," he said.

Despite the absence of Joey in any of the video, Megan decided that it had still been an enjoyable morning.

She sighed as Scott adjusted her head against his shoulder and jotted down another notation. She'd given up hope of finding any footage of Joey and now was content with exploring the sculpted ridges of Scott's chest. It was odd but rather nice, just hanging out.

"So this is what you meant about relaxing on the sofa and watching TV," she said.

"This doesn't compare to watching football, sweetheart, but we have to start somewhere." He brushed her forehead with a kiss. "Besides, you can learn a lot about racing. Watch how the rider on the inside gets her horse up on the rail. She's patient, waiting for an opening. Then two jumps and she almost caught Jake and Miguel."

"Miguel looks taller than the other riders," Megan said. "Heavier too." She hadn't noticed how different he looked in the saddle. She'd been too busy handling her own horse.

"Yes, that's one of my questions for Garrett," Scott said. "The school has restrictions on height and weight, but it doesn't seem to apply to foreign students. Not to Miguel anyway. He's certainly an aggressive rider. Looks like he's shutting down the hole. Damn!"

Megan jerked upright as the horse on the inside abruptly flipped over the rail, his legs wind milling helplessly. Someone hollered and the screen turned gray. Scott grabbed the remote, jabbed to rewind, and they both leaned forward on the sofa.

"Son of a bitch," Scott said, after watching the replay again. "He deliberately put that girl through the rail."

Megan stared in shock, her nails curved tightly into her palms. It seemed horrifyingly blatant. Miguel had checked over his shoulder, spotted the rider gunning for the hole, but had tugged Jake to the left, forcing the streaking horse into the rail.

"But that's reckless riding," she said, horrified that Eve had to gallop with someone as dangerous as Miguel. "They'd kick him out for that... Wouldn't the school kick him out?"

"One would think," Scott said.

Megan stacked the pile of clean clothes on her bed, stepping sideways so Tami could reach past and grab her jeans.

"Thanks for washing my stuff," Tami said. "I'm going to wear these this afternoon. Miguel is taking me for a drive." Her voice turned sheepish. "That is, if you let me borrow your truck."

"I thought you didn't like the noisy muffler?" Megan teased.

"We're getting used to it. And today I want to cheer him up. We're going someplace where we can be totally alone." Tami tugged on her tight jeans, her eyes glinting with curiosity. "How's the studly professor?"

Megan shrugged and continued folding clothes but couldn't stop the smile that split her face.

"Obviously good," Tami said, grinning back. But her

expression turned wistful. "It's going to be horrible when they leave."

"What do you mean?" Megan asked. "Where's Miguel going?"

"Back to the Baja Tinda. He's driving down with Ramon and the horses."

"Oh, I didn't know. That's tough." But Megan's hands stilled over the shirt she was folding. It was also odd. Miguel hadn't been at the school very long, had only arrived after her first week. It didn't seem possible that he'd finished any modules that would count toward graduation.

"How many more courses did he need?" she asked, keeping her voice light.

"I don't know." Tami scowled and flopped onto the bed. "But he hasn't said anything more about my job in Mexico. He was in a really bad mood this morning, especially since Lydia made him scrub water buckets."

Megan laughed and resumed folding clothes. She was beginning to like Lydia. Ramon let Miguel do anything he wanted, but Lydia wasn't swayed by the fact that his father owned the Baja Tinda.

"It wasn't fair." Tami's voice turned petulant and she clearly didn't appreciate Megan's amusement. "It was Peter's turn to water, but Rambo kicked one of the grooms when they tried to oil his hooves and Lydia asked Peter to take over. So then she made Miguel do Peter's job. She wants Rambo all gussied up because his old owner is adopting him. But now they're short a horse for the trailer, and Miguel is mad." Tami wrinkled her nose. "He's no fun when he's mad."

"But if Rambo isn't any use to the Baja Tinda," Megan said, "why does Miguel even care? He's already refused to ride him."

"My Spanish isn't great and they talk too fast," Tami said. "But I overheard his father yelling that he needed four horses to cross the border." She pulled out her phone and checked her messages. "I'm going to push Miguel about that job down there," she added. "He's always nicer when he wants sex."

Megan's mouth tightened but she continued sorting clothes, relieved Miguel was leaving. Tami would be better off when he was gone. The ruthless way he'd forced that horse and rider through the fence was sickening. And if he was indicative of the type of people at the Baja Tinda, it wouldn't be a safe place for Tami to work anyway.

Baja Tinda. Even the name left a sour taste in her mouth.

"Tami," she said slowly, "I've seen Miguel's tat sleeve but not the rest. Is it a tattoo of a horse?"

Tami shook her head, concentrating on her phone. "No, it's just a bunch of stuff...stars, numbers, a snake. But the one on his stomach is totally cool. It goes real low. You should see where the arrow points."

"Oh, wow," Megan said, repressing a shudder. "I'd love to see that."

"Maybe I'll take a picture."

"Great," Megan said. "And in return, you can borrow my truck, today and tomorrow."

Tami gave a delighted smile. "That's a great deal."

Scott frowned after Snake finished reciting Joey's surprisingly short record. "That's it?" he asked. "Nothing more than possession? Maybe T-Bone missed something. You sure he found it all?"

"Boss, T-Bone can find out how many times I had sex last week."

"That I don't want to know," Scott said. "But send me everything you have on this Joey Collins kid. Go deep. School, record, family, friends. He might be a user, but at this point he doesn't sound like much of a dealer."

"This isn't our typical case." Snake's voice lowered, and Scott guessed Belinda was walking down the hall. "Are we working drug cases now?"

"No," Scott said. "Just a favor for a friend."

"Must be a special friend."

Scott leaned back in his chair, glad Snake couldn't see his silly smile. Megan was special. When she looked at him with those big beautiful eyes, he turned to putty. He wanted to look after her, take away that wariness and erase the sadness that crept into her face when she thought he wasn't looking.

"So this is for your lady friend," Snake said. "Want me run a background check on her?"

"Absolutely not."

Snake chuckled. "Then it must be serious. Good for you, man. About time too. Belinda will be ecstatic. Guess that's what fixed your headaches. When you coming home?"

"Soon," Scott said. He dragged a hand over his jaw. The school's permits had been renewed. Garrett had made it clear that his services were no longer required and that a new instructor could take over the class. But leaving midstream didn't feel right. Neither did leaving Megan.

Of course, she'd finish her program soon and then they'd both be in LA. Except for her occasional evasiveness, everything between them was good. And it was only natural she'd hold a few things back. She didn't let people get too close, something he intended to change.

Snake was now ranting about uncooperative LAPD, and Scott checked the time. Megan had only been gone an hour. But already he missed her. "So there's nothing very pressing then," he said.

"Nothing pressing?" Snake said. "Have you been listening? The cops want to block access, that lady at the club won't give up her list to anyone but you, and my snitch at the dock has been missing for three days."

"I'll make some calls." Scott jotted down a reminder on his yellow pad. "Don't worry about it."

Snake was silent for a moment, then snorted. "Damn," he said. "You got it bad."

Megan finished her barn chores then walked down the aisle, pausing to look into Rambo's stall. He was tied to a ring at the back of the stall, looking very disgruntled while Peter tidied his mane.

"Lydia seems to think I'm a groom," Peter said. However, his good-natured grin showed he didn't really mind. "This is earning me enough bonus points to graduate a week early," he went on. "Not to mention I'm happy for the horse. Can you stay here and hold his head? You're the only person he tolerates, but Lydia thinks you've been up too late and need a rest."

Megan steadied Rambo's head, turning so Peter wouldn't spot her blush. She didn't know what Scott had said, but he'd certainly smoothed her way with Lydia. And now he was going to find Joey. Everything was falling into place.

"You're going to look handsome for your new home," she said, scratching Rambo's polished neck. "I'll bring you some carrots as soon as Peter is finished."

"Yeah, I saw the truckload of carrots dumped behind our barn." Peter wrapped the comb around a strand of black mane and yanked. Rambo's ears flattened but he didn't move. "Why did Garrett arrange that?" Peter went on. "He doesn't strike me as a man who worries about animal treats."

Megan shrugged. Peter was right, but it was nice to have carrots for the horses. Besides, it saved bagging alfalfa and messing up Scott's car.

"Rambo looks super," she said. "Thanks for looking after him."

"I knew you were otherwise occupied." Peter gave a knowing wink. "Too damn busy to even turn on your phone."

She quickly pulled out her cell and switched on her phone. When she wasn't riding, she always kept it on, hopeful Joey might call. She'd only turned it off when she and Scott were lying on the sofa this morning, watching video. But that had been a waste of time since Joey hadn't been in any of the footage.

Not really a waste of time though. Being with Scott was a natural high, and she was eager to return to his villa for supper. He'd suggested she invite Eve too so he could conduct an informal interview. Finally, he'd learn the truth about Joey. The truth about everything.

And even though Eve distrusted Scott's friendship with Garrett, that was no longer a concern—not since Megan and Scott had reached a new level of intimacy. Megan was confident now he wouldn't put the school's wellbeing above hers. He was ethical, dependable and he wanted to see her back in LA. He'd probably try even harder to solve the case once he learned Joey was her brother.

"Someone's in love," Peter teased, jerking back her attention.

She didn't want him to see the dreamy look on her face so pretended to straighten Rambo's already neat forelock. The horse tolerated her fiddling with only a swish of his newly conditioned tail.

"Scott scares me a little," Peter went on, "but you were never afraid of anyone, even Lydia. I hope it works out."

Megan traced the white hair on Rambo's scarred cheek. She wasn't used to showing her feelings, particularly to a guy, but there was something about being in a barn that made deception unnecessary. Maybe the horses' innate honesty was contagious. She quit trying to hide her expression and shot Peter a tremulous smile. "Thanks," she said. "I really like Scott so I hope it works out too. Luckily we both live in LA."

Peter nodded. "Wish I had met someone here too, someone who likes horses as much as me." He gave a wistful sigh and tossed the comb in the grooming kit. "Rambo looks ready to race again. Bet Eve wishes she were riding horses half as good."

Eve might not be riding anything for nine months, Megan thought. She removed Rambo's halter and followed Peter from the stall, wondering if Eve would tell Scott she was pregnant. Wondered what he'd think when he heard Megan was Joey's sister and intended to help Eve with the baby. What did Scott even think about babies?

She latched the stall door, her fingers clumsy with anticipation. This was going to be a big interview, an all-important evening. And Eve could give Scott a much clearer picture of Joey since she didn't have a sister's perceived bias.

"With Eve gone," Peter went on, "that leaves Miguel as top jockey. Although he didn't look much like top dog when he was scrubbing buckets."

Megan's head jerked up. "What do you mean? With Eve gone?"

"Thought you knew. She left late this morning. Some guy Garrett knows offered her a job."

"A job? A riding job?"

"Yeah. The offer came in and she packed her helmet and left. She was sure excited. They were all celebrating at the jockey barn, even sharing their coffee with us. Did you know they have their own fridge? And washing machines?"

"Sorry, Peter," she said. "I have to go."

She charged from the barn, checking her phone as she ran. The screen was blurry and she could barely see but she wasn't sure if it was because of her tears or her jerky movements.

She whipped through her messages and finally spotted Eve's texts. She'd sent three. The last one said she'd call sometime and that was it. While Megan had been lying on the sofa, watching TV with Scott, her pregnant friend and Joey's only other supporter had packed her bags and left. To ride dangerous horses.

Megan bolted toward the parking lot, ignoring the stares of two curious grooms. Eve was probably travelling by bus. Maybe she was still at the station and Megan could catch up in her truck. She needed to talk to her about so many things. Wanted to plead for her to be careful. To consider the baby and not ride. And to beg her to stay and talk to Scott.

Eve was impulsive but inherently kind. Megan just needed to talk to her. Help her see reason. She fumbled in her pocket for her keys, then remembered. Tami had her truck.

She groaned, wishing now she hadn't loaned it. Wished she hadn't been lying on the sofa with Scott. She'd been far too complacent, certain that after he talked to Eve, he'd be motivated to find Joey.

She thumbed a frantic text message then stared at the screen, willing Eve to answer. Nothing. She tried calling her number. But a mechanical recording stated the phone was out of the service area.

Eve was gone, truly gone.

Megan's knees buckled. Gravel bit through her jeans, but she was unable to move. Could only press the phone to her face, trying to hold back her crippling despair.

CHAPTER TWENTY-NINE

"It's okay, sweetheart," Scott said. "Take some big breaths."

Megan flung her overnight bag in the corner by the door and paced around the table. "But you don't understand," she said. "Eve left!"

"It's not the end of the world. I can still interview her over the phone." Although he did prefer to talk to people in person. Liked to see their reaction to tough questions. "Where did she go?" he asked, keeping his voice mild.

"That's the problem." Megan whipped her head back and forth. Despite her reddened eyes, she looked beautiful. Beautiful but achingly vulnerable. "She's gone to ride real racehorses! Santa Anita, I guess."

He didn't see why it was such a problem but Megan looked shattered, frightened even. It left him uneasy. "Just give me her cell number," he said. "I'll call her."

"She's not answering. It's off. Or out of range." Her voice rose in distress. "Just like Joey's."

"Whoa, Megan. This is not the same thing at all." He couldn't stand it any longer and wrapped his arms around her, shocked at the tautness of her body. "Try to relax. This is a good move for Eve. Of course you'll miss her but she came to the school to be a jockey.

"I'll talk to Garrett," he went on. "Find out what trainer hired her. Maybe we can watch her races on the Internet."

"But she could get hurt. She shouldn't even be riding!"

"Why not?" His eyes narrowed as he pictured Eve. Pretty, petite, talented. Definitely a jockey's build. And she rode like a hellion with probably a temperament to match. But maybe she relied on drugs to boost her courage. She'd bolted from his class once, displaying erratic behavior.

Garrett thought Joey was slinking around the school, which meant drugs were still available. Someone must be helping Joey hide. Quite possibly that person had been Eve. But without Joey's girlfriend around, it'd be easier to find him, obtain answers. And ease Megan's mind. He hated seeing her anguish and intended to sort this out, even if it meant diverting his best investigators to the Joey Collins' case.

Megan was shaking her head now, her mouth set in a stubborn line. "I'm going after her. She's not thinking straight. I just need to know what trainer she's working for."

"You can't just leave," he said, rubbing the sudden ache in his temple. "That needs to be cleared with the school first."

"But I have to see her. You don't understand."

"Then tell me so I do understand." His jaw felt frozen, his words clipped.

"I can't." She wrung her hands, looking everywhere but at him. "It's her business, not mine. But it's important. *She's* important."

And he wasn't.

That thought wormed through his head no matter how hard he fought it. He'd always known he wasn't first on Megan's agenda—ironic since the only two women he'd ever wanted had secret passions he didn't understand. And now she was blocking him out again.

He tried one last time. "Tell me about Eve," he said. "Maybe I can help."

"She told me not to say." Megan shook her head and rushed toward the door. "But Tami's coming back soon and then I'm going to Santa Anita. I just need you to find out the trainer's name. I'll drop back after I get my truck."

She slammed the door behind her.

He sank down on a chair, rubbing his throbbing head. Santa Anita racetrack. Ten hours' drive, up and back. Garrett and Ramon would be irate. But maybe they'd cut her some slack if he explained the situation.

Unfortunately he didn't understand the situation. And 'to talk to Eve' wasn't much of an excuse. But maybe Megan would change her mind and not go.

He glanced toward the front door, somewhat consoled that she'd left her overnight bag.

***

Megan charged past the paddocks toward the barn. Her truck was back in the parking lot so fortunately Tami and Miguel had returned. She'd be able to find Eve and plead with her to consider the baby. She'd bring her checkbook too. She should have discussed child support and reviewed all the options. However, Eve's job offer had been so unexpected.

She waved at Peter but didn't stop to talk, just booted up the dorm steps, slipped the key from the planter and flung open the door.

The curtains were drawn, the room strangely dark for mid-afternoon.

She switched on the light then jerked in horror. Tami curled on the bed, her eyes so swollen she was barely recognizable.

"I look awful, don't I?" Tami mumbled. "We went for a walk in the woods. Guess I'm allergic to something."

Allergic to Miguel. Megan hid her dismay and rushed across the room, dropping to her knees by the bed. "What happened? Was the job offer bogus?"

"It's nothing. You know how my eyes swell when I cry."

"But why are you crying...so much?"

"You must think I'm stupid." Tami's shoulders shook in a shuddering sob. "*He* sure does."

"You're not stupid. Miguel is an asshole. Not worth the tears. And you'll find a job without him." Megan couldn't resist checking her watch. She really had to catch that bus. "There are a lot of other jobs," she added. "Eve's already been hired at Santa Anita."

"I know. I heard Miguel and Ramon talking." Tami rolled over on her side and gave a wan smile. "I figured you asked Scott to pull some strings and find Eve a job. You're always nice to everyone."

Megan shook her head. "I didn't know anything about the job. She was already gone when I left Scott's place today. What did Miguel and Ramon say?"

"Nothing much." Tami averted her gaze. "But they found another Thoroughbred from the ranch next door so the trailer's leaving tonight. I won't see Miguel for a while...and he doesn't even care."

Megan reached out to give Tami's arm a consoling squeeze but felt her wince. And Tami wore a long-sleeved shirt. A strange choice for this hot day.

She pulled up Tami's sleeve, her eyes widening when she spotted the ligature marks banding her wrist. "Was that Miguel?" Her voice rose in horror. "He can't get away with this. We have to tell Garrett. Or Lydia."

Tami yanked her sleeve back down. "I'm fine," she muttered. "And don't you dare tell anyone. It wasn't Miguel's fault. I agreed."

The welts were raw and angry. Clearly at some point, Tami hadn't been in agreement. "Then I'm going to talk to Miguel," Megan said.

"No, really. I'm fine. It was my fault. Besides, I got your pictures." Tami leaned over and grabbed her phone. "Look. You can see the tattoos on his chest."

"Was this because of me?" Megan's voice thickened with regret. "Was he mad because you took a picture?"

"He didn't even know." Tami gave a watery smile and shoved the phone in Megan's hand. "See. His eyes are closed."

Megan scrolled along the screen. There were several excellent pictures, but a few she definitely wouldn't share with Scott. Even her cheeks burned. "Can I forward the first three to Scott? Not any of the last," she added hastily. "We just want the tattoos, for...research."

Tami nodded and Megan quickly sent the pictures. "Thanks, Tami." She passed back the phone, not quite able to banish her guilt.

"Don't look so worried," Tami said. "Miguel's kinkiness makes me sick and if I didn't like my phone so much, I'd stick it up his ass. I'm definitely not covering for him again."

"What do you mean? Covering for him?"

Tami shrugged but wouldn't meet Megan's eyes. "Just little things," she muttered. "He didn't want Ramon to know we were spending so much time together, you know. Nothing important."

Megan just waited, adopting Scott's method. The silent stare. She'd seen him use it several times and it was difficult to remain silent. Tami broke in twenty seconds.

"Like I said," Tami went on, "it was nothing important." She clasped her hands, looking at her fingers and fiddling with a silver pinkie ring. "A couple times he wanted me to say I was with him, you know, when I'm not certain we were...but I don't actually remember."

"Look at me, Tami," Megan said. "This is important. The night Rex was hurt. Were you really with Miguel?"

"For a bit. It was dark when he arrived though. I think that's why he gave me the phone. He said he was sneaking a joint and needed my help. But when he showed up, he was sweaty and out of breath."

"That sonofabitch." Megan groaned. "He must have been the one who hurt Rex. Lock the door. I have to talk to Scott. But stay away from Miguel."

"He's busy the rest of the day anyway," Tami said. "He's working with Ramon. And I'm sorry I lied. I was positive he wouldn't hurt a dog. But I've been thinking about it more and more, and now..."

Megan looked at Tami's hunched shoulders and bit back her frustration. "It's okay," she said. "I really appreciate you telling me the truth."

"But I should have told you before. Lies always come back to bite you in the ass."

Megan forced a weak smile, aware she was just as guilty. She'd been evasive with Scott from the very first day. But no longer.

She'd postpone her search for Eve and tell Scott everything. She couldn't imagine why Miguel had attacked Rex, but it proved he was capable of violence. And he'd definitely hurt Tami. Maybe now both Garrett and Scott would look at Joey's disappearance with fresh eyes.

CHAPTER THIRTY

"Megan needs a day off to clear up some things with Eve." Scott crossed his arms, hating to ask Garrett for another favor. "So I need to know what trainer Eve is riding for."

"Jack Zeggelaar," Garrett said. "One of his riders was hurt and Jack is supportive of apprentices." He leaned forward, frowning. "What do you mean? Is Megan going to Santa Anita?"

"Yes. She'll miss a couple lectures tomorrow, along with her ride."

"Ramon is hauling horses," Garrett said, "so Lydia is looking after the jock class. You'll have to tell her." He rubbed his forehead. "Megan wants to go to Santa Anita? I thought with Eve gone that this whole thing would die down.

"Do you want to go with her?" Garrett added. "That'd be okay. I could have the new guy teach. He's arriving in the morning. Or we could give everyone the day off. Call it a 'Farewell to Rambo' holiday."

"Not necessary," Scott said. "I just needed the trainer's name so she can find Eve."

"You're not going with her?"

"I think she already left, although her bag is still here." Scott was careful to keep his voice level. "Anyway, she didn't invite me."

"Well, that's a switch," Garrett said. "Let's take a drive into town. I know a couple ladies who don't need much invitation. Good lookers too. It'll be like the old days."

"No, thanks."

Garrett's eyes widened and he stared at Scott. "Oh, buddy," he said slowly. "I didn't see this coming. Well, we'll just go out and get drunk. Hell, we can drive to Santa Anita too. Surprise Megan... And maybe give Eve one last warning."

"Warning?"

"Yeah." Garrett's voice lowered. "It's nothing to do with Megan, but Eve has some drug problems. She's tied in tight with Joey. It was Ramon's idea to bring in Miguel. Flush her out. Eve tried to sell him some smack so we had to get her off the property. Who knows how many students she approached. I'm sure it's nothing to do with Megan though," he repeated. However, the forced heartiness in his voice was noticeable.

Scott felt his face freeze. "I'd like to talk to Miguel about this," he said. "And Eve." *And Megan too.*

"Certainly," Garrett said. "I'll ask Miguel to drop by before he leaves for the Baja Tinda. And if you want to go back to L.A. now, I certainly understand. It's best if you and Megan sort out your personal affairs away from the school. There are only so many concessions I can make without it looking like favoritism."

Scott remained silent for a moment, still grappling with the nature of Megan's connection to Eve. "Yeah, sure," he said.

His phone rang. He grabbed it on the first ring. But it wasn't Megan.

"Hey, boss," Snake said. "Not much on the Collins kid. Three pops, all drug related. No priors except petty possession. He was in juvie for a while. Got in a little heavy after that. Some stints in rehab. The last one was the longest, but nothing since."

"So," Scott twisted, shooting a relieved glance at Garrett. "He doesn't look like a dope runner?"

"Not to me," Snake said. "Most of his running was with a soccer ball. Pretty cool actually. Scored four goals in a game against the cops. He's either clean or very careful."

"What about family. Are they connected?"

"Don't think. Father bolted the country a week after the first charge against Joey's sister, Megan Spence. The mother is white bread."

"Can you repeat that?" Scott guessed his voice had risen because he felt Garrett's curious stare.

"White bread. Stay-at-home mother. Remarried five years ago. Plain vanilla."

"No, the part about the sister. Megan Spence is Joey's sister?"

"Bingo," Snake said. "And she's interesting but clean. Pot possession at fourteen followed by community service. Guess that was because her dad wasn't around to wield the punishment. She's the only possibility for the drug running. She has serious money sliding in and out. Apparently from jewelry but Belinda is checking the legitimacy. I'll get back to you with that, as well as information on those tattoos you sent."

An ache attached itself to Scott's left eye. "Thank you, Snake."

He lowered the phone and looked at Garrett who appeared just as stunned.

"Well, this is a surprising development," Garrett finally said. "That explains why Megan always pretends Joey is innocent. I have to take a piss."

Scott remained rooted to the sofa then slowly unclenched his fists and pressed Megan's number.

"Hi, Scott," she said. "I'm not sure about going to Santa Anita today. Some things came up. Important stuff I need to tell you."

"Good," he said. "Some things came up here too."

He heard Tami giggling in the background, probably laughing at how easily they'd pulled the wool over his eyes. My God, he felt like an idiot.

"My bag is by the door," Megan said. "It has my notes from calls to Joey's mother. She answered all the questions you gave me. And Scott," she added, "thanks for your help."

She hung up, sounding breathless.

Scott stared down at the floor, shaking his head in disbelief. Joey's mother. Megan's mother. No wonder Megan had insisted on calling the family. He must be the world's lousiest investigator.

Garrett reappeared but didn't sit. "I'm sorry, buddy," he said, his voice thick. "But it's not like Amanda. Megan knew you were a private investigator. Only natural she'd want your help. Do whatever she had to do..."

Scott pulled in an achy breath. Garrett was just trying to make him feel better, but it only emphasized the real reason why Megan had ended up in his bed. He gave a dismissive shrug, hiding his pain. "Yes, that's understandable. But it's not natural to lie."

"Maybe she had good reason," Garrett said. But when Scott raised an eyebrow, Garrett stopped making excuses for Megan and blew out a sigh.

"I asked Miguel to come by," Garrett added. "He never said anything about Megan, but he might know something. The kids see him as another student and talk more openly. Lydia did notice there's been a steady stream of students visiting Megan's room. It's clear now she's selling something they want."

Scott stubbornly folded his arms. "If Megan was using, I'd have noticed."

"Sure you would," Garrett said. However, they both knew he hadn't noticed with Amanda, not until it was too late. He'd been so involved in his job, helping everyone outside the home, too driven to notice his desperate fiancée.

"She drives a noisy truck," Garrett added. "Guess if she were working with Joey, she'd have money."

Scott squeezed his eyes shut, hating to admit the most recent news. "Didn't you hear Snake?" he asked. "She has considerable cash flow."

"Why doesn't she spend it on a nicer vehicle?"

Scott shrugged. He didn't feel like talking to Garrett about this, only to Megan. He'd thought she made cheap dollar-store jewelry but couldn't remember if she'd actually said that. He'd made assumptions. And let emotion cloud his brain.

He rose and walked Garrett to the door. "I think this conversation is best suited for two," he said wearily. "Megan's on her way now. I'll call you later."

"But Miguel is coming over."

"And when he does," Scott said, "I'll talk to him." But what Megan said would be far more important to him than anything Miguel said.

"Don't be too hard on her. I'm sure she's not involved." Garrett reached out to pat Scott's shoulder but took an awkward step and stumbled over the top of Megan's bag.

Garrett regained his balance then stilled. He stared down, his eyes widening. Scott followed his gaze. Someone cursed and Scott realized it was him. But it felt like his chest was imploding. And all he could do was curse. Because a plastic bag was visible...a plastic bag full of white powder.

"Now we know why she had to see Eve," Garrett said. "Dammit, she was selling to my students." And for the first time that day, anger clipped his voice. "I'm sorry, buddy. I have to call the police."

Scott crouched down and pulled the zipper wider on Eve's bag. Lifted out the plastic bag and opened it. This wasn't cheap black tar heroin. It was the good stuff—fine, white and highly processed. Over a pound and a half. Aw, hell. His legs felt rubbery. He didn't move. Could only stare, mesmerized by the smack...and the initialed iPod lying beneath it.

Joey had taken that iPod from Lydia's villa, and now Megan had it. She knew exactly where her brother was. Her plea for help, her fake concern. She'd had an entirely different agenda. The whole thing had been a pretense.

Garrett was still talking, but it was hard to make sense of his words. Scott rose stiffly, feeling ten years older than when he'd woken this morning.

Garrett glanced out the window and quickly zipped Eve's bag shut. "Miguel's coming up the walk," he whispered, a tormented look twisting his face.

At least for now Garrett was hiding it from Miguel. Maybe, just maybe, they could keep the police out of this. But it was a damn lot of heroin intended for a lot of unfortunate souls. Obviously, Megan was in this up to her pretty little neck. And Scott's balloon of disbelief burst, leaving behind only a bitter anger.

Megan rushed toward Scott's villa, texting Eve as she walked. Still no reply. Maybe Eve was on the bus, out of range or perhaps her battery was dead. Sighing, she slipped the phone back into her pocket.

The baby would be fine, she told herself. Eve was a good rider. It was early in her pregnancy. And Megan would sit down with her, and they could calmly review all the options. Eve probably felt she was in this alone. She wasn't thinking straight. But for the baby's sake, she really shouldn't be riding spirited racehorses, not while she was pregnant.

Megan just prayed she'd stay pregnant. And not do anything hasty. It would be a priceless gift to have Joey's baby in her life. In her mother's life. Whatever Eve needed, Megan would help. Money, support, love. Maybe she hadn't made that clear enough? But Eve had been reluctant to talk about baby plans and little wonder. Joey was gone, and a pregnancy would effectively postpone any jockey aspirations. No doubt, Eve felt as if her world had been shattered.

Megan wished she'd been able to catch her before she climbed on the bus. But she couldn't desert Tami. Not after what Miguel had done. The shattered look on Tami's face, the angry welts on her wrists, were seared in her mind.

Miguel had lured the girl with talk of a fictional job then used her like toilet paper. Tami was young and impressionable. She didn't deserve that. Damn Miguel. Megan's hands tightened into fists and her stride quickened.

She was going to tell Scott everything. He had a strong code of honor. He'd never tolerate such brutal behavior. She hoped the school would banish Miguel, but not before Scott tore a strip off him.

Maybe she'd ask Scott to drive with her to Santa Anita tomorrow. There was a new instructor hired and apparently Miguel was leaving tonight, although she wanted to confront him first. He shouldn't be allowed near students, or on the track, or anywhere near the school. He was a lying, swaggering rapist.

She rounded the corner and spotted three men standing in Scott's driveway. Miguel, Scott and Garrett. Miguel was speaking, waving his hands as though holding court, and she couldn't wait to wipe the cocky look off his face.

"Ramon asked me to come up," Miguel was saying. "Discover how many students Joey was supplying. As far as I can tell, it was only Eve."

He glanced over Scott's shoulder and saw Megan approaching. But he didn't look at all abashed. In fact, a triumphant smile lifted the corners of his mouth.

"Know anything about Megan?" Scott asked, his voice toneless.

Miguel looked past Garrett and Scott, still smirking at Megan. "She's my girlfriend's roommate. Of course, I know what's going on. She and Joey have a good drug business."

Megan slammed to a stop, her breath incredulous. "You liar," she said.

Scott wheeled, his face impassive. He didn't step forward. Didn't smile. Didn't even look embarrassed. He was actually asking that jerk about her?

"I don't believe this," she sputtered, staring at Scott in disbelief. "You're listening to *him*? About me? About Eve?"

Garrett stepped forward, his voice troubled. "The game's over, Megan. Miguel told us about Eve's...problems."

"What?" Her fists tightened, her gaze shooting from Scott to Miguel. "What are you talking about?"

"Eve likes her drugs," Miguel said. "And she's a *puta*. Many people had sex with her, including me."

"You liar." Megan shot forward and slammed her hands into his chest. His arm flashed. She saw his coiled fist, knew it was going to hurt, but was too incensed to even duck. However, Miguel jerked in the air like a rag doll and she was slammed into something so hard, her breath escaped with a whoosh.

"Calm down," Scott said, throwing Miguel to the ground then trapping Megan's wrists.

Miguel scrambled to his feet. "See, she's nuts." His eyes glittered and he tapped his head. "She and Joey, they're both loco."

"You asshole." She lurched at Miguel, trying to twist from Scott's hold. But he flattened her arms, anchoring her legs with his.

"Stop," Scott said. "Let's talk about this."

Garrett edged around Miguel, staring at Megan in wide-eyed dismay. "Don't you have some cuffs or something? She's going to hurt herself."

"Yes, tie her up." Miguel sneered. "She loves that. Her roommate loves it too."

Megan's brain exploded with red. She jerked up, butting Scott's head and twisting sideways. He yanked her arm behind her back, but the pain was little compared to her fury.

"Cuffs are in the dash," Scott said. "Get out of here, Miguel."

Miguel crossed his arms, raking her with a taunting smile. Megan bit her mouth so hard she tasted blood. She needed to get closer, wanted to kick him again but Scott had done something to her arm and it hurt. She jerked her head back, trying to escape his hold but it was impossible.

"Goddammit, Miguel. Leave," Scott snapped. "Now."

A car door opened and closed. Her ears roared but she heard Garrett say Miguel wasn't the criminal here. She tried to launch herself again but something yanked her arms. Metal bit into her flailing wrists.

Miguel was smirking and waving his arms while hers were cuffed, and her sheer impotence only stoked her fury.

"I'll call the police," Garrett said.

She tried to jerk around but Scott was still holding her, his face impassive.

"You idiots," she managed, but her voice cracked and she shivered in helplessness, her throat so tight the words sounded feeble.

Scott and Garrett were talking around her. Her head throbbed, and the whole world seemed off kilter. She caught Miguel's snide wink as he turned to leave, but her rage had drained now, leaving her exhausted.

Scott and Garrett were arguing. Scott didn't want any police and Garrett did, but at least Miguel was gone. Her head throbbed, her wrists were cuffed and confusion left her numb.

She was guided around the back of the villa, an implacable hand on her arm. Twice she stumbled and was literally picked up, and then she was sitting in Garrett's house, and Scott and Garrett were talking again. Scott wouldn't look at her and she couldn't believe he'd snapped stupid cuffs on her, and she was so stunned she wanted to curl up in a corner until this nightmare was over.

And then Scott walked out the door, and it was only her and Garrett.

Garrett gave her an odd look. Tears trickled from her eyes and her nose itched. He walked over and wiped her face, and she thought maybe everything was going to be all right, and that Scott would come back any minute and say it had all been a bad joke.

"What's going on, Garrett?" she finally asked, hating the wobble in her voice, the tears that dripped down her cheeks.

"You'll have to stay here until you're calm. Then you will leave the school. But Scott insisted that I don't involve the police."

"The p-police?"

"It's okay. I promised him you won't be charged. However, I want you off the grounds. Immediately. Your possessions will be collected from your room and brought here, along with your vehicle. Please don't interact with any students." Garrett dragged a tired hand over his jaw. "Just go."

A warm wetness gushed from the corners of her eyes. She guessed she was bawling but couldn't wipe her face. "You're k-kicking me out because I'm Joey's sister?" She bent her head, trying to dry her face on her arm. "I want to see Scott," she added weakly.

"But he doesn't want to see you, Megan. Ever again. He's gone. He had a fiancée who was an addict. To him, dealers are the lowest form of scum."

"Gone? He's gone?" She sniffed and Garrett's face blurred.

"Don't worry. He left the key to his cuffs. Made me promise to take them off once you're calm." Garrett frowned. "Do you want to use the bathroom? Wash your face?"

She nodded, trying to work the words around the lump in her throat. Scott was gone? Really gone?

"I was going to tell him," she whispered. "About Joey. And that Miguel hurt Tami."

"Well, unfortunately it's too late for that." Garrett's eyes looked sad as he pulled the key from his pocket. "Stand up."

She lurched to her feet. Garrett moved behind her, fumbled for a moment. Then the cuffs clinked off.

"Bathroom is second door on the right." He pointed down the hall.

Her throat felt too raw to talk so she merely nodded and stumbled down the hall to the bathroom.

Her reflection in the mirror was scary. She looked like a stranger with frayed eyes, blotchy skin and unkempt hair. Her head spun so she splashed water on her face, holding onto the sink for long minutes.

This was crazy. And Scott was almost as big a jerk as Miguel. To cuff her and leave without any questions. He hadn't even tried to understand. Maybe she should have told him earlier, but at the time she'd mistrusted his tight relationship with Garrett. All his talk about dependability, about sticking around. What a load of bullshit.

She blinked, trying to soothe the sting behind her eyes. Then splashed more cold water on her face until finally it seemed as though her brain was working again. She had to leave the school. But that was okay. She still had her plan to travel to Mexico and look for Joey...minus Scott.

Asshole. She ached all over, especially her chest. Probably because of the way he'd manhandled her. She checked her arms, even lifted her shirt, but couldn't find a single bruise. She pulled her shirt back down with a sniff. Cops probably learned how to muscle people around without leaving any mark. No wonder people resisted arrest. It was horrible, humiliating and frightening.

"Asshole," she muttered, aloud this time. Still, it was over. Not really a big deal except for the ignominy of being kicked out. So now she'd just drive up to Santa Anita and find Eve. Sort that out first. She pulled out her phone and checked her messages. Nothing from Eve but a rather frantic one from Tami.

Lydia is here packing your stuff!! *WTF*???

Wow. Garrett hadn't wasted much time although at least it wasn't Ramon pawing through her drawers, handling her underwear. She clamped her mouth, fighting her regret at not being able to say goodbye to Tami, or help her obtain some retribution. At least Miguel would be gone. He wouldn't be around to hurt Tami any longer.

Her fingers felt clumsy as she pressed a message. *Talk later. Is Lydia still there*?

Yes, Tami texted back.

Will call. Stay away from Miguel. You can keep my necklace.

Awesome. I luv u, Tami messaged.

Megan smiled, stiffly but still a smile. She slipped her phone in her pocket and carefully folded Garrett's plush towel back over the heated rack. She hadn't noticed the bathroom earlier, had been too staggered by events, but it was utterly luxurious with fancy fixtures and elaborate lighting that emphasized the rich tones.

Maybe she'd renovate her bungalow when she went home. She didn't want the inconvenience of major changes, but a little decorating might be good. Buy some new furniture, a nicer TV, a sofa for two... Her heart cracked.

And I won't think of Scott anymore.

She yanked the door open. He'd cuffed her, handing her off to Garrett like a common criminal. And even though she was drained of tears, the stabbing in her chest wouldn't quit. Because she had dared to imagine a future, had pictured Scott sprawled on her couch, tussling with her over the remote.

Asshole. She tramped down the hall.

Garrett raised an eyebrow. "Would you like some coffee?"

She jammed her hands in her pockets and shook her head. Refused to let him pretend this was a normal visit. "So am I allowed to leave now?" she asked. "Gather my stuff?"

"Lydia is getting it. And then you'll vacate the property. I want you to stay away from the students." He paused, his blue eyes glittering. "And I expect you to stay away from Scott too. Although since he despises traffickers, it's obvious your relationship is finished."

"Our relationship is definitely finished," she said. "Although I might charge you both with unnecessary roughness." She paused. "What do you mean, trafficking?"

Garrett shrugged, still studying her face with a peculiar intensity. "I should have guessed you were related to Joey, the way you insisted on digging up every damn detail. But I never dreamed you'd drag Scott into it. Do you intend to continue this ridiculous search?"

"It's not ridiculous. I'm going to find out what happened to my brother."

"But Scott won't help you any longer," Garrett said, turning and pouring himself a cup of coffee.

"Joey's not a trafficker," she said. "And I wish you'd believe that."

"Doesn't matter what I believe. We've obtained a five-year mandate now and the school's operations can continue." He walked to the front door and glanced out the window. "Ah, the ever-competent Lydia has arrived. Wait inside. I'll get your bag, then escort you to your truck."

He wasn't even going to let her explain to Lydia. "You're carrying this too far," she said.

He shot her a warning look so she blew out a resigned sigh and flopped on the sofa. But as soon as he stepped outside, she whipped out her phone and called Tami.

"What the hell!" Tami said, her voice rising. "Lydia said you were kicked out because of heroin possession. Half a million dollars in street value. I told her she was crazy, but she said both Garrett and Scott saw the drugs."

A chill swept Megan. Her legs turned so numb she was relieved she was sitting. "That's not true. Garrett is kicking me out because I'm Joey's sister...and I concealed it."

"You're Joey's sister?" Tami was silent for a moment. Then her words came in a rush. "Well, that's good. You could say it was Joey's heroin. And I'll vouch I never saw you selling. That's not a lie."

"But I don't know anything about heroin," Megan said, rubbing her forehead. "I think you must have misunderstood."

"No. Lydia was shocked too. Said you weren't even allowed to go to Rambo's retirement party. She thought you should go, you know, because you found Rambo the home. But Garrett refused."

Megan shook her head. It seemed as though Tami was speaking a different language. "Tell me about the heroin," she said.

"I told Lydia the only person with drugs was Miguel," Tami said. "But Scott and Garrett saw heroin in your bag."

"Oh, no! So that's what Garrett meant. They think I was trafficking." She glanced up as Garrett opened the door and stepped inside, carrying her duffle bag. "This is all a big mistake, Tami. I'll call you back."

She cut the connection and leaped to her feet. "Garrett, you have to listen."

"Who were you talking to?" he asked.

"My roommate. She told me about the heroin. But it wasn't mine. I swear. Someone must have put it there. I didn't even understand why you and Scott were so angry, and I lost my temper because of Miguel and how he hurt Tami. Please, you have to believe me. It's not mine."

Garrett's face darkened, and he didn't look at all pleased. "I think the best thing is for you to go home and forget this. Just give it up." His eyes narrowed. "Or I *will* call the police. Scott doesn't believe you either. In fact, you sicken him."

She flinched as though slapped.

"I'll refund your tuition," Garrett added. "Go and wait for your brother to come home. No one wants you around."

"F-fine." Her voice quavered. "But you should kick out Miguel too. He's a creep and he hurt Tami and he might hurt other students—"

"I'll look after Miguel. Now let's get your vehicle. You have a long drive." Garrett's phone rang. He checked the display, then pressed it to his ear.

"Yes. Everything's fine," he said, turning his back and pacing to the window. "She's leaving the property now. Meet me here, but don't worry. Everything's fine," he repeated, glancing over his shoulder.

He closed his phone. "Better hurry before I change my mind." He scooped up her duffle bag and her smaller overnight bag.

"May I see it?" she asked. "The drugs you saw in my bag."

"Dammit, this is over." Garrett's mouth flattened. "And if you talk to anybody about what happened here, I'll be forced to report you to the authorities. In spite of my promise to Scott."

"But I'd like to see it," she said stubbornly. "There must be some mistake."

"Don't be silly," he said. "We're not letting you keep the drugs. They were in your small bag, along with Joey's iPod."

She squeezed her eyes shut, remembering how Scott had raked her with such contempt. The same expression her father had worn when the police charged her with drug possession. *He'd left then too.*

"Of course he left," Garrett said. "And no ridiculous explanation will change Scott's mind. So forget about calling him."

She realized she'd been speaking aloud and opened her eyes. "Scott's the last person I'd call," she said dully. "He didn't care enough to listen."

"Precisely." Garrett had the door half open when his phone buzzed again. He glanced at the display, stepped back and dropped her bags on the floor. "Just a minute," he muttered.

"Hey!" He spoke into the phone with such forced joviality, she leaned against the wall, guessing he was going to be more than a minute. Despite Garrett's intention that he escort her off the grounds, she intended to pop up to her room and say goodbye to Tami. Surely they'd let her do that?

"Yeah," Garrett was saying. "She's fine. The cuffs have been off for a while."

She straightened away from the wall and stared at Garrett. Obviously he was talking about her. Must be Scott on the other end. A pang shot through her.

"She's...almost calm," Garrett added, turning his back to Megan. "I think, maybe she'd been a little cranked. That explains the mood swings." His voice lowered. "Naturally really, considering..."

Megan frowned. She didn't want to talk to Scott—after all, he'd deserted her—but she was more than calm and she resented the inference that she was a raving junkie.

"Sure, I'll tell her," Garrett said, his voice almost jovial. He closed the phone.

"And of course he's hardwired to help," Garrett muttered, as if talking to himself. "It's in his DNA." He swallowed then squared his shoulders.

"Just a moment," he said to Megan. "I need to make a call." His gaze flickered over her face but didn't meet her gaze. "Ramon," he said, pressing his phone back to his ear. "We have a problem."

She gulped. Garrett's voice sounded different. Resigned, flat. She backed up a step, uncertain. But the skin on the back of her neck prickled, and the adrenaline rush made her stomach roil. "I need to use the bathroom again," she muttered.

She turned and stumbled down the hall, her legs so wobbly she felt drunk. She locked the door and stared wide-eyed at the knob while her heart hammered with a sickening dread. The drugs had been in her overnight bag. In Scott's villa. The only people near it were Scott and Garrett. Scott would never plant drugs in her bag.

So it had to be Garrett... But why?

She pulled out her phone and tapped Tami's number, her fingers clumsy. "Tami," she whispered. "I'm in Garrett's bathroom. If I don't call you back in half an hour,

I'm in big trouble."

"You're already in big trouble," Tami said.

"Even bigger," Megan said. "Never mind, I'm going to sneak out the back door. See you in a minute."

She opened the bathroom door and listened. Garrett was still on the phone but speaking Spanish now. There was a door off the patio to the pool. She remembered it from her interview. She crept down the hall and peered around the corner, watching as Garrett paced. He was doing more listening than talking, his face so twisted it looked like a stranger's.

She waited until he'd turned back to the front door then dashed across the opening and down the hall. Fumbled with the door, then slid it back, no longer caring about the noise. She just wanted out.

She lurched across the pool deck, briefly blinded by the sun reflecting off the blue water. Spotted a gate to the right just past a stainless steel barbecue. She swung it open.

Squeaked in fright when she saw Ramon looming on the other side.

"Hi," she managed, her breath escaping in short gasps. "Garrett's busy on the phone. I'm just going to get my truck."

Ramon said nothing, his dark eyes flat. She backed away. He stepped closer, blocking the way, and pressed a phone to his ear.

"Got her," he said.

She bolted around the pool, but he caught her arm in two strides and yanked her roughly back into the house.

"Damn that Scott," Garrett said. He pulled her hands in front of her and clicked the cuffs back on. "She's got a phone somewhere," he added.

Ramon patted around her pockets, extracting her phone, but she could only stare at Garrett in bewilderment. "Why?" she asked. "Why are you doing this?"

"I can't have Scott poking around. He's too relentless," Garrett said. "I thought the drugs would turn him off, but I underestimated your charms. Inconvenient for all of us." His voice turned regretful. "Especially for you."

"But Scott's gone." Her voice cracked. "And I'm just going home."

"Unfortunately, I don't think you'll ever stop looking for your brother. Will you?" He tilted her face so she couldn't jerk away then sighed and dropped his hand. "Scott's determined to help. So you see how it has to be."

"N-no, I don't see. How does it have to be?" Her body trembled along with her question, but Garrett had already turned to Ramon.

"Take her to the cowshed," Garrett said, tossing a key. "Stick to the back lane. I'll get her truck."

Ramon grunted and propelled her out the door. Her legs wouldn't work and she stumbled on the cobblestones. He yanked her up and shoved her headfirst into Garrett's car. At least her hands were in front. Scott had cuffed her from behind, a much more helpless feeling.

In fact—she eyed the door handle, resolving to jump out as soon as they were out of Garrett's sight, whatever the speed. She only wished her knees would stop shaking.

"Don't worry," Ramon said. "Everything will be all right." But the door locks clicked and when she jerked her head around, he wouldn't look at her, and it was clear he was lying.

She fought the bile rising in her throat. "Is this what happened to Joey?" she asked.

"If you don't make any trouble, we'll take you to see him," Ramon said with an insincere smile. "No problem."

"Oh, that's good then." She hoped he didn't hear the wobble in her voice. She was terrified and sweating, her mind and body disjointed, but did he really think she was such a fool?

Maybe.

"Garrett told me what you two were doing," she added, forcing a smile. "And of course, I'm cool with that, making money... I think you guys are actually rather clever."

Ramon gave a satisfied shrug. "We've moved over twenty million for the Baja Tinda."

Her hands clenched on her lap. "That's a lot of money," she croaked, deciding she really didn't want to hear anymore.

"It was Garrett's idea to bale the money in the hay," Ramon said. "But it wouldn't have happened without my cousin's connections."

"Your cousin?"

"Hugo, Miguel's father. Someday he'll be as powerful as Sanchez."

Megan gripped her hands so tightly her nails bit into her skin. The Sanchez cartel—even she had heard of them. They were rumored to have more guns than the California Police. And Miguel's people were taking them on.

"Do you hide guns in the hay too?" she asked, her voice almost hysterical.

"Only money," he said. "Four horses, eight bales. Just enough for the journey. Not enough hay to draw suspicion."

A sickening nausea lodged in her stomach. Now she knew what had happened to Joey. Somehow he'd stumbled onto this. No wonder he hadn't called. She stared at Ramon, her face frozen. "Is my brother at the Baja Tinda?"

"Of course." But the edge of his mouth tightened, and she fought the urge to leap across the seat and scratch out his lying eyes. "We'll take you to him," Ramon added.

"Great." She nodded, trying to fake a calmness she didn't feel. "I can help load the horses. But what about my passport? I hope Lydia put it in my bag. Maybe we should check—"

"Don't worry about it," Ramon said.

The horrible pressure in her chest tightened. She forced her head to nod again, the only part of her that seemed capable of movement. "Guess you have lots of contacts at the border. I haven't been to Mexico in years. Can't even remember if I need a passport," she babbled. "But this is going to be fun."

She felt his assessing gaze and forced a vacuous smile even as she scanned the drive, praying she'd see someone, anyone. But this road was deserted, out of bounds to all students.

No wonder Garrett had moved Braun. He hadn't wanted Scott anywhere near the cowshed. And despite the car's air conditioning, sweat beaded every inch of her body.

They crunched into the parking lot and stopped beside Ramon's truck, now hooked up to the gleaming horse trailer. "Oh, you're all ready," she said. "That's great. If you unlock these cuffs, I'll help load the horses."

"Miguel will handle the horses." Ramon cut the engine and stepped out. He walked around the back of the car and opened her door. "Come inside and wait for Garrett."

She didn't want to wait. Garrett would be much harder to trick, but Ramon took her arm and guided her into the arena. However, his grip wasn't as tight as when he first shoved her into the car.

"Wait with me," Ramon said, "while I start the baler."

"Okay." She gave an enthusiastic nod. Icy clarity now replaced her earlier bout of panic. They were going to kill her, somewhere between here and the Baja Tinda—unless she escaped. She trotted beside Ramon, as though he were her best friend and she didn't want to ever leave his side.

"It must be hard to bale money," she said.

"Not with the modifications. They bring the money already bagged. I just have to drop it between the flakes before the bales are tied."

"That's so clever." She forced an admiring smile, and he even gave her a tentative smile back. Ironic, she thought. Finally she was able to get him to smile. And now she understood why the loose alfalfa was in the arena, why Garrett hadn't wanted her to use it.

Somehow Joey had figured it out, maybe when he was helping Ramon fix the baler. He'd probably dropped his iPod then. Knowing her brother, he'd been fighting for his life, not trembling like a coward. Like her. A tear slid down her cheek. She raised her cuffed hands and wiped it away.

Ramon hit the starter and the machine rumbled to life. He forked hay into the feeder. A square bale slid out the other end. It was fast and efficient, an excellent baler. But Ramon scowled. "*Dias*. I thought that was fixed."

She tilted her head, studying the banana-shaped bale. The left side of the twine hadn't fastened, leaving only one string and an extremely vulnerable bale of hay. "That's just the bill hook," she said. "When it only ties on one side, that's generally the problem."

Ramon kicked the bale and it burst apart. "It worked yesterday," he said.

"Aw, that sucks." She strained to hear beyond the arena, praying Garrett wouldn't arrive with her truck.

Ramon rubbed a sheen of sweat on his forehead, looked at the door, then grabbed a wrench. "They won't like this," he muttered.

"Who won't?" She glanced over her shoulder, following his nervous gaze.

"It's Sanchez money," Ramon admitted. "We only move it for a cut."

"Oh." Her heart sunk. The Sanchez cartel—people with less reluctance to kill than both Ramon and Garrett. And Ramon's apprehension made her knees knock. She had to get out of here before they arrived.

"I can fix it for you," she said. "Joey showed me."

Ramon snorted. "Joey caused all our problems. The baler hasn't worked since he tinkered with it."

Good for you, Joey. "Yeah," she said, giving a knowing nod. "I always had to fix our equipment after him. We had a machine like this and ours wouldn't tie on the left either. It was a broken pin in the bill hook. If the tension isn't right, the string never ties." She reached down and tugged the useless twine hanging from the banana bale. "Believe me. That's your problem."

"Can you fix it?"

"Sure." She leaned over the baler, grateful she'd just read Joey's magazine and was full of tractor terms. She didn't know enough to fix the bill hook, but she certainly knew how to sabotage it. And if Joey had caused a problem, it must have been deliberate. He was a born mechanic. All the neighbors had called him whenever they needed help.

"Pass me the wrench," she said, trying to sound like an authority.

Ramon turned to the toolbox and she quickly leaned over the frame, snagging her cuffs around the billhook pin. She yanked as hard as she could, praying the hook would twist and screw up the tension. For good measure, she'd also remove some nuts.

She turned and raised her hands. "The space is too small for both my hands. Just unlock these cuffs so I can reach in."

Ramon passed her the wrench, studying her with his familiar dispassionate expression.

"Come on, Ramon," she said. "You don't want to be fighting with this baler when the big guys arrive with the money."

"I am a big guy. Hugo is my cousin." But he pulled the key from his pocket and her cuffs fell off with a satisfying clink.

She bent over the baler, shifting so he couldn't see her trembling fingers, then loosened a bolt. It dropped silently into the deep dirt. "Do you have another pin?" She glanced innocently over her shoulder. "This one is broken and the tucker finger isn't giving enough tension."

"We're not baling a damn field." Ramon's dark eyes narrowed. "It only needs to tie eight bales."

It's not going to tie one bale. She subtly palmed another nut. "Here we go," she said. "That should work. Now I'll grab another pitchfork and help you load the hay."

"No. Stay here." Ramon pulled the wrench from her hand. He turned and picked up the pitchfork, his back to her.

She wheeled and bolted for the door.

Ramon cursed and thudded after her, but fear gave her wings. She blasted across the arena and into the sunlight—smack into Miguel's wiry chest.

"In a hurry, *puta*?" Miguel asked, laughing with a complete absence of humor. He yanked her arm behind her back and pushed her back to Ramon. "You idiot. Garrett said you had her."

"She seemed obedient," Ramon muttered.

A hand grabbed her hair, and she squealed at the painful jerk. "Does it look like she's obedient? Do I have to do every fucking thing around here?"

They switched to an angry flurry of Spanish, but the grip on her arm and hair remained tight. Her head was tilted back at an impossible angle. It was difficult to see Miguel, but she could smell his breath, heavy with coffee, along with the stink of stale sweat and cologne. She didn't move, just stood there while they argued, her neck exposed and vulnerable.

Ramon didn't talk as much as Miguel now. His voice was low, almost resigned. Miguel abruptly kicked her feet out, shoving her to the ground. "Watch her," he said, and stalked to the stalls.

Ramon stared down without meeting her eyes. She tried to rise to one knee but he pushed her down with his boot. Her breath shuddered out, her insides shriveling.

"If you kill me," her voice quavered, "you'll never get that baler working."

"What?"

"You heard me." She cleared her throat, sensing she was fighting for her life. "I bet your cousin won't like that."

Ramon's nostrils flared. Miguel strode back through the doorway, a thin lead rope gripped in his hand.

Ramon gestured at the baler and muttered in Spanish. Miguel's face darkened. He jerked to a stop, staring at her in frustration. At that moment, he looked so much like a petulant kid—a spoiled boy who toyed with innocents like Tami—that her ball of fear burst.

"Your daddy can buy you all the horses and women you want," she said, "but you'll never ride worth shit."

He shot forward, cursing, and wrapped the rope around her neck.

She rose on her toes, jerking backwards, fighting the vise that gripped her throat. Part of her hadn't believed he'd really do it.

She heard Ramon's urgent voice and a rumbling—her truck? She hadn't realized her muffler was so loud. Then she could suck in wonderful air again. She was pushed into the dirt, sprawling and gasping for breath, just grateful that the horrible rope was off her neck.

Garrett's voice cut through her haze. He spoke rapidly to the two men and even though he was a lying scumball, she was glad he was here.

He crouched down but stayed on his feet, careful not to get dirt on his impeccably creased pants. "What did you do to the baler, Megan?" he asked.

She looked up at him, but his face was spotty. And her breath came in painful bursts, her throat too sore to speak.

"I don't think you understand your situation," he went on, his voice grim. "We have company arriving. And we need that baler."

"I thought," she sputtered, still clasping her throat, "I thought that I fixed it... Hard to remember anything though since that creep with the cheap cologne tried to strangle me."

Miguel shot forward with a torrent of Spanish, but Garrett motioned him back. His voice lowered. "My power is limited here and Miguel has a temper. For Scott's sake, let's not make this any harder than it has to be."

"If you let me go, I won't say anything." She hated the squeak in her voice, hated that she was pleading. She clamped her arms around her chest, trying to hide her trembling. "Besides, I won't ever see Scott again."

Garrett's smile looked pained. "That's what I thought. But he's not giving this up. He's already called twice. And he's too good at his job."

"But he'll wonder where I am. He'll look for me." She tried to sound confident but she wasn't sure Scott would even care.

"It won't be a surprise when he can't find you," Garrett said. "Drug dealers often disappear. He's just grateful I promised not to involve the police. I told him you left with Joey."

"Where is Joey?"

"Somewhere in Mexico. Frankly, my dear, I don't want to know where they dumped him."

A burning pain exploded in her chest and she was glad she was already on the ground. She'd sensed Joey was dead, but to have Garrett casually confirm it was devastating.

"Why?" Her voice cracked.

"He was helping Ramon with the baler. Came back with some special screws at a very bad time."

"But he d-died in Mexico?"

"That's right. We didn't want any trouble close to the school, not when our license was up for renewal."

Megan couldn't breathe. Joey had been killed three months ago. Then dumped like garbage. She wanted to launch herself at Garrett's head, but her body felt impossibly numb. And cold. So very cold.

"You don't understand," Garrett said, his voice slightly aggrieved. "It's impossible to cross these people. I didn't want to ship this month, not while Scott was around, but you saw what Miguel did to my dog. Now, please, fix the baler."

"Why bother," she said dully. Her adrenaline rush had flattened and now she only felt Joey's loss along with an incredible weariness. "You're going to kill me anyway."

"There are many ways to die," Garrett said. "The men that are coming are experts. Best to choose the easy route."

Miguel rattled off a string of angry words. His boots loomed closer but Garrett snapped something, and Miguel quit talking.

"See." Garrett turned his attention back to her. "I won't let Miguel hurt you. I respect Scott far too much for that."

Oh, that's rich. She drew her trembling legs to her chest, appalled her choices were to die quickly now. Or slowly later. Even more terrifying—that she was actually weighing the pros and cons.

CHAPTER THIRTY-ONE

Scott whipped his car around a sharp corner then hit the brakes. He veered onto the shoulder of the road, bumping over the gravel and sending up a swirl of dust.

Dammit. He slammed his fist into the dash, still struggling to accept the facts. Megan was a drug dealer. Drug dealers were scum. He'd fallen in love with scum.

He'd always considered traffickers to be bottom feeders, pulling victims into a sinkhole of doom and despair. After Amanda's downward spiral, his already-low tolerance had turned razor thin. It had been easier to leave the LAPD than to read dealers their rights—especially when he really wanted to crack their skulls open for taking away the only woman he'd ever loved.

Until now.

Groaning, he dropped his head in his hands. Didn't know how long he sat or at what point he decided to turn his car around. But he couldn't drive away. Couldn't just leave her. He'd failed someone before. Maybe this time he could make a difference.

Garrett had promised he wouldn't involve the police. Besides, it was probably Megan's brother who was the biggest criminal. All Scott knew was that he had to help her.

She'd left with Joey a half hour ago, heading south, but he knew her license plate. He could call in a few favors, track her down before she disappeared in Mexico.

It had all happened so blurringly fast. He should have asked more questions. She was inherently kind. Maybe she was trying to raise money for tsunami victims or buy a kidney or help more horses like Rambo. It didn't matter. If he had to cuff her to his side, he'd do it. He'd do whatever it took to help straighten out her life.

He wheeled his car around, tires screeching but this time they burned rubber on the opposite side of the road. He hugged a familiar corner, recognizing the spot where they'd first met, the place where she'd stopped to help. When she'd wiggled that beautiful ass beneath his car and pulled him from the ditch. He'd known then she had a generous heart.

The question was would she choose to go clean?

Buzz. The number on his screen was unfamiliar, and he almost didn't answer.

"Taylor," he said.

"Hi." The voice was high pitched and breathy. "Is this Scott?"

"Yeah."

"Oh, hi," the voice said, happy now, and then he recognized the youthful bounce.

"Hi, Tami," he said, watching the twisty road for an old blue truck. Maybe Megan would change her mind and return to L.A. Garrett said she was heading for Mexico, but he didn't believe that. Didn't want to believe it.

"It was hard to find your number," Tami said. "I didn't want to ask Garrett, of course, and your office refused to give it to me. But then I remembered Megan used my phone to send the tattoo pictures. Do you have a massage business?"

"What is it, Tami?" He clutched the wheel, hope rising at the approaching sound of a noisy muffler. But it was only an ancient sun-bleached Chevy, chugging around the bend, trailing a plume of exhaust.

"Megan said if she didn't call back in half an hour, she was in big trouble."

"I know," he said, "but we're going to sort out her problems. I'm trying to catch her truck now."

"But she's not in her truck. She's hiding in Garrett's bathroom. And she hasn't called back. I'm not sure what that means—"

"Slow down. When did she call?"

"Almost an hour ago. It took me a really long time to find your number." Tami's voice turned reproachful. "That woman who answers your office phone wasn't very helpful."

"Did you see Megan when she gathered her things?"

"No. Lydia did it. She tossed everything in Megan's duffle bag."

Scott winced. Garrett hadn't even let Megan pack. "What about when she picked up her truck?" he asked. "Did you see her then?"

"No, and she would have called to say goodbye. You know she would."

"Yeah." He dragged a hand over his jaw. Megan was extremely loyal to her friends. To her brother. "All right," he said slowly. "I'll call Garrett again. See what's happening."

When he disconnected, Tami was still talking, complaining that Lydia had confiscated all their chocolate bars. He cut her off, his mind processing this new scenario. Hiding in the bathroom? What the hell? A chill slid down his neck.

Seconds later, the phone rang again and he guessed it was Tami calling back. But the display showed Snake.

"Got some news, boss," Snake said. "That tattoo you sent belongs to a splinter group of the Sanchez cartel. They control a piece of the west coast. Headed by Hugo Torres."

Scott squeezed the wheel in dismay. That explained the lab quality of the heroin. Megan was swimming with the big boys. And those people were ruthless. No one was safe dealing with them.

Miguel was obviously the key. He'd set up dealers like Megan and Joey, right beneath Garrett's nose. But no...that didn't make sense. Scott gave his head a shake, feeling out of sync. Megan had sent him the pictures. She was the one who'd asked him to check out Miguel's tattoos.

"I'm thinking Miguel is at the center of this," Scott said slowly. "Not Megan."

"Oh, yeah," Snake said. "That girl is clean. She's the lady behind the Megan Spence Collection. All Internet jewelry. Belinda said she even bought a Spence necklace once, custom made stuff with silver feathers and some kind of blue rocks—"

"What! She really does make jewelry?"

"Yeah. But she donates most of her profits to troubled teens. There's a bunch of organizations on her list. All legit. Belinda already checked for laundering."

Scott groaned, gripping the wheel so tightly that a knot settled between his shoulder blades. Megan had claimed Miguel was lying. But he hadn't listened. He'd chosen the coward's route and when Garrett had urged him to go, he'd fled.

At least she was away from Miguel. Safe with Joey. "What's your take on Joey Collins?" he asked, surprised his voice sounded so level.

"Kid had some addiction troubles. Looks to be clean now. But if he crossed this bunch, it's not surprising he disappeared. That Miguel dude is bad news. Cops got nothing on him, but the ink says enough. The star indicates his rank, the teardrops his kills. There's a lot of intercartal rivalry, and the Torres name is popping up everywhere."

Scott's knuckles turned bloodless. "I have to call Garrett. Dammit, he's sending horses to those people."

"Boss." Snake cleared his throat. "It doesn't appear that horses are the Baja Tinda's main industry. The place is a fortress, not a training track."

"You checked that on the street?"

"And with our inside sources. Maybe Garrett doesn't know but..."

Scott didn't like Snake's inference and didn't bother to answer. Garrett wouldn't have invited him down if the school was dirty. Then again, Garrett had originally only wanted to use his name.

Had Garrett invited him or had it been Belinda's suggestion? Once the school received its approvals, Garrett had stressed it would be okay to leave—even though the course had just started. It was hard to remember the details when he'd been falling so hard for Megan.

But maybe that had been the plan? Garrett and Megan's plan.

His car squealed around another corner, propelled by his jumbled thoughts. But Garrett hadn't introduced him to Megan. He'd met her on the road. And despite Snake's warning, he couldn't accept that Garrett was involved with any criminal aspects of the Baja Tinda.

The man had always been drawn by a quick buck but to climb into bed with a cartel was nuts. Besides, there was no obvious gain in letting Miguel hobnob around the school.

"Boss?" Snake said. "Just keep your head up. That's

all I'm saying."

"I'm only twenty miles from the school," Scott said. "Think I'll stop in." He punched the gas. He could detour there and still catch Megan's ancient truck before she reached the Mexican border.

But right now, he had some hard questions for Garrett.

CHAPTER THIRTY-TWO

Scott turned his car into Garrett's driveway and jerked to a stop behind the BMW. He strode up the walkway and pushed open the door without bothering to knock.

"Garrett!" His shout trailed off. Megan's overnight bag still lay by the wall. Beside it sat a larger duffle bag tagged 'MEGAN SPENCE.' Lydia had been thorough. Megan's white riding helmet was buckled around the hand straps.

He swallowed but couldn't ease the dryness of his throat. Garrett had assured him Megan had driven off with Joey. Why would she leave her stuff? He yanked out his phone and called Garrett.

"Just checking on Megan," he said, as soon as Garrett answered.

"I told you she left with her brother," Garrett said. "No worries. I'm not going to press charges. Or involve the police. We all want to forget this."

"She was driving her own truck? What was Joey driving?"

Garrett's hesitation was palpable. "I'm not sure," he finally said. "Joey stayed by the gate. She called him on her phone. You know he's not welcome here. They're probably halfway to Mexico by now.

"Hey," Garrett went on. "The vet called. I can pick Rex up next week."

"That's nice," Scott said, but he knew Garrett's tactics and wasn't going to be diverted. "So Megan just packed up her bags, got in her truck and drove off? That's the end of it? No police involvement?"

"Yes. Like I promised, that's it. Where are you now?"

Now it was Scott's turn to hesitate. He'd never lied to Garrett in his life, but his instincts were screaming. "About three hours from L.A.," he said. "Is that a horse I hear? Are you in the cowshed?"

"Yeah. Let me step outside." A horse neighed, more muffled now. It sounded like Garrett was walking, his breathing slightly ragged. "We're loading the horses for the Baja Tinda."

"You taking them down yourself?" Scott asked, already loping toward his car.

"No, Ramon does that."

"Must be a lot of paperwork," Scott said, quietly easing his car door shut. "Crossing the border with animals."

"Not with racehorses. They have their papers and health certificates. And the officials know us so we're fast tracked." Garrett sounded rather smug. "They like what we're doing. Supplying horses, training their students. It's good for both sides."

Someone spoke in the background. "Gotta go. I'll call you next week." Garrett said. "Thanks for the help down here, buddy."

Then he was gone, and something sharp and sour spread in Scott's chest. His hand was shaking when he called Megan. Her happy voice, almost bizarre in the situation, invited him to leave a message.

He pulled his Glock from beneath the seat, laid it on his lap and called Snake.

"Damn." Garrett strode back into the arena, his phone gripped in his hand. "They're already here. Ramon, open those end doors and let them in. Miguel, put that last horse on the trailer."

Miguel's hand tightened around Megan's hair, his gross touch sending creepy crawlers down her spine. "Get Ramon to load the horse," Miguel said. "This *puta* has to fix the baler."

"Megan, fix it. Now!" Garrett shoved his phone back in his pocket. "Don't you understand? I can't help you anymore."

Thud.

She cringed as Ramon dropped the bar securing the far doors. Seconds later, a blue Monte Carlo with two Hispanic men cruised into the arena. The driver lowered the window, his eyes flat. He said something in Spanish, then frowned at Miguel's reply. When he scowled, the scar by his mouth distorted his cheek. He did a careful unhurried sweep of the arena before opening his door and stepping out, bringing with him an air of menace.

Her breath turned shallow. Coming now in short gasps.

Garrett abruptly moved. Something hard pressed against her head. Oh, God.

"Fix it, Megan." Garrett's voice was urgent, and the way his hand shook scared her almost as much as the gun. "They do the wet work. And they enjoy it. Don't make this harder than it has to be."

"Too fucking late," Miguel snarled. He yanked her up, shoving her against the car. Her knee slammed into the fender, but she was too paralyzed with fear to feel any pain. If he hadn't been holding her so tightly, she would have fallen.

The man from the passenger's side didn't even look at her. He just opened the trunk and began removing neat stacks of money. But the man with the scar reached into the trunk, past a selection of guns, and pulled out a black-handled knife. The anticipatory gleam in his eyes turned her legs boneless.

"My friend says a string won't tie." Scarface said to her, speaking in clipped and dispassionate English. "I get annoyed when the bales aren't tight."

The knife loomed closer. She squeaked. Tried to jerk away but the cold blade flattened against her neck. For a terrifying moment, she quit breathing.

The man glanced over her head at Garrett, his eyes flat. "This is the second time we've had a problem here."

"I could have made her cooperate." Miguel's voice rasped in her ear. He yanked her head further back. "But *he* wouldn't let me."

Scarface's gaze shifted to Miguel. "Your father wants you to stay clean this side of the border." The knife skimmed along her neck. She wanted to tell him she'd gladly fix the baler but her mouth was so dry, she could only whimper.

"But I want to do this one. He'll understand." Miguel squeezed her breast. She jerked. The knife sliced into her skin and she stilled. No pain, only warm liquid on her neck.

"P-please...I'll fix it," she squeaked but Miguel was talking and Garrett was protesting and such nausea swept her, she thought she'd vomit.

Scarface waved a dismissive hand at Garrett who immediately silenced. The man looked back at Miguel. "My son would like to be a jockey," Scarface said. "Can you arrange that?"

"Of course," Miguel said. "Your son will be accepted in the fall classes."

Scarface stared at Miguel for a long moment. "All right." He lowered his knife. "But gag her first. And don't let her scratch your face. Fifteen minutes. No more."

"*Gracias,*" Miguel said. His erection pressed into her and she could smell his pulsing eagerness.

"No, please—" But an oil-stained rag cut off her words. Someone roughly tied her wrists behind her back. Not Miguel because he was standing in front of her, yanking down the zipper of her jeans. His rough hands groped between her legs.

He gave a coarse laugh. "Now I'll show you how I can ride, *puta*—"

"Step back! Hands behind your head."

She was released so quickly she fell to the ground. Scott stepped through the end door, his face as grim as the gun in his hand. A relieved sob caught against the rag in her mouth.

But he was alone. One man against five.

She tried not to move, willing them to do what he asked. *Please, just raise your hands.* But they had guns too, much bigger than his, and there were more guns in the trunk. Already Miguel was edging toward them.

"Get your goddamn hands up!" Scott snapped.

Scarface showed no emotion. Then slowly, so slowly, he lifted his hands and flattened them over the back of his head. Garrett stared at Scott, his gun at his side, face ashen.

"You too, Garrett. Drop the gun. And, Miguel, get away from the trunk." Scott's voice was as menacing as Scarface's, his face so ruthless it was almost unrecognizable. She would have put her hands in the air too if they hadn't been tied.

Maybe it was going to be okay. Even though Scott was outnumbered, he looked supremely confident.

Formidable. Her eyes darted from Scott to the five men standing by the car. And then she realized—there were only four.

She thrashed and yelled beneath the gag, trying to warn him. Jerked her head at the horse stalls, frantically rolling her eyes.

But it was too late.

Ramon stepped from the darkened aisle. *"Suelta el arma!"* he said. Sweat dripped down his forehead. His gun hand trembled.

"It's over, Ramon," Scott said, keeping his gun trained on the four men in front of him. "Police are on their way."

"Shoot the fucker," Scarface yelled, his hand creeping to his side.

"No! I'll take care of him." Garrett stepped forward, raising his gun. "He'll go quietly."

Scott and Garrett's gazes locked over their guns. They seemed to stare at each other forever. The arena was silent except for the ticking of the car engine.

Scarface cursed and grabbed for the gun in his waistband. Garrett abruptly twisted and shot at Ramon, and all around her the air exploded.

She gave a muffled squeal. But Scarface was down and motionless. So was his quiet partner. Movement flashed as Miguel snatched a gun from the trunk. She kicked at his legs but he shot over her head, the pop surprisingly quiet.

Whump. Miguel jerked back with the sound, red blossoming over his chest.

He slumped at an odd angle, one arm draped against the back tire. A trickle of blood snaked from his mouth. His eyes met hers then bulged and lost focus.

Her frantic sob escaped, and she glanced around, helpless with her tied hands. Everything seemed to be moving in slow motion. Ramon held his thigh and cursed. Everyone else was down except Scott who circled the car, taking Ramon's gun and kicking everyone else's away.

He squeezed her shoulder, hard, then knelt beside Garrett.

"I always was a lousy shot," Garrett said, so faint she could barely hear, even though he lay only ten feet away.

"Hang on, buddy," Scott said. He pressed his hands over Garrett's chest, but his fingers were turning redder and redder.

Uniformed men swarmed through the doorways. A grim-eyed man with an earring helped her up, removed the rag from her mouth and untied her hands. Someone draped a blanket over her shoulders and wiped her neck but she was gagging and couldn't stop shaking, and she was glad when they put her in a warm car.

"Better take her to the hospital first," someone said through the window. The driver nodded, but she told them she wasn't hurt and managed to zip up her jeans.

They drove to a police station. She waited in a bare room with very hard chairs. A nice lady with a calm voice brought her coffee and asked a lot of questions, and even though the coffee was black and strong, she drank three cups. She told them about Joey and the lady asked more questions and then she signed some papers and they moved her to another room with windows, and she was surprised to see it was already dark.

A man with a clipboard appeared and told her it was okay to leave. She just stared, not even sure where her truck was, and then a scowling man with a shaved head and a flaming viper tattoo burst through the door.

She tried not to cringe but he turned to her with a smile that transformed his face.

"I'm Snake," he said. "Scott sent me. Your stuff is already in my car. Come on."

She nodded but didn't move. He took her hand and gently guided her to his black Hummer, and he was so big and the vehicle so solid, she quit worrying and fell asleep.

When she woke, she was in her driveway and her truck was parked by her bungalow. Maybe jockey school had been a bad dream. But then she looked at Snake sitting patiently behind the wheel, gun in his lap, and she knew it was real.

"You should have a lawyer," he said, his dark eyes concerned. "Scott hopes they won't need your testimony and is working at getting you removed from the witness list but until then I'll be sticking around."

"Where is he?" She rubbed her eyes. Despite the coffee, she felt exhausted.

"At the hospital. With Garrett."

"What about...everyone else?" Her mouth twisted with revulsion. It was impossible to say Miguel's name.

"Two dead, three injured. One of the injured, Miguel

Torres, is Hugo Torres' son." Snake's wary eyes swept his rearview mirror. "We're not sure what Torres' reaction will be if he dies. We'd like to keep you out of it."

She stared into the black night, too drained to be afraid. "But they killed my brother. I want to help."

"Yeah. Guess I'd feel the same way." He paused but she could feel his careful scrutiny. His voice lowered, so soft she could barely hear him. "And now I understand why Scott didn't miss the office."

He shoved the gun against the hollow of his back and clicked open the door. "Let's get you inside. You've had a helluva day."

CHAPTER THIRTY-THREE

"You're not scaring her, are you?" Scott asked.

"No, boss," Snake said. "She's gutsy. And understands the situation. She went to visit her mother once but mainly she stays inside, making jewelry."

"So the house is secure?"

"She goes jogging in the morning."

"But you're with her?" Scott's gut tightened with dread. "When she goes out?"

"Yeah, but it's isolated here. Ramon is the one who needs to worry."

"You still have to watch her." Scott's fingers tightened around his phone. Ramon had agreed to testify in exchange for a reduced sentence. He was the only one able to talk since Miguel had died on the way to the hospital. And Garrett...

He glanced at the unconscious man lying on the hospital bed, his throat thickening with a mixture of rage and regret. He'd entrusted Garrett with Megan. Yet, she'd been brutalized, almost murdered. He couldn't say her name without feeling a crushing guilt.

Snake's sigh sounded loud. "She doesn't blame you."

"Yeah, well, she should," Scott said. A pulse throbbed above his left eye and he paced around the sterile hospital room. "I'll be here awhile. Just watch her until this is sorted out. I'm sending you some help."

"Maybe you should get your ass back here and take care of your woman yourself."

"Not yet. There's been infighting. The Baja Tinda cell is vulnerable. "

"If that cartel is on the way out, why am I sitting here watching Megan's grass grow?"

"I have to make sure." Scott dragged a hand over his

jaw. "Can't fail her again."

"You didn't fail her. And why the hell are you waiting on Garrett? You want to kill him when he wakes up?"

Scott studied the man in the bed, confused by his ambivalence. Garrett's face looked unfamiliar, the beeping monitors the only sign of life. The bastard had set up Megan, then saved their lives. He wanted to throttle Garrett, thank him, then throttle him again.

Megan had wanted to keep their relationship and his investigation of Joey private. Despite that, he'd revealed it all to Garrett—with tragic repercussions. He'd mishandled everything. He was hell on women.

"I have to clean up some loose ends," he muttered.

"You want me pass on any messages to Megan, you know, while you're so busy down there?"

The disapproval in Snake's voice was obvious, but Scott didn't much approve of himself either.

"Just keep her safe," he said, then he cut the connection.

Megan angled the topaz over the thin silver wire then glanced up from her work board. A panel van had pulled into the driveway. Snake materialized—for a big man, he moved quickly—and leaned over the van's side window. The two men looked friendly so she relaxed, reaching for her pliers to secure the link.

She didn't think there was much danger. According to Snake, the incident at the school had sparked an intercartal rivalry and now Miguel's father was busy fighting for his own survival. For her, life had returned to normal. Except for the black Hummer parked in her driveway and the ache in her chest that refused to go away.

Garrett had died two days earlier without regaining consciousness, and Snake neatly sidestepped any questions about his absent employer. Clearly, Scott blamed her for Garrett's death yet felt a warped responsibility for her safety. Maybe Garrett *wouldn't* have died if she hadn't enrolled in his school. Yet the man had been a murderous criminal, and her feelings about him were clear.

Even though Garrett hadn't pulled the trigger, he'd been an accomplice to Joey's murder. And he'd been more than willing to let them kill her, just not so keen to see her raped.

A shudder wracked her body. She dropped the wire, torn by her conflicting feelings—because in the end, Garrett had saved them. And a part of her was grateful.

Of course, it was Scott he'd been protecting. Garrett had cared so much for his friend, he'd taken a bullet. If not for his sacrifice, her body would have been stuffed into that trunk. Garrett would never have been able to control Miguel or Scarface; he was merely the American contact who helped move their drug money. The school provided a legitimate reason for border crossings, but Garrett had been expendable.

She jerked to her feet, consumed with restlessness. Jogging, not jewelry, was her release now. Some days, she felt like she was drowning.

The police doubted they'd ever recover Joey's body. Scarface and the other man were dead, silent forever. Joey could have been dumped anywhere. Ramon knew nothing, only that Joey had been shot twice in the head, fifty miles after crossing the Mexican border.

He could be buried in an unknown grave, or stacked in a Mexican morgue or worse, tossed in a ditch, his bones picked apart by scavengers. She squeezed her eyes shut, trying to block the gruesome images.

Her mother was still numb. Without a body, Joey's death was difficult to accept.

Megan wished she hadn't given Joey the tuition money. Wished she could erase the last three months. Earlier, she had a mission to find her brother. Now her existence seemed aimless.

She also missed Tami and Eve. The school was finishing the current students, under the direction of Lydia, and a Kentucky school had generously loaned one of their riding instructors. Garrett's facility wouldn't be open next fall, but this year's students would graduate.

Eve was another matter. They'd talked several times, and Eve still waffled about the baby. At least she knew Megan would help, to whatever extent permitted, but it tore Megan up to have no say about Joey's baby. Now she dreaded Eve's calls, afraid Eve would announce that she had an abortion. All Megan could do was hope and pray—and try not to badger Eve.

But she'd love a baby in her home. Even if it were just for a visit. Her bungalow felt lonely, stripped of spirit. Often she woke up trembling, certain Miguel lurked in the dark corners. Sometimes she wished she were back in the dorm, with Tami snoring in the adjacent bed.

Or Scott.

He constantly crept into her thoughts. But he hadn't believed her, hadn't trusted her. Instead, he'd chosen to listen to his lying friend. At the first whiff of trouble, he'd fled. Worse, she'd let herself believe he might be more than a school fling. But where was he now? Just another coward who didn't care enough to call.

Of course, she was absolutely fine with being alone. It was what she'd expected. Besides, it had only been six weeks. She'd get used to the quiet again. She loved her solitude.

Snake rapped on the door with his typical coded knock—four times, a three-second pause then twice more.

She smiled, despite her melancholy. He was so protective. She didn't think Miguel's father would hunt her down, but Snake looked hurt when she didn't follow his careful directions. "Who is it?" she asked.

"Terrence," he said.

She opened the bolt almost before he'd finished saying the password. Maybe today he'd accept a coffee and visit for a bit.

The retired teacher who lived next door was terrified of Snake. Sure, the guy was as big as a Clydesdale, sported a shaved head and aggressive tattoos, but anyone could see Snake was really a marshmallow. And he had the best stories, usually involving Scott. If only half of them were true, the Taylor Investigative Agency certainly had some interesting cases.

"Come in—"

Her greeting jammed in her throat. A German Shepherd charged forward with a thumping tail and ecstatic whines. Rex leaped in the air and licked her face then wheeled in dizzying circles, unable to contain his joy. His ribs were visible and his leg had been shaved, but there was no cast and if he was limping, it wasn't obvious.

She sank to the floor, holding open her arms. His wet

tongue swept her nose, her forehead and both sides of her cheeks. She glanced over Rex's beautiful head, her sniffs blending with his excited whines. Snake shuffled his feet, as though embarrassed to witness such an emotional display.

"Scott thought you might like to keep the dog," he said. "But he wasn't sure. Looks like you're okay with it?"

"Keep him? You mean, he's mine? Oh, wow." She leaped to her feet and hugged Snake's thick neck. "I'm so okay with it!"

He flushed and backed up, almost stumbling on the doorstep. "Well, that's good. I've got vet instructions and dog food and medicine and all kinds of stuff that Scott sent. I'll bring it in."

"Scott? Is he still at the school?" She despised the quaver in her voice but had to ask. Yes, he'd sent her this wonderful dog, but the significance was blindingly clear. He wasn't going to be around...and he didn't want her to be alone.

"Yeah." Snake adjusted his sunglasses. "He's working down in that area. Looks like his license will be reinstated soon."

"I didn't know he'd lost his license."

"Well, he didn't wait for the police." Snake shrugged. "Plus he shot four people, three of them fatally."

"But that's not fair. It was self-defense. He saved my life." Her voice rose. Rex stopped wagging his tail, looked at Snake and gave a warning growl.

"Of course," Snake said. "And those facts were all considered." His gaze shifted to Rex. "Looks like that dog is serious about protecting you too."

She gestured and Rex sank to the floor. She'd forgotten he'd been trained as a guard dog, although it was now clear why Garrett had wanted him. "I'll be careful with him around other people," she said, giving Rex a reassuring pat. "We'll be fine...at least he's loyal."

"Scott's loyal too," Snake said. "But he feels responsible for what happened."

She sighed. "And Garrett was his best friend and now he's dead."

"He doesn't blame you." But Snake spoke so quickly she knew he was lying, and any hope that Scott would call was painfully squashed.

"It doesn't matter," she said. "I understand." She busied herself with scratching the base of Rex's ear, determined to hide the wobble in her voice. "Just tell him thanks. And that I'll take good care of Rex."

"Sure. I'll tell him," Snake said, not meeting her eyes.

She closed and locked the door behind him.

Rex followed her into the kitchen, wagging his tail and whining, but the happy click of his nails was only a partial balm to the aching rip in her heart.

CHAPTER THIRTY-FOUR

"Guess what!" Tami squealed so loudly Megan moved the phone another inch from her ear. "They offered me seven thousand dollars for that video of Rambo."

"Who did?"

"The helmet company," Tami said. "For the video I took of Scott and Rambo. When he was bucking in the round pen. They want to say 'this is the helmet experts choose,' that sort of thing." She squealed again. "I'm going to be rich!"

Megan squealed along with her.

"Well, I will be rich if I can get Scott's release on the picture," Tami added. "So, will you ask him for me?"

"Ask him?" Megan's voice faltered. "I haven't spoken to him since I left the school."

"But couldn't you ask? I figure he'll agree if you're the one to call."

"I can't," Megan said. She circled the kitchen table while Rex whined, his soulful eyes anxious. The dog knew her so well. Only two weeks, and she couldn't imagine being without him.

"Please." Tami's voice rose. "Remember who called Scott to get help. If not for me, you'd still be hiding in Garrett's bathroom."

Megan swallowed. She knew where she'd be now, and it wouldn't be hiding in a bathroom. "You know Scott too," she said. "He's either going to say 'yes' or 'no.' It doesn't matter who calls."

"Then he's going to refuse," Tami said glumly. "He's helping a woman clear out Garrett's house. He barely cracked a smile when I dropped by."

Megan couldn't stop herself. "What woman?"

"Garrett's ex-wife. They both looked really sad. And

the police are always around. But Lydia turned nice. She likes being in charge, and she even lets us ride on the ridge behind the barn, well, everyone can except the grooms. They're still trotting in the field. Hang on a sec." The phone muffled and Tami returned, giggling. "Peter says 'hi.' We've been hanging out a lot," she added.

"Oh." Megan blinked in surprise then smiled. "I'm glad to hear that. Peter's a nice guy."

"Yeah, real nice," Tami said. "I never noticed him before but since Miguel is well, toast—"

Megan's mouth twitched, and she couldn't stop herself. She started laughing and then laughed so hard, her gut hurt. "Oh, Tami," she finally managed, clutching her stomach with her left hand. "I miss you."

She wiped the tears from her eyes. Rex trotted to her side and cocked his head, studying her with grave concern. He probably hadn't heard her really laugh before, she realized with a pang. And that was going to change.

"You go, girl," Megan said, "and heck, yes, I'll call Scott." She wasn't going to pussyfoot around anymore. She was the one who should be angry, not him. He had pushed and pushed until she fell in love and then he'd dumped her. Just because he thought she had a little heroin—okay, a lot of heroin—in her bag.

Tami squealed in the phone. Megan could hear Peter chuckling, and they sounded so happy that for a moment it was possible to believe she was happy too.

"This isn't a good way to run a business," Belinda snapped. "Just give it up and come home."

"How many John Does are left?" Scott asked.

"Three, and the morgue knows you're coming." Her voice softened. "You have to forgive yourself. You weren't responsible for Garrett's death, any more than Amanda's."

Scott flinched. Belinda hadn't mentioned Megan's near-murder but other than that, she'd pretty much summed up his failures. He certainly hadn't helped Megan's trust issues.

"I'll call on Friday," he said, before disconnecting. "Thank you, Belinda."

He checked the car's navigation system. One last

Mexican morgue at a tiny hospital close to the border. Ramon had helped narrow his search, but Scott was only guessing at the dumping grounds. He prayed someone had discovered Joey's body. Drug dealers were lazy. It was unlikely Garrett's associates had made much effort to hide their bloody trail.

He still couldn't believe it... Garrett working for a cartel? A disbelieving sigh leaked out. How had he missed it? What kind of piss-poor judgment did he have? Sure, Garrett's ethics had always been a little murky but to condone murder. God, he wished the man had lived so he could choke him with his bare hands.

But that thought no longer roused much fury. It only exacerbated his deep sense of hopelessness. He drove into the back of the sun-beaten parking lot, feeling as lifeless as the bodies inside.

He showed his creds to the receptionist and signed a sheet. A short man in a blue medical robe and white plastic cap appeared through a swinging door. "This way, *senor*," he said, pausing to unlock a thick door.

Scott followed him into a walk-in refrigerator stacked with cadavers. Chlorine couldn't mask the nauseating smell of decay.

"We have several males," the man said. "Still unidentified. The first one is the headshot, two are knives. We have seven more without heads."

"Start with the headshot," Scott said, exhaling through his nose.

The man checked some tags then unzipped a stained white bag and pulled it open. Scott stared. A sour taste filled his mouth but he couldn't turn away... It was Joey. Looking very much like the pictures in his file. The resemblance to Megan was obvious, the same mouth...oh, God.

Two holes in the forehead—at least, Ramon was playing it straight. The body was in fairly good shape, and the morgue would have the bullets along with the autopsy report. He struggled to think objectively but his throat was spasming. It wasn't Megan stuffed in that bag but it could have been. It easily could have been.

He'd cuffed her. Then passed her over to a ruthless cartel.

Bile rose in his throat, a monster wave he couldn't

stop. He turned and rushed for the bathroom.

"Door to the left, *senor*," an attendant called.

He wrenched the door open just in time.

He retched violently, then splashed his face with cold water. Grasped the sink and studied his reflection. His face looked desolate in the cheap mirror. She'd been totally innocent, seeking only to clear her brother's name. And she'd almost been murdered, just like Joey. *Christ, how can I ask her to forgive me when I can't even forgive myself?*

His cell vibrated and he pulled it out. Megan, oh hell.

He stared at the display as if it were a coiled rattler. Then sucked in several frantic breaths, trying to shake the smell of formaldehyde. His hand shook. He jabbed three times at the buttons before managing to press 'talk.'

"Hello?" she said. "Scott?"

"Yeah," he said, realizing he hadn't spoken.

"It's Megan. Sorry to bother you..."

She paused for a moment, as though giving him a chance to speak. And he wanted to, he really did, but his throat had dried up. She didn't seem to have a similar problem. In fact, her voice sounded bright and lilting, filling him with such an intense longing he feared his heart might pound out of his chest.

"Tami made a video of you and Rambo," she went on. "And wants to know if you'll sign a release. So she can sell it."

He wet his mouth, struggling to speak, struggling to even breathe.

"Scott?" Her voice changed, turning quiet. "So, what do you think? Is that okay?"

"Sure," he managed, unable to make any sense of her words. But if Megan wanted something, he'd get it for her. That he knew.

"All right," she said. "Guess we'll fax your office the release?"

"Sure," he repeated. It seemed he could manage that one word. He swallowed, opened his mouth to tell her about Joey then clamped it shut. Her dead brother lay twenty feet away—the brother she'd steadfastly believed in. The brother for whom she'd nearly sacrificed her life.

But US authorities had requested confidentiality and the Mexican Federales wanted first dibs. Identity needed to be confirmed. It would all take time. Right now, she sounded so happy. He just wanted her to remain like that, happy and safe.

"All right then. Thanks," she said. "Bye." Her voice wavered as if looking at someone, and he wondered if Snake were in the room.

"Megan," he croaked but she was already gone. Besides, he really didn't have anything to say.

Rex's wet nose pressed against Megan's neck. She slumped on her new sofa, phone clutched in her hand, face pressed against the dog's shoulder. Her eyes felt swollen and itchy, and she was embarrassed to let Rex see her distress. She hadn't cried like that since her father left.

The conversation hadn't gone at all like she hoped. Scott had sounded so curt, as if they were strangers. Deep down, she'd nursed a glimmer of hope. Had thought they just needed a chance to talk. He would apologize for cuffing her, she would thank him for saving her life, although maybe not in that order. Then maybe they'd meet for a cup of coffee. Possibly, she'd show him the coyote den Rex had discovered.

Just friend stuff. She wouldn't invite him in to see her new purchases: the extra-wide sofa and her huge TV loaded with sports channels. She didn't want a relationship anyway. Not anymore. Which was good because he obviously didn't want one either.

He was still affected by Garrett's death and the heroin in her bag—which wasn't even hers. It was impossible to fight something like that, and wily Garrett had known exactly which of Scott's buttons to push. And now she had Garrett's ghost hanging over them as well.

She jerked from the sofa and keyed in a number. After she told Tami the good news, she'd take Rex for a walk and then finish some jewelry. She had several big orders to fill but lacked the creative energy, and customers were turning impatient.

Tami answered on the first ring. "What did Scott say?"

"Yes."

Tami squealed, but Megan was prepared and had already repositioned the phone for minimal damage.

"So what now?" Tami said. "Wait a sec. I'm sending the release. Along with the link to the video and some pictures. Oh my God. Seven thousand bucks!"

"I don't think he even wants to see the video." Megan moved to her computer and opened her email, waiting for the document.

"But what did he say?" Tami asked. "He has to sign it. It has to be legal. Oh, and check out the other attachment."

Megan clicked on the screen. Then shot forward, studying the attached horse pictures, her mouth curving in a smile. "Rambo sure looks happy."

"Yeah, Lydia wanted them sent. You sure found him a good home."

Megan absorbed the three pictures: one of Rambo rolling in knee-deep grass, one of him playing halter tag with a stocky gray, and another of him staring into the camera with a look that seemed to contain a message of thanks.

"Wow," she repeated, her throat in a tangle. It was lucky Tami was talking because for the next three minutes she could only stare mutely at the contented horse.

"So that's what Peter and I are doing," Tami said. "Checking out retirement homes."

"The school horses are being retired?"

"Yes, at the end of the season." Tami sounded frustrated. "Haven't you been listening?"

"Sure, I have," Megan said, smiling as she changed her screen saver to a picture of Rambo playing with his new friend. At least one good thing had come out of her time at the school. Plus she'd met Tami and Eve.

She opened Tami's second attachment.

"The release looks good," Megan said. "I'll give it to Snake and he can get Scott to sign."

"Who's Snake?" Tami asked.

"One of Scott's employees. He's around here a bit." Megan hesitated. She didn't know what Tami had been told and didn't want to hurt her with further news of Miguel and his multi-million-dollar crime family. Few details had been released, only that Garrett and Miguel had been killed, and that the investigation was ongoing. "Snake mows the lawn and stuff," she added.

"Wow." Tami giggled. "Scott is sure ape over you.

First he chases your truck to Mexico and now he sends his employee to do yard work."

"What do you mean? Chased my truck to Mexico?"

"You know, when I called to say you were in Garrett's bathroom. He said he was already trying to catch your truck. Catch up to you and Joey."

"But that's when he thought I was a drug dealer," Megan said. "Garrett told him I'd joined Joey."

"That's right." Tami blew out a satisfied sigh. "I straightened that all out."

"You mean he wasn't going home when you called? He was trying to find me? Even then?" A burst of happiness sparked in her chest. She knew Scott had received Snake's warning about Miguel, but now she understood how he'd arrived at the cowshed so quickly. He hadn't driven back to L.A. at all. Garrett had lied—or been misinformed.

"Thank you, Tami. I really needed to know that."

"No problem. There is one other thing." Tami took a big breath. "We're having our graduation and I was hoping you'd come as my guest."

"But each student is only allowed two tickets."

"That's right. And I want you. It's at the cafeteria, but not for another month so that's good. Maybe by then you'll feel better about visiting the school?"

Megan's lower lip quivered with emotion. "I feel better already," she said.

Megan threw a stick along the trail. Rex ran and scooped it up, then promptly dropped it.

"He's not much of a retriever," Snake said, as he waited for Megan to step over a fallen log.

"I don't think Garrett played many games with him. He wanted a guard dog." She gestured at Rex. His limp was barely perceptible, just a slight hitch to his trot. "Animals sure heal fast. Does Scott ever ask about him?"

Snake's mouth hardened and he made a show of scanning the hillside for the coyote den. "No, Megan. He doesn't." His voice gentled. "It's not that he doesn't care. He feels guilty and to a man like him, guilt is one of the hardest things to handle."

"It's because of Garrett, isn't it?" she said, knowing

they were no longer talking about Rex. "He can't forget Garrett."

"Maybe. Or maybe it has something to do with his old fiancée." Snake reached up and snapped off a low-lying branch. "He wants to save people, not hurt them."

Megan crossed her arms, fighting her bleakness. "But he did save me. In the end, he did."

"Not in his mind. He feels he put you in tremendous danger."

"Well, yes, but..."

"You see. It's black and white to him." The muscles in Snake's arm bunched as he tossed the stick along the path, much further than she could ever throw. Rex watched as the soaring stick disappeared then he flopped to the ground and licked his paws.

"So he'll always blame me for Garrett's death?" she said, her voice thick with misery.

"Hard to say what he's thinking. He's walled himself off." Snake waved another stick at Rex who was pretending not to notice. "At least he's taking on some fun work."

Snake's eyes gleamed and she hated to envision what he considered fun. Now that Hugo Torres was fighting for his own survival, Snake would soon leave for another assignment.

"So you'll be giving up our regular dog walks?" she asked, trying to keep the regret from her voice. She enjoyed Snake's company—and he was her only link to Scott.

"I'm joining Scott soon."

"Oh?" She perked up. Scott was rumored to still be at the school but Tami said he disappeared for long stretches. And Snake was frustratingly close-mouthed about his absentee boss. "So you'll be out of town for a while?" she asked.

"Yeah, until the job's done. Private investigators can go places the police can't." He grimaced, realizing he'd just told her they wouldn't be working in L.A. "Maybe you should go visit your mom again. I heard you talking on the phone. Sounds like she's doing better."

"Yes, she's okay now. I'm not sure when we'll have Joey's body back, but it really helped...finding him. And she has a supportive husband. She said the authorities were amazingly helpful. A much different experience than before."

"Good. I'll tell Scott."

Megan pivoted, her eyes widening. "Did he have something to do with recovering Joey's body?"

"Of course," Snake said. "He always intended to find your brother. If Scott says he'll do something, he does it."

"But where is he now?" Her voice quavered, so much that she pretended to cough.

Snake bent over and scooped up another stick, clearly uncomfortable with her questions. "You know I can't say. But maybe I'll stop by when I come back. Bring some balls or something. See if we can teach that damn dog a few tricks."

She forced a smile. Snake was a kind man, always trying to cheer her up. However, Rex cocked his head and stared at Snake as though aware he was being criticized. As Scott had once said, he was a very smart dog.

And thinking of Scott only choked her up so she resolved not to think of him at all. If only that were possible.

CHAPTER THIRTY-FIVE

Would love to see you. Can you drop by barn before races?

Megan replayed Eve's text for the tenth time as she parked her truck in the spacious Santa Anita parking lot. Clearly, Eve had made a decision about the baby but her words revealed nothing. A few more weeks and it would be too late for an abortion. Or maybe the timing meant she'd already made her choice.

Oh, God, please. Megan fumbled with the remote, her fingers stiff with apprehension. Finally the truck locks clicked. She shoved the keys in her pocket and headed to the backside, her heart beating a staccato. The last time she'd talked to Eve was when she called to tell her that they had recovered Joey's body. But all Megan's invitations to meet had been politely declined.

The job is really busy, Eve had said, and I need time to think.

Away from the pressure of Joey's sister. Megan totally understood, but it didn't stop the butterflies from churning in her stomach.

A uniformed guard monitored the horse lane heading to the backside, and she hesitated. She hadn't even thought about the need for a visitor's pass, but of course there would be stringent security. She reached for her phone to call Eve but spotted a cameraman walking along the horse track and veered to join him.

"That camera looks awkward," she said with a smile.

"It's the tripod that's a pain." His eyes glided over her with lazy approval. "You work here? Packing up for Del Mar?"

"Just here to see a friend." They were only ten feet

from the security booth now, and she kept her attention on the cameraman, pretending she was with him and hoping the guard wouldn't ask for a show of credentials.

"Busy day here," the cameraman said. He wore a bright Hawaiian shirt and his forehead gleamed with perspiration. "It's the last weekend and I need a few more close-ups."

She nodded, understanding now the reason for Eve's message. Santa Anita's spring meet was over today, and the horses would be moving to Del Mar. Eve would soon be a hundred miles away. Maybe that's why she'd waited to send the text. Which might mean she'd chosen to keep riding. That she didn't want to postpone her career for a baby.

Or maybe it just meant she wanted to see Megan while she was still in the area.

Megan tugged at her lower lip, so concerned with the ramifications she forgot to worry about the security guard. She was ten feet past the guard before she realized he hadn't asked to see her credentials.

"Maybe I'll see you later," the photographer said. "There are some good races today."

She nodded, her mind still wrapped around Eve. "Good luck with your pictures," she said. "Do you know where Jack Zeggelaar's barn is?"

"Sure. Down that road to the left. About five barns down. His name is on the sign."

She headed in the direction the man had pointed, passing busy shedrows with circling hot walkers, bright flowers, and leg wraps drying in the sun. The smell of hay and horses was everywhere, filling her with nostalgia. This had been Joey's dream—Joey's and Eve's. At least Eve was still pursuing it, galloping horses every morning, trying to break her way into the jockey lineup.

Megan checked the Internet every night, scanning stable notes for Eve's name. She even watched the live web cam during morning gallops, trying to spot her. She just prayed Eve would be careful and keep the baby safe. Apparently Jack Zeggelaar was a respected trainer and often gave apprentices a chance—and that would all be wonderful if only Eve wasn't pregnant.

If she still was pregnant.

Megan sucked in a fortifying breath. Okay, there was

Jack Zeggelaar's shedrow. She wasn't sure if she should walk in or hang around outside and wait for Eve. Music was playing and someone called in Spanish. She stuck her head in and peered down the shedrow. An inquisitive bay gelding stuck his head over his door and stared back.

"Are you the new exercise rider?" A man in a blue polo shirt stepped out, wiping his hands on a rag.

"No," she said. "I'm here to see Eve."

He thumbed over his shoulder. "She's with Marshall. By the wash rack."

"Thanks." She turned in the direction of his thumb and immediately spotted Eve. She held a handsome gray gelding and was hosing water over his left front leg. Her jeans were slightly wet from the spray and her T-shirt was tucked in.

Megan's heart kicked with dismay. But that didn't mean anything, she told herself. Eve was tiny and might not be showing, not yet. She paused and at that moment Eve looked up. Her face lifted in a sparkling smile and Megan quit worrying. Whatever Eve had decided was the right choice. She no longer looked mournful but happy, almost light.

"I'm so glad you came." Eve dropped the hose and flung her free arm around Megan's shoulder. "Sorry I've been so quiet," she said. "It took some time to get my head straight."

Megan ignored the cold water spraying her leg and hugged Eve back.

"And now you caught me doing a groom's job," Eve added. But she was still smiling as she bent and rescued the wayward hose. "This is Marshall. He's running in the sixth race today. Jack has assigned me three of his quietest horses."

Marshall definitely looked like a sensible horse. He hadn't minded when the hose dropped, spraying his belly and Megan's legs with cold water. But Eve? A groom? At the school, the jockeys had all considered the grooms a notch or two below.

"He looks great," Megan said cautiously. "Maybe Jack will give you a shot at galloping him some time?"

"He sure will, but not right now." Eve smoothed the front of her shirt and gestured at the graphic—a picture of a big bellied mare, contentedly grazing in a lush field.

Megan's eyes widened. That was one very fat mare. It must mean... She sucked in a breath, feeling almost lightheaded. "You're having the b-baby?"

"I am." Eve beamed. "I had a fall last week and it terrified me. Jack said I could stay on and work as a groom—he really is a decent guy—and then start galloping whenever I'm ready."

"But that's fantastic! I can babysit, anything."

"And I'll be needing your help," Eve said. "But my mother loves children and we'll live with her until I can start riding again. Jack said it's better if I learn everything from the ground up anyway. He says nothing is better than experience, even though Garrett's school was good—" She broke off, shaking her head in disgust. "Guess I shouldn't mention that man's name. I thought Garrett was so nice finding me this job, but he just wanted me far away from you. I'm glad he's dead." Her eyes turned fierce but she kept her voice low. "I can't let Jack hear me say that though. He and Garrett were good friends."

Megan swallowed. Scott and Garrett had been good friends too. That was the root of the problem.

"I'm looking forward to meeting your mother," Eve went on. "Is there a date yet for Joey's funeral?"

"They haven't released his body yet." Megan stepped over the pooling water. Her eyes kept shooting to Eve's stomach, and she quit worrying about Scott and all she felt was a bubbling joy. A baby, Joey's baby!

"I took one of those new gender tests," Eve said. "It's a boy. And if he takes after the paternal side, he'll be loyal and brave." Her eyes misted. "I'm so grateful he'll have you for an aunt."

Aunt. Megan grinned and wrapped Eve in an impulsive hug. "I hope you're happy with this," she said. "Because I'm ecstatic. I'm going to buy a bigger house and make a special room for the baby."

"But what will Scott think?" Eve asked. "You know, if you're babysitting a lot?"

Megan's smile slipped a notch. She stepped back and patted Marshall's neck. "I haven't seen him since I left," she said. "Anyway, that was just a school fling."

"Really?" Eve said. "Because I never got those vibes. He seemed like a standup kind of guy. Not the fling type."

"It doesn't help that I'm the reason his best friend

died." Megan forced a careless shrug, showing that she didn't care in the least.

Eve wasn't fooled for a minute. "But that's crazy. He shouldn't blame you. Anyone who deals with a cartel risks a very short life span." She shook her head, her dark eyes flashing. "What exactly did he say?"

Megan stooped and picked up a sponge, desperately needing something to do with her hands. Scott hadn't cared enough to say anything. He'd been almost mute the one time she'd called, when she asked about the photo release. At least he'd sent Snake, and given her Rex. It seemed he was still protective of her. It was rather confusing.

She squeezed the sponge, watching the sudsy water soak her fingers. "He doesn't want to talk," she admitted, misery flattening her voice. "So I don't know what he's thinking. Guess he's too busy cleaning out Garrett's house."

"Call the moron," Eve said, temper spicing her words. "You can't go around wondering the rest of your life. Besides, you asked him to find Joey. So in a sense, he works for you."

"But I didn't pay him," Megan said. Still, she couldn't help but smile. It was nice to have someone finally agree that Scott was acting like an idiot. She was tired of Snake and his unswerving loyalty to his boss.

She remembered Snake's words. 'You know Scott. If he says he'll do something, he does it.' But he had said a lot of things, including that he'd meet her in the paddock on April 30th. Clearly today's date was trashed. It felt like a lifetime since she'd pulled his car from the ditch.

Maybe she'd call him tonight. Claim she'd waited by the paddock. Maybe he'd feel a teensy bit guilty knowing she'd driven to Santa Anita to meet him. At least then she'd finally have a chance to thank him because even though he'd carved out her heart, he had saved her life. And found Joey. So of course she'd always be grateful.

"I will call him." She tossed the wet sponge back into the bucket, splashing water over the sides. "I'll call tonight," she said, her voice firming, "and be done with it. And since this is the last day of the meet, I might hang around and watch a few races. When's post time?"

"One o'clock," Eve said. "But don't go yet. I want to

introduce you to a few people. All the guys are staring."
Her eyes flashed with mischief. "Bet they're hoping you're
our new exercise rider."

CHAPTER THIRTY-SIX

A burly man blocked Megan's view and she edged sideways, straining to see the horses in the paddock. Race one, and already spectators were gathering. She wouldn't watch long—just enough so that when she told Scott she had been here, it'd be the truth.

Besides, she had a dog waiting. Rex had been dejected when she'd told him to stay home. He was utterly loyal. He wouldn't heroically save her life then disappear without a word. But there would be no more agonizing about Scott. She was going to be an aunt!

She was still pumped by Eve's decision. They'd briefly discussed plans to visit Megan's mother and break the bittersweet news together.

I'll be there for your baby, bro.

She ignored the little lump in her throat and turned her attention to the nine Thoroughbreds circling the walking ring. Horses were the perfect tonic. The animals shone with vitality, their sleek coats gleaming. The number three horse had a haughty expression and reminded her a bit of Rambo, as though he considered himself too good for current company. She wasn't going to buy a program, not for a single race, but she would make a bet on the three horse, in honor of irascible old Rambo.

Her eyes drifted over the excited owners, catching the gaze of the photographer in the Hawaiian shirt. She hoped he was getting some good pictures. He smiled and winked. She waved but looked away, uncomfortable with the masculine interest in his eyes. She scanned the spectators gathered around the paddock.

Oh, God! A familiar head. For a moment, it hurt to breathe. Scott's hair was longer, his tan deeper, and dark stubble covered his jaw. But it was him. Unmistakably.

He wasn't away with Snake on some clandestine job but he was here. Right where they'd arranged to meet. Her breath escaped in a shuddery sigh. He hadn't called once in the long lonely weeks, but at least he'd remembered this date. It must mean something. Maybe he'd finally come to terms with Garrett's death.

She clasped her hands, drinking in his face. The scar on the side of his head was barely visible now. He looked good, but different. Lean, hard, dangerous. Spectators skirted around him, leaving a slight gap at the rail.

Except for the lady in the red suit. She didn't leave any space at all. In fact, she gave a vivacious smile, stepped closer and placed a familiar hand on his arm. His head tilted an inch, and he nodded.

Megan jerked convulsively. No mystery now why he hadn't called. Of course, he'd shown up for his date. It just wasn't with her.

Despair overwhelmed her, leaving no room for hurt or even anger. She'd deluded herself into believing they might be able to work things out, but clearly Garrett's death had left an impossible chasm.

Scott's head turned, as if sensing her presence. She tried to duck behind the stocky man on her left but was too slow. Scott spotted her, his deep smile changing his face. He no longer looked lethal. Was once again a gorgeous hunk of man...but a man who took the easy way out. Would he have even called if she hadn't showed up?

He approached with an easy grace. The crowd parted, opening a respectful path. But the woman in red trotted behind him, and Megan's resentment overrode her despair, leaving her entire body stiff.

Scott's smile turned wary, his intent gaze not leaving her face. "Hello, Megan," he said, passing her a program.

She automatically accepted it, hiding her confusion. He had another program in his hand so obviously he'd purchased two. Was he actually expecting to meet today?

"I can pick you up a *Racing Form* if you prefer," he said, his voice quiet.

"No, this is fine." She stared down at the program. Her hands were shaking and she had to steady them against the rail.

"There's no need to worry about the cartel anymore." He cleared his throat. "The Federales raided the Baja

Tinda two days ago. Hugo Torres is dead."

She glanced up. Couldn't remember his voice ever sounding so ragged. Lines fanned from his eyes and his strong jaw appeared even more chiseled.

"There's no need to worry anymore," he repeated. "You're safe." He edged closer, so close she could feel the heat radiating from his body.

She hated her shiver of awareness.

The three horse pranced by, newly saddled and awaiting his jockey. She had a program now. She could look up the horse's name and race record. Maybe he was even related to Rambo. But her mind was sluggish, still struggling to make sense of Scott's presence.

He was here, and seemed glad to see her. He didn't look at all remorseful. In fact, his expression was so shuttered she had no idea what he was thinking.

"Perhaps you should introduce us, Scott," a feminine voice said.

Megan steeled her shoulders and turned toward his companion in the artfully cut suit. The lady was flamboyant, beautifully groomed, with a smiling red mouth and an intricate gold necklace. She and Scott made an eye-catching couple.

Megan's voice wasn't quite steady but she made a valiant effort. "Hello," she managed. "I'm Megan Spence."

She glanced toward the turnstiles, desperate to escape. She'd been a fool to fall in love, to let herself believe he cared. She'd convinced herself that Garrett's death was the problem, that Scott just needed some time. She'd misinterpreted his touch, those tender whispers, the extra things he always did. This was embarrassing for them both.

And yet he remained cool and calm, just watching her with those hooded eyes, silent in the middle of all the chattering spectators.

"I'm Vanessa Grant," the woman said, smoothing her immaculate hair and peeking up at Scott. "I know you're busy and Scott said this wouldn't be the best time, but there are a few things we need to discuss."

Discuss? Surely she didn't want to exchange notes on how wonderful Scott was in bed. Megan willed her face to remain as expressionless as Scott's, but he was much better at it than her, and her lower lip gave a telltale quiver.

"Not now, Vanessa," Scott said.

"We just need a few details for the fall schedule," Vanessa continued brightly. "Our memorial races are listed on the website. Since you're both here—"

"Call my office," Scott said, his voice cracking like a whip.

Vanessa murmured something else but Megan could only concentrate on her breathing. In and out. She didn't know what was going on, but the steel in Scott's voice didn't bode well for Vanessa.

"I apologize," Scott said, his voice softening. "I thought the memorial would be a good idea. Maybe you'd like something else?"

Megan glanced past him. Vanessa had turned and retreated toward the clubhouse, her flashy suit out of place against the more casually dressed race goers.

"Oh." She swallowed, wetting her throat. "Vanessa works here?"

"Marketing manager," Scott said. "I'd like to sponsor a memorial race for the fall meet."

"I see." She nodded, staring at the horses, wishing she'd remembered her sunglasses. He was much too good at reading her emotions. She didn't want him to see her blinding spike of relief that the lovely and eager Vanessa wasn't his date.

"So? What do you think?" He edged closer, dipping his head with the question.

His breath was warm against her neck, his familiar scent a cocoon. For a jumbled moment, she just wanted to melt into his chest. Then she wanted to berate him and thank him and ask why he hadn't called, and the torrent of emotions left her much too shaky to speak.

"We could have an apprentice race or a memorial race," he went on. "Perhaps you and your Mom can decide? Or Eve too, if you like?"

"Okay," she said, guessing her voice now sounded as thick as his. But she'd assumed the race was for Garrett. She swallowed, still staring at the horses. A memorial for Joey? It was difficult to absorb such a thoughtful gesture, not when her heart pounded with renewed hope.

"But we can discuss that another time," he said, following her gaze. "Do you like a horse in this race?"

"Number three," she managed. The jockey was

already in the saddle. She didn't remember hearing the call for riders up. Couldn't remember seeing the jockeys parade from the jock room.

"Want me place a bet for you?" Scott asked, his voice only inches from her ear.

She mutely shook her head. He was still talking about horses? How could he act as if nothing had happened? The last time she'd seen him, he'd been pressing his hands over Garrett's bloody chest. In that terrible, horrible cowshed.

A shiver escaped and she gripped the rail. "I didn't have a chance to thank you," she said, "for saving my life. You were amazingly brave and—"

"Don't. Please, don't." He gave a racking groan and splayed his fingers over hers.

She stared down at his hands so dark against her paler ones. Three knuckles were freshly torn, and the sun-bleached hairs on his forearms were stark against the tan of his skin. And then she understood. He'd been in Mexico. He'd had something to do with the collapse of the Baja Tinda. He'd been completely and utterly busy

Still, her hurt was overwhelming. "You didn't even call," she whispered.

"I had to fix things first. Needed to bring Joey back. But I can't fix what I did. How I jumped to conclusions. I didn't realize you were riding for your brother. I thought... His voice faltered. "Megan, all you ever did was sell chocolate bars. And I'm sorry. So damn sorry."

She tried to twist around, but his arms tightened and he pressed her against his chest, his head close to her ear. "I'm sorry," he repeated.

A tear trickled down her cheek. She started to lift her hand but he was stroking the back of her wrists, his light touch at odds with the anguish in his voice. And she didn't really want to move. Not now, not when she'd feared she'd never be this close to him again. So maybe his heartbreaking silence hadn't totally been about Garrett. A nugget of hope sparked in her chest.

"Belinda's pushing for a release," Scott went on, his voice still ragged. "I have some guys down there. You'll have Joey home by next week."

It took a moment for her to digest that news. Her mother received regular updates and had said officials were surprisingly cooperative. It appeared Scott's influence had a long reach, and that he was determined to hobble Miguel's family, but oh God, she didn't want anyone else hurt.

"Where's Snake?" she asked.

He paused, as though surprised by her question. "Still at the Baja Tinda. But the Torres cell is broken. You don't have to worry any longer."

She hadn't really worried. Had never thought Miguel's father would target her for revenge. It seemed more likely he'd go after Scott—the shooter. If she'd known Scott had been working south of the border, she would have been terrified. But at least he was safe now. She shivered with relief. "You came back before Snake?"

"This is the 30th. I had to meet you."

She squeezed her eyes shut. What kind of man would take off to Mexico, recover Joey's body, participate in some kind of cartel invasion, then honor a date made months earlier? Yet not even call? She couldn't understand his thought process.

Yet her chest thumped with hope, and when she opened her eyes the sun seemed a little brighter, the air sweeter. His hands remained linked over hers, but neither of them spoke. The announcer warned 'two minutes to post.' Two women agonized over their bets, a pigtailed girl begged for a pony ride, and a man with a hotdog dropped ketchup on his shirt. Her hearing—every one of her senses—seemed to have kicked into overdrive.

"I love the track," she said. "The smell of horses, beer, hotdogs."

"Me too," he said. "Want some?"

Her appetite had vanished over the last month but now she could almost taste the mustard. Hotdogs were always good here. She didn't want Scott to move though. Wanted to absorb his presence a bit longer. Somehow he'd wrapped himself around her, had tucked her head beneath his chin.

It seemed as if they were the only ones here now. She peered sideways. Actually they were the only ones by the paddock. The last of the spectators had disappeared, trailing toward the track to watch the race.

"The hotdog and beer I can get you now," he said.

"The horse later."

Her knees turned rubbery but it didn't matter. He was literally holding her up. Was he saying he'd buy her a horse? She'd always thought that would be the ultimate gift. "My place is too small for a horse," she managed.

"Mine isn't."

"I see." Her voice was breathy, so low she could barely hear it over the thumping of her heart. But she didn't understand. He acted as though everything was cool between them. Maybe he had a trace of amnesia? She pulled in a deep breath. "What about Garrett?" she asked.

He slid his hands up her arms, wrapped them around her shoulders and turned her around. "What about him?" His gray eyes were unreadable.

Now she wished she hadn't mentioned the man. Not today. It was enough that Scott was here, that he'd cared enough to come. He was even talking about getting a horse and riding together. Surely they could build on that.

But she couldn't stay silent.

"You didn't call." Her voice quivered with the pain of all those sleepless nights. "Wouldn't even talk when *I* called. Do you blame me for Garrett's death?"

He recoiled as if shocked. "It wasn't that. But I cuffed you, handed you over." His voice broke.

"But then you came back and saved me," she said. "It's in the past."

However, she could feel the tension in his body and it was apparent it wasn't in *his* past. His face had stiffened to a stony mask. Oh, God. What if he took off on another job, seeking some crazy kind of redemption? She didn't want him anywhere near Mexico.

"There is something you can do for me though." She spoke fast, before she lost her nerve.

"You got it," he said. But he lowered his hands from her arms, his chest so tight now she could see the ridges beneath his shirt.

"Eve is having Joey's baby," she said. "He'll need a man in his life, someone dependable."

"Eve's pregnant? So that's why you insisted on riding Rambo." He paused then tilted his head, eyes flaring with hope. "You think I'm dependable?"

She nodded. Tears stung the back of her eyes. He was the most dependable, the most decent man she'd ever met.

But he just stared, motionless. He certainly made no

move to close the gap.

She crossed her arms, pretending an interest in the paddock screen. Two galloping horses strained for the wire. Looked like number three, the Rambo look-alike, would win. She couldn't bring herself to care, not with this clawing fear that paralyzed her body.

Scott's withdrawal was ominous. No doubt she'd scared him with talk of a baby. Sure, he'd take a bullet for her—but he was a natural-born protector. That's what he did. Didn't mean he wanted to be around for the long haul.

She fumbled with her program. Spectators trickled back to the paddock as the horses arrived for race two. In a few minutes, the area would be crowded again. She scanned the entries but the writing was indecipherable, and she realized she was holding the pages upside down.

"Forget I asked that of you," she said. "I know it's a big commitment..." Her voice trailed off in misery. She couldn't stop blinking, trying to block the prick of tears.

He cursed. Pried the program from her distressed fingers and pulled her along the concrete, moving against the flow of race fans.

They rounded a corner. He turned, panther like, and pulled her against the wall. It was much quieter here but she could still hear the loudspeaker, the crowd...his ragged breathing.

He raised his hands, cupping the sides of her face, the center of his eyes as dark as his gunslinger stubble. "You need to know right now that I love you. I was a goner since the day you wiggled under my car." He cleared his throat. "And I'm honored to help in any way with the baby. I wish I could have known Joey."

She stared up at him. Tenderness blazed in his eyes along with a strange uncertainty. He loved her? In spite of everything? But he didn't know all of it. However, his thumb stroked her cheek and as usual, his touch made it difficult to think.

"I..." she sucked in a quivery breath, not certain if he'd even hear her confession over the thudding of her heart. "I experimented with drugs when I was younger," she said in a rush.

"So did I."

"But I ended up in Juvenile Court," she said. "Just like Joey. After Dad left I was a bit of a rebel."

"I know, sweetheart."

She stopped talking. He knew? But of course he did. At some point, he'd been investigating her. But he wasn't revolted? Garrett claimed Scott hated drugs. And anyone who ever used them. Something warm flooded her chest. "I do not wiggle under cars," she added, her voice bubbling with so much joy it sounded unfamiliar.

"Megan, you have an irresistible wiggle." His thumb skimmed along her cheek and his voice turned fierce. "And I *will* make you love me. No matter how long it takes."

She flung her arms around his neck. "That's not something you have to do," she said. "In fact, it's way too late. I already subscribed to all the sports networks. Even bought a sofa for three."

His eyes widened. A group of teenagers brushed past. Someone muttered a hasty apology but he didn't take his gaze off her face. "You mean a sofa that fits you and Rex. And me?"

"That's exactly what I mean." Her smile turned tremulous. "I love you too."

He tunneled his hand through her hair, still staring, as if in disbelief. Then his head swooped and his mouth covered hers in a kiss filled with promise. A kiss that left her breathless and slightly dizzy and totally loved. And when he lifted his head, his eyes looked wet, but it was hard to see because everything blurred through her own haze of tears.

"Let's go home, sweetheart," he said gruffly.

Home. She already felt like she was home, along with something else...a presence she hadn't sensed for a long time. And she was swept with a profound sense of peace, knowing Joey was close. And that he was smiling.

***

ABOUT THE AUTHOR

Bev Pettersen is a three-time nominee in the National Readers Choice Award, a two-time finalist in the Romance Writers of America's Golden Heart® Contest as well as the winner of other international awards including the Reader Views Reviewers' Choice Award, Aspen Gold Reader's Choice Award, NEC-RWA Reader's choice Award, the Write Touch Readers' Award, a Kirkus Recommended Read, and a HOLT Medallion Award of Merit.

Bev competed for five years on the Alberta Thoroughbred race circuit and is an Equestrian Canada certified coach. She lives in Nova Scotia with her family and when not writing novels, she's riding. If you'd like to know about special offers or when her next book is available visit her at http://www.bevpettersen.com

Made in the USA
Columbia, SC
07 May 2024